Don't Cry

Beverly Barton

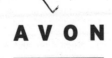

AVON

AVON
A division of HarperCollins*Publishers*
77–85 Fulham Palace Road,
London W6 8JB

www.harpercollins.co.uk

This paperback edition 2011
1

First published in the U.S.A by Kensington Publishing Corp as *Don't Cry*
New York, NY, 2010

A catalogue record for this book is available from the British Library

ISBN-13: 978-1-84756-248-7

Printed and bound in Great Britain by
Clays Ltd, St Ives plc

FSC
www.fsc.org
MIX
Paper from responsible sources
FSC™ C007454

FSC™ is a non-profit international organisation established to promote the responsible management of the world's forests. Products carrying the FSC label are independently certified to assure consumers that they come from forests that are managed to meet the social, economic and ecological needs of present and future generations, and other controlled sources.

Find out more about HarperCollins and the environment at
www.harpercollins.co.uk/green

To Billy, for a million and one reasons, but most of all because he loves me

&

In memory of Pelham, Alabama,
Police Officer Philip Davis,
who lost his life in the line of duty, December 4, 2009

Acknowledgments

I owe a special debt of gratitude to Lt. Tim Carroll, Commander Major Crimes Division, Chattanooga Police Department, for his invaluable assistance.

In an effort to help me get my facts straight, Tim answered numerous questions and gave me an officer's view of police work and of the brave men and women who risk their lives on a daily basis to protect the citizens of Chattanooga, Tennessee.

Any errors are entirely mine, either because I assumed I knew something that I didn't or because I didn't ask the right questions.

In several instances, I used a writer's prerogative to alter minor facts, but it is my hope that I have written a realistic fictional novel.

Prologue

Thirty years ago

The Humpty-Dumpty night-light cast a soft, honey-white glow over the nursery, from the 5' x 7' Mother Goose rug on the wooden floor to the fluffy clouds painted on the ceiling. A large Raggedy Andy doll, with a mop of red hair and a perpetual smile, sat atop a brightly decorated toy box in the corner. Billowy blue and white gingham curtains covered the double windows that overlooked the backyard, and a matching gingham quilt, neatly folded, lay at the foot of the baby bed in the center of the small room.

Humming quietly, Regina Bennett sat in the white spindle rocking chair, her precious little Cody asleep in her arms. Even in sleep, he still clutched his favorite toy, a little yellow teddy bear. Earlier that evening, he had been terribly fussy, crying incessantly, the sound of his pitiful gulping sobs breaking her heart. But after she had given him his medication, he had gradually quieted and gone to sleep.

But for how long? An hour? Two hours? The medication's effects seemed to wear off more quickly with each passing day. Eventually, the medication wouldn't ease his pain.

She brushed aside his damp blond curls, leaned down,

and kissed his warm forehead. Before the chemotherapy treatments, his hair had been thick and shiny, but the new growth was thin and dull. "You won't suffer anymore, my precious darling. Mommy promises."

Rocking back and forth, she cuddled Cody protectively against her breast. Still humming "Hush Little Baby," an old Southern lullaby, Regina slid her hand down to the side of the rocker and grasped the small pillow she had placed there earlier that evening.

"Mommy loves her little boy. Mommy's going to do what's best for you."

Regina lifted the pillow off the floor.

Rocking.

Humming.

Smiling sadly.

Tears misting her eyes.

Singing softly.

"Hush, little baby, don't you cry."

Regina laid the handmade pillow over her son's nose and mouth. Tears seeped from the corners of her eyes and cascaded down either side of her face. She pressed her hand in the center of the pillow and held it in place until she was certain Cody was at peace. She lifted the pillow, tossed it aside, and looked at her tiny two-year-old son.

No more pain. No more suffering.

Chapter 1

J.D. Cass listened to his breakfast date's end of the telephone conversation and knew it was bad news. In his profession, bad news was the norm, as it was in Holly's, so he wasn't surprised. When a guy was dating an assistant district attorney, even in an on-again/off-again relationship, he became accustomed to their dates being interrupted by business. Of course, it worked both ways. How many times had one of Holly's meticulously planned romantic evenings ended abruptly when he'd gotten an urgent call?

They hadn't managed to get together for the past three weeks, and J.D. was way past horny. So, yeah, his invitation for them to share an early breakfast today was his selfish way of wooing her back into his bed, and the sooner the better. Since he and Holly were both early risers, a 6:30 A.M. breakfast date had seemed the perfect chance to see each other and the least likely time that their professional lives would intrude. So much for great ideas.

"My God!" Holly Johnston's big blue eyes widened and her full lips parted in a silent gasp. "Who found her? Hmm . . . When? Is the press already there?"

Curious about the identity of the person who had been found and eager to hear the details, J.D. frowned when his own cell phone rang. He checked caller ID and grunted.

He hit the On button. "Cass here. What's up?"

"They found Jill Scott." His boss, Special Agent in Charge Phil Hayes, had a deep baritone voice made even rougher and throatier from a lifetime of smoking.

"Alive?"

"No."

"Where?"

"How close are you to Lookout Valley?"

"Why?" J.D. got a sinking feeling in the pit of his stomach.

"Because we're fixing to get dragged into this mess, so I want you to head on over to the crime scene pronto."

"Shit! Why is the TBI getting involved?"

"Because the DA wants us to be on standby. It turns out that there is a second missing woman. Debra Gregory, the mayor's wife's cousin, disappeared sometime late last night."

"Doesn't the mayor think his own police force can handle the investigation? This isn't our—"

"His Honor wants to use every resource available to him," Phil said. "And that includes us, buddy boy. The mayor called the DA and then Everett Harrelson called me personally fifteen minutes ago. Last night, the Chattanooga PD had two missing persons cases. This morning they have a murder case and a suspected kidnapping case. Since both women fit the same profile, there's a chance the same guy kidnapped Jill and Debra."

"When I show up at the crime scene, just how official am I?"

"You're unofficial for the time being. We'll ease into this gradually. Tell the investigators you're there in an advisory capacity. Assure them that the TBI isn't taking over their case."

"Yeah, sure. Like they're going to believe that."

After J.D. returned his phone to the belt holder, he looked across the table at Holly. She slid her phone into an outer pocket on her shoulder bag and shrugged.

"Bad news?" he asked.

She nodded. "What about you?"

"Yeah. That was Phil. They believe they've found Jill Scott, the woman who's been missing for the past two weeks."

Scott, a local middle school teacher, beloved by students and parents alike, had mysteriously disappeared two weeks earlier. Her parents, her fiancé, and her friends assured police that Jill would never leave without a word to anyone. They were convinced that she'd been abducted. Thanks to local media coverage, there probably wasn't a man, woman, or child in Hamilton County who didn't know the teacher's name.

"It seems our calls were about the same case," Holly told him. "Of course, I'm not actually involved with the case, not yet, but—"

"But your nephew was in Jill Scott's seventh-grade class and her murder is semipersonal for you, right?"

Holly nodded. "So, did the TBI get drafted to—?"

"Unofficially at this point," J.D. said. "But that status can change at any time." He offered Holly a life-sucks-sometimes frown. "I have to head over to the crime scene." He stood, pulled out his wallet, and laid down a couple of twenties to pay for their meal, plus a generous tip.

"Mind if I go with you?" she asked.

When he gave her an inquisitive stare, she said, "I'll stay out of the way. I know that I'm nothing more than a concerned citizen." She smiled. "Okay, a nosy concerned citizen."

"And I'm a TBI agent sticking my nose in where I may not be wanted and probably won't be welcomed."

* * *

Audrey Sherrod swallowed her tears. Although she would never apologize to anyone for her emotional involvement with her clients, she did her best not to let the empathy she experienced override her professionalism. Caring about people was a plus in her business. Allowing her personal feelings to affect a patient's treatment was unacceptable, so she walked an emotional tightrope, balancing the two sides of her personality.

Mary Nell Scott's daughter Jill had been missing for fifteen days. The Scott family was surviving on hopes and prayers. Mary Nell's husband had turned to their parish priest for solace and advice. Jill's sister, Mindy, relied on her best friends for comfort. Mary Nell had chosen to seek the help of a mental health therapist. She had chosen Audrey because several years ago, she had been one of Audrey's first clients. At that time, Mary Nell had been dealing with her husband's infidelity. After months of counseling, she had come to terms with what had happened and realized she wanted to save her marriage.

"I can't bear to hear Father Raymond's voice," Mary Nell had confessed when she had first arrived at Audrey's office today. "I know the man means well, but my faith isn't strong enough to simply leave everything in God's hands."

Mary Nell had been raised Presbyterian and converted to Catholicism when she had married Charles Scott. She had brought up both of their daughters in the Catholic faith, but she seldom attended mass and readily admitted that she had doubts about God's existence.

When the one-hour session ended, Mary Nell sat there calmly, with her head bowed and her folded hands resting in her lap. Audrey got up and retrieved a bottle of water from the mini-fridge in her office.

She truly understood the hell Mary Nell and her family were living in right now. Not knowing what had happened to a loved one was heartbreakingly unbearable. And yet they had to bear it. They had no other choice.

But that's not true. Mary Nell does have one other choice. A selfish, unthinkable choice.

Audrey pushed aside the memories from her own past about the choice her stepmother had made when she had found life unbearable. A choice that had destroyed a family already in crisis.

"I don't have another client until regular office hours at nine this morning, so if you'd like to stay longer, you may." Audrey handed Mary Nell the bottled water. She had come in early to see Mary Nell, who had left her a frantic phone message at five o'clock that morning.

"No, no." Mary Nell shook her head. "I'm meeting Charlie at seven-thirty and some of our neighbors are going to help us put up new posters all over Hamilton County. We're offering a reward of twenty-five thousand to anyone . . ." Pausing, her upper teeth biting down into her bottom lip, she closed her eyes as fresh tears trickled down her cheeks.

Suddenly Mary Nell's cell phone rang. When she struggled to open her purse, Audrey eased the leather clutch out of her trembling hands and retrieved the phone for her.

"Want me to answer it?" Audrey asked.

Mary Nell shook her head, and then reached out and took the phone.

"Hello," Mary Nell said. "What? Yes, I'm still with Audrey. Why? Oh, all right." She held out her phone. "It's my daughter, Mindy. She wants to speak to you."

Eying the phone in Mary Nell's outstretched hand, Audrey instinctively knew that whatever Mindy had to say would not be good news.

"Hello, Mindy, this is Audrey Sherrod."

"Dr. Sherrod, they've found her. They've found Jill. She's dead."

"Who contacted you with this information?"

"No one, not yet." Mindy whimpered softly. "It's already on the news, on the TV and the radio. They found a body. The newscasters are saying it's probably Jill, that the woman fits her description and she's wearing a gold cross. Jill always wore the gold cross Daddy gave her for her sixteenth birthday."

"Don't jump to conclusions."

"It's her. I know it is. Dad knows it is. I just didn't want Mom to be alone and see it on the news or hear about it on the radio. Dad and I are coming by there to pick up Mom. We're driving out to Lookout Valley where they found the body. They haven't moved her yet. She's still there. Oh, please, Dr. Sherrod, please come with us. Mom's going to need you. We all are."

"Yes, of course. I'll have my secretary cancel my morning appointments, just in case," Audrey said.

When she returned the cell phone to Mary Nell, her client looked at her pleadingly. "Don't lie to me. Tell me what Mindy said. It's Jill, isn't it? She's . . . oh, God, she's dead, isn't she?"

Audrey dropped down on her haunches in front of Mary Nell and grasped the woman's clutched hands. Their gazes met and held.

"The police have found a body that fits Jill's general description," Audrey explained. "The information is on the TV and radio. Mindy didn't want you to hear it and assume the body is Jill's. She and Charlie are on their way here now. They want me to go with y'all to the crime scene. They want to make sure it isn't Jill."

Just one little white lie to ease Mary Nell into the situation and allow her a few final moments of hope.

When half an hour later, at approximately 7:45 A.M., J.D. and Holly arrived on the scene at 50 Birmingham Highway in the Lookout Valley area, they found semicontrolled bedlam. They had missed the initial frenzy, the first responders' attempt to secure the site, the wail of sirens, and the rush of emergency vehicles. The area around the Cracker Barrel restaurant buzzed with official personnel, the first of many yet to come. Before the end of the day, the scene would be investigated by as many as fifty law enforcement and civilian specialists. The police had roped off the crime scene and strategically placed officers to keep the foot traffic to a minimum. One way in and one way out. News crews, barely held at bay by the uniformed officers, kept cameras zeroed in on the cordoned-off area and reported live to their television audience.

J.D. gained immediate entrance to the sealed area as soon as he flashed his badge. When he glanced back at Holly, she smiled and nodded, letting him know she'd be fine on her own. He'd never doubted it for a minute. Holly was a modern, I-can-take-care-of-myself woman.

Careful not to disrupt the ongoing investigation, J.D. took in the crime scene with a subtle visual inspection. He recognized a lot of the personnel, including the Hamilton County ME, Dr. Peter Tipton, and a couple of members of his team, one taking photos and another talking to two CPD investigators. J.D. knew the guy he assumed was the lead detective. He and Sergeant Garth Hudson had worked a case involving a gang-related murder eleven months ago, shortly after J.D. had been transferred from Memphis to the TBI Chattanooga Field Office. Hudson was a decorated, twenty-five-year veteran of the CPD. A smart guy, a good cop, a little on the cocky side. J.D. didn't know the officer with Hudson, an attractive African American woman with a dark caramel complexion and petite, curvy body. As he approached them, she turned and glowered at him, her coffee brown eyes surveying him from head to toe.

"Who sicced the TBI on us?" Hudson growled the question as he glared at J.D. "The mayor, no doubt."

"I'm here strictly in an advisory capacity," J.D. assured him. "This is the CPD's case." J.D. smiled at the pretty lady with Hudson. "Introduce us."

Hudson grunted. "Officer Tamara Lovelady, my partner. Tam, meet TBI Special Agent J.D. Cass."

Tam nodded, her expression neutral.

"So, how about letting me take a look at Jill Scott," J.D. said, then added, "if it is Jill Scott."

"There's a good chance it is Ms. Scott's body, but no positive ID. Not yet." Hudson glanced at his partner. "Tam will go with you. Look all you want, but don't touch."

J.D. wanted to remind Hudson that he wasn't some rookie who needed instructions, but he kept quiet. For now, he wasn't assigned to this case, and any privileges Hudson afforded him were at his discretion. He had worked with police and sheriffs' departments throughout the state and understood how territorial local law enforcement could be. Trying not to step on any toes was just part of his job. A part he damn well hated. He wasn't known for his diplomatic abilities. He supposed that was one reason he was still a field agent. That and a hot temper he'd been trying to control all of his life.

The TBI's role was to assist local law enforcement in investigating major crimes, the operative word being "assist."

When Officer Lovelady motioned to J.D., he followed her past the swarm of investigators and onto the restaurant's wide porch.

Peter Tipton spotted J.D. and Tam heading his way. He paused in his examination of the body and moved aside to give J.D. a complete view of the corpse.

The victim—not yet positively identified as Jill Scott—sat upright in one of the numerous rocking chairs on the Cracker Barrel porch. Her eyes were shut and at first glance she seemed to be sleeping. Something swaddled in a delicate blue baby shawl lay nestled in her lap. J.D. strained to get a better look at the object.

He took a step closer, and then stopped.

"We thought at first it was a doll," Tam told J.D. "But it's not."

Good God almighty!

"It's real," J.D. said.

"Oh yeah, it's real all right," Tipton replied.

J.D. had seen some weird sights in his time, as well as several sickeningly gruesome scenes, but never anything like this.

"It's a first for me," Tipton said.

"Yeah, me, too. Any idea who . . . what . . . ?" J.D. found himself stammering, something he never did. But then he'd never seen a fresh corpse cradling the skeletal remains of a small child. He cleared his throat and asked, "Any idea how either of them died? The woman—?"

"Asphyxiation."

J.D. studied the dark-haired victim sitting so serenely in the wooden rocking chair. Traffic from the nearby interstate hummed over the din of voices, conversations blending with news coverage and bystanders' comments. Overhead the September sky was clear, the morning sun warm, the temperature somewhere in the high seventies. The beginning of a perfect pre-autumn day. But not so perfect for Jill Scott.

"Method of asphyxiation?" J.D. asked.

"Probably suffocation," Tipton replied. "There's no sign of strangulation."

"How long do you think she's been dead?"

Tipton glanced at the corpse. "She's in full rigor. Time of death—six to twelve hours ago. I'd guess eight to ten."

"You don't think she was killed here, do you?" J.D. asked.

"She was probably killed somewhere else sometime before midnight and then brought here while it was still dark so it would be less likely anyone would see what was happening."

"Yeah, not much chance anyone saw something."

"Whoever killed her staged this little scene," Tam Lovelady said. "He painted us a picture."

"Mother and child," J.D. surmised.

"He's a sick son of a bitch, whoever he is." Tam stared at the victim. "She looks so damn peaceful."

"He went to a great deal of trouble to dispose of her body in such a dramatic fashion." J.D. remembered a bizarre case in Memphis when he was a rookie agent where the killer had placed his victims by the river, sitting up in a camp chair and holding a fishing pole. Weirdest thing he'd ever seen. Until now. "He's telling us something. We just have to figure out what it is."

"He's telling us that he's fucking crazy," Garth said, his voice a low grumble, as he came up behind them.

"What about the child?" J.D. asked.

"At this point, nothing more than the obvious—that the woman and the child didn't die at the same time. So, if that's all, J.D., I need to get back to work," Tipton said. "We're about ready to bag the body and the skeleton."

"Yeah, sure thing." As Tipton walked away, J.D. called to him. "We'll talk again later."

Tipton threw up his hand in a backward wave as he walked off.

"Are you hanging around?" Garth asked J.D.

"I thought I would, if you have no objections."

Garth shook his head. "My crime scene is your crime scene."

With a hard, craggy face, deep-set hazel eyes, and thinning gray hair, Garth Hudson looked every one of his fifty-some-odd years. Borderline butt-ugly, the sergeant wouldn't win any beauty contests, but he was neat as a pin. Whenever

J.D. saw the man, Garth was wearing neatly pressed slacks, a jacket, and a tailored shirt.

J.D. and the investigators watched quietly while Tipton slipped the blue baby blanket and its contents into a body bag and then carefully handed the tiny unknown child to one of his assistants. That done, he went back to the woman in the rocking chair. He covered the victim's head, feet, and hands with individual bags and secured them with tape.

They stood by respectfully until the body was bagged and removed from the scene.

Before they could resume their conversation, a series of ear-piercing screams and mournful cries stopped everyone in their tracks.

"What the hell?" Garth's gaze traveled around the crime scene and beyond, searching for the source of the noise.

"I want to see her!" a female voice shouted. "If it's my baby, I want to see her!"

A uniformed officer rushed over to Garth. "It's the mother. Jill Scott's mother."

"Damn!" Garth huffed. "How the hell did she find out?"

"My guess is from the live TV coverage." Tam motioned past the crime scene tape to the horde of reporters chomping at the bit for a closer view.

"The whole family just showed up," the officer said. "Mom, Dad, and kid sister. The mom's screaming her head off."

"Keep her out of here," Garth said. "But tell the guys they're to handle the family with kid gloves."

"Want me to take care of it?" Tam asked. "I can go talk to the family."

"Yeah," Garth said. "You can handle a hysterical woman a lot better than I can."

When Tam gave her partner a you're-a-chauvinist-pig glare before walking away, J.D. fell into step beside her.

"Do you do that a lot?" J.D asked.

Without slowing her pace, Tam said, "Do what?"

"Handle the unpleasant tasks for your partner?"

"Sergeant Hudson and I have been partnered for less than a month. I'm the new investigator on the homicide squad. But before then, yeah, I usually handled anything my partner thought was woman's work. Other women. Kids. Anything that had to do with emotional issues."

"And you don't mind?"

"I don't mind. I don't have anything to prove. I know I'm a very good police officer and I'll be a very good detective. And I don't think of it as a negative thing that I'm capable of handling some of the most difficult aspects of being a police officer."

"And one of those difficult aspects is dealing with the victim's family."

"Can you think of anything more difficult than telling a mother that her child is dead?"

Debra Gregory tugged on the ropes that bound her red, chafed wrists to the arms of the rocking chair. Her seemingly useless struggles to free herself had eaten away skin, leaving her wrists and ankles bruised and bloody. He had secured her feet together and tied her wrists before he had left her. She had screamed for help until she was hoarse, but had soon realized no one could hear her and that's why he hadn't gagged her. Wherever he was holding her captive was so isolated that there was no danger of anyone hearing her screams.

Dark and damp. And as silent as a grave.

Terror had given way to frustration, and frustration to anger.

She had lost count of how many hours she'd been in this horrible, obsidian hell. He had left her alone for what seemed like days, alone in the pitch-black darkness. She didn't think she'd been here days. Not yet. Only a few hours. Maybe a little longer. God help her, she wasn't sure.

The last thing she remembered before waking up here was coming out of the gym late Tuesday night. Days ago? Hours ago? She'd been one of the last to leave shortly before closing at eleven and noticed that only two other cars remained in the parking lot. She had hit the Unlock button on her keypad before reaching her Lexus, and just as she'd opened the door, someone had grabbed her from behind. It had happened so quickly. A strangely sweet odor coming from the cloth he cupped over her nose and mouth. Her senses dulling as the anesthetic took effect. The weightless feeling as he lifted her off her feet. And then unconsciousness.

The police are looking for me. My family is doing everything possible to find me. I'll be rescued soon. I can't give up hope. I have to stay alive, no matter what.

When would he come back?

She was alone in the darkness, strapped to a chair, unable to escape, going slowly out of her mind. Suddenly a dim light instantly obliterated the darkness.

She turned her head sideways, but couldn't see the source of the light. It came from somewhere across the room. A candle? A lantern? Maybe a night-light?

Light had to mean that he had returned. Not enough light to see anything clearly, just enough to make out shapes and shadows.

Debra's heartbeat pounded in her ears. Her fear escalated quickly as she sensed him moving toward her. Closer and closer.

"Did you have a nice rest while I was gone?" he asked from where he stood behind her.

"Please . . . please let me go." Her voice quavered. "I haven't seen your face. I don't know who you are. I can't identify you." She was bargaining for her life, pleading with this unknown, unseen devil.

He stroked her hair, his touch terrifyingly tender. "You're talking nonsense. Of course you know who I am." He untied her left hand and rubbed her chafed, bloody wrist before pulling her arm inward toward her waist.

"I don't . . ." She drew in a sharp breath when he reached over her head and around her shoulder and placed something in the curve of her arm. She looked down at the bundle lying in her lap and was able to make out the form of what she thought might be a baby wrapped securely in a blanket.

No, no, it couldn't be a baby. It wasn't moving, wasn't crying. It wasn't warm and alive.

"He needs you," the man told her. "He won't rest unless you sing to him."

She swallowed the fear lodged in her throat. Was she holding a doll, a very large baby doll? As her vision adjusted to the semidarkness, she looked right and left, then upward, trying to catch a glimpse of her jailor. All she saw were his legs clad in jeans and the sleeves of his dark jacket.

"Sing to him. You know the song he likes," he told her, his voice soft yet stern. "Rock him to sleep the way you do every night."

"I—I don't remember the song."

"Of course you do. Now sing to him."

She forced out the words of the most familiar lullaby she knew. "Rock-a-bye baby—"

"That's not the right song!" he shouted. "Sing the right song. He wants you to sing the song you always sing. You know the words!" And then he sang the first verse. "Hush, little baby, don't say a word . . ."

On the verge of screaming hysterically, Debra somehow managed to sing as she held the blanket-wrapped bundle in her arms. She vaguely remembered the tune, but not the lyrics. *Sing, damn it. Make up the words. Improvise! Your life could depend on it.*

"Hush, little baby, don't say a word, Mama's going to buy

you a golden ring." Her voice quivered. "If that golden ring don't shine, Mama's going to sing, sing, sing."

"You're mixing up the words." Leaning over her, watching her, his breath warm against her neck, he whispered, "But he loves the sound of your voice. We both do. Keep singing."

Debra forced the words, making them up as she went along, trying her best to fit them to the tune she barely remembered. She tried not to cry, not to panic, not to say or do something that would upset her captor. He held her life in his hands. As long as she cooperated and played his little game, she had a chance of staying alive.

Why she chose that moment—midsong and midthought of doing whatever was necessary to stay alive—to glance down at the doll, she would never know. With her eyes fully adjusted to the dim, distant light, she was able to see the object in her arms. Not a doll at all.

The song died on her lips, and the scream vibrating in her throat remained trapped there by sheer paralyzing horror.

Chapter 2

Charlie Scott kept his arm clutched tightly around his wife's shoulders, the strength of his hold the only thing stopping her from breaking through the yellow barricade tape that separated the onlookers from the crime scene. While Mary Nell pleaded with her husband to release her, Audrey held eighteen-year-old Mindy's damp, shaky hand as she tried to talk to Mary Nell. But Mary Nell was beyond listening, beyond anyone helping her at this point. There would be a time, later on, days from now or perhaps weeks or months, that Audrey might be able to help her. But not today.

"Why won't someone tell us if it's Jill or not?" Mindy's soft voice was barely audible over her mother's loud, pitiful cries.

"The police probably haven't identified the victim," Audrey said. "Until they do, we cannot lose hope that the woman they found isn't Jill."

"I can't stand it." Mindy gripped Audrey's hand. "Mom's falling apart and . . ." Unable to control her tears, Mindy jerked away from Audrey and dropped her head, hunched her trembling shoulders, and covered her face with her hands.

As Audrey turned to comfort Mindy, she spotted her friend Tamara Lovelady, lifting the crime scene tape, walking under it, and heading in their direction. She and Tam had been friends all their lives. Both of their dads had been Chattanooga policemen. Oddly enough, she and Tam had been born exactly two days apart. How many birthday parties had they shared over the years? Their last party had been four years ago when they turned thirty, an event hosted by Tam's parents.

Tam's eyes widened with a hint of surprise when she saw Audrey. Despite Mary Nell reaching out to Tam, she passed by Jill's mother and came straight to Audrey.

"Are you here with the Scott family?" Tam asked.

"Yes. Mary Nell—Mrs. Scott—was with me when we got the news about the body being found here in Lookout Valley." Audrey leaned down and whispered, "Is it Jill Scott?"

Tam, who stood five-three in her bare feet, looked up at Audrey, who towered over her at five-nine, and replied, "We'll need a family member to officially ID the body, but, yes, we're pretty sure it's her."

"What are y'all talking about?" Mary Nell demanded, her eyes wild with fear. "Tell me! I have every right to know if . . ." She gulped down her hysterical sobs. "If it's Jill, I want to see her."

"Mrs. Scott, I'm Officer Lovelady." Tam's gaze settled sympathetically on Mary Nell. "The body is being taken to the ME's office. We'd appreciate it if a member of the family"—Tam looked directly at Charlie Scott —"would identify the body."

Mary Nell keened shrilly, the sound gaining everyone's immediate attention.

"Isn't there some way that Mr. and Mrs. Scott could see the body now?" Audrey asked.

"I don't know. I'll check with Garth—"

"Please, let me see her," Mary Nell whimpered.

"Why don't y'all give me a few minutes," Tam said. "Audrey, want to come with me?"

"Sure."

When they were out of earshot of the Scott family, Tam said, "Mrs. Scott is going to fall apart if she sees her daughter's body."

"I've already called her GP to alert him that she's going to need medication."

"Good."

Tam took Audrey with her past the tape barricade as she rushed to catch up with Pete Tipton's assistants, who were carrying the body bag toward the ME's van parked in the restaurant's back parking lot.

"Wait up, guys," Tam called to them.

Tipton, who was still talking to Garth and another man, someone Audrey didn't know, quickly ended his conversation and threw up his hand. "What's wrong?"

"Nothing," Tam said. "I just need y'all to wait a couple of minutes."

Tipton, Garth, and the stranger came over to where Tam and Audrey stood only a few feet away from the body bag.

"Look, the parents want to see the body now," Tam explained. "The mother is hysterical as it is. I don't think letting her see the body can make it any worse."

"If anything, it might help her." Audrey injected her opinion. "The not knowing is often far worse than the knowing." She glanced at Garth, her step-uncle, and saw the flash of painful memories in his eyes. "If it is Jill, then why make her parents wait any longer to find out the truth?"

"And you are?" The tall, rough-around-the-edges stranger

looked right at Audrey. The midday sun turned his salt-and-pepper hair to black-streaked silver.

Garth looked questioningly at Audrey and asked, "What are you doing here?"

"I'm here with—" Audrey said, but Tam interrupted her and rushed straight into introductions.

"Audrey, this is Special Agent Cass with the TBI."

Garth added, "J.D., this is my niece, Dr. Sherrod."

Audrey and J.D. Cass exchanged quick, intense inspections. She wasn't sure exactly what he thought of her and really didn't care. As a general rule, people tended to like her and she liked almost everyone she met. But there was something about the way this man looked at her, as if he found some flaw she wasn't aware of, that annoyed her.

His black-eyed gaze settled on her face and then he smiled. "You're not an M.D., are you?" He rubbed his chin. "Hmm . . . Let me guess—"

"Doctorate of philosophy in psychology," Audrey told him. "I'm a mental health therapist."

"Audrey is Mary Nell Scott's counselor," Tam explained. "She came here with Jill Scott's family because Mrs. Scott is one of her patients."

"Damn," Garth grumbled under his breath.

"Is it your professional opinion that Mrs. Scott can handle seeing her daughter's corpse?" J.D. asked, his gaze intensely focused on Audrey

"It's my opinion that seeing her daughter's body—if indeed that's Jill"—she nodded toward the body bag—"will harm her less than not knowing."

Audrey glared at J.D. Cass. Admittedly, she found him attractive. Who wouldn't? He was about six-three, broad shouldered, and extremely masculine, although not classically handsome. But for some reason, he irritated her. Maybe it was because of the almost condescending way he'd said,

"You're not an M.D." Or it could be because she sensed that he found her lacking in one way or another?

And that bothers you, doesn't it?

Damn right it did. After all, she was reasonably attractive, some even said pretty. She was highly intelligent and well educated and possessed more than competent social graces. Who was he to look down his imperfect nose at her?

"Let's get this over with," Pete Tipton said. "Bring the parents over and let them ID the body." He motioned to his assistants.

"Thank you." Audrey focused on the ME, offering him a genuine smile.

"I'll tell the Scotts." By the time the statement left her lips, Tam was in motion.

Garth received a phone call, excused himself, and left Audrey and the TBI agent standing side by side. Usually quite adept at conversation, even idle chitchat when necessary, Audrey suddenly found herself unnaturally silent.

Sensing the TBI agent looking at her, she turned back around and faced him. "Is there something you wanted to say, Special Agent Cass?"

With a sly smile curving his lips, the man shrugged. "No, ma'am, Dr. Sherrod."

"Here they come," Pete Tipton said as the Scott family approached. "No matter how many times I've done this, it doesn't get any easier."

Tam escorted the Scotts, Charlie with his arm around Mary Nell, and Mindy following her parents.

"May we see her, please?" Charlie asked.

Tipton nodded. Tam led the family to where the ME's assistants held the body bag. Tipton unzipped the bag, removed the small, protective bag covering the victim's head, and stepped back to allow the family an unobstructed view.

Mary Nell gasped and then burst into tears as she crumpled right before their eyes. Weeping uncontrollably, she doubled over in pain. Charlie held her, his arms circling her waist, supporting her twisted body. Mindy stood silent and alone a few feet behind her parents. She had turned an ash gray, her glazed eyes overflowing with tears.

Charlie pulled Mary Nell up and into his arms. He looked Peter Tipton right in the eye. "It's our daughter. It's Jill."

Tam and her husband Marcus, an engineer with the Tennessee Valley Authority in Chattanooga, met Audrey and her current boyfriend, Porter Bryant, for dinner that evening. Audrey and Tam arrived late, less than two minutes apart, so they paused outside J. Alexander's for a quick chat before entering the upscale restaurant on Hamilton Place Boulevard. Neither had changed clothes from earlier that day. Tam still wore black slacks, a lightweight camel blazer, and sensible but stylish one-inch pumps. She had discarded her shoulder holster, something she had forgotten to do a few weeks ago when the foursome had met for dinner. Of course, it had been her first week as a detective.

How Tam could look so good with practically no makeup at the age of thirty-four, Audrey would never know. Maybe it was her flawless golden brown skin or her large, luminous, dark chocolate eyes and thick black lashes.

Although Audrey hadn't taken time to change from her tailored navy pin-striped slacks and matching jacket into something more femininely casual, she had added fresh blush and lipstick, which she kept in her handbag. She had almost phoned Porter and canceled, but a girl had to eat, and what better company could she find tonight than three good friends? The last thing she wanted to do after a day like today was go home to an empty house. She kept thinking about getting a pet, a cat or a dog or even a goldfish. She thought about it, but never did it.

"You look beat," Tam said. "Have you been with the Scotts all this time?"

She nodded. "Yes, I stayed and talked to Charlie and Mindy after Dr. Jarnigan's nurse practitioner came by and gave Mary Beth an injection. A strong sedative. And I helped Charlie deal with countless phone calls and an endless parade of family and friends who came and went all afternoon. Their priest is there with them, as well as Charlie's sister and her husband and several cousins."

"It's been a difficult day all around," Tam said. "I left your uncle Garth at headquarters. No wonder he's been divorced four times. What woman would put up with a man married to his job?"

"Every missing persons case is personal for him."

"Because of Blake," Tam said. "Garth is a dedicated policeman for the same reason you're a dedicated counselor. You both want to help people in pain."

Although Audrey managed to go days, often weeks, without thinking very much about Blake, any missing persons case stirred up old memories. And when she was personally involved in the case, a counselor to someone with a missing family member, she occasionally still had nightmares, decades-old nightmares, about her little brother Blake's disappearance. The two-year-old had been abducted twenty-five years ago and was still missing. Missing and presumed dead.

"I know you can't talk about evidence and all that," Audrey said. "But can you tell me one thing—do y'all think that whoever kidnapped and killed Jill Scott is the same person who abducted Debra Gregory?"

"Possibly. It's common knowledge that the two women are both in their mid-twenties, both average height and weight, both white females, both brunettes with long dark hair. The *Chattanooga Times Free Press* ran their photographs side by side on the front page this morning. At the mayor's insistence, I'm sure. Did you see it?"

"I saw it. And before you ask, yes, I thought there was a resemblance."

"Enough of a resemblance that they could pass for sisters," Tam said. "Debra Gregory looks more like Jill than her own sister Mindy does."

"But the CPD is downplaying the resemblance, aren't they? The fact that the women resembled each other wasn't mentioned in the press conference."

"We don't want to panic all the young, dark-haired women in Hamilton County who fit the same description. Not when we can't be a hundred percent sure the two cases are connected. Debra hasn't been missing twenty-four hours."

"Then why bring in the TBI?" Audrey asked.

"They're not officially involved. Not yet." Tam forced a smile. "We'd better find our dates. We're already twenty minutes late. Marcus has called me twice since he arrived."

As they entered the restaurant, Audrey asked, "How well do you know Special Agent Cass?"

Tam spoke to the hostess, who offered to show them to their table.

"I never met him before today," Tam replied. "Why do you ask?"

"No reason. Just curious."

"There they are." Tam waved at Marcus and Porter, who were seated in a booth halfway across the restaurant. "FYI—the DA called in the TBI. We did not request assistance."

"He seems like the type who'd expect to take over."

"Who? Special Agent Cass? What makes you think that?" Tam's smile widened. "Yeah, I know. He was sending out some powerful He-Man vibes, wasn't he? And I noticed the way you two kept looking at each other. What was that all about?"

"I have no idea what you're talking about," Audrey lied.

When they approached the booth where their dates sat, both men stood, gentlemen that they were. Marcus gave Tam a quick kiss on the mouth and a big I'm-glad-to-see-you smile. Porter gave Audrey a peck on the cheek. She and Porter had been dating for nearly six months now and she suspected he was ready for more than the friendship they shared. He hadn't pushed her into a sexual relationship and she was grateful, although she knew that it was only a matter of time. More than once recently, he had hinted about them moving in together, but she had ignored the hints. She had no desire to live with Porter or any other man. And marriage was out of the question. No way, no how.

"Sorry I'm late," Tam said. "We're in the middle of—"

"No shop talk this evening," Marcus told her. "We're going to have drinks and a nice dinner and relax."

"Sounds good to me." Tam picked up her husband's glass of Chardonnay and took a sip. "This could be the last halfway relaxing evening I have for quite some time."

J.D. dropped his keys on the kitchen counter as he entered his Signal Mountain rental house through the door that led inside from the two-car garage. By the time he reached the living room, he had removed his jacket and his hip holster. He tossed the jacket over the back of the nearest chair and dumped the holster down on the coffee table. It had been a long, seemingly endless day and he was tired. And still horny. He had hoped his breakfast date with Holly that morning would lead to an invitation for him to come over to her place that night. So much for well-laid plans. Per his boss's instructions, he had stuck with the lead investigators on the Jill Scott case all day and had finally left Sergeant Hudson at the police station half an hour ago. The man was dedicated beyond the norm for any officer.

It wasn't that J.D. didn't give his all to his job. He did. But he didn't live and breathe his job 24/7. There had been a time when he had. Now he couldn't even if he wanted to. He had other responsibilities, ones in his personal life that required his time and attention.

Just as he kicked off his shoes and wiggled his sock-clad toes, he heard the phone ring. Not his phone. The ringtone belonged to his daughter. Some idiotic song titled "Boom Boom Pow" by a group Zoe had informed him was called the Black Eyed Peas.

Even now, after she'd been living with him for more than a year, he still sometimes forgot he had a kid. A fourteen-year-old daughter. A teenager with an attitude. Zoe was far too pretty and looked way too mature not to gain male attention. When he had told her that she was too young to date, she'd thrown a hissy fit. The girl had a temper. And as much as he'd like to blame her mother for that genetic defect, he couldn't. Carrie Davidson had been promiscuous, self-centered, vain, and sexy as hell, but not once during their brief affair had he ever seen her lose her temper. No, Zoe had inherited that personality flaw from him.

J.D. traipsed into the kitchen, opened the refrigerator, and retrieved a bottle of beer. Just as he removed the cap and took his first sip, he heard a loud crash, followed by a string of equally loud curse words. Carrying the beer with him, he went through the living room and down the hall and stopped outside his daughter's closed bedroom door. He knocked.

"Go away!" she screamed.

"What's going on in there?"

"Not a damn thing. All my friends are together and having a good time tonight and I'm stuck here in my room, a virtual prisoner."

"It's a school night," J.D. reminded her. "I hardly think all your friends are out partying tonight."

"A bunch are studying together over at Presley's house.

They ordered pizza and are having fun. Fun that I'm missing, thanks to you." Zoe eased open her bedroom door and peered out into the hall. "Hi. How was your day?"

"Rough," he replied. "How was yours?"

"It was okay, but it could end really good." She opened the door all the way and plastered a big smile on her gorgeous face.

What the hell was she wearing? They'd had more than one row about her clothes. Tonight it was green tights, suede knee-high boots, a too short, too tight knit sweater, and a skirt that barely covered her butt. All the clothes she had brought with her last year when he'd moved her in with him had looked like they belonged to a hooker. She'd promptly informed him that her clothes were what girls were wearing these days, as opposed to when he'd been a kid, back in the Dark Ages.

"What do you want?" J.D asked. From his experience, whenever Zoe was pleasant to him, she wanted something.

"Let me go over to Presley's. Please, please. I promise I'll be back by eleven."

"I don't think so. It's after eight now. Besides, I'm too tired to drive you over to—"

"That's okay, J.D." Zoe came out of her room, her leather shoulder bag slung over her arm. "Presley's brother Dawson will pick me up. All I have to do is call her back right now." Zoe held up her bright pink cell phone. "Please."

He didn't like playing the stern, disciplinarian parent, but God knew it was way past time that someone did. Apparently Carrie had allowed Zoe to do whatever she wanted to do. And now that she was forced to live with a parent who more often than not said no to her demands, she was a miserable young girl.

"Not tonight," J.D. told hcr. "It's a school night. You know the rules."

"Screw your rules! I hate you! I hate living here with

you!" She scrunched up her face, glowered at him, and then went back into her room, slamming the door behind her.

J.D. heaved a deep, labored breath.

What had he ever done to deserve this?

You got Carrie Davidson pregnant, that's what.

J.D. took a hefty swig from the beer bottle as he walked back to the kitchen. He wasn't cut out to be a father. Although he was doing his best with Zoe, his best wasn't good enough. She was miserable and she made him miserable. She was his daughter. The DNA tests proved it beyond a shadow of a doubt. He should love her. She should love him. But she hated him and he tolerated her.

He finished off the first beer as he made himself a couple of ham and cheese sandwiches and then drank another beer with his meal.

He wondered what Dr. Audrey Sherrod would think of his relationship with Zoe. They were a dysfunctional family if ever there was one. Neither had known the other existed until eighteen months ago when Carrie, dying from breast cancer, had called J.D. to say, "Congratulations, you're the father of a bouncing baby girl."

Burrowing into his worn leather lounge chair, J.D. picked up the remote and channel surfed, finally pausing on CNN.

Why was he thinking about Audrey Sherrod? Why had she suddenly popped into his head?

He had gotten the distinct impression that the lady didn't like him. She certainly had looked down her nose at him. And she had a cute little nose and a rather pretty face. Not beautiful, but pretty enough if you liked her type, which he didn't. She was tall for a woman, a good five-nine. Slender, but not quite skinny. He had noticed the way her breasts filled out the neat pin-striped jacket she had been wearing. Sufficient but not large by any means.

If you had gotten laid recently, you wouldn't find Audrey Sherrod the least bit attractive.

Maybe. Maybe not.

Just because he had always preferred his women hot and eager didn't mean it might not be interesting to see just what it would take to defrost Dr. Sherrod's icy façade.

What the hell was he thinking? He sure didn't need another woman in his life. The casual relationship he shared with Holly suited them both just fine. He didn't think Audrey Sherrod was the type for casual, and that's all he wanted from a woman, all he could ever offer, especially now that he had Zoe in his life.

J.D. was ashamed of the way he felt, that he considered Zoe a nuisance. What kind of parent was he?

Think about what the Scotts are going through tonight. They've lost their daughter, and here you are moaning and groaning about your kid. You should be thankful that she's alive and well and creating havoc in your life. I'd bet Charlie Scott would tell you that you're one lucky SOB.

Two hours later, after consuming his third beer and falling asleep in front of the TV, J.D. woke, gathered up his shoes, jacket, and holster, and headed down the hall. He paused outside of Zoe's closed door. He knocked softly. She didn't respond. He turned the doorknob and to his surprise found the door unlocked. He eased open the door and peered inside the semidark room. With her hair still damp from her recent shower and wearing an oversized Jeff Gordon NASCAR sweatshirt, she lay asleep atop the covers.

J.D. slipped into the room, freed one hand from the load he was carrying, and then drew the folded bedspread up and over his daughter. He stood there for a few minutes and watched his little girl sleep. In the looks department, she'd gotten the best of Carrie and him. Actually, she looked a lot like J.D.'s sister Julia.

I'm sorry I'm not a better father. I'm sorry that I never knew you existed. I'm doing the best I can, kiddo. I promise that I'll try not to screw things up too bad.

He reached down and ran his fingertips across her forehead, brushing aside a strand of long black hair.

You deserve better than me, Zoe. But you're stuck with me. Like it or not, I'm your dad.

Chapter 3

For most of her life—certainly after the car wreck that had claimed her mother's life when she was six—Audrey had enjoyed a close bond with Tam's parents, Geraldine and Willie Mullins. Geraldine was the type of mother every little girl should have—loving, caring, attentive, putting her child's needs before her own. A mother to her child, not a girlfriend. Tam had been raised with a strict set of rules and regulations, but at the same time her parents had trusted her completely.

"I trust Tam to always do the right thing," Geraldine had said. "And until she proves to me that I can't trust her, I will always believe what she tells me is the truth."

Audrey was pretty sure that Tam's parents felt that she had never disappointed them. She'd been salutatorian of her high school graduating class, graduated magna cum laude from UT, and had gone on to graduate first in her class at the police academy. Although Geraldine would have preferred her daughter choose a less dangerous profession, Willie had been a very proud papa when his only child chose to follow in his footsteps and join the CPD. Willie had worked his way up the ladder from patrolman to chief of police.

Audrey envied her best friend her parents and the nurturing environment in which she had grown up. And even if they had known about Tam's one and only fall from grace, they would have forgiven her and not loved her any less. Audrey's earliest memories were of her parents arguing. Wayne Sherrod's job as a Chattanooga policeman had come first with him. His wife and daughter had come in a distant second. Why the bubbly, sweet-natured social butterfly Norma Colton had married a stoic, cynical, hard-nosed cop, no one understood, least of all Audrey. Maybe it had been nothing more than opposites attracting.

She had always believed that if she'd been a boy, her father would have paid more attention to her. And that theory, one she had formed early on, had been proven correct when his second wife had presented him with a son. From the moment he was born, Blake had been the center of Wayne's life, even more important to him than his job.

She had been jealous of her baby brother and had sometimes resented him terribly. But she had also loved him. Blake had been so sweet, so adorable, so very precious. When, a month before his second birthday, he had disappeared—assumed kidnapped—she had been consumed with guilt. Had it been her fault in some way because she had resented that her father so obviously loved Blake more than he did her? In her nine-year-old mind, she had felt somehow at fault. It hadn't helped that, in his desperate grief, her father had accused her and her stepbrother Hart of being glad that Blake had been abducted.

As an adult, she had come to realize that her father had known what he'd said wasn't true, that later, he had probably regretted the harsh, unjust accusation. And although her father had never apologized, Audrey had long ago forgiven him for lashing out at two innocent children. But she hadn't forgotten, couldn't forget no matter how much she wished she could. She wasn't sure her father even remembered that day in detail. But that one moment in time, that one unjust accusation, had erected a barrier between father and daughter that still existed.

Audrey saw her dad infrequently—holidays, mostly. She called him occasionally—on his birthday and on her birthday—but he seldom called her. Her dad's relationship with his stepson Hart wasn't any better, but at least Hart had his uncle Garth, who had stepped in and become a surrogate father to him. And even though she thought Garth was a brash, cocky, womanizing SOB, she respected him for being a dedicated policeman and for looking after Hart, for always being there for his nephew. Her stepbrother practically worshipped the man.

Audrey would have felt completely alone in the world if not for the love and attention Tam and her parents had shown her over the years. But that was only one of the many reasons she adored Geraldine and Willie Mullins.

It was her love for Tam's parents that had brought her there tonight despite the emotionally grueling day she'd had. Nine days after her murder, Jill Scott had been laid to rest. Audrey had cleared her afternoon schedule so she could attend the funeral and be available if Mary Nell needed her. But it had been obvious to everyone that Mary Nell had been medicated, possibly overmedicated. She had done little more than sleepwalk through the church service and the burial ceremony.

It had been nine days since Jill's parents learned their daughter's fate. Nine days since Jill's body had been found in a rocking chair on the Cracker Barrel porch in Lookout Valley. Nine agonizing days, and the police still didn't have a suspect. Nine days, and Debra Gregory was still missing.

When Audrey entered the Read House in downtown

Chattanooga, she searched the lobby area for Porter. They had agreed to meet there instead of him picking her up at home. He wasn't difficult to find since he was waiting right inside the front entrance.

Spit and polish. That was Porter Bryant to a T. Always dressed impeccably, clean-shaven, styled hair, manicured nails buffed to a gloss finish, and wearing a delicate hint of expensive men's cologne.

Porter was to the manor born, so to speak. His father had been a wealthy, high-profile lawyer and his mother a socialite who had dabbled in interior design. Audrey suspected that Porter's mother and her mother would have gotten on famously.

"Sorry I'm late," she told him. "After I left the Scotts, I barely had time to go home and change clothes."

"You missed Chief Mullins's grand entrance and the big surprise moment." Porter's tone held a note of censure. When she gave him a screw-you glare, he quickly added, "You look lovely, so it was worth the wait. And I'm sure with so many people here, the chief and Mrs. Mullins weren't aware of your absence."

When he held out his arm for her to take, Audrey graciously accepted and they walked across the lobby and entered the Hamilton Room. Geraldine and Tam had rented that room and the adjoining River City Room for the surprise sixtieth birthday party they were hosting for Willie. The moment the door opened, music, laughter, and the roar of at least two hundred voices enveloped them.

"My God, I know Geraldine didn't invite half of Hamilton County," Audrey said. "She wanted it to be a close friends and family event."

"Well, if only a third of the invited guests brought a date, that would dramatically increase the number of people attending tonight. Considering that Willie Mullins is the Chattanooga police chief, one would expect a large gathering.

Certain things are expected of a high-ranking public servant."

"I'm sure Geraldine was pressured into expanding the guest list." No doubt by some well-meaning bureaucrat whose opinions matched Porter's. Tam had told her there were rumors circulating that the state Democratic Party was interested in backing Willie for the U.S. Congress in the next election.

"If so, then she was a wise woman to agree. What the Mullins family does now can affect his political future," Porter said as if Audrey was clueless about how the game of politics was played. "And Mrs. Mullins showed remarkable good taste in adhering to acceptable social etiquette for such a huge party by requesting no gifts."

Audrey had to bite her tongue to keep from snapping at Porter. His last comment had come across as a backhanded compliment if she'd ever heard one.

Dating Porter had become a habit, one she needed to break sooner rather than later. He was handsome and could, on occasion, be charming, but he was such a snob. He seemed to be every woman's dream—intelligent, well-mannered, attentive, and handsome. Everyone said that he was a young man with a bright future. Even Tam had liked him when he and Audrey had first started dating, but had revised her opinion within a few weeks.

"Porter's okay," Tam had told her. "If you like the stuffed-shirt type. But, girlfriend, he's so not the man for you."

Despite Tam's opinion and her own nagging doubts, Audrey had fallen into a comfortable routine with Porter. And what she had liked most about dating him was the fact that he hadn't been demanding. Whenever she had to break a date, he was more than understanding. When she continuously told him she wasn't ready for a serious relationship, he accepted the fact that she wasn't ready, that she wanted to wait.

But wait for what? She hadn't been specific. He hadn't asked.

What are you waiting for, Audrey?

As Porter led her through the throng of celebrators, he said, "This is a come-and-go thing, so we don't have to stay the entire four hours. I thought you could make your presence known, wish happy birthday to Chief Mullins, grab a few tidbits from the buffet table, drink a glass of bubbly, and then—"

"I intend to stay for a good while," Audrey informed him.

"How long? I had hoped—"

"Porter, do not go there. Not tonight of all nights. You have to understand what a difficult day this has been for me."

He pouted like a petulant child who had been sent to bed without his supper. "Yes, of course. I'm sorry. No pressure, darling."

She paused alongside the dance floor and turned to the ever-accommodating Porter. "Willie Mullins is my dearest friend's father. I love the man. I think of him and Geraldine as family. I'm not going to make a brief appearance at his sixtieth birthday party and just disappear."

"Yes, of course, I really do understand." Porter released his hold on her elbow. "Why don't I find a waiter and get us some champagne."

"Thank you. That would be nice."

As if from out of nowhere, Tam appeared the minute Porter left. Wearing a lemon yellow silk dress that clung to her rounded curves and a pair of dewdrop pearl earrings as her only jewelry, Tam was stunningly beautiful.

She slipped her arm around Audrey's waist. "Look at Mom and Dad. It must be wonderful to still be that much in love after all these years."

Audrey gave her friend a squeezing hug and then glanced at the dance floor where Geraldine swayed dreamily in Willie's big, strong arms. "Your parents are proof that there really is such a thing as happily-ever-after."

"Your dad's here," Tam said. "He and your uncle Garth. And Hart."

"Hart's here?"

Tam nodded.

"How is he?" Audrey asked.

"Clean and sober, at least for tonight. He looks nice. I think he's wearing that new suit you bought him for his last job interview."

Audrey forced a smile. She loved her stepbrother. After Blake's disappearance twenty-five years ago, they had bonded as siblings. They had both known that they were the expendable kids, the ones who would never be as important to her father and his mother as Blake had been. And each of them had dealt with their family's tragedies in different ways. Audrey had focused all her energy on a profession where she could help other people deal with their own tragedy, with grief, with suffering of any kind. Hart had sought solace in drugs and alcohol. He'd been in and out of rehab half a dozen times during the past two decades, and he'd never held down a job for more than six months at a time.

"I wish I could do more to help him than just buying him a new suit."

"My God, you've done all you can. And you've done it over and over again. What more could you do? I'm not saying Hart's a lost cause, but . . ." Tam grimaced. "Hart's got problems that you can't fix, problems that maybe nobody can fix."

"I know. In here"—Audrey tapped her head—"I know. But in here"—she patted her chest—"I want to believe that somehow, some way, someday . . ."

"Fairy Godmother Audrey." Tam smiled. "Always wishing you could wave a magic wand and make everything all right for everyone."

Audrey snorted, the sound quite unladylike. "Yeah, all the good that wishing does me when my damn magic wand is broken."

Tam laughed.

"It's good to hear you laugh," Audrey said. "Neither of us has done much of that recently, have we. You know, in a way, it seems strange to be enjoying such a happy occasion tonight when only a few hours ago I was at Jill Scott's funeral."

"I try to keep my professional life and my personal life separate," Tam said. "Most of the time, I can, but sometimes . . . He's still out there, the guy who kidnapped and murdered Jill Scott. We're no closer now to catching him than we were nine days ago. And unless all the experts are wrong, there's a good chance that the same man abducted Debra Gregory and will kill her, too."

"I shouldn't have mentioned Jill tonight," Audrey said. "I'm afraid I'm seldom able to separate myself from my client's problems. What does that say about my professionalism?"

"Screw your professionalism. Caring too damn much about everyone else is what makes you you, and I wouldn't change that or anything else about you."

"Only because you love me like a sister."

"Got that damn straight." Tam's gaze fixed on something or someone behind Audrey. Her eyes widened and a quirky smile played at the corners of her mouth. "Don't look now, but tall, dark, and could-eat-him-with-a-spoon is here, right behind us and coming this way."

"Who are you talking about?"

When Audrey started to turn around, Tam grabbed her by the forearms. "Don't turn around. Not yet," Tam said under her breath. "Damn, he's not alone."

"For goodness sakes, who are you—?"

"Well, hello there," Tam said to the person standing behind Audrey. "How are you tonight?"

Why was Tam acting so odd? Audrey turned and, despite her six-foot height in her three-inch heels, had to look up slightly to be face-to-face with the man. J.D. Cass, the TBI agent she'd met nine days ago when she had accompanied the Scott family to the Lookout Valley Cracker Barrel, smiled at her. He was the guy whose "you're not an M.D." comment had irritated her. Not only that, but the way he'd looked at her had irritated her, too. And the fact that she had found him attractive irritated her. Hell, everything about the man irritated her.

"Audrey, you remember Special Agent Cass, don't you?" Tam glanced from the TBI agent to the bosomy woman hanging on his arm.

For some reason, Audrey disliked the lovely blond on sight. It wasn't like her to feel instant hostility toward someone. Maybe it was because the woman was so gorgeous and obviously sexy, her attitude all but screaming, *I'm prettier than you are. Ha-ha-ha.*

Okay, so she still had a few hang-ups about her looks, especially whenever she compared herself to someone as blatantly feminine and sexy as J.D. Cass's date. Audrey had always been big for her age. Above average height, small breasts, big feet, and at best moderately attractive instead of beautiful. And she'd certainly never filled out a dress the way this woman did.

"Nice to see you again, Tam," J.D. said, but he was looking at Audrey. "And you, too, Dr. Sherrod." Without taking his eyes off Audrey, he introduced the woman at his side. "You both know Holly Johnston, don't you?"

"Ms. Johnston and I have met," Tam replied.

Before Audrey could mention that she didn't know Ms. Johnston, Porter reappeared with their champagne. When he saw the other couple, he smiled at the voluptuous blonde in the slinky red dress. The dress barely reached the woman's knees, revealed a great deal of cleavage, and dipped to her waist in the back.

"You're looking beautiful, as always, Counselor," Porter said, his glance blatantly enjoying the scenery. "Holly, have you met my date, Dr. Audrey Sherrod?" He placed his arm possessively around Audrey's waist. "Sweetheart, you've heard me mention Holly. We work together."

"We were just getting around to introductions." Audrey did her best to smile. She had learned over the years how to put on a pleasant face and act agreeable regardless of how she actually felt.

So, Holly, the blond goddess, was an assistant district attorney, just as Porter was. She vaguely remembered him mentioning this drop-dead-gorgeous woman in the DA's office who was a real barracuda in the courtroom. Audrey suspected that J.D. Cass's date was a barracuda in the bedroom, too.

"Y'all will have to excuse me," Tam said. "I see my husband motioning for me. I think it's almost time to bring out Dad's birthday cake."

Within minutes of Tam's departure, DA Everett Harrelson joined them and the conversation quickly turned into shop talk with Porter, Holly, and their boss. Audrey took several discreet steps back and away from the foursome, hoping she could inconspicuously slip away so that she could wish Willie a happy birthday before they presented him with his cake. Audrey thought she wouldn't be missed for several minutes and was about to make her escape when Special Agent Cass smoothly maneuvered himself away from Holly, who didn't seem to notice that she was losing her date. At least temporarily.

J.D. came up beside Audrey. "Looks like our dates are ignoring us." He held out his hand. "Would you care to dance, Dr. Sherrod?'

Audrey hesitated for half a second. "I . . . uh . . ."

"It's just a dance, not a lifetime commitment," he said jokingly.

"Thank you, Special Agent Cass, I'd love to dance."

She took his hand and he led her onto the dance floor.

"My name's J.D.," he told her as he slipped his arm around her.

"I'm Audrey."

"Now, that wasn't so hard, was it?"

"What?" She eyed him quizzically.

"Our getting on a first-name basis."

"Are we playing some sort of game, J.D.? If we are, clue me in."

He chuckled, and damn it, she liked the sound. Deep and robust and genuine.

"You have a nice smile," he told her.

She hadn't even been aware that she was smiling. "Do you always flirt with every woman you meet?"

"Who says I'm flirting?"

"Isn't that what you're doing, flirting with me because you're aggravated that your date is distracted by her boss and coworker?"

He chuckled again, as if he found her comment highly amusing.

Audrey felt a flush of heat warm her from head to toes. She hoped her sudden awareness of just how close her dance partner was holding her didn't show on her face.

"You're an open book," Tam had once told her. "Everything you're feeling shows on your face."

"Holly and I don't have that kind of relationship," J.D. said.

"What kind is that?"

"The kind where I'd be aggravated or jealous that she's ignoring me in favor of spending time with her boss and her coworker."

"Then you two aren't seriously involved?"

"I'm never seriously involved. Not since my divorce six years ago. What about you—are you and Beau Brummell engaged, going steady, or just sleeping together?"

Audrey laughed spontaneously, thoroughly amused by J.D. dubbing the fastidious Porter with the name of the best-known dandy of all time.

"Porter and I are not engaged," she said. "And we're a little too old to go steady. Besides, I think that term is passé, but I have no idea what teenagers call it these days." She gave her last statement several moments of consideration before saying, "And whether or not we're sleeping together is none of your business."

J.D. grinned.

Damn if the man wasn't dangerously sexy. And he probably knew it. Guys like that always did, didn't they?

"You're absolutely right," he said. "It would be my business only if you and I were—"

"And we are not!" *Audrey, Audrey, why did you finish the man's sentence for him? Why such an adamant statement of fact?*

With that damn sexy smile unwavering, he agreed. "No, we aren't."

As if on cue the music stopped, the dance ended, and J.D. led her off the dance floor. She pulled away from him.

"I'm going to find Willie and wish—"

Too late. The waiters wheeled out an enormous six-tier cake placed in the center of a serving cart and the band played "Happy Birthday." The partygoers, including Audrey and J.D., joined in the song. As the well-wishers crowded together around the guest of honor, J.D. eased his arm around Audrey's waist. Ambivalent feelings toward the man warred inside her and a damn army of butterflies did a war dance in her belly.

* * *

Debra didn't know if it was daylight or dark outside in the real world. Here in the macabre otherworld in which she existed, it was always night. It could be twelve noon or twelve midnight for all she knew. It could be Monday or Friday. Perhaps she had been here for a week, or it could have been a month.

What did it matter?

"Rock him to sleep," the voice told her. "Lovingly. Tenderly. He needs a mother's gentle touch."

She held the bundle in her arms and immediately began crooning the lullaby she knew he expected her to sing to the object wrapped in the soft blue blanket. How many times had they repeated this ritual? Dozens? Hundreds? She had lost count. Odd how rocking and singing to the skeleton of a small child had become a routine, one she no longer viewed with utter horror. Her entire world was now confined to this small space, an area with hard floors and walls too distant to see in the semidarkness in which she now lived. As far as she knew, the rocking chair where she was confined was the only piece of furniture in the room.

He had not harmed her, at least not physically. He kept her feet loosely bound so that even when she was allowed to move around, she had to hobble. And whenever he left her, he tied her wrists to the chair arms. He brought her food and water. He allowed her to wash herself and even brush her hair; and he provided an old-fashioned slop jar for her to use. But the indignity of having to bathe in front of him and even relieve herself with him standing nearby had added to the emotional trauma she had endured every moment of her captivity.

In the beginning, she had been afraid that he would rape her, but it soon became apparent that his reasons for abducting her and holding her prisoner had nothing to do with sex.

Then she'd wondered if he would eventually torture her. He hadn't. But the psychological torment was just as bad as physical torture would have been, perhaps worse.

She felt him move away from his stance behind the rocker, where he always stood when she performed. And that's what it felt like—a performance. Where was he going? His leaving while she still held the blanket-wrapped bundle was not part of the normal routine.

Her voice momentarily faltered.

"Keep singing," he told her.

She continued with the lullaby, repeating the words over and over, making up new verses as she went along.

Within minutes, he came up behind her again, but instead of standing guard over her, he reached around her and laid a small pillow across her lap. Since that first time when he had placed what she had thought was a doll in her arms, she had avoided glancing down at it, but she looked at her lap, at the age-yellowed white satin pillow trimmed with tattered blue ribbons. It was a baby's pillow.

"Do what you know you must do," he said.

"I don't understand."

"You must send him to heaven where he'll be one of the little angels."

"What? I don't know what you mean. What do you want me to do?"

"Pick up the pillow."

She did.

"Lay it gently over his face."

She did.

"Hold it there and keep singing and rocking him until he goes to sleep."

Until he goes to sleep?

Realization dawned. *Until he's dead.*

"You want me to smother him?" she asked.

"You don't want him to suffer any longer, do you?"

She lifted the pillow and placed it over the bundle she held.

"It'll all be over soon," the man's voice whispered softly . . . sadly.

Believing he meant the make-believe child in her arms would soon stop breathing, she felt a sense of immediate relief when he lifted the pillow, put it in her lap, and took the bundle from her. For now, it *was* over. He would tie her wrists to the chair and leave her here. Until the next time.

In the beginning, she had tried to get away from him, but each time he'd caught her before she had gotten more than a few feet. After being shoved onto the floor, face down, several times, she had stopped trying to escape.

She waited there in the rocking chair, waited for him to tie her wrists to the arms and then leave her. But when he reached around her from behind, there were no ropes in his hands.

Instead, he lifted the pillow from her lap and brought it up and over her face. She didn't realize what he intended to do, not until he pushed the pillow against her face and held it there.

Chapter 4

Audrey had spent a restless night, tossing and turning, waking every hour or so from the time she had finally fallen asleep at midnight until a few seconds ago when she had shot straight up in bed. She glanced at the bedside clock—5:40 A.M.—and groaned. Damn it, she'd been dreaming. Crazy dreams. The kind that didn't make any sense, but that were nevertheless all too real and somewhat unnerving. As a child, she had been prone to nightmares, especially after Blake's disappearance. Jumbled, chaotic, frightening dreams. But as an adult, she rarely remembered her dreams.

Unfortunately, she recalled exactly what she'd been dreaming when she awoke so suddenly. She and J.D. Cass had been dancing, just as they had been last night at Willie's birthday party. Except in the dream, they had been alone, just the two of them, and he had kissed her.

It would never happen. Not in a million years.

If and when you see him again, you'll be cordial to him and yet distant. Whatever was going on last night between the two of you meant no more to him than it did to you. It was nothing more than a harmless flirtation.

But her unwanted attraction to J.D. Cass was minor compared to what was really troubling her. If only she could lay all the blame for her restless night on her encounter with J.D., it would be easy enough to dismiss. In the course of that one evening, she'd come face-to-face with far more than an unwanted attraction to a man she instinctively disliked. Troubled family relationships and personal insecurities were far more to blame for her discontent.

She couldn't dismiss her concerns about Hart or her regrets about her relationship with her father. Until last night, she hadn't seen her stepbrother in weeks, not since she had bought him the new suit for his job interview. When she hadn't heard from him and he hadn't answered her phone calls, she had contacted Garth. He'd told her that Hart had gotten cold feet at the last minute and had blown off the interview.

"He can't face you right now," Garth had said. "He feels pretty lousy about disappointing you again, especially after you not only lined up the interview for him, but bought him some new duds, too."

Uncle Garth always made excuses for Hart, always played the role of protector. They had disagreed more than once on what to do to help Hart. She had finally given up trying to persuade Garth that maybe a little tough love would do more good than continuously enabling Hart to make poor choices.

Garth Hudson had his faults, but no one could accuse him of not loving his nephew. He had gone that extra mile for Hart so many times she'd lost count. He had paid for Hart's repeated rehab treatments. He'd given him a place to live when he'd been between jobs, which he was on a regular basis. And he'd called in favors several times to keep Hart out of jail.

Hart had faced her last night with a shy smile and a sincere apology. He'd been apologizing to her for one thing or another since they were kids. And she always forgave him for whatever misdeeds he'd committed. With his big blue eyes, so like little Blake's, and his sweet, boyish smile, Hart could be irresistibly convincing.

God knew Hart was his own worst enemy. If only he could get his act together and not keep screwing up. And if pigs had wings, they could fly.

"I don't know what I'd do without you, sis. You and Uncle Garth," he'd said last night during their brief conversation. "I don't know why either of you put up with me."

"Because we love you."

She did love Hart. He was family. They shared a history. They had survived Blake's kidnapping, Enid's suicide, and her father's complete emotional withdrawal. They were irrevocably bound by the scars of their childhood tragedies.

Hart had promised they'd get together soon, that he'd drop by or they could meet for lunch one day. "I've got a line on another job," he'd told her. "It's minimum wage, but at least I could start paying Uncle Garth some room and board."

That indefinite promise from Hart that they'd see each other again soon had been more than she'd gotten from her father during their brief conversation. Her dad had mentioned how pretty her dress was and told her he was glad to see her. But he hadn't looked her in the eye, hadn't smiled at her, and certainly hadn't hugged her. She had asked how he was enjoying his retirement and he'd mentioned that he was doing a lot of fishing. Audrey couldn't remember one time in her thirty-four years that she and her father had ever had a meaningful conversation.

Enough introspection, especially this early in the morning.

She might as well get up. There wasn't much chance she'd go back to sleep. She needed her morning cup of hot tea, something she looked forward to every day.

After a quick trip to the bathroom, Audrey headed for the kitchen. She filled the white enamel kettle with fresh water and placed it on the Jenn-Air range to heat. A hint of daylight peeked through the closed blinds of her Walnut Hill town house as she padded around on the Brazilian cherry hardwood floor, set out her favorite teacup on the granite countertop, and removed a bag of Earl Grey from the maple cupboard. If anything, Audrey was a creature of habit. She lived her life on a flexible schedule, appreciating the peace that the familiar gave her on a daily basis.

As a child, she had experienced enough drama to last her a lifetime. She supposed that was why she craved normalcy, why she chose to live a quiet, uneventful life. Beginning with her parents' divorce, her childhood had been riddled with tragedy. Only a year after her parents' bitter divorce when she was five, her mother had been killed in a car wreck when a drunk driver swerved into oncoming traffic. Then her baby brother Blake—her father's pride and joy—had mysteriously disappeared. And a few months later, her distraught stepmother had committed suicide.

Just as Audrey opened the blinds to let in the morning light, the kettle whistled and the phone rang. On her way to take the kettle off the stove, she grabbed the portable phone and hit the On button without checking caller ID. It was barely six o'clock, so odds were that the caller had bad news.

"Hello." Audrey tipped the kettle and poured boiling hot water into her tea cup.

"Audrey, this is Don Hardy."

Why is the mayor calling me? "Good morning, Mayor Hardy." She set the kettle on the counter and dunked her tea bag down into the steaming water.

"My wife is going to need you this morning," he said. "Can you come to our house as soon as possible?"

"Yes, sir, but I don't understand. Why does—?"

"I just got off the phone with Sergeant Hudson. He thinks they've found my wife's cousin, Debra."

Audrey swallowed. Instinctively she knew without asking that the police had not found Debra Gregory alive.

"I see. It's not good news."

"No."

"I'm so sorry."

"Our worst fears have been confirmed," Don Hardy said. "Sergeant Hudson was on the scene when he called me. A passerby on his way to work just happened to see something he thought was odd and called the police. The officers first on the scene found a dead woman sitting in an old, broken rocking chair at an illegal dump site out in Soddy-Daisy."

"And Garth believes the woman is your wife's cousin?"

"Yes. She fits the general description, and your uncle said that she looks exactly like the photo the police have of Debra. If it is Debra, and I'm pretty sure it is, Janice is going to fall apart. They were very close. Debra was like a kid sister to my wife."

"Do you want me to come to your home or—?" Audrey asked.

"Yes, please, as soon as possible. I . . . uh . . . I haven't told Janice yet, but I can't put it off much longer. I'll have to leave her to go ID the body. Janice is Debra's closest relative here in Chattanooga."

"If you'll give me your address and directions, I'll be there within the hour."

"Thank you." He hurriedly rattled off the street address and then went over the driving directions with her twice.

Audrey laid the portable phone on the counter, picked up her cup, took two quick sips, and then dumped the tea into the sink before heading straight back to her bedroom. There was no time for breakfast or even a leisurely cup of morning tea.

* * *

J.D. had left Zoe a note stuck to the refrigerator with an orange and white UT emblem magnet. They had pretty much fallen into a routine during the past year, each giving the other plenty of space, neither able to truly connect with the other. Most weekday mornings, they ate breakfast together and he dropped her off at Baylor—the outrageously expensive private school she attended—on his way to the office. But whenever he was called out before breakfast—weekdays or weekends—he'd leave her a note as he had done this morning. Since it was Sunday, he wouldn't have to make arrangements for someone to take her to school, and at fourteen, she was old enough to be left alone without adult supervision during the day.

After several come-to-Jesus talks with Zoe, he pretty much trusted her to do what she was told. She didn't like it, but that's just the way it was. She was a kid. He was her father. He made the rules. She followed them or else.

Or else what?

Damn it, sometimes he had no idea how to handle her.

She had pushed him to the limit more than once. He had grounded her, taken away certain privileges, and tried to talk sense to her. Only once had he threatened to send her packing. The fear he had seen in her eyes that day was something he never wanted to see again. As much as she hated living with him, as often as she grumbled and complained about how much she disliked him and what a piss-poor excuse for a father he was, Zoe knew he was the only game in town. Nobody else wanted her. If not for him, she would be living in foster care.

The thought unnerved him more than a little. He had heard the horror stories. He'd run across more than one juvenile delinquent who had come out of the system the worse for wear, neglected, and occasionally abused. If Carrie hadn't gotten in touch with him before she died, if she hadn't told him he had a daughter . . .

Pushing aside thoughts of how bad he sucked at being a father, J.D. took the Soddy-Daisy/Hixson Pike exit off US-27 North and followed Garth Hudson's directions to the illegal dump site in Soddy-Daisy. After taking TN-319 and following Tsati Terrace, he veered off onto what appeared to be little more than a winding, narrow paved lane. Within minutes, he saw the row of emergency vehicles lined up along the roadside and the swarm of personnel already on site. He carefully parked his '68 Dodge Charger at the end of the line, got out, and then walked a good two hundred yards before reaching the edge of the crime scene. Ordinarily, he didn't use his dad's old car as a daily driver, but his '07 Chevy Camaro convertible was in the body shop. Some goofball had rear-ended him last week.

In a semiwooded area, less than twelve feet from the road, a band of investigators milled around a fifteen-by-fifteen-foot pile of discarded items. An old refrigerator. A ratty, seen-better-days love seat. A twin-size mattress. Empty paint cans. Several overflowing plastic garbage bags. And one old, broken rocking chair, the floral cushions faded with age and stained from exposure to the weather.

Tam Lovelady turned just as J.D. flashed his badge to the officer guarding the entrance to the cordoned-off area. She threw up her hand and motioned to him. As he approached Officer Lovelady and Sergeant Hudson, his gaze focused on the woman in the rocking chair. Her body sat upright, rigid, as if made of stone. Her pretty face was unblemished, her long, dark hair had been draped about her shoulders, and a small skeleton, wrapped in a blue baby blanket, lay nestled in her lap.

"Looks familiar, doesn't it?" Tam said.

"Yeah," J.D. replied. "This is too similar to the scene at the Lookout Valley Cracker Barrel to be a coincidence."

"You think?" Garth Hudson said sarcastically.

J.D. grunted. "So, are you sure she's Debra Gregory?"

"Ninety-nine percent sure," Garth replied. "Mayor Hardy will ID the body. But for now, we're working under the assumption that whoever killed Jill Scott killed Debra Gregory. Two abductions. Two murders. The skeletal remains of two babies left with the murder victims. It's the same MO."

J.D. took a step closer to the body and paused beside ME Peter Tipton. Pete watched while the photographer, working under his supervision, snapped shot after shot of the body and the skeleton.

"Asphyxiation," Pete said.

"Huh?"

"Cause of death. She was probably smothered. Just like Jill Scott."

J.D. pointed to the bundle in the victim's lap. "Not a doll this time, either."

"No, not a doll. Another child. About the same size. Probably about the same age."

"So far, we don't have any idea who the first child was, only that it was a male about two years old," J.D. said. "Once we get the DNA results back . . . Hell, we haven't identified the first child, and now we have another one."

Pete glanced away from the body in the rocking chair and looked at J.D. "I hate to say it, but it appears we may have a really bizarre serial killer on our hands. A little profiling hoodoo"—Pete gestured with his hands—"might be in order about now."

"Are you suggesting we involve the Feds?"

"Not unless you state boys can't handle it," Pete said. "I heard you've got some experience in that department."

"Where'd you hear something like that?"

"Word gets around."

"I'm just an amateur compared to the real thing."

Only when Tam cleared her throat was J.D aware that she was standing nearby. "Sorry to interrupt, but I overheard the tail end of what y'all were saying, something about Special Agent Cass being familiar with profiling."

"I know a little something," J.D. admitted. "But if the CPD wants a profile of the killer, then I can put in a call to a buddy of mine at the Bureau or either of you can call the BSU."

"I'll run that by Sergeant Hudson." Tam glanced at her partner, who was talking to one of the uniformed officers. "I don't think he'll object. As long as both the TBI and the FBI keep in mind that this is a CPD case and we're in charge—"

"Enough said." J.D. knew the drill.

Local law enforcement could be territorial, even if they wanted and needed assistance. When he'd been assigned to the Memphis field office, he'd had a bad run-in with a local county sheriff. The sheriff, a good old boy with a lot of influential friends, had come out of the confrontation smelling like a rose. J.D. had come out of it smelling like shit. He had learned his lesson the hard way, one of many. Not the first, of course, and God help him, probably not the last either.

"Unofficially, the three of us just talking among ourselves, do you have any gut feelings about this guy—a man who abducts pretty, young, dark-haired women, holds them hostage for a couple of weeks, smothers them, and then poses them in a rocking chair with the skeletal remains of a toddler?" Tam's gaze connected with J.D.'s.

"Just the three of us talking among ourselves, I'd say this guy's got some kind of mommy problem." J.D. looked at the body in the rocking chair. "Maybe some sort of mommy and baby thing. Think about it—a rocking chair, a blue baby blanket, a dead child . . ."

"Makes sense," Tam said. "But what you just said is pretty much a given, don't you think?"

"Yeah, sure, but why put a dead child in her arms?" Pete asked. "What does that mean?"

J.D. shrugged. "Beats me. Unless, in his mind, he's mimicking something."

"What I want to know is where he got the two little skeletons," Tam said. "There are no reports in Tennessee or any of the surrounding states about the graves of any children being dug up, no bodies reported being stolen."

"Which leaves us with what?" J.D. asked.

Tam and Pete stared questioningly at J.D.

"The bodies probably belong to missing children."

"Are you saying you think our killer murdered these little boys years ago and kept their bodies hidden away?" Tam asked.

"Possibly," J.D. said. "Either that or he knew where whoever killed them had buried the bodies."

Chapter 5

After Audrey's arrival at his home that morning, Mayor Don Hardy had left his wife in Audrey's capable hands—his assessment, not hers—and gone to the Forensics Center on Amnicola Highway to ID Debra's body. Although understandably distraught over her cousin's murder, Janice Hardy had managed to hold it together and not fall apart completely. What she had needed was to talk about Debra, about their close sisterlike relationship and how very much she would miss her cousin. Naturally, Janice had questioned how something so horrible could have happened. Why would anyone want to kill Debra? Or Jill Scott? Two lovely young women apparently killed without rhyme or reason, simply because they fit a certain profile. Young, slender, attractive, brown-eyed brunettes.

An hour ago, shortly before leaving the mayor's home, Audrey had received a call from Tam. She had told Audrey that their lunch plans were unfortunately canceled, and then she had asked her to stop by headquarters that afternoon.

"Dad's here with us," Tam had said. "We're putting our

heads together and trying to make sense of things. Dad wants to talk to you, so would you mind dropping by as soon as you can?"

Audrey was supposed to have Sunday dinner with Tam and Marcus and Tam's parents, but the discovery of Debra Gregory's body that morning had changed everyone's plans. Assuming that no one else had eaten lunch either, Audrey had stopped by the River Street Deli downtown and bought lunch for four. She figured the "we" Tam had referred to were Tam and Garth and Willie.

Audrey parked her cocoa brown Buick Enclave in the civilian parking lot adjacent to the Police Service Center, across the highway on Wisdom Street. She hoisted her embossed black leather Coach bag over her shoulder and picked up the large sack from the passenger seat. Using the crosswalk between Amnicola Highway and Wisdom Street, she approached the 911 Center and the CPD headquarters housed in the two-story gray buildings.

Everyone at the police department knew Audrey. The old pros had known her all her life and there actually were a few of those still around, men like her uncle Garth and Willie Mullins. Some of the young guns were her friends and a few of them were childhood buddies, as Tam was. Others were acquaintances. She had worked, in an advisory capacity, with the CPD in the past, so no one raised an eyebrow when she showed up at headquarters on a Sunday afternoon. Normally, visitors had to be accompanied by police personnel beyond the front information center desk lobby area.

Audrey went up to the second floor of the PSC, where the patrol squad rooms were located. The door to the office that Garth now shared with Tam stood wide open. Just as Audrey approached, Garth must have sensed her presence. He turned and glared at her, not looking all that happy to see her. She held up the sack and waved it slowly back and forth to let him know that she came bearing gifts. Shaking his head as if reluctantly agreeing for her to join him, he motioned to her. Tam, who stood in the corner of the office, was on the phone. She glanced at Audrey and forced a weak smile.

Willie—Police Chief Mullins—sat behind Garth's desk, his attention focused on the papers and photographs lying on the desktop in front of him. As a general rule, the chief didn't come to headquarters on a Sunday afternoon. But there was a good chance the CPD was dealing with a serial killer and not your regular run-of-the-mill murderer. Both the mayor and the DA were probably breathing down Willie's neck.

She often wondered if Willie missed being an investigator, if he missed working with his old partner, her dad. Of course, no one had forced him to take the police chief position. He could have taken the route her uncle Garth had and turned down chances for promotion just so he could stay in the field.

"I don't want a desk job," Garth had said more than once. "And I sure as hell don't want to play politics."

But Willie excelled in his new position. He had an even temper, an easygoing manner, and a keen intelligence that made him an excellent diplomat and a great leader. Garth was smart—street smart and book smart—but he was also temperamental, moody, not easy to get along with, and known for his hard drinking and womanizing.

"Thanks," Tam said to the person on the other end of the line just before she ended their conversation. "Pete Tipton said that if or when another similar murder occurs, the TBI will send in a crime scene vehicle, either from Nashville or Knoxville. A third murder would erase all doubts about our having a serial killer on our hands."

"Is there any doubt now?" Garth grumbled.

"He's killed twice that we know of," Willie said. "He'll

kill again. It's only a matter of time before he kidnaps another woman."

"And we don't have a clue who he is or when and where he'll strike again." Tam looked from her father to Audrey. "What's in that sack?"

Audrey placed the sack on Tam's desk. "Sandwiches from the River Street Deli. One for each of us."

"You're not part of this investigative team," Garth told her. "We've got a job to do. So thank you for the sandwiches. Leave them with us and go."

"No," Willie said. "Stay. We can take a break, long enough to eat together." He looked right at Garth. "I want to talk to Audrey. I had Tam ask her to stop by. There are things she needs to know."

Garth mumbled under his breath, but didn't contradict his boss. Instead he said something about getting coffee and disappeared around the corner.

"He's frustrated," Willie told Audrey. "We all are. You know how Garth is."

"Yes, I know only too well," Audrey replied.

Tam opened the sack and removed the four sandwiches, but before handing them out, she looked to Audrey for information.

"Here, let me do that." Audrey handed Willie a sandwich. "Roast beef, rare." Then she placed a sandwich in front of Tam and laid another aside for herself. "A couple of their Elana Ruz sandwiches for us—turkey, cream cheese, and strawberry preserves."

Tam sighed deeply. "If you weren't already my best friend, you would be now."

Audrey and Tam exchanged smiles.

Garth returned with two cups of coffee, gave one to Willie, and kept the second cup. "I figure you girls will want to doctor up your coffee to suit yourselves. I've got no idea how either of you want it."

"I'll get us both a Coke," Tam said. "Does that suit you?"

"A Coke's fine," Audrey replied

"I'll make yours regular and mine diet."

Audrey nodded. She and Tam had different body types and different metabolisms. Tam was always dieting. Audrey had never dieted. But she suspected that eventually, probably in her fifties, that would change.

When Tam walked off, Audrey noticed that Willie was once again engrossed with some of the papers and photos spread out on Garth's desk.

"Would I be out of order to ask what you're looking at?" she asked.

"You know better than to ask," Garth told her.

"Sorry." Audrey eased away from the desk.

"It's something we chose not to share with the media." Willie glanced from Garth to Audrey. "But Audrey isn't the media."

"She's not one of us, either," Garth reminded the chief.

Choosing to ignore Garth's comment, Willie said, "It's something that we all find odd about how both bodies were staged."

"Everything's odd," Garth said. "There's nothing normal about it either."

Willie glowered at Garth before turning back to Audrey. "It's about what the two women held in their laps."

"Jill Scott was holding a doll, right? Or at least that's what everyone assumes. That's what the reporters said. So, what was Debra Gregory holding?"

"The media present at the scene where Jill Scott's body was discovered were kept at a distance and assumed they saw a doll lying in her lap." Willie shuffled through the photos in front of him, chose two, and held them up to show Audrey. "It wasn't a doll."

Audrey stared at the crime scene photograph of Jill Scott.

It took her brain several seconds to grasp the reality of what she saw. Her mouth parted to release a soft, startled gasp.

"It's a . . . a skeleton." Audrey took the photo from Willie and studied it more closely. "Oh my God! The killer laid the skeleton of a small child in Jill's lap."

"It's horrible, isn't it?" Tam said as she came back into the office.

"Then it's real," Audrey said, barely believing her own eyes. "It's the actual skeletal remains of a human child?"

Tam set two colas on the desk, one by her sandwich and the other by Audrey's. "All too real. We're waiting on DNA results in the hopes we can identify the child, but the UT Body Farm has identified the remains of the child found with Jill Scott as a white male, probably between the ages of twenty and thirty-six months."

"What about Debra Gregory? Was there a . . . ?" Audrey couldn't bring herself to say the words.

"Yes, there was another child found in her lap," Tam said. "About the same size."

Willie stood and placed his big hand on Audrey's shoulder. "Pete Tipton will examine the remains, take DNA samples from bone and teeth, and forward them to the lab."

Audrey suddenly felt as if someone had dealt her a body blow hard enough to knock the wind out of her. For a few seconds, she couldn't breathe, couldn't think, couldn't allow herself to accept the impossible possibility. *Not now. Not after twenty-five years.*

"Is there any chance that one of those little bodies could be . . ." She swallowed hard. "Could be . . ." She couldn't get the words out, couldn't say the unthinkable.

"It's possible," Tam said. "We'll know as soon as the DNA testing is completed."

"Oh, God, does my father know?" Audrey asked.

* * *

Whitney Poole hated her job, especially when she drew the Sunday lunch shift at Callie's Café. Crowds of church-goers descended on the restaurant in droves, and many of those good Christian people treated the waitresses as if they were unemotional robots. As if being yelled at, ordered around, and occasionally cursed wasn't bad enough, the cheapskates who ate at Callie's because they could buy a meat and three vegetables for $5.99 were definitely not big tippers.

Whitney glanced at her wristwatch—4:15 P.M.—and smiled when she realized her shift would end in fifteen minutes. Her feet ached, her head hurt, and she probably had a bruise on her butt from where a customer had pinched her. The son of a bitch had actually pinched her ass. When she'd given him a nasty look and told him to keep his hands to himself, he and his two buddies had whooped loudly in her face.

After going from table to table and refilling coffee cups and tea glasses, she hurried to print out the bills for her two remaining tables. One was a blond guy sitting all alone. He seemed quiet and shy and hadn't said another word to her after placing his order. He had simply answered when asked if he wanted more tea or a dessert. He had declined both. He'd been pleasant enough, although he hadn't smiled at her or anyone else, but she had caught him staring at her a couple of times, and the way he'd looked at her had sent chills up her spine. She couldn't pinpoint what it was about him that spooked her; she just knew that he did, despite the fact that he was young and good-looking.

She laid his check on the table, asked if he wanted anything else, and turned to go to the next table.

"Wait," he called to her.

She hesitated, feeling a sense of dread spreading quickly through her; but she turned, smiled, and said, "Yes, sir?"

He held up a five-dollar bill. "I just wanted to make sure you got your tip."

She stared at the money in his hand for a couple of seconds, then snatched it away from him and said, "Thank you."

He rose to his feet so quickly that before she had time to move, he was facing her, only a couple of inches separating their bodies. Instinctively, she moved backward, forced another smile, and rushed to the next table. By the time she laid down the check and glanced back, the man was walking out the door. She released a heavy breath, glad to see him leaving.

But suddenly he stopped, glanced over his shoulder, and smiled at her.

The only thought that came to mind was something her grandmother had said whenever she got a peculiar feeling. *I feel as if somebody just walked over my grave.*

Get real, Whit. Just because that guy was sort of creepy doesn't mean you should freak out or anything.

By the time 4:30 rolled around, she had all but forgotten her weird customer. The only thing on her mind was her Sunday night date with Travis. He was bringing over pizza and a DVD. They'd eat, watch the movie, and then do the nasty. They'd been dating a couple of months. Nothing serious. At least not yet. But neither of them was seeing other people. That meant something, didn't it? He hadn't said the L-word and neither had she, but she already knew she loved him. And she knew better than to push him. She'd done that before, with disastrous results. Danny had walked away and never looked back, leaving her with a broken heart. That had been nearly two years ago. She wouldn't make the same mistake with Travis. She'd wait for him to make the first move, to say "I love you," and take their relationship to the next level.

Whitney dug the car keys out of her Wal-Mart red purse and slung it over her shoulder as she exited Callie's Café through the back entrance. When she reached her Honda Civic, a reliable used car she'd bought last year, she paused when the hair on the back of her neck stood up. Someone was watching her. She could feel it.

Play it cool. Don't panic. It's broad daylight. You aren't alone. There are people inside the restaurant and probably out here, too.

She glanced around casually, doing her best not to draw attention to herself. Besides the other employees' vehicles, she counted three other cars, all three empty. And she didn't see another soul anywhere in the parking lot. No one was following her. No one was watching her.

After hurriedly unlocking her car, she slid behind the wheel, closed the door, locked it, and tossed her purse into the passenger seat. While starting the engine, she surveyed the parking lot again and saw nothing out of the ordinary. But just as she drove into the street, she spotted an older-model car parked across the road at the nearby Kangaroo gas station and mini-mart. A man stood beside a white Lincoln, the driver's door open, and he was looking right at her.

My God, it was the weirdo from the restaurant, the one who had given her the five-dollar tip.

Her heartbeat accelerated.

What would she do if he followed her?

You'll drive to the nearest police station, that's what you'll do.

For the next few blocks, she kept looking in her rearview mirror to see if he was following her. He wasn't. No sign of his big old car or one that even vaguely resembled it.

If that guy ever came back to Callie's Café, she'd ask one of the other waitresses to take his order. And if he ever dared to follow her when she left the restaurant, she'd sic the cops on him.

She was the one. He had known the minute he saw her. Everything about her was familiar, everything from her long, dark hair to her young, slender body and full, round breasts.

Her name tag had read Whitney.

But she couldn't fool him.

He knew who she was.

He always recognized her.

I'm going to take you home, where you belong. I need you. We need you, Cody and I.

A child needs his mother. Someone to love him. Someone to rock him and sing to him. Someone to ease his suffering when he's in pain.

I've taken very good care of Cody. I've made sure you will be with him forever so he will never be alone again. I'll keep my promise. I'll help you make everything right.

It's what you need in order to rest in peace. It's what Cody needs so that his little soul can go to heaven and the two of you can be together for all eternity.

He drove out of the parking area there at the gas station/mini-mart and slipped unobserved into the late Sunday afternoon traffic. His plans to follow her to wherever she was staying now went up in smoke the minute he realized that she had recognized him standing there across the street from Callie's Café. Why she always resisted when he tried to take her home, he didn't know. She always pretended she was someone else, someone who didn't know him, someone who had no idea why she was so desperately needed.

Now that he had found her again, all he had to do was wait for the right moment to approach her when they could be alone. Just the two of them.

Chapter 6

Audrey disagreed with Garth. And not for the first time. They came at life from two different angles. Always had and always would. Her step-uncle was relentlessly stubborn and refused to accept anyone else's viewpoint. He felt that he was right and everyone else was wrong. No opinion mattered except his. Audrey could be stubborn and fought for what she believed in, but she tried to keep an open mind and was willing to listen to other opinions and be proven wrong in any argument.

"Wayne doesn't need to know about this," Garth repeated adamantly. "We have no proof that either of those toddler skeletons is Blake." His brow furrowed deeply as he scrunched his face in a surly scowl.

"I think my father should be told," Audrey said, keeping her voice calm and even. "If he finds out that we kept this information from him, he'll be very upset. He won't appreciate us trying to protect him."

"God damn it, Audrey, there's nothing to protect him from!" Garth shouted. When Willie gave him a concerned glance, Garth lowered his voice. "The odds of either child being Blake are slim to none. Why put Wayne through hell all over again?"

"But what if this turns out to be a one-in-a-million coincidence and somehow—"

"Neither of them is Blake!" Garth cut her off midsentence. "The very idea that those two little skeletons might somehow be connected to a string of toddler kidnappings more than twenty years ago is a far-fetched notion. We are not digging up ghosts that are better left buried. We are going to keep Wayne out of this. Do you hear me?"

"Wayne Sherrod is one of my closest friends," Willie said. "He has been for a good thirty-five years, and I think I know him as well as anybody." Willie glanced from Audrey to Garth. "I'm calling him. We'll tell him together, the four of us. No matter what, he would want to know, even if there's only a slim possibility that either of those poor little boys is Blake."

Garth grumbled a string of partially incoherent obscenities so quietly that the words were barely audible, but his disapproval came through loud and clear.

When Garth stomped off, went downstairs, and headed toward the exit, Audrey followed him, leaving Willie to telephone her father. She caught up with her uncle in the parking lot adjacent to the Police Service Center. He pulled out a pack of cigarettes from his jacket pocket, removed one, and stuck it in his mouth. After replacing the pack, he lifted a lighter from his pants pocket and lit the cigarette.

Audrey walked up beside him. "Are you okay?"

Garth puffed on the cigarette, his eyes downcast, his shoulders hunched. "Yeah, sure."

"I almost wish one of those skeletons would turn out to be Blake."

Garth took several more drags off his cigarette, tossed it on the pavement, and ground it into pieces with the toe of his shoe. He gave Audrey a sideways glance. "Do you really think that would make it any easier for Wayne?"

"Maybe. I don't know. In most cases, closure is a good thing."

"Closure my ass. That's psycho mumbo jumbo. How's it better to know for sure your son is dead than to hold on to hope that he's still alive out there somewhere?"

"Because we both know that statistics, logic, and hard, cold facts tell us that there is practically no chance that Blake is still alive," Audrey said. "You and Willie and Dad and everyone on the force, back when Regina Bennett was arrested, said that more than likely Blake was one of her many victims. Of the six toddler boys who were abducted, only one survived. The last one. And only because he was rescued before she killed him."

"Yeah." Garth lifted his gaze and faced Audrey. "Blake probably was one of her victims, but we have no proof that the skeletons found with Jill Scott and Debra Gregory belong to any of those missing toddlers."

"No, not yet."

Audrey's gut instinct told her that there was a connection, that after twenty-five years, they were finally going to bring Blake home.

J.D. kept the different parts of his life separated as much as possible. Of course, there were times when the various parts of a guy's life overlapped whether he wanted them to or not. His job as TBI agent J.D. Cass comprised the bulk of his waking hours, five days a week and sometimes on Saturday and Sunday. The man J.D. was a loner for the most part who ventured into short-term relationships for a little female companionship in and out of the bedroom. The family guy J.D. had lost his parents years ago, but he kept in touch with his kid sister, Julia, and usually spent Christmas with her in Nashville. And now J.D. had to include fatherhood as a subcompartment under the family guy heading. Admittedly the role of parent didn't come easy to a confirmed bachelor who had sworn off committed relationships when his shipwreck of a marriage finally sank.

Just when a man thought he had everything under control was usually when fate threw him a curveball. Zoe had sure as hell been one of those totally unexpected pitches. And he had a stomach-knotting feeling that Dr. Audrey Sherrod just might be another one.

Holly Johnston, on the other hand, was exactly what he wanted, a woman who wasn't any more interested in a commitment than he was.

Holly had invited him to a late lunch today, lunch that she had assured him would include dessert.

"Something hot and spicy and oh so sweet," she'd promised. "I'll serve it to you au naturel on silk sheets."

Since Holly hadn't phoned him until ten o'clock that morning, he'd already halfway promised Zoe that they'd go to the movies that afternoon. Lucky for him, a group of her classmates was going to Hamilton Place to shop until the mall closed, and she'd been happily surprised when he'd changed his mind and told her she could go. Since Jacy Oliver's aunt was chaperoning, he figured the woman would keep an eye on the girls.

With Zoe off with friends and far happier than she would have been spending the afternoon with him, J.D. had the rest of the day for himself since, at that point, he wasn't officially assigned to either Jill Scott's or Debra Gregory's murder case. Until his boss told him anything different, he wasn't going to stick his nose any farther into CPD business.

When he arrived at Holly's, as promised, she provided a late gourmet lunch—no doubt ordered from a nearby restaurant—and did indeed deliver a delectable dessert in her bed, on her hot pink silk sheets. The lady sure did have a way with her hands and mouth. Years of experience had honed her bedroom skills. If there was one thing Holly Johnston did well outside of her profession as an ADA, it was sexually pleasing a man.

After a second vigorous round of hot and heavy, J.D. lay there completely spent, his hips and legs tangled in the top sheet. Holly rested beside him, her luscious body uncovered, a fine sheen of perspiration glistening on her skin from forehead to knees. As she sighed contentedly, she turned over and propped her elbow on the pillow as she looked down at J.D.

When she continued staring at him without saying anything, he grinned. "What?" he asked.

"If I were a different kind of woman, I think you would be on my top ten list of candidates."

If he didn't know Holly so well, her statement might have unnerved him. "Candidate for what?"

She laughed. "For a husband, of course."

"God forbid." He lifted his hand and ran his index finger over her throat and down between her large, round breasts. "I tried that once. I made a lousy husband."

She caught his caressing hand and lifted it off her naked body. "I have no doubt of that." She sat up, twisted around, and placed her feet on the carpeted floor. Glancing over her shoulder, she ran her tongue across her lips in a playfully seductive manner. "If all I wanted in a husband was a big dick and mind-blowing sex, you'd be my number one candidate, but when I eventually get married, it won't be for sex or even for love."

Holly got out of bed, picked up the satin robe lying on the floor, and slipped into the semisheer knee-length garment.

"I believe that was a backhanded compliment." J.D. untangled his legs from the sheet and shot up off the bed. When he reached out and grabbed Holly from behind, she didn't protest.

Just as she turned in his arms and lifted her face for a kiss, his phone rang. He eyed the pile of clothes on the floor where his phone lay atop his slacks.

"Let it go to voice mail." Holly rubbed herself against him.

"I would, but I've got a kid, remember?"

Holly moaned. "You have my sympathy." She disengaged herself from his loose hold and headed toward the bathroom.

J.D. bent down and picked up his phone. The caller I.D. read Cara Oliver. Damn! He figured Cara Oliver was Jacy Oliver's aunt, the one who was chaperoning Jacy, Zoe, and their friends at the mall.

So help me, Zoe, if you've done something stupid, I'm going to—!

The incessant ringing reminded J.D. that instead of assuming the worst about his daughter, he should simply answer the phone and find out what was what.

"J.D. Cass," he said when he took the call.

"Mr. Cass, this is Cara Oliver," the soft, concerned voice said. "I'm Jacy's aunt."

"Is something wrong, Ms. Oliver?" *Please, God, please let her say no.*

"I—I don't know quite how to say this, but . . . well, Zoe is missing."

"What!"

"I take full responsibility," Cara Oliver said. "The girls were sitting in the food court. We'd just gotten ice cream and . . . I went to the restroom and when I came back, the girls were gone."

"Are all the girls missing?"

"No. I found Jacy, Presley, and Reesa, but when I asked them where Zoe was, they swore they didn't know. But . . ."

"But?" J.D. demanded.

"But I think they know something."

"Are you still at the mall?"

"Yes. We're here at the food court."

"Stay there. I'm on my way."

"Mr. Cass, I am so very sorry about this."

"It's not your fault, Ms. Oliver. Zoe is a very resourceful girl and if she wanted to slip away from your watchful eye, she'd have found a way regardless of what you did or didn't do."

J.D. tossed the phone on the bed, picked up his clothes, and dressed quickly. He didn't have time for even a quick, much-needed shower. Just as he slipped the phone into the belt holder, Holly came out of the bathroom.

"Leaving?" she asked.

"Yeah, sorry, babe. Fatherhood duties call."

Holly raised an inquisitive eyebrow.

"Zoe's pulled a disappearing act. I have to go find her."

"I hate to hear that. Since our acts one and two were so exciting, I was really looking forward to act three."

"Yeah, me, too." He gave her a quick peck on the cheek and then swatted her behind. "I'll call you later."

"And I may or may not be available."

J.D. chuckled as he walked toward the door, but by the time he exited Holly's apartment, his thoughts had turned completely to his daughter.

Damn it, Zoe, what are you up to now?

At sixty-one, Wayne Sherrod was still a good-looking man. Tall, robust, broad shouldered. He kept his thick, silvery white hair cut short and was, as he always had been, clean-shaven and neat. A medic in Vietnam when he'd been barely nineteen, Wayne never spoke of what had to have been a horrific experience. Audrey could never remember a time in her entire life when she'd heard her father talk about his past. Nothing about being a child, a teenager, or a soldier. During her lifetime, he'd always been a police officer, and according to those who knew him best, he'd been a damn fine lawman.

But he'd been a terrible father, especially after he and her mother had divorced. Maybe, if Blake had lived . . .

When her father entered the second floor of the PSC, she wanted to rush to him, put her arms around him, and tell him she was there for him. How stupid was that? After a lifetime of being mostly ignored and often neglected by her dad, a part of her still longed for a genuine father/daughter relationship. Just once, she wanted to hear Wayne Sherrod tell her that he loved her.

Head held high, shoulders squared and straight, he marched toward Garth's office, the door open and the four of them waiting anxiously as he approached.

Willie cleared his throat. "Let me do the talking."

"For the record, I'm against doing this," Garth told them for the umpteenth time since Willie had phoned Wayne.

Standing at her side, Tam reached down and grasped Audrey's clenched fist. Audrey looked at her best friend, relaxed her fingers, clutched Tam's hand, and gave it a hard squeeze.

Wayne paused in the doorway, surveyed the foursome, and settled his gaze on Willie. "What's this about?"

"Come on in and close the door," Willie said.

Hesitating only momentarily, Wayne did as his old friend had asked. Once they were enclosed privately in Garth's office, he glared at Audrey. Instead of averting her gaze, she stared right back at him. The days when her father could intimidate her with a hard, cold glare were long gone.

"Take a seat." Willie indicated a wooden chair to the right of the desk.

"I'll stand, thanks."

"We're not all in agreement about this," Garth said. "If it had been up to me, we wouldn't be doing this."

"Doing what?" Wayne's brow furrowed with curiosity and concern as he focused on Garth. "What the hell's going on? Whatever it is, just spit it out." Wayne narrowed his gaze and directed it toward Willie.

"We've had two young women abducted and murdered," Willie said.

"Two?" Wayne asked.

"Yeah. Debra Gregory's body was found this morning. Same MO as the Jill Scott murder."

"I hate to hear that, but what does either murder have to do with me?"

"Not a damn thing!" Garth stomped across the room until he stood in front of his brother-in-law.

Puzzlement clear in Wayne's brown eyes, he ignored Garth and asked Willie again, "What do the murders of these two women have to do with me?"

"The information I'm going to share with you hasn't been released to the public and it won't be for as long as we can possibly keep it under wraps," Willie said. "Both women were found sitting in rocking chairs, as everyone knows. Both were holding blanket-wrapped bundles in their arms. The press has stated that they assume the women were holding dolls."

"But they weren't, were they?" Wayne glanced at Audrey.

She forced herself not to look away, to hold her gaze steady and not to back down from the coldness in her father's eyes.

"No, both women were holding the skeletal remains of what have been identified as human males, probably between two and three years old."

Wayne didn't move, didn't flinch, didn't so much as blink. He stood there so quiet, so rigid, that he could have been mistaken for a marble statue.

"Wayne?" Willie called his name.

He didn't respond.

"Daddy?" Audrey said. And when he didn't reply, she walked over and laid her hand on his arm. He stiffened instantly. "They haven't identified the remains," she told him. "Not yet. It's possible that neither—"

"You think one of them could be Blake, don't you?" Her father glanced at where her hand rested on his upper arm. He pulled away from her and confronted Willie. "That's what this is about. You think . . ." He gulped hard. "You believe it's possible that one of the bodies—one of the skeletons—is my son."

"I tried to tell them that there's no way in hell that either could be Blake." Garth gripped Wayne's shoulder.

Wayne took a deep breath. "No one can be that certain. And if there's one chance in a billion . . . I want to know. You'll need a DNA sample. I assume mine will do. If not, I still have . . ." He closed his eyes for half a second. "I have Blake's hairbrush, his toothbrush. . . ."

Oh, Daddy . . . Daddy.

Tears choked Audrey, tears that threatened to escape and overflow.

Poor Daddy. Poor little Blake.

If he hadn't been so damn pissed at Zoe, he might have appreciated what a lovely woman Cara Oliver was. Late twenties, big brown eyes, and a mane of thick auburn hair that framed a face blessed with attractive features. Even in jeans and an oversized cotton sweater, she couldn't hide the appeal of her slender yet curvy body.

"Mr. Cass, I am so very sorry about this." Cara gazed up at him pleadingly.

J.D. offered her a forced smile. "Don't blame yourself.

It's not your fault. Zoe's a handful. This isn't the first time she's pulled a stunt like this."

"I've spoken to the girls again and I'm sure they know something. But they're not talking." She glanced at the threesome, who sat with eyes downcast at a nearby table in the food court.

"Mind if I talk to them?"

"No, please, be my guest." Cara huffed in exasperation.

When J.D. approached the girls, they scooted their chairs closer together. He looked from one to another. Jacy had the same dark red hair and brown eyes as her aunt, but was not as pretty. Presley was cute as a button, with curly brown hair and a smattering of freckles across her pert little nose. And blond, blue-eyed Reesa possessed the promise of becoming a real femme fatale in the tradition of a long list of bosomy Hollywood blondes.

J.D. grabbed an empty chair, turned it around, and sat down, straddling his legs around the back and resting his arms on the top of the frame. "Where's Zoe?"

Silence.

"Jacy, where's my daughter?"

Jacy hazarded a glance at J.D. "I don't know." She quickly cast her gaze downward again.

"Presley?"

She stared at him, a look of sheer terror in her hazel eyes. "I—I don't know where she is, Mr. Cass. I don't."

"Reesa?"

She smoothed nonexistent wrinkles from the long sleeves of her colorful T-shirt, then lifted her head and smiled at him. "Zoe's all right. You don't have to worry about her. She'll come home when she's ready to."

"Hush," Jacy warned.

"You promised," Presley chimed in simultaneously.

"Oh, get over it," Reesa told her friends. "I didn't promise

Zoe anything. You two did. And I'm not going to be given the third degree by her dad, who I'm sure knows all kinds of ways to make us talk since he's a TBI agent." Reesa batted her eyelashes at J.D.

Good God, the child is actually flirting with me.

"Aunt Cara," Jacy wailed. "You won't let him give us the third degree, will you?"

Cara managed to keep a straight face. "Actually, I've already given Mr. Cass . . . uh . . . Special Agent Cass permission to do just that, if he believes it's necessary."

Tears filled Presley's eyes. Jacy whimpered.

Reesa snorted. "You two are pathetic. He can't do anything without your parents' permission." She looked at J.D. "Can you?"

"Is that what you girls want?" he asked. "You want to involve your parents?"

"Zoe's with my brother Dawson," Presley blurted out.

J.D. grimaced. His daughter was with some boy doing God only knew what. "How old is Dawson?"

"He's sixteen," Presley said.

Well, at least the boy was just that—a boy. "Where did Zoe and Dawson go?"

"I honestly don't know." Presley looked him in the eye.

He could tell that she wasn't lying. She was too frightened to lie.

"They just went for a ride in his new car," Reesa said. "They wanted to have some fun, to be alone together. There's no crime in that, is there?"

Reesa was a little smart aleck, but she was not his problem. Zoe was.

"He'll take her home," Presley said. "It's not as if they've eloped or anything like that."

"Thank God for small favors," J.D. grumbled under his breath, then told Presley, "Call Zoe. She won't answer her phone if she sees I'm the one calling her. Tell her that her father said to get her butt home ASAP if she knows what's good for her."

"Er . . . ah . . . yes, sir."

Presley placed the call and they all waited for Zoe to answer. And then Presley gasped, "What? Oh my God, no! Are you okay? Is Dawson okay?"

"What's wrong?" J.D. asked, his heart beating ninety-to-nothing. When Presley stared at him wide-eyed and her mouth agape, he snatched her phone out of her hand and said, "Zoe, this is your father. What the hell is going on?"

"Oh, J.D., please help us." Zoe sounded desperate.

"Are you all right? Where are you? What's happened?"

"Don't be angry. Please don't be angry."

"Zoe!"

"We're in jail."

Chapter 7

Wayne Sherrod couldn't get away from headquarters fast enough. He had hated the pity he'd seen in Willie's eyes and the sympathetic expression on Tam's face. He hated that Garth was in denial and preferred to dismiss the possibility that one of the dead toddlers might be Blake. He understood that Garth simply couldn't accept the fact that Blake was dead. It had taken Wayne years to accept the truth. Yeah, sure, somewhere deep down inside him a glimmer of hope still existed, but he knew only too well how illogical that hope was. Blake was dead. The odds were that he had been one of Regina Bennett's victims. Wayne had visited the crazy bitch in the mental hospital twice, and both times he had come away with more questions than answers.

Just as he started to open the door to his Chevy Silverado, he heard footsteps behind him and knew without turning around that Audrey had followed him.

Go away, girl. Go away and leave me alone.

"Daddy . . . ?"

He gripped the door handle with bone-crushing strength. Keeping his back to her, he said, "I'm okay."

"No, you're not."

"Don't worry about me. I don't need your sympathy or your comfort."

"No, you never did, did you?"

Without so much as glancing over his shoulder, Wayne climbed up into the cab of his truck and slammed the door. After starting the engine, he buckled his seat belt and put the gear into reverse. As he drove out of the parking area, he caught a glimpse of his daughter in his peripheral vision. She stood alone, tall, slender, and elegant, and looking so much like her mother.

I'm sorry, little girl. Sorry I've been such a worthless father. I'm sorry for so many things.

If he could go back to when Audrey had been a baby, to when he'd been madly in love with Norma, there were so many things he'd do differently. But he couldn't go back. A guy didn't get any second chances in this life. He had loved two women and he'd lost them both. And he'd fathered two children and had lost both of them, too. Death had taken Blake from him. And his own stupidity had lost him his daughter.

As he made his way down Amnicola Highway and hit 153, his mind swirling with memories and an ache in his gut growing more painful by the minute, Wayne wanted only one thing—to forget. He didn't want to remember Norma Colton. How beautiful she'd been. How he had adored her. How she had felt lying beneath him. How sweet her lips had tasted. How badly he had disappointed her by being unable to give her all the love and attention she craved. He hadn't understood why she'd had to be so possessive, so demanding. The more she had clung to him, the more he had pulled away.

I'm sorry, Norma. God, I am so sorry. I wish I had been able to give you what you needed. I wish I had realized that you were the love of my life. I wish I'd had the chance to tell you.

The late-afternoon sun sank low on the eastern horizon, a blaze of color spreading across the sky. Wayne sucked in a long, hard breath. He had made more than his share of mistakes, and others had paid the price. Not that he hadn't suffered, wasn't still suffering, but he deserved it. Neither of his wives had. And God knew, neither of his children had.

Where Norma had been effervescent, giggling and talkative and loving all the time, Enid had been a quiet, reserved woman with a gentle nature. He had fallen in love with her and her son, Hart, too. In the beginning, they'd had a good marriage—or so he'd thought—and he'd been content. But even before Blake's birth, he had begun to notice little things about Enid's behavior, things that he later realized were signs of her mental illness. But he had chosen to ignore those signs. After all, his life had been good, hadn't it? There had been no need to make mountains out of molehills.

If only . . . Famous last words. If only he had paid more attention to Enid's strange behavior. If only he had admitted that after Blake's birth, she had needed professional help. But a quarter of a century ago, people didn't talk much about the various types of mental illnesses, about things like bipolar disorder or postpartum depression.

I'm sorry, Enid. I'm sorry I didn't realize you were sick, that you had suffered with mood swings and severe bouts of depression since childhood. Sorry that I didn't realize until it was too late.

Wayne turned onto Meadow Hill Drive and slowed his truck to the neighborhood speed limit of twenty-five as he drew near his destination. The three-bedroom, two-bath red brick ranch house with the neatly manicured lawn and rose bushes lining one side of the concrete drive beckoned to him as it had for so many years. Inside this house, he would find, as he always did, warmth and caring, understanding, and a few hours of forgetfulness.

He had already rung the doorbell before he thought that maybe he should have called first. But when Grace Douglas opened the door and stood there smiling up at him, every thought except what a wonderful sight she was left his mind.

"What a pleasant surprise," Grace said as she stepped back to allow him into her home. When he remained silent, simply looking at her, drinking her in, her smile disappeared. "Wayne, what's wrong?"

The moment he closed the door behind him, she opened her arms and wrapped them around him. When she laid her head on his chest, he enclosed her soft, womanly body in a tender embrace and the weight of the world dropped from his overburdened shoulders.

"Whatever it is, you can tell me," Grace said as she lifted her head from his chest and gazed lovingly up at him.

He reached down and cradled her face with both hands. "Have I told you lately how very important you are to me?"

Her lips curved in a fragile smile. "Not lately, no, but you don't have to tell me for me to know, because I feel the same way." She took his hand in hers and led him through the living room and into the kitchen at the back of the house. "Sit down and I'll put on a fresh pot of coffee."

When she pulled away from him to prepare the coffee, he grasped her wrist. She looked back at him.

"I guess the coffee can wait," she said.

He slid out a chair from the table, sat down, and then eased her onto his lap. She draped her arm around his neck.

Grace Douglas was round and plump, with wide hips and full breasts. She was a kind, giving woman with a heart as big as Texas. He doubted most folks ever noticed the sadness in her pretty blue eyes, a sadness that he understood in a way no one else in her life did.

He ran the back of his hand gently across her cheek. She closed her eyes and quietly sighed.

"Could we talk, later?" he asked. "I promise I'll explain everything. But right now . . ." He glided his hand down her neck, across her shoulder, and opened his palm to cup one breast.

Right now, he needed to forget. He needed to lose himself in this beautiful, loving woman. There would be time enough later that evening to tell her about the unidentified skeletons of two toddler boys. Skeletons that might be the remains of his son Blake and her son Shane.

The minute J.D. entered police headquarters, he spotted his daughter. She rose from the chair where she sat alongside a tattooed, nose-ringed boy with scraggly brown hair and a surly expression.

When a uniformed police officer said something to her, Zoe cried, "But it's my father. Please, let me tell him what happened."

The officer nodded. Zoe came running toward J.D. and hurled herself at him. Instinct took over and he put his arms around her in a comforting, fatherly way.

"I wasn't drinking," Zoe told him. "I swear to God, I wasn't drinking. Not even a beer."

The young officer, who looked all of twenty-five, lean, blond, and clean-cut, walked over to J.D. "Special Agent Cass?" He offered J.D. his hand. "I'm Officer Karns. Ryan Karns."

"Yeah, I'm J.D. Cass." He shook the man's hand. "So, what's going on here?" He glanced from Zoe to Officer Karns.

"Your daughter isn't under arrest, but we had to hold her, of course, until a parent could pick her up," Karns said. "The boy she was with was speeding not two miles from here, and when a patrolman tried to pull him over, he raced off doing close to a hundred. Lucky for him and your daughter, he didn't wreck."

"Dawson just panicked, J.D." Zoe grabbed his arm. "He'd been drinking a beer and he didn't want to get a DUI. That's why he ran."

J.D. glowered at his daughter.

"Whatever possessed you to go off with that boy?" J.D. glanced at the sulking young hunk who glared back at him.

"Dawson's my boyfriend," Zoe snapped angrily.

"Like hell he is. You're fourteen. You're not old enough to have a boyfriend."

When she opened her mouth to protest, J.D. gave her a warning stare and said, "Not another word out of you."

"Young lady," she mumbled under her breath.

"Is my daughter free to go?" J.D. asked Officer Karns.

"Yes, sir, she is."

"No, damn it, I won't leave without Dawson." Zoe planted her hands on her slender hips and shot her father a challenging glare.

"You'll leave," J.D. told her. "Either under your own power or thrown over my shoulder like a sack of potatoes. Your choice . . . young lady."

"I'm afraid Dawson isn't free to go," Officer Karns explained. "Not only was he speeding, but he was driving under the influence, endangering himself and others. He failed the breathalyzer test. He had a BrAC of 0.09."

"He was just drinking beer," Zoe told them, adamant in Dawson's defense.

"Whatever he was drinking doesn't matter," J.D. informed her. "A reading of 0.08 is considered intoxicated, and the number drops even lower for anyone under the age of twenty-one. Dawson's sixteen."

"We've contacted Dawson's parents. They're out of town, so we'll be holding him at the Hamilton County Juvenile Detention Center until they get back in town."

When J.D. refused to help Dawson, Zoe began mouthing off again, threatening all sorts of outlandish things. The wayward teen was his parents' problem, not J.D.'s. He had enough trouble with Zoe.

In the middle of his daughter's tirade and just as J.D. was at his wits' end, he heard a calm, soothing female voice ask, "Is there anything I can do to help?"

"Evening, Dr. Sherrod." Officer Karns's shoulders drooped wearily, as if he, too, were at the end of his rope. No doubt he had counted on J.D. being able to control his fourteen-year-old daughter since he wasn't sure how to deal with the hysterical girl.

Apparently, Audrey Sherrod had been visiting her uncle and had just walked out of his office. However, it wasn't Garth Hudson who accompanied her, but Chief Mullins. The chief gave Audrey a quick, fatherly peck on the cheek and whispered something to her, then nodded to Officer Karns and headed for the exit.

Dr. Sherrod's question had startled Zoe into complete silence. She stood there staring at the woman as if she were an alien who had just stepped out of a spaceship from Mars.

"I . . . uh . . . I don't know if you can help." Karns looked from Audrey Sherrod to J.D. "It's up to you, Special Agent Cass."

J.D. surveyed the woman from head to toe. Sublimely cool and controlled, Audrey looked him right in the eye. Despite the unseasonably hot and humid September day and the warm pink flush on her cheeks, she was perfectly groomed, not a silky brown hair out of place, her makeup flawless, her slacks and sweater unwrinkled.

J.D. didn't want her help. Didn't need her help. But he was in no position to be rude. All he wanted was to take Zoe home and ground her for the rest of her life. Well, at least until she was thirty. Apparently Dr. Sherrod was well-known and respected here at police headquarters and no doubt on as friendly terms with the chief as she was Officer Lovelady, the chief's daughter.

"If you think you can help, then by all means help." J.D. resented Dr. Sherrod's interference. Resented it like hell. "I didn't realize that your area of expertise included soothing smart-mouthed, disrespectful teenage girls."

Audrey's hazel brown eyes glimmered as she settled her gaze on him, a sure sign she recognized his comment as an insult as well as a challenge. Turning up her haughty little nose, she said, "There is usually a reason behind such behavior." She turned to Zoe. "Hi, I'm Audrey Sherrod. I'm a professional counselor and occasionally I work with the police in an advisory capacity. If you think I can help you, then tell me how and I'll see what I can do."

Zoe kept staring at Audrey for several moments as if she wasn't quite sure how to respond. Finally, she said, "I'm Zoe Davidson."

"Nice to meet you, Zoe. Is there anything I can do to help you?"

"Dawson is the one who needs help, but my father won't help him."

"I see." She glanced at J.D., a questioning look in her eyes. "And what do you expect your father to do?"

"Get Dawson out of this mess," Zoe replied. "My dad's a Tennessee Bureau of Investigation agent. He could take care of this for Dawson if he wanted to, but he doesn't like Dawson because he thinks I'm too young to have a boyfriend."

"How old are you?"

"Fourteen."

"Hmm . . . I had a boyfriend when I was fourteen, and my father didn't like him."

Zoe smiled at J.D. triumphantly. Great. Just what he

needed. A damn female shrink who apparently agreed with his daughter.

"Ryan, what are the charges against Dawson?" Audrey asked.

Officer Karns rattled off a list of offenses, everything from reckless driving to resisting arrest, with half a dozen other complaints in between, including DUI, resisting stop and frisk, and reckless endangerment.

"I see. I assume you've contacted his parents."

"Yes, ma'am."

"And is there anything Special Agent Cass can do for Dawson, any way he can take the boy with him when he and Zoe leave?"

"No, ma'am. Dawson Cummings is going to be spending the night in juvenile tonight. Once his parents arrive and his bond is posted, he'll be released into their custody."

"Zoe's very concerned about Dawson," Audrey told Officer Karns. "Can you give her some kind of reassurance that he'll be well treated and no harm will come to him until his parents can arrange for his release?"

J.D. watched and listened, completely dumbfounded by the way Zoe was reacting to Audrey Sherrod. Hadn't he been saying pretty much the same things to her? Why was she paying attention to a stranger when all she'd done was scream at her own father?

"Yes, ma'am." The young policeman looked directly at Zoe. "I give you my word that Dawson will be okay until his parents can take him home. He's drunk and belligerent and he's mouthed off and, yes, he's in big trouble. But his folks will get him a good lawyer and since this is his first arrest, he'll probably wind up with nothing more than a slap on the wrist."

"There, Zoe, Officer Karns has given you his word." Audrey placed her hand on Zoe's shoulder. "I'm sure if you go home with your father now and apologize to him for some of the things you said to him, you and he will be able to come to an understanding about Dawson." Audrey looked at J.D. "Isn't that right, Special Agent Cass?"

J.D. snorted. Damn her. She'd put him on the spot. He nodded. "Yeah, okay."

When Audrey turned to go, Zoe called, "Wait. Don't leave."

Audrey paused and glanced over her shoulder.

"Uh . . . J.D. and I, we don't communicate all that well. We both always wind up saying the wrong things." Zoe gazed pleadingly at Audrey. "Was it like that for you and your dad?"

J.D. noted the slight hesitation and the quickly concealed odd expression as it crossed Audrey's face.

"Yes, Zoe, it was. My father and I had communication problems, too."

"Are all fathers like that? I mean, do all of them think you're still a baby when you're not? Do they all try to run your life and assume they know what's best for you even when they're wrong?"

"Yes, to some extent all fathers are like that, so it's up to daughters during their teen years to be patient and understanding and do their best not to give their fathers a heart attack. Of course, giving him a few gray hairs is a different matter. That's a given."

Zoe looked at J.D., and she and Audrey laughed.

Yeah, funny. He hadn't missed the joke. His hair had already begun turning prematurely gray before Zoe came to live with him, but he had to admit that it was getting grayer every day.

Zoe went over and stood in front of J.D. "If I apologize to you, will you let me say good-bye to Dawson before we leave?"

Letting his daughter anywhere near that young hoodlum was the last thing J.D. wanted to do, but when he glanced at

Audrey, she gave him a cautionary meet-your-child-halfway stare.

"Yeah. Okay," he said reluctantly.

"I'm sorry I said all those awful things to you. I—I didn't mean them." Zoe gulped. "Well, I didn't mean most of them."

J.D. nodded. At least she was truthful. That alone was a step in the right direction. "Apology accepted."

"Now, may I say bye to Dawson?"

"Make it quick."

"I will."

Everything was going along just fine. Everybody was calm and rational, even Zoe. And J.D. managed to keep his resentment of Audrey Sherrod's interference under control. Okay, so the woman had worked some kind of magic on Zoe, but she'd had no right to—

God damn it. What the hell?

Zoe stood on tiptoe, wrapped her arms around Dawson's neck, and kissed him. Kissed him on the mouth. And both his mouth and hers were wide open!

J.D. growled like the papa bear he was and felt like ripping Dawson apart, limb from limb. Just as he moved forward, intending to grab Zoe, Audrey reached out and clamped her hand over his forearm.

"Don't," Audrey whispered. "It's just a kiss. Give her that much."

J.D. snapped his head around and glared at Audrey. "She's a child. My child."

"She's a child on the verge of womanhood. And unless I miss my guess, your daughter is strong-minded and stubborn, and the more you object to something, the more appealing it is to her. The harder you push, the harder she'll push back."

J.D. clenched his teeth. He wanted to tell Audrey Sherrod

to go to hell. But he didn't. As bad as he hated to admit it, she was right. Zoe was just like him, God help them both. She was as strong-willed and stubborn as he was, and she reacted just as he did to being issued orders.

The kiss ended before J.D. could explode. And when Zoe came back to him and said, "I'm ready," he noticed that Audrey's long, slender fingers still circled his forearm.

"You can let go now," he told her.

She jerked her hand away as her gaze flashed from his face to Zoe's. "If you ever need someone to talk to, give me a call."

J.D. barely managed to keep from telling Audrey to back off and leave his daughter alone.

"Thanks," Zoe said. "I just might do that, Dr. Sherrod."

Audrey smiled warmly before turning and walking away.

"I like her," Zoe said. "Why can't you date somebody like Dr. Sherrod instead of that stuck-on-herself-because-she's-so-wonderful Holly Johnston?"

"Whom I date is none of your business," J.D. told her as he escorted her downstairs and out of the police station.

"That should work both ways," Zoe said.

"It will when you're twenty-one."

Zoe groaned and rolled her eyes skyward.

Damn. Fatherhood should come with a how-to book.

Chapter 8

After they had made love, while he held her close, Wayne had told Grace about the two toddler skeletons found with the bodies of the two murdered women. He hadn't needed to say more than that. She had guessed what he had dreaded telling her. She hadn't cried. She hadn't said much. But he knew she was as torn up inside as he was.

Now she lay cuddled against him, her breast pressing into his side and her head resting on his shoulder. He had known her for almost twenty-five years, but they hadn't become lovers until ten years ago. They had met under the most horrific circumstances—Grace's two-year-old son, Shane, had been abducted not long after Blake had been kidnapped. Their mutual hurt and anger and unbearable grief had created a bond between them, a bond that intensified because they each not only lost a child, but lost a mate. Enid had committed suicide, leaving Wayne alone and lost in his agony. Grace's husband had become an alcoholic and drank himself to death less than five years after Shane's disappearance, leaving her to raise their older son Lance alone.

Over the years Wayne and Grace had stayed in touch. In

the beginning, it had been nothing more than Wayne sharing information with her whenever he heard about anything that might possibly be remotely connected to their sons' abductions. Eventually, they started meeting for coffee, and that led to getting together for dinner, and after fifteen years of gradually becoming dear friends, they had become lovers.

Grace was a part of his life that he didn't share with anyone else. Willie and Geraldine knew about Grace and he was pretty sure Garth did, too. But the kids didn't know, Audrey and Hart. Hell, they didn't know much of anything about his life, and he knew very little about theirs. And it was his fault that things were the way they were. He had been the one who had abandoned them. Emotionally abandoned. While they were growing up, he had kept them housed, fed, and clothed, and had paid the bills, but he had ceased being a father to either of them years ago.

Grace eased out of bed and headed toward the bathroom. He watched her, enjoying the view. No longer young, firm, or slender, her body still looked damn good to him. She was a giver, his Grace, not a taker. Looking back over the past twenty-five years, he wasn't sure he would have survived without her.

He got out of bed and joined her in the bathroom. She had already freshened up and slipped into a floor-length blue cotton robe.

"While you're cleaning up, I'll go fix us some supper," Grace said.

"Don't go to any trouble, honey." He nuzzled the side of her neck as he pulled her backward against him.

She rested there in his arms for a couple of minutes, then pulled away from him. "How about scrambled eggs, bacon, and toast?"

"Sounds good."

When she left the bathroom, Wayne stared at himself in the vanity mirror over the sink. His brow was deeply furrowed and his eyes and mouth were framed by wrinkles. And his once-dark hair was now light gray, almost white. How the hell had he gotten so old so fast? Sometimes it seemed as if it had been only yesterday that he'd been twenty-one, his whole life ahead of him. Now he was sixty-one, most of his life behind him.

He turned on the cold water, cupped his hands to catch the water, and tossed it into his face. Then he filled the sink with warm water, picked up the soap, and lathered his genital area. Afterward, he retraced his steps, picked up his discarded clothing, and dressed.

Entering the kitchen, he found Grace at the stove. With the bacon sizzling on one electric eye, she busily poured whisked eggs into a hot skillet.

"What can I do to help?" he asked.

"Put on some coffee and fix the toast."

As he set about preparing the coffeemaker, he asked, "Do you want to talk about it?"

She kept stirring the eggs, focusing her attention on the job at hand. "What more is there to say?"

"I guess you're right. Until we know for sure if those little bodies are Blake and Shane, then . . ." He didn't know whether he hoped they were his son and Grace's son or if he hoped they weren't.

She lifted the skillet and spooned the scrambled eggs onto two plates, then set the skillet aside. "You'd think that after all these years, it wouldn't still hurt so much."

Wayne poured fresh water into the reservoir and punched the On button to start the coffee brewing. He moved closer to Grace and slid his arm around her waist.

She closed her eyes. Tears trickled down her cheeks.

Wayne turned her in his arms, reached up, and wiped away the tears with his fingertips. He leaned down and kissed her closed eyelids as his unshed tears caught in his throat.

* * *

Zoe hadn't said a word all the way home, and the minute they entered the house, she headed for her room.

"We need to talk," J.D. told her.

"I don't want to talk."

"Too bad. Come back here and sit down."

Zoe plodded reluctantly from the hallway into the living room and slumped down on the sofa.

God, he didn't want to do this. But he had to do it. He was Zoe's father.

"What you did today—running off with Dawson—was not only irresponsible and thoughtless, it was dangerous," J.D. said, doing his level best not to raise his voice.

Zoe remained sullen and silent.

"I expect you to acknowledge what I just said," he told her.

She lifted her downcast gaze, her eyes bright with anger and a hint of tears. "It's all your fault.'

Stunned by her accusation, he stared at her as he tried to figure out her illogical reasoning. "How is it my fault that you slipped away from Jacy's aunt, who, by the way, was worried sick about you, and ran off with a boy who'd been drinking? How is it my fault that you could easily have been killed in a car wreck because he was driving drunk? And how is it my fault that you and Dawson were picked up by the police?"

"Because . . . 'cause . . ." She swallowed her tears. "If you'd just let me date Dawson, let him come here and let me go out with him—"

"You are fourteen years old. That's too young to be dating."

"My mother was dating when she was fourteen!" Zoe shouted.

"Yeah, and see how she turned out." The moment the words left his mouth, J.D. wished them back. Maybe Carrie had been a very untraditional parent, maybe she'd been irresponsible and flighty, but she had been Zoe's mother.

"How dare you say that about my mom!" Zoe shot up off the sofa. "She was a better parent than you are. At least she loved me."

When Zoe ran out of the room, he cursed softly and called himself a few choice names, *idiot* heading the list. Why was it that no matter how hard he tried to do the right thing where Zoe was concerned, he always wound up making a mess of things?

Because you don't know the first thing about raising a teenage girl. Because Zoe knows that you really don't want her and that even though you should love her because she's your daughter, you don't.

Tam didn't like it when Marcus was away, but in his job as a TVA engineer, he had to travel on a fairly frequent basis. Their apartment seemed so empty without him. He had phoned to let her know he had arrived safely and promised to call again in the morning before she left for work. The luckiest day of her life was when she met Marcus Lovelady, and the second luckiest day was the day they got married. He was such a good man. Kind, considerate, and reliable. And he loved her with his whole heart.

They had discussed having children and she knew that at thirty-four, her biological clock was ticking faster and faster. But she wasn't sure she wanted to try to combine motherhood with a career. Although Marcus would be as wonderful a father as her own dad had always been, she doubted she could ever be half the mother her mama was. Besides, she wasn't sure she deserved to be a mother. Not after . . .

That was over fifteen years ago. You were barely eighteen.

Tam poured herself another glass of Merlot, flipped on

the TV, and kept the sound muted as she sat in her favorite easy chair. She glanced down at the wedding band and one-carat diamond on her ring finger.

She admired and respected Marcus. And she loved him. But had she cheated her husband by marrying him when she would never be able to love him with her whole heart? If she could give him a child, would that make up for the fact that she would always be in love with another man?

Oh, dear Lord, don't think about him. He isn't a part of your daily life and hasn't been for a long, long time.

What was wrong with her tonight? Why was she in such a melancholy mood? Why was she thinking about him, remembering . . . ? She didn't want to think about him, didn't want to remember the child she had aborted, a child who would be nearly fifteen now, almost as old as she had been when she'd gotten pregnant.

It had all been so hopeless, so impossible. And she had been so completely in love.

The saddest part of all was that he had loved her, too, just as much as she had loved him.

Tam gulped down the remainder of her wine and let the empty glass fall from her hand onto the carpeted floor beside her chair. She closed her eyes and allowed the memories to wash over her, warm and sweet like low tide in the heat of summer.

She could almost feel his lips on hers, feel their naked bodies joined, feel him buried deep inside her. She could hear his voice, deep and sultry, saying her name, telling her how much he loved her.

Tears escaped from the corners of her closed eyelids and crept slowly down her cheeks.

Tam wrapped her arms around her body and hugged herself as she sucked back the tears. *Don't do this to yourself. Stupid. Stupid. Stupid.*

If only Marcus were there she wouldn't be wallowing in self-pity. But Marcus wasn't there to reassure her, to make her smile, to remind her of all her many blessings.

Tam got up, grabbed the receiver from the portable phone on the nearby desk, and dialed her best friend's number.

Audrey answered on the third ring. "Hey there."

"Are you busy?"

"Not really. What's up?"

"Marcus left on another business trip this afternoon and I'm lonely," Tam said. "I've been sitting here downing a couple of glasses of wine and am on the edge of a self-pity jag."

"Want me to come over?"

"Would you?"

"Give me thirty minutes." Then Audrey asked, "Have you eaten dinner yet?"

"No, I—"

"Drinking on an empty stomach?" Audrey clicked her tongue to make a disapproving noise. "You know better."

"I have salad fixings."

"Good. Why don't you take a shower and put on your pajamas and when I get there, I'll prepare the salad. I have leftover chicken I'll bring with me to add to the salad. But until you eat something, no more wine for you. Promise?"

"I promise."

Tam hung up the phone. Audrey always knew the right thing to say and the right thing to do to help her. Maybe it was because they knew each other so well, because they'd been close friends since childhood. If Audrey thought that Tam wasn't completely in love with Marcus, she had never said a word. However, she suspected that her best friend knew the truth. She needed to talk to someone, to admit the truth out loud, and who better to be her father confessor than Audrey, her best friend who just happened to be a shrink? Well, a counselor, which was the next best thing to a shrink. Maybe even better.

* * *

Audrey parked her Buick Enclave, unbuckled her seat belt, and reached for the shoulder bag and the plastic sack containing the cold chicken she had promised to bring for their salad. Her phone rang. After retrieving it from an outer slot on her purse, she checked the caller ID. Zoe Davidson.

"Hi, Zoe," Audrey said when she answered.

"Hi, Dr. Sherrod." Zoe's girlish voice sounded even younger than her fourteen years. "I—I . . . uh . . . You said if I needed to talk, to call you. You probably didn't expect to hear from me, at least not this soon, but . . ."

"It's all right," Audrey assured her. "I don't mind that you called. What can I do to help you?"

"You can get me a different father."

"Oh, I see. I had hoped maybe once you and your dad got home, you might have been able to talk things out and—"

"He doesn't want to talk things out. He just wants to issue orders. I hate him. And I hate living with him. And he hates me, too. He doesn't want me. He just keeps me because he knows I don't have anywhere else to go."

Oh, Zoe, you poor, sweet girl.

The similarity between the way J.D. Cass's daughter felt now and the way Audrey had once felt about her relationship with her own father was too obvious to ignore. Audrey understood how it felt to believe your father hated you, that he tolerated you because it was his duty, not because he loved you.

"My guess is that your father doesn't hate you," Audrey said. "And even if you hate living with him and having to adhere to his rules, you don't really hate him."

Silence.

"Zoe, do you think your father would allow you to set up an appointment with me?"

"You mean as one of your patients?"

"Although my specialty isn't family counseling, I am qualified—"

"J.D.'s the one who needs counseling," Zoe said.

"That's probably true and ideally I would counsel both of you, together and separately. But, honey, you need someone to talk to, someone who'll listen and—"

"And care about me. About how I feel and what I think. Could you do that, Dr. Sherrod? Could you care about me, even just a little?"

A hard knot of emotion formed in the center of Audrey's chest. She drew in and released a deep, cleansing breath. Would it be a mistake to counsel Zoe Davidson when she knew, even now, that she would become emotionally involved with this young girl?

"Zoe, if I counsel you, it would be my job to care about what you think and how you feel. And I already like you, you know."

"You do?"

"Well, of course I do."

"I—I like you, too."

"Would you like for me to phone your father and ask his permission for us to set up your first appointment?"

"Oh, I don't know. What if it pisses him off?"

"Why don't you leave your father to me? I'll call him in the morning from my office and either he or I will let you know the outcome."

"Thank you, Dr. Sherrod. Thank you so much."

"You're welcome, Zoe."

Ending her call, Audrey slipped her bag over her shoulder, picked up the plastic sack, and opened the car door. Before Zoe's phone call, Audrey's main concern had been her best friend. She'd heard an odd hint of desperation—almost panic—in Tam's voice. Now not only was she concerned about Tam, but her conversation with Zoe Davidson had aroused a barrage of mixed emotions. She felt a sense of kinship with Zoe, seeing some of herself at fourteen in the rebellious, unhappy teenager. Her desire to help Zoe went beyond the professional and into the personal realm. Would it be better if she referred J.D. and his daughter to another therapist? Yes and no. It would be better for her not to become involved with either the daughter or the father. But Zoe trusted her. She might not trust another counselor so easily.

All the while Audrey went from the parking area to Tam and Marcus's apartment, her mind focused on one thing—making the correct decision where Zoe was concerned. It wasn't until she rang the doorbell several times, waiting a minute or two between rings, that Audrey's full attention returned to her friend. Tam was expecting her, so why wasn't she answering the door?

Maybe she's still in the shower.

Audrey rang the bell again. No response. Just as she reached down into her purse to find her key ring, intending to use her key to Tam's apartment, the door swung open and Tam stood there smiling, the phone to her ear.

"It's Marcus." Wearing her pajamas and a matching knee-length robe, Tam mouthed the words as she motioned for Audrey to enter.

Audrey returned her friend's smile. While Tam continued her conversation with her husband, Audrey headed for the kitchen. She placed her purse on one of the two bar stools and laid the plastic sack containing the chicken on the counter. After removing an unopened bag of fresh spring-mix greens from the refrigerator, along with cherry tomatoes, a cucumber, and bottled ranch dressing, Audrey set about preparing their salads. She sliced the chicken into small chunks, added it to the salads, and sparingly sprinkled the dressing over her creation.

When she heard Tam laugh, she breathed a sigh of relief. It wasn't often that Tam went into a blue funk, but when she did, it was usually a doozie. The last time had been more than a year ago and had been precipitated by two factors—Marcus was out of town and Tam had come face-to-face with her teenage sweetheart—factors that Audrey realized hadn't been repeated until quite recently.

Still smiling, Tam came into the kitchen. "Marcus said hello and sends his love."

"Feeling better?"

"Much, thanks."

Audrey studied Tam briefly, then set their salad plates atop the placemats on the small kitchen table. "Do you prefer herbal tea or water with lemon or another glass of wine?"

"Before Marcus called, I'd have said more wine. But now, I think water with lemon. You get the crackers out of the pantry and I'll take care of our water."

Half an hour later, with their meal eaten and the dishwasher loaded, Audrey and Tam curled up together on opposite ends of the plush chenille sofa in Tam's living room. Each held a cup of herbal tea.

"Want to tell me?" Audrey asked.

Tam glanced down at the cup of tea that she cradled in both hands. "No. I don't want to tell you. I don't want to admit what a stupid, ungrateful bitch I am. I don't want to say it out loud."

"If you don't want to, then don't. But if you think it will help, maybe release some pent-up emotions, then tell me. Whatever you say, you know I won't repeat it to another living soul. And I won't judge you."

"You never have," Tam said. "My parents think I'm practically perfect. And Marcus . . . oh, Audrey, he does think I'm perfect."

"No one is perfect, but you come mighty damn close."

"How can you say that when you know . . . ? Oh God, you know me better than anyone else on earth. You know how far from perfect I am. If my parents knew how I'd let them down, they'd be so disappointed. If Marcus knew . . ."

"You have never disappointed Geraldine and Willie, and if they knew, they would be loving and supportive. And if Marcus knew, he would understand. You were barely eighteen. You did what you thought was best for everyone involved. And I was right there with you, agreeing with your decision and holding your hand."

Tam looked at Audrey, her brown eyes filled with unshed tears. "If you had been in my situation, would you have . . . ? Would you have killed your own baby?"

Audrey set aside her tea, then took the cup from Tam and set it beside hers on the coffee table. She scooted across the sofa, draped her arm around Tam's shoulders, and leaned her head over against Tam's.

They sat there in silence for quite a while, two friends remembering a tragedy from the past. Audrey understood that even after all these years, Tam still felt regret, remorse, and guilt. She managed to keep that long-ago heartbreak buried deep inside her, but occasionally it resurfaced.

"What do I tell Marcus when he wants to have a baby?" Tam asked. "He hasn't come right out and said he's ready, but he's dropped a few subtle hints."

"Tell him the truth. Tell him about the abortion."

Tam inhaled deeply and exhaled strongly. "I don't know if I want a baby. Hell, I don't even know for sure I can have one."

"There is no reason to think that because of the abortion, you can't get pregnant," Audrey assured her. "But being able to get pregnant and wanting to have a baby are two different things. If you don't want a baby because of what happened when you were a teenager, then I recommend some counseling to help you—"

Tam laughed, but when Audrey glanced at her face, she saw tears running down Tam's cheeks.

"Well, that was a really impersonal and rather condescending statement, wasn't it?" Audrey said. "I'm sorry, Tam. I let Dr. Sherrod inject herself into a situation where she had no business being. This talk is between you and me, Tam and Audrey, best friends since we were babies."

"It's all right," Tam said. "And it's not as if you haven't been trying to get me into counseling for years."

"I'm a bossy know-it-all."

"Yes, you are, but I love you anyway."

"I know. Thank you."

"Audrey?"

"Hmm . . . ?" She didn't know if she was prepared for whatever Tam wanted to tell her. They had shared all their secrets over the years, trusting each other completely, but Audrey suspected there was one secret that Tam hadn't shared with anyone.

"You know that I love Marcus. He's the best thing that ever happened to me. He makes me so happy."

"I know, and I'm very grateful to him. I love seeing you happy. I want only good things for you because you deserve only good things."

"Do I?"

Audrey took Tam's hands in hers. "Yes, you do."

"I love Marcus, but . . ."

"But?"

"I don't know if I can say it out loud. I don't know if I dare."

She squeezed Tam's hands.

"A part of me—that stupid teenage girl—is still in love with Hart."

Audrey released the breath she'd been holding and wrapped her arms around Tam, who clung to Audrey as she cried.

"How stupid does that make me?"

Oh, Tam, I knew. I knew, but I didn't want to know.

And she also knew that no matter how much Tam and Hart had loved each other, how much they still loved each other, there was absolutely no hope for them as a couple. Not then. Not now. Not ever.

Chapter 9

Audrey balanced her briefcase in one hand and a mocha latte in the other as she approached her office. At the locked door, she maneuvered the latte out of her right hand into her left, then removed the key ring dangling from her clenched teeth and inserted the door key into the lock. Most mornings, she arrived before her receptionist, Donna Mackey, who usually arrived by eight-thirty, once she had dropped her twin grandsons at preschool. Her son-in-law, an army corporal, was stationed in the Middle East and her daughter worked the morning shift as a Burger King assistant manager. One of the reasons Audrey had hired Donna was because her grandmotherly appearance and personality immediately put patients at ease.

After making her way through the small waiting room and into her private office, Audrey dumped her briefcase in her swivel chair and set the latte on her desk. Just as she opened the window blinds to let in the morning sunlight, the phone rang. Before Donna arrived to take calls, the answering machine picked up and recorded messages, so Audrey continued moving through her office and back into the waiting room opening blinds and getting things in order for a busy Monday work schedule.

After the recorded message ended, a male voice said, "Dr. Sherrod, this is J.D. Cass."

Audrey stopped and listened.

"I . . . uh . . . I was wondering if I could set up an appointment to talk to you."

Audrey walked over to the telephone on her desk and laid her hand atop the receiver.

"It's about Zoe," J.D. said. "She seems to have taken a shine to you, and since she did . . . well, I thought maybe you could help her." He paused for a moment, and then added, "Help us."

Just let the answering machine take the call. Donna can contact Special Agent Cass later and arrange for an appointment. J.D. and his daughter are simply potential clients. Nothing more.

Her hand tightened on the receiver and before she could stop herself, Audrey disregarded what her common sense had told her.

She lifted the receiver. "Special Agent Cass. This is Dr. Sherrod."

"Oh." He seemed surprised to hear her voice. "Yeah. Good morning."

"Good morning."

"I guess you heard what I said about Zoe liking you and how I wanted to talk to you about helping us work out some father/daughter problems."

"Yes, I heard. And I'd be happy to check my appointment book and set a time for you and Zoe to come in for your first counseling session."

"Thanks, but I'd rather see you alone before we bring Zoe

into it. I'm not even sure she'd go for the idea. She might not want to try counseling."

"She does," Audrey said.

"How do you—?"

"Zoe called me last night. She and I had a nice chat."

"She didn't say anything to me about calling you. But then she doesn't tell me much."

"The truth of the matter is I promised Zoe that I'd phone you this morning and talk to you about the two of you beginning family counseling."

"You're kidding."

"No, I assure you that—"

"Tell me something, Doc, what kind of spell did you put on my daughter?"

"What do you mean?"

"You only met Zoe yesterday, and already you seem to have her eating out of your hand. How did you do it? She's been living with me for over a year, and I swear to God getting her to listen to anything I say is like pulling eyeteeth."

"No spells of any kind, I assure you. All I did yesterday at the police station and last night during our phone conversation was listen to what she had to say."

"Are you saying I don't listen to her? Well, I do, but everything that comes out of her mouth is 'I won't' and 'I'm miserable' and 'I hate you.' Believe me, my listening to her has been a total waste of time."

"Then perhaps that is the first problem we need to address in counseling."

"Yeah, maybe it is," J.D. said. "So, when can you work us into your busy schedule? It would be better for Zoe if I didn't have to take her out of school. And as late in the day as possible would work for both of us."

"I'll check my appointment calendar and have my receptionist get back to you."

"Couldn't you check your calendar now?"

Yes, of course she could. But she wouldn't do it. The fact that this man was practically demanding preferential treatment irritated her.

"I'm afraid I don't have time. I'm quite busy and—"

"Maybe I should check with another counselor who isn't as busy as you are."

Damn him. She wanted to tell him to go right ahead, that the last thing she needed was to get involved with him, even on a strictly patient/therapist level. "After I promised Zoe that I'd contact you, I actually considered the option of putting you in touch with another therapist, but I decided that Zoe might rebel against the idea of seeing someone else. Your daughter trusts me."

"And likes you."

"Yes, she likes me and I like her."

"You're one up on me, Doc. She doesn't like me very much."

"Maybe that's because she knows you don't like her."

J.D. didn't respond, didn't say one word.

"I'm sorry," Audrey told him. "That was unprofessional of me."

"Maybe so, but it was the truth."

"I think you and Zoe have a great deal to work through before you can find common ground and possibly learn to like each other."

"You might be right," he replied. "So, how about that appointment?"

Audrey gritted her teeth as she picked up the appointment book and flipped through the pages. "The earliest appointment I have after three in the afternoon is Friday at four-thirty. It's the last hour-long appointment of the day."

"I'll take it. Put me down."

"I'll put y'all down, you and Zoe, for your first session of family counseling."

"Okay, Dr. Sherrod, we'll do this your way."

"Thank you for being so agreeable, Special Agent Cass."

He chuckled. "Yeah, sure. We'll see you Friday at four-thirty."

As soon as she replaced the receiver, Audrey released an exasperated breath. She was out of her mind to accept J.D. Cass as a client. She didn't like the man, and he knew that she didn't like him. Her personal feelings for him were a problem. Was there any way she could be objective where he was concerned?

You'd better be. Zoe needs you. If you don't suck it up and learn to put aside your dislike for J.D., Zoe's the one who will suffer.

The last thing Garth wanted to do was dredge up the past, a past he thought was long dead and buried. But these new kidnapping cases had dug up ghosts and all but resurrected the dead. God help him, he had no choice but to tell Hart. Sooner or later, the information about the toddler skeletons being found bundled in Jill Scott's and Debra Gregory's arms was bound to leak out and become front-page headlines. He couldn't let Hart learn about those skeletons from anyone else. There was no telling how his nephew might react. Blake's disappearance—Blake's death—twenty-five years ago had altered the course of so many lives, Hart's more than anyone else's.

Unfortunately, Hart had inherited Enid's emotional weaknesses. As a child, he had been quiet and shy and gentle. And Garth had tried to take care of him and protect him as he always had Enid, even though she'd been his older sister. Although physically, he and Enid had resembled each other just enough so that people recognized they were related, in every other way, they had been as different as night and day. He had taken after their none-too-handsome old man, a hard-drinking, womanizing son of a bitch. Their father's only saving grace was that he had taken care of his own, making sure his wife and kids never went without the necessities. Garth was like his father in that way, too. He'd done his level best to take care of Enid, and after her divorce from Hart's good-looking, worthless dad, he'd taken care of his nephew, too. Garth had inherited one redeeming quality from his sweet mother—his ability to love. He doubted his old man had ever loved anyone except himself.

Garth loved Hart as if he were his own son. Always had. Always would.

Glancing at his wristwatch, he noted that it was nearly eight-thirty. He had called Tamara to let her know he'd be running late that morning. She hadn't asked why, but he figured she knew. He never mentioned his nephew to his partner. No need to dredge up old memories for either of them. Tam was married now and appeared to be happy. He hoped she was. She'd always been a good kid. It wasn't her fault that things hadn't worked out between her and Hart. Of course, Garth knew that the two of them going their separate ways had been for the best. Hart hadn't been ready for marriage at seventeen, still wasn't, and probably never would be. Besides the racial factor—which, despite the gradual changes in people's attitudes, still mattered to a lot of folks—there was Hart's alcohol and drug abuse, his inability to hold down a job for more than a few months at a time, and the boy's mental instability.

Garth had hoped that Hart would wake up earlier that morning than his usual ten or eleven o'clock, but it seemed that unless he wanted to wait around and waste half the morning, he'd have to rouse his nephew.

He knocked on Hart's closed bedroom door, and to his surprise, the boy answered him.

"Yeah?"

"Are you up?"

"Yeah, just woke up and took a piss. Why?"

"How about having a cup of coffee with me before I head out this morning?"

Hart opened the door and looked at Garth. "What's up? You're usually long gone by now."

"Come on in the kitchen and we'll have that coffee."

"Sure."

Barefooted and bare-chested, Hart followed Garth into the small galley-style kitchen and watched while Garth poured black coffee into a couple of mismatched mugs. When he handed his nephew one of the mugs, he took that moment to study him closely but quickly. The boy was every bit as good looking as his father had been, blond, blue-eyed, and almost too pretty to be a guy.

He noted that Hart appeared to be sober and alert and in a good mood.

"I need to talk to you," Garth said.

"Yeah, sure. Shoot." Hart took a sip of coffee. "This would be better if it was Irish."

When Garth narrowed his gaze, Hart chuckled good naturedly. "Don't worry, there's no liquor in the house and I haven't had a drink in weeks. And I'm still going to my meetings every day."

"Good for you."

Would telling him about the skeletons send him off on a bender or to the nearest drug dealer?

"Is something wrong?" Hart asked. "Nothing's wrong with Audrey or Dad or—"

"No, no, they're fine. It's about the case Tam and I are working on."

"How's that going? You're treating Tamara right, aren't you?"

"Tamara's a good police officer. She and I work just fine together."

"I'm glad."

"Hart, son . . ." Garth set his mug down on the counter. "I don't know any easy way to say this, so I'm just going to say it. The case I'm working on . . . the two kidnapping and murder cases are connected. We're pretty sure the same man kidnapped and murdered Debra Gregory and Jill Scott."

"A serial killer?"

"More than likely. What I'm going to tell you is something we've kept from the press, something when I tell you, you're going to have to—" Garth growled with frustration. "I wouldn't be telling you anything because there's nothing to it, nothing to concern us, but God almighty, Willie Mullins took it upon himself to tell Audrey and Wayne, and Audrey's convinced herself of something that's impossible and Wayne's all torn up about it and—"

"For God's sake, just tell me."

"You might've heard that both of our murder victims were found sitting in rocking chairs and holding a blanket-wrapped doll in their arms."

"Yeah, I guess everybody in Chattanooga's heard the weird details."

"You see, the problem is, in neither case was it a doll wrapped up in the blanket. It was the skeleton of a baby . . . a toddler, actually. The experts say the skeletons belonged to boys between two and three years old."

Hart stared at Garth, his blue eyes wide with uncertainty, as if he thought he had misunderstood.

"What are you trying to tell me?" Hart asked, his voice a raspy whisper.

"Audrey and Wayne think there's a possibility that one of those toddlers might be Blake."

Hart's coffee mug dropped from his hand and hit the floor with a loud crash. Hot liquid poured across the tile floor.

"That's not possible," Hart said.

Ignoring the spilled coffee and broken mug, Garth reached out and grasped Hart's shoulder. "Of course it's not, and once the DNA tests are run, Wayne and Audrey will know neither boy is Blake."

"But they hope one of them is Blake, don't they? They want to find him. How many times did I hear Dad say that he wanted to bring Blake home and bury him beside Mom?"

Garth squeezed Hart's shoulder. "Now, you listen to me, son. There's no reason to get upset about this. It'll amount to nothing. I wish to high heaven that this hadn't happened and reopened painful old wounds for all of us. Don't let this set you back. You've been doing real good lately. You're clean and sober and you're taking your meds and—"

"I'm sorry, Uncle Garth. I'm so sorry."

Garth hugged the boy to him and held him. "You've got nothing to be sorry about. Do you hear me? You do the best you can, and that's all anybody can ask of you."

Garth released Hart, forced a smile, and then cleaned up the coffee and broken mug before he left for work.

J.D. knew former Special Agent George Bonner, now retired and serving his second term as mayor of nearby Cleveland, Tennessee, only by reputation. The two had never met, not until now. Bonner carried three hundred pounds quite well on his six-four frame. He was a big, bulky guy with a shock of auburn hair streaked with silver and a set of keen brown eyes.

"Mayor Bonner, this is Special Agent J.D. Cass," Chief Mullins said.

Bonner stuck out a meaty hand and he and J.D. exchanged a solid, man-to-man handshake as the two sized up each other. The corners of Bonner's lips lifted slightly and J.D. sensed that he had just passed muster.

Chief Mullins indicated the other two men in his office. "You already know Mayor Hardy and DA Harrelson."

Both seated, neither the mayor nor the DA stood, but each acknowledged J.D. with a nod and he did the same.

"Take a seat, J.D.," Chief Mullins said.

J.D. sat in the chair the chief indicated.

"The DA has put in a request to the TBI asking that you be officially assigned to what the press"—the chief tapped his index finger on the copy of the *Chattanooga Times Free Press* lying on his desk—"as of this morning's headlines is referring to as the Rocking Chair Murders and the UNSUB as the Rocking Chair Killer."

The announcement didn't surprise J.D. He'd halfway expected it. What he hadn't expected was to be called to the chief's office for a meeting with the mayor and the DA. And what was Bonner doing there?

"You'll be working with Sergeant Hudson and Officer Lovelady," the chief told him, then glanced at Bonner. "They'll be brought up to speed later today when you and I meet with them. We're going to have to handle everything from here on out very carefully. If our suspicions are correct, then things could quickly turn into a media nightmare."

J.D. glanced around the room, inspecting all the somber faces. An odd, off-center twitch in his gut warned him that there was more to this bigwig powwow than met the eye.

"It's complicated." Chief Mullins glanced from J.D. to George Bonner. "There is a possibility that our Rocking Chair Murder cases are connected in some freakish way to a series of kidnappings that occurred in and around the Chattanooga area over a five-year period that began twenty-eight years ago."

That information piqued J.D.'s interest and aroused his curiosity.

"I was the FBI agent in charge of the task force that investigated the Baby Blue toddler abductions," Bonner said. "I'll give you the basic info now and you can go over all the files later and bring yourself up to speed on the old cases."

J.D. nodded.

"Over a five-year period, six toddler boys, all fitting the same general description, were abducted, and the first five have never been found, dead or alive."

Bonner's facial expression didn't alter, but J.D. noted the flicker of pain in the former federal agent's eyes.

"Until now," Bonner said. "Maybe."

"We won't know for sure until we get the results of the DNA tests on both toddler skeletons found with our murder victims." Chief Mullins cast a sympathetic glance toward Mayor Hardy, whose wife's cousin had been the second victim.

"If the skeletons turn out to be two of the Baby Blue abductees, then there will be no doubt that there's a connection between the two cases despite a quarter of a century separating them," Bonner said.

J.D. took a couple of minutes to assimilate the info. Years ago, someone had kidnapped six toddler boys. Their bodies were never found. Now someone had killed two young women and placed the skeletal remains of the toddlers in the murder victims' arms.

Whoa, wait a minute. Did Bonner say five of the toddlers had never been found?

"You said five of the bodies had never been found. What about the sixth toddler?"

"Jeremy Arden," Bonner said. "We rescued him and arrested the woman who kidnapped him. He's alive and well. I checked, and he's living here in Chattanooga now."

"The woman who kidnapped him—did she abduct the other five boys, too?"

"We weren't sure then and we're not sure now. Regina Bennett was declared legally insane and spent the rest of her life in a mental institution. The psychiatrists who examined her at the time explained the death of her own toddler had sent her already unbalanced mind over the edge. She admitted to killing her terminally ill two-year-old, and from her rambling confessions, we gathered that she kept putting the child out of his misery over and over again. The only thing was, we believe that she was actually killing perfectly healthy little boys after she kidnapped them."

A tight knot formed in J.D.'s belly. "She never told you what she did with the bodies?"

Bonner shook his head. "From what we could gather and what her doctors explained, Regina Bennett believed that she mercifully ended her son's suffering. In her mind, there had been only one child."

"Her own son," J.D. said.

"And before you ask, yes, we tried to find out where Cody Bennett was buried, and we found something mighty peculiar. There was no record of Cody's birth or his death."

"Are you sure the child existed?"

"We're sure. There are hospital records. The boy existed and he was diagnosed with acute lymphocytic leukemia. Thirty years ago, the survival rate for children with the disease was much lower than it is today. For many children it was a death sentence."

"Ever figure out why there was no record of Cody Bennett's birth or death?" J.D. asked.

"The best we could ascertain, Regina Bennett was raped,

hid her pregnancy, and then gave birth to the child at home on her aunt and uncle's farm." Bonner held up a restraining hand. "Again, before you ask, yes, we covered every inch of that farm—all eighty-nine acres—with a fine-tooth comb. We didn't find any human remains."

"If the skeletal remains found with Jill Scott and Debra Gregory are two of the missing toddlers, someone knew where Regina Bennett buried those little boys," Chief Mullins said. "And that somebody is, more than likely, our killer."

Chapter 10

After her uncle's phone call that morning, Audrey had asked Donna to reschedule her eleven o'clock appointment for one this afternoon. That gave her exactly two hours to drive from her office downtown on McCallie Avenue to Parkridge Valley, a twenty-minute drive if she took Interstate 75, have lunch with Hart, and get back on time. When she had last seen Garth at police headquarters late yesterday, she had thought she'd convinced him to wait before he told Hart about the toddler skeletons. He had argued that Hart had as much right to know as Wayne did.

"Dad isn't emotionally unstable," Audrey had said. "Hart is. We have no idea how the news will affect him or what he might do. He hasn't been out of the rehab program at Parkridge for very long, and although he's been clean and sober for weeks now, it wouldn't take much to send him off the deep end again."

Garth had agreed with her, but apparently sometime between late yesterday and this morning, he had changed his mind. He had called her at the office shortly before her first patient arrived.

"I told Hart" was the first thing Garth had said when she took his call.

Groaning silently, she had replied, "How is he?"

"Not good," Garth had admitted.

"Where is he or do you know?"

"Don't worry. He's still here at my place," Garth had told her. "I've talked him into letting me take him over to Parkridge for a meeting this morning and I thought maybe you could go over and pick him up afterward."

It wouldn't be the first time that she and Garth had worked as a tag team to take care of Hart. "What time?" she had asked.

"Eleven-thirty."

"Okay. I'll have to get Donna to rearrange appointments, but I'll pick him up at eleven-thirty and see if I can talk him into going to lunch with me."

"Don't try to psychoanalyze him during lunch. Don't be a counselor. Just be his sister, okay? You can do that, can't you?"

Just be his sister.

Dear Lord, if only things were that simple. Hadn't she always been his sister first and foremost in the years after Blake's disappearance? A loving, caring, supportive sister who had made excuses for him, forgiven him time and again, and seen him through crisis after crisis. How many times had he sworn that if she would give him just one more chance, he would, in his own words, straighten up and fly right?

She had made far too many excuses for Hart. She had told herself repeatedly that maybe he simply couldn't help it, that he'd always been emotionally fragile, that Blake's disappearance and his mother's suicide had sent him on a collision course with alcohol and drugs.

So, here she was at Parkridge, waiting for Hart to emerge

from the outpatient meeting. She had uttered more than one "Please, God, please" prayer on the drive there. Even though Garth had been Hart's primary caretaker over the years, she was Garth's backup. Not once in all these years had Garth let Hart down; and not once had she turned her back on her stepbrother. Not even when he got her best friend pregnant.

Trying to be as inconspicuous as possible, Audrey stood back and away from the exit door as the support-group session ended. She saw Hart before he saw her and she noticed he was talking to another man, a guy who looked a little younger than Hart, possibly in his late twenties. When Hart spotted her, he visibly tensed, as if he knew that Garth had sent her to baby-sit. Their gazes connected for just a second. She kept her expression neutral, uncertain how he would react if she smiled or frowned.

When Hart walked over to her, the younger man came with him. He was of medium height and build, his dark blond hair curled over his ears and down the back of his neck past his collar. His blue eyes were bloodshot. And he sported several days of light brown beard stubble. His jeans were faded and worn, and his long-sleeved cotton shirt was wrinkled.

"Hi, sis." Hart kissed her cheek, then turned to the other man. "See, I told you she'd be here. I can always count on Audrey and Uncle Garth, no matter how bad I screw up."

Ignoring Hart's comment, she held out her hand. "Hello, I'm Hart's sister, Audrey."

The young man hesitantly accepted her hand. His grip was soft and weak, as if he were unsure of himself. Audrey had found that quite often when she shook hands with another woman, the woman's grip would be unnaturally limp, which reflected a lack of confidence. She had a firm grip that often surprised men who were not accustomed to what they considered a bold attitude.

"Nice to meet you, Audrey." He kept his gaze averted, seeming unable to make direct eye contact with her. "I'm Jeremy."

"Have you two known each other for very long?" Audrey asked, assuming that they had gone through rehab together.

"A few weeks," Jeremy said.

"We met at one of these support meetings," Hart told her. "And the really crazy thing is that, as it turns out, we've got a lot in common. Not only are we both recovering addicts, but we've both been fucked up since we were kids."

Not knowing what Hart expected her to say, Audrey didn't respond at first. Instead she glanced from Hart to Jeremy and said, "I've come to invite you to lunch, Hart. Maybe Jeremy would like to go with us."

"I . . . uh . . . thank you, but I've got to get to work." When Hart patted him on the back in a we're-buddies fashion, Jeremy said, "See you tomorrow?"

"Yeah, see you tomorrow." As soon as Jeremy walked away, Hart faced Audrey. "You don't know who he is, do you?"

"Should I know him?"

"Probably not. I didn't recognize him either. All I'd ever seen were photos of him when he was a little kid."

Puzzled by Hart's comment, Audrey stared at him with a wrinkled brow and narrowed gaze.

"Maybe you'll recognize his name—Jeremy Arden."

Audrey's mouth flew open on a silent gasp. *My God!* "Jeremy Arden? The little boy the FBI rescued from Regina Bennett?"

"One and the same."

"Does he know who you are? Who we are?"

"Yeah, I told him. He knows our little brother was abducted, that the authorities believe he was one of Regina Bennett's victims."

"I had no idea he still lived in the Chattanooga area."

"He just moved back here last year. He's lived pretty much all over the country, bumming around, trying to figure out how to live with what happened to him." Hart fixed his gaze on Audrey's face. "Jeremy doesn't have a big sister who's never given up on him. The poor guy doesn't really have anybody. His dad's dead and his mother remarried years ago and pretty much disowned him."

"I can't imagine a mother disowning her child."

"Not everybody's as caring and forgiving as you are. He really doesn't blame his mom. Believe it or not, sis, Jeremy is a lot more screwed up than I am. He actually remembers being with Regina Bennett. Not all of it, but bits and pieces."

"But he was so young. It's more likely that he thinks he remembers because of what he's been told."

"Maybe. Maybe not. But he was older than Blake. Jeremy was small for his age and looked younger than he was. He was nearly three years old when he was abducted."

"I don't know that I ever knew how old he was," Audrey admitted.

"Neither did I. He told me."

"Has he talked to you about it?"

"Nah, not really. It's not something he can talk about easily."

"I hope he's talked about it to the doctors here at Parkridge."

"I guess he has, but sometimes talking doesn't help."

Hart grabbed Audrey's arm beneath her elbow. "Come on, sis, take me to lunch. That's why you're here, isn't it?"

Relaxing a little, Audrey allowed herself to smile. "You know me too well."

* * *

It was time for her to come home. Cody missed her. He missed her. She had to know how much they needed her. And she needed them. They belonged together, the three of them.

Using the binoculars, he watched her through the window of her apartment, the open curtains revealing her arguing with a man. Why was she living with someone else, with a man he didn't know? And why did she keep using different names? This time, she was calling herself Whitney Poole.

Why did she keep going away? Why wasn't she helping him keep his promise?

He laid the binoculars on the car seat and rubbed his temples, trying to relieve the pounding in his head. The headaches were getting worse. He wasn't sleeping well at night. It was happening again. He couldn't rest without the sound of her voice lulling him to sleep.

Hush, little baby, don't say a word.

He had to bring her home soon. If he didn't, he would lose his mind. Even knowing that she wouldn't stay—couldn't stay—for very long, it didn't matter. A few days, a few weeks, that was all he needed.

She would leave him, of course, as she always did. But eventually, he'd find her again and bring her home.

He had sent Cody with her twice now.

He was keeping his promise.

He picked up the binoculars, and when he saw the man slap her, he wanted to kill the son of a bitch.

It's all right. I'll take you away soon, back home, where you belong. You'll be safe. You'll be loved and cherished.

When he saw the guy slap her again, he balled his hands into tight fists and pressed his head against the steering wheel. As he pounded the seat on either side of his legs, he beat his head repeatedly against the steering wheel.

Soon, very soon, I'll come for you. I'll take you away from that horrible man. I promise I will. And I always keep my promises.

J.D. had spent most of the day poring over the copies of the old Baby Blue kidnapping files. He hadn't even taken a lunch break. He'd spoken briefly to Garth Hudson and Tam Lovelady about the Rocking Chair Murders, making sure he had all the information, no matter how insignificant. But for the most part, he had read reports, looked at photos, scanned old newspaper clippings, and familiarized himself with the six abduction cases that the FBI had investigated during a five-year period. Six toddlers. Seven, if you counted Cody Bennett, a child who, except for hospital records of his illness, hadn't existed. At least not on paper. No birth certificate. No death certificate. And yet, his mother had admitted to "putting him to sleep."

Had Regina Bennett killed her own child, as she had claimed? Had she also killed five other toddlers?

As the day wore on, J.D.'s vision began to blur, his shoulders ached, and his belly growled, reminding him that he had skipped lunch. Information overload had scrambled his brain temporarily. He dropped the ballpoint pen on top of the yellow legal pad and stared sightlessly down at his scribbled notes. Despite hours of uninterrupted reading and studying, he had barely made a dent in the mile-high stack of files pertaining to the Baby Blue cases. But so far, he hadn't found anything that might possibly link those cases to the present-day Rocking Chair Murders.

Regina Bennett's parents were dead, had died when she was a child. The childless aunt and uncle she had lived with were both dead now, too, and the farm they had owned had been sold years ago. The aunt and uncle had belonged to some fundamentalist sect of the Holy Brethren Church, a denomination J.D. had never heard of, but then not being a religious man himself, his knowledge was limited. There was no record that Regina had ever been married, just as there was no record of her son's birth.

J.D.'s phone rang. As he rubbed the back of his neck with one hand, he grabbed the phone with his other. "Yeah, Special Agent Cass here."

"Are you going to pick me up sometime before dark or not?" Zoe sounded more than a little put out with him.

Damn! What time was it? He glanced at his wristwatch. Five forty-three. "Sorry. I lost track of time. You should have already called. Practice was over a good while ago, wasn't it?"

"Just come get me, will you?"

"I'm on my way."

"You'd better be."

He didn't respond. If he did, he and Zoe would simply continue their verbal sparring match because she was always determined to have the last word, no matter what. And that, too, was so much like him. His father used to say that J.D. would have the last word even knowing he'd get his backside tanned for doing it.

J.D. gathered up the assortment of documents on his desk and stuffed them back into their designated folders. He chose two folders to take home with him and locked the rest up in the file cabinet behind his desk. Once his desk was cleared, he removed his jacket from the back of his chair, slipped it on, and pulled his car keys from his pants pocket.

He headed southwest on Highway 58, took a left on Chestnut Street, then a right on West Fourth and ramped onto U.S. 27 North. Thinking ahead, J.D. decided that after he picked up Zoe, they'd head over to McAlister's and get takeout for supper. He wasn't a great cook, but he occasionally prepared their meals. They ate out every once in a while, but mostly he bought takeout for them. Except for his three-year marriage to Erin, he'd been a bachelor his entire adult life. And except for adding a teenage daughter to the mix, he still lived a bachelor's life.

After exiting onto Signal Mountain Boulevard, he turned left at New Baylor School Road. The uniformed sentry standing outside the guard shack glanced his way. After the guard noted the round red sticker emblazoned with a large white *B* for Baylor adhered to the lower left corner of the Camaro's windshield, J.D. was allowed to follow the line of vehicles entering the campus. There was no way he could have afforded to send Zoe to this exclusive old school if Carrie hadn't left a decent life insurance policy. Apparently despite Carrie's party-girl lifestyle, she had loved Zoe enough to think of the child's future. A scholarship to Baylor had been out of the question since her grades weren't all that great despite her having a high IQ. And although she was a decent athlete, she wasn't a star player and therefore not eligible for an athletic scholarship. He had debated about spending the nearly twenty grand a year to put Zoe in private school, but he'd decided that a top-notch education would do her far more good in the long run than a hundred grand in the bank.

She wore one of the mandatory school uniforms, her apparel today consisting of a red blouse and plaid skirt; and she had her dark hair pulled into a ponytail. With her book bag slung over her shoulder, Zoe opened the passenger door, removed the book bag, and threw it into the back floorboard. She fell into the front bucket seat and slammed the door.

"Bad day?" he asked.

"Bad life." She snapped the reply as she folded her arms across her chest and stared straight ahead, not bothering to even glance his way.

He didn't respond, knowing if he did it would lead only to more squabbling. In the beginning, he had hoped that they would learn to like each other and their daily lives would fall into a peaceful routine. No such luck. If the counseling sessions with Dr. Sherrod didn't work, then he didn't know what else to do except take Holly's advice and change Zoe's status at Baylor from day student to boarding student. At least that way, they'd have to tolerate each other only on occasional weekends and during summer vacation.

"I thought we'd pick up takeout from McAlister's," J.D. said.

"Whatever." Zoe shrugged.

"Decide what you want." J.D. followed the line of traffic off campus and back onto Signal Mountain Boulevard.

"You mean I have a choice? I figured you'd just choose for me since you're determined to run my life."

"I'm not arguing with you this evening," he told her. "I've had a long day and I'll be up late tonight going over some files I'm taking home with me. I know you're upset with me for picking you up late. I've already apologized for that, so drop it. Whatever other complaints you have, save them for our appointment with Dr. Sherrod on Friday."

Much to his surprise, Zoe didn't come back with a smart-mouth response. And when they arrived at McAlister's, she told him she wanted a Super Spud with chicken and sweet tea. On the ride home up the mountain and during dinner together, she didn't talk except to reply succinctly to whatever he said.

She rose from the kitchen table, picked up the Styrofoam container that held the remnants of her meal and the empty cup. "May I be excused? I've got a lot of homework."

He glanced up at his daughter and nodded. "Yeah, sure. I'll come in and say good night at ten."

"Yeah, sure." She mimicked him.

He grinned. "If you need any help with your homework—"

"Thanks, I won't." She dumped the foam container and cup into the garbage can and left the kitchen.

J.D. cleaned up, took out the trash that had accumulated for the past couple of days, and then settled down in front of the TV with a beer and the two file folders he'd brought home from work. He kept the sound muted after he caught the weather forecast for the next day, lifted his feet onto the coffee table in front of him, and opened the first folder.

Blake Wayne Sherrod had been three weeks shy of his second birthday when he had disappeared from his home. His mother, Enid Hudson Roberts Sherrod, suffered from migraines and had taken prescription-strength medication and had lain down while her son took his afternoon nap. Blake's older half siblings, Audrey Sherrod and Hart Roberts, had been outside playing with neighborhood kids. Enid had asked them to periodically check on their little brother, which both later swore that they had done. The police and the FBI had questioned both children, but not the day Blake disappeared. Garth Hudson, a young officer on the Chattanooga police force, had been the first on the scene, and only he had questioned his niece and nephew. Wayne Sherrod had stated that he'd been concerned about his wife because she hadn't been feeling well that morning and had asked his brother-in-law to drop by and check on Enid if he got the chance during his afternoon lunch break. Days later when the children were questioned, neither child had remembered seeing anyone enter or leave their home.

J.D. laid the report aside and took a hefty swig from the beer bottle.

Twenty-five years ago, people didn't always lock their doors, even at night. And with the two older children playing outside that day and coming in occasionally to check on their sleeping baby brother, Enid wouldn't have locked either the front or back door. Although unlikely, it was possible that someone had sneaked into the house, unseen and unheard, snatched Blake Sherrod out of his crib, and escaped without being seen.

After downing a few more sips of beer, J.D. set the bottle on the coffee table and leafed through the Blake Sherrod file until he found photos of the house, the front yard and backyard, and the little boy's bedroom. As he flipped through the other photos, one in particular caught his eye. A photo of Hart Roberts and Audrey Sherrod that someone—the police photographer?—had snapped the day of the abduction. If he'd ever seen two shell-shocked kids, it was Audrey and her stepbrother, ages nine and eight. Hart clung to his older stepsister's hand and she held a thin arm around his shoulders. His head was bowed, his gaze riveted to his feet. Audrey stared into the camera, her eyes wide, her little chin lifted bravely, almost as if she was daring anyone to harm Hart.

Who took that picture and why?

Not that it made any difference. He was just curious.

Enid Hudson had committed suicide a few months after her son's disappearance. Apparently, the woman had suffered not only from migraines, but from depression most of her life. And although she'd been treated for the debilitating headaches, she'd never sought professional help for her mood swings.

J.D. considered the evidence. Just because five other little boys were presumed kidnapped and murdered by Regina Bennett did not mean that Blake Sherrod was one of her victims. There was no evidence that linked Blake's disappearance to the woman. But then again, there was no hard evidence linking any of the missing toddlers to Regina, except Jeremy Arden, the little boy the FBI had rescued.

What if the DNA tests on the skeletons found with Jill

Scott and Debra Gregory revealed that they were two of the missing toddlers from the Baby Blue kidnapping cases? What would that prove? It certainly wouldn't prove a connection between Regina Bennett and the toddlers, only a connection between the Baby Blue kidnappings and the Rocking Chair Murders.

Chapter 11

The hot, humid summer breeze did little to cool the heat of that July afternoon. Sweat beads dotted the faces of her playmates and trickled down her own neck and dampened her hair. At least keeping her almost waist-length hair in a high ponytail allowed the air to hit the back of her neck. As she did every morning, she had ironed her clothes and Hart's and fixed their breakfast of cold cereal and fruit. She didn't mind being helpful. And it was like Daddy had said—Enid had her hands full taking care of Blake, so he expected Audrey to pitch in and help. But sometimes, she missed just being a kid with no responsibilities, a kid who didn't have to do laundry, iron clothes, prepare breakfast, run the vacuum, and make up her own bed. When her mother had been alive . . . But she'd been a little kid then. Now she was half grown. She was nine.

"Come on, Audrey," Shanna Moore called. "We're going to race around the block and see who's got the fastest bike."

Audrey jumped on the shiny new bike that Santa Claus had brought last Christmas. Her father thought she still be-

lieved in Santa and since Hart did, she pretended that she did, too.

"Hey, it's your turn to check on Blake," Hart hollered at her just as she lined up with the other three girls to start the big race.

"You do it this time," she pleaded. "I'll do it the next two times."

"You'd better," Hart grumbled. "I don't see why we have to keep checking on the little spoiled brat. It's not like he's going to run off if he wakes up. He'll come out here crying his head off."

"Just go check on him, okay?"

And Audrey sailed off on her bike, determined to win the race.

Audrey came awake suddenly, her mind in a fog, her senses still reliving a day twenty-five years in the past. Her eyes flew open. She gulped for air.

The dream had seemed so real. But then, those dreams always were.

She shoved the sheet and blanket off her, slid to the edge of the bed, and sat up. It had been several years since she'd dreamed about the day Blake disappeared. As a child and teenager, she'd been haunted by dreams about that fateful day, but eventually the frequency of those nightmares lessened until eventually they had gone away completely, or so she had thought.

It didn't take a genius to figure out why the dreams had returned. The possibility that one of the two toddler skeletons might be Blake had revived all the old memories.

Audrey glanced at the bedside clock. 5:06 A.M. Too late to try to go back to sleep. She slid her feet into her house shoes there by the bed and went to the bathroom.

If they had finally located Blake, did that mean her family would be able to find a sense of closure? Her father and Hart and Uncle Garth. *And you, too, Audrey.* Would holding a memorial service and burying him beside his mother give them—those left behind—some measure of peace? God, she hoped so.

And if neither toddler is Blake, what then?

Either way, whatever the DNA tests proved, the past had been resurrected, their grief and anguish and guilt dredged up from the murky depths of their souls.

An hour later, as Audrey finished her third cup of hot tea and downed the last bites of a whole wheat muffin, the phone rang.

Please, don't let it be bad news.

Caller ID was a great invention. Audrey answered on the third ring. "Good morning."

"I didn't wake you, did I?" Tam asked.

"No, I've been up for a while and already had breakfast."

"Have you talked to your uncle Garth this morning? Or—or last night?"

Oh, shit, what now? "No, why?"

"I guess he didn't see any point in worrying you."

"You're worrying me right now. What's going on?"

"Hart didn't go home—back to Garth's place—last night."

Great. Just great.

"Hart's okay," Tam said hurriedly. "We don't know where he'd been or who he'd been with. Garth was out looking for him well past midnight."

"Where did he find him?" *Not in an alley somewhere, please.* "Was he . . . had he been—"

"Yeah, he'd been drinking." Tam cleared her throat. "And Garth didn't find him. I did. Sort of. Hart showed up here around two this morning, so drunk he could barely walk.

Apparently somebody had dropped him off outside my house."

"Oh, Tam, I'm sorry. What did Marcus say?"

"Marcus is still away, thank goodness."

"I assume you called Garth and he came and got Hart."

"I called Garth and he came over, but . . ."

"No, please, don't tell me that Hart is still there."

"Garth and I both thought it best to just let him sleep it off here, in my guest room. Garth's coming back here around seven-thirty and he may need backup. He wants to put Hart in Parkridge again."

"I'll be over as soon as I can grab a shower and get dressed."

Tam hadn't slept a wink after her doorbell rang at two o'clock that morning. A staggering, blubbering, barely coherent Hart had fallen into her arms when he'd tripped over the threshold of her front door. She had draped her arm around his waist, pulled him inside, and somehow managed to hold on to him while she closed and locked the door.

"You're so beautiful," he had told her, his bloodshot eyes focused on her face as she'd helped him to the sofa.

"Why are you here, Hart?" she'd asked. "Why didn't you go home?"

"Can't. Don't want to. I'm a mess, babe. Such a mess."

He had curled up on her sofa and closed his eyes. She had sat on the edge of the coffee table and watched him for several minutes before she got up, took the afghan from the back of the sofa, and covered him with it. He'd mumbled her name in his alcohol-induced sleep.

She had called Garth and he'd shown up half an hour later. They had roused Hart enough to get him on his feet, but he had adamantly refused to leave with Garth. Short of knocking him out or calling for help to subdue Hart, they'd had little choice. Garth had helped her walk Hart into the guest bedroom.

"I'm damn sorry about this," Garth had said. "I don't know why he came to you. He knows to leave you alone. Even when he's not himself, he knows better."

"It's all right. We'll deal with things the best we can."

"Maybe Audrey was right. Maybe I shouldn't have told him about the toddler skeletons, but . . ."

No matter what Garth did for Hart, nothing seemed to help. If she hadn't walked away from him years ago and done her best not to look back, she would be caught, as Garth and Audrey were, in the vicious cycle of Hart's never-ending melodrama.

Showered, dressed, and ready for work, Tam paced the floor as she waited for Audrey and Garth to arrive. If Hart woke before they got there, how would she handle the situation? She had no idea what to expect.

"Morning," Hart said.

Tam nearly jumped out of her skin when she heard the sound of his voice. He stood at the end of the hallway leading to the bedrooms. His golden hair stood on end as if it had been styled with an eggbeater, and an overnight growth of light brown beard stubble added to his disheveled appearance.

They stared at each other for several seconds before Tam broke eye contact. She didn't know what to say. Apparently, he didn't either. He walked into the living room in his sock feet. Garth had removed his shoes beforc putting him to bed at three this morning. When he approached her, she glanced at him and saw that his gaze was still locked on her face. Unnerved by the way he was looking at her, she backed away from him.

He stopped dead still. "I'm sorry. I shouldn't have come here." His gaze shot nervously around the room. "To be honest, I don't remember how I got here."

"I don't know either," she replied. "Maybe a friend dropped you off or maybe you took a cab or—"

"Where's your husband? I'm surprised he didn't kick my ass out. Nobody could have blamed him."

"Marcus is away on business."

"Good. Uh . . . I mean it's good I didn't cause trouble for you with your husband. I want you to be happy. I don't ever want to hurt you again. I swear."

Steeling her nerves, Tam swore to herself that she could handle this situation, that she was in control of her emotions. "I believe you."

The tension between them tautened with each passing second, like a wire tightening almost to the breaking point.

The doorbell rang.

Tam actually swayed on her feet as her body relaxed and she released a pent-up breath. "That's probably Audrey."

"You called in reinforcements," Hart said.

Tam didn't reply, nor did she glance back at him as she headed straight for the front door.

Audrey didn't know who looked worse, Tam or Hart. Her stepbrother appeared to have sobered up after his drinking binge last night. Tam looked like she'd spent the night in hell.

"Go ahead," Hart said. "Chew my ass out. I deserve it. I fucked up once again."

Audrey shook her head. What a sad state of affairs for all of them. "Garth will be here soon and we're taking you to Parkridge." No need to beat around the bush. Straight talk was what Hart needed.

"One little slip and it's back to the dungeon." Hart grimaced.

"Do you have a better idea?" Audrey asked.

"Yeah, why don't I just go jump off the Walnut Street Bridge and put us all out of our misery?"

Audrey cut her eyes toward Tam in time to see the stricken look on her face as she bit down on her bottom lip. Audrey glared at her stepbrother. "Damn it, Hart, think about how what you say and what you do affects other people, the people who love you."

Hart stared at Tam, his gaze filled with a mixture of self-contempt and a plea for forgiveness. "I'm not worth loving."

How many times had Audrey heard those words come out of Hart's mouth?

And how many times had she heard him threaten to kill himself?

What could she say? How do you convince someone who hates himself that he deserves to be loved?

As the three of them stood there in Tam's living room, the silence deafening, the doorbell rang. Tam sucked in a startled breath. Hart cursed.

"That's probably Uncle Garth," Audrey said. "I'll let him in."

When she opened the door, Garth stepped inside as his gaze swept over the living room. With a snarl on his lips and weariness heavy on his thick shoulders, he surveyed Hart from tousled hair to shoeless feet. "Get your shoes."

Hart made no move to obey.

"He doesn't want to go back to Parkridge," Audrey said.

"Too bad," Garth said. "He's going."

"*He* is in the room, standing right here," Hart told them. "Don't talk about me as if I'm not here." He glared at Garth. "I'll continue going to Parkridge as an outpatient. You can drive me over there yourself for the first available meeting today, but I don't need—"

"You don't know what you need!" Garth growled the words. "Were you or were you not drunk this morning when you showed up on Tamara's doorstep?"

"Yeah, I was. And I admit that I didn't handle the news about—" Hart glanced at Audrey and then refocused on his uncle. "The news about the toddler skeletons shook me up. But I'm okay now. I swear I am. I promise I won't act crazy about this. I can deal with the possibility that one of them could be Blake."

"Can you?" Garth asked.

"I can. I swear I can."

Garth turned and faced Tam. "Did he say anything stupid or do anything that—?"

"No," Tam replied.

"You don't have to worry about anything, Uncle Garth," Hart said. "I didn't accidentally let any top-secret information slip out while I was drunk." Hart laughed, the sound horribly hollow and sad.

"Shut up, will you? You're talking nuts." Garth grabbed Hart's arm. "You don't have to go back into rehab, but you're going to continue with the outpatient program, no ifs, ands, or buts about it. Understand?"

Hart saluted his uncle and tried to click his sock-clad heels. "Yes, sir."

Fifteen minutes later, with Hart tucked in the front seat of Garth's '06 Mercury, Tam sat down on the sofa, leaned over, and placed her open palms on either side of her face. Audrey sat beside her and flung her arm across Tam's trembling shoulders.

"He'll never get any better, will he? He's always going to be . . ." Tam's voice trailed off midsentence as she looked at Audrey with teary eyes.

Audrey hugged Tam. "Don't do this to yourself. Hart is not your problem. You don't owe him anything. Do you hear me? You have a husband who loves you. Don't do anything to risk your future with Marcus."

* * *

Jeremy Arden faced himself in the mirror as he shaved. He was young, good looking, and reasonably intelligent. He shouldn't be living in a dump like this, working as a busboy at a local restaurant, and fighting his inner demons every waking minute just to stay clean and sober. If his father hadn't died and if his mother hadn't married that jerk-off second husband, maybe things would be different for him. When a kid went through the kind of trauma he had, more than anything, he needed the love and support of his parents.

He really didn't remember much about what had happened when he'd been kidnapped. Not consciously. But more than one shrink had made him realize that on some subconscious level, he remembered more than he was willing to admit. Occasionally, a thought crossed his mind—a memory?—and he was never sure whether what he was thinking about had actually happened or if somebody had told him it had happened.

The dreams weren't real. They were just nightmares. Frightening nightmares that ate away at his brain like drops of acid. Only when he was drunk or high could he escape the reoccurring dreams, the night sweats, the sound of a voice singing inside his head.

Hush, little baby.

When he was seven, his parents, with the assistance of the shrink he was seeing at the time, had explained exactly what had happened to him when he was three. The psychiatrist had told his parents that he was old enough to understand and that knowing the basic facts would help him fully recover.

"Those bad dreams you have are because when you were three, this woman—this mentally unstable woman—kidnapped you," his father had said. "She took you out of our car where you were sleeping while your mom went into the service station to pay for the gas she'd just pumped."

"This woman kept you with her for a long time." His

mother had wrung her hands continuously as she talked. "Months and months. We nearly lost our minds worrying about you, but . . ." His mother's voice had broken and she'd turned away from him in tears.

His father had taken his hand. "The police found you and took you away from this woman and brought you home to your mama and me. It was the happiest day of our lives."

During the following years, Jeremy had learned more about the woman who had abducted him. Oddly enough, he had become fascinated by Regina Bennett. An unhealthy fascination. And he had visited her several times at the mental institution before she died. Even in her fifties, she had still been a rather pretty woman, bosomy and slender, with pensive brown eyes and thick, dark hair.

She had called him Cody.

And the last time he saw her, shortly before she died, she had caressed his cheek and hummed a familiar tune. "Remember, Cody? Remember how you loved for me to sing to you?"

Did he remember? He thought he did. Flashes of memory. Nothing definite. Maybe not even real memories, just thoughts planted in his head by an insane woman.

Ouch! Jeremy had cut himself with the razor and a spot of blood appeared on his chin. The momentary physical pain snapped him out of his thoughts and temporarily relieved him of the emotional pain that never left him.

He didn't have time to question the past, to wonder what if. What if he'd never been kidnapped? What if his father hadn't died? What if his mother hadn't married an asshole? What if he'd never visited Regina Bennett and gotten to know her?

He needed to finish up here, grab a shower, and get dressed. He had places to go, people to see, things to do.

* * *

J.D. took a sip from his mug and frowned when the taste of the cool coffee reminded him how long it had been sitting on his desk. After dropping Zoe at school, he had come straight to the office, poured himself a mug of hot coffee, and tossed the two Baby Blue files he'd taken home with him on his desk. By the time he had finished thoroughly studying the Blake Sherrod files, it had been past eleven last night, so he'd never gotten around to the other file, the Jeremy Arden file.

This morning, he had decided to study the same aspects of each of the six cases simultaneously instead of going through each file separately, one at a time. First things first, the point where each case had begun—with the abduction.

Blond, blue-eyed Keith Lawson, twenty-nine months old, only child, abducted twenty-eight years ago from a sandbox in his grandmother's backyard when she went inside the house to answer a ringing telephone and left the child alone.

Blond, blue-eyed Chase Wilcox, twenty-five months old, the younger of two children, abducted twenty-seven years ago when the teenage baby-sitter was in another room having sex with her boyfriend.

Blond, blue-eyed Devin Kelly, twenty-seven months old, only child, abducted twenty-six years ago when his divorced father's girlfriend left him sitting in his stroller at a department store, outside the dressing room while she tried on a pair of jeans.

Blond, blue-eyed Blake Sherrod, twenty-three months old, one of three children in a blended family, abducted twenty-five years ago from his baby bed while his mother slept in her bedroom and his older siblings played outside.

Blond, blue-eyed Shane Douglas, thirty months old, younger of two sons, abducted twenty-five years ago from his hospital room where he was recovering after having minor surgery to put tubes in his ears because of chronic ear infections. The nurses had persuaded his mother, who hadn't left his side, to go to the cafeteria for a bite to eat.

Blond, blue-eyed Jeremy Arden, thirty-four months old, only child, abducted twenty-four years ago from his mother's car when she left him in his car seat to go inside a mini-mart to pay for the gas she had just pumped. Found four months later with Regina Bennett, who lived in a small house on her aunt and uncle's farm in Sale Creek, not thirty miles from his parents' home.

Regina's aunt and uncle had sworn they had no idea that their niece had kidnapped Jeremy or any other child. Although the authorities doubted their complete ignorance, they had no proof of the couple's culpability in the Baby Blue cases.

J.D. got up, went into the bathroom, and dumped his cold coffee in the sink. After pouring his mug full with semifresh hot coffee, he returned to his office. Standing beside his cluttered desk, he thought about the information he had just finished reading. The obvious came to mind first. Each child fit an almost identical profile. Blond, blue eyed, somewhere between two and three years old. Six toddlers, kidnapped a year apart over a period of five years.

No, that wasn't right. Six kids, five years. Something didn't add up. J.D. set his mug down as he flipped through the files until he found the exact dates. The five-year period was correct. That meant if Regina Bennett kidnapped all six boys, she had abducted two of them the same year. J.D. checked the abduction dates again and when he found the discrepancy, his gut tightened, but his mind cautioned him not to read too much into the information.

Blake Sherrod had gone missing in July and Shane Douglas had disappeared in August. Only a month apart.

J.D. triple-checked the dates.

Why had Regina Bennett changed her pattern of taking

only one boy a year? Had something gone wrong with one of the kidnappings? Had she killed one of the boys too soon? Had someone else taken one of the boys?

Once again, J.D. skimmed through the files, checking the exact dates each boy had disappeared, thinking perhaps the month or the day might be the same. Keith and Chase had both disappeared in the month of June, a year apart. Devin and Blake had both disappeared in July, a year apart. Shane had disappeared in August, as had Jeremy Arden. The day of the month differed with each boy. The only similarity was that each of the boys had disappeared in the summer.

There had to be a reason that Blake Sherrod and Shane Douglas both went missing the same year. His gut instinct told him that this fact was significant. J.D. doubted that he was the first person to question why, if Regina Bennett had kidnapped both boys, she had changed her MO that year.

J.D. picked up the phone, removed the business card from where he'd clipped it to his desk calendar, and dialed George Bonner's number.

Chapter 12

Jeremy caught a glimpse of the dark-haired waitress at the back entrance of Callie's Café as soon as he parked his motorcycle. The guy with her looked angry, his face splotched with red and his slim body coiled tight with anger. He was yelling at the waitress, but Jeremy was too far away to hear what he was saying. When he drew back his hand and slapped the woman's cheek, it was all Jeremy could do to stop himself from intervening.

If he hits her again . . .

Thankfully, it didn't happen. The guy turned and walked off, leaving the waitress in tears.

As soon as the man he assumed was her boyfriend got in his car and drove off, squealing his tires in the process, Jeremy approached the young woman.

Play it cool. Don't scare her. And whatever you do, don't touch her.

Approaching her slowly, Jeremy called out, "You okay?"

She jerked her head up and a pair of teary brown eyes stared at him, a look of surprise and unease etched on her pretty features. As she swiped away tears and sniffled a couple of times, she took several steps backward toward the restaurant's exit by the large metal Dumpster.

Realizing she was wary of him, Jeremy stopped a good ten feet from her. "Sorry. I couldn't help seeing what happened. That guy's a real jerk. You should get rid of him."

She nodded. "Yeah, I know."

"If you're okay, I'll leave you alone."

"I'm okay."

When Jeremy turned around and headed toward the restaurant's front entrance, she called out to him. "Hey, I've seen you in here before, haven't I?"

"Yeah, a few times." He glanced over his shoulder and smiled at her.

"Thanks for . . . well, for asking if I was all right." She studied him for a minute, as if trying to decide whether or not she could trust him.

Keeping his smile in place, he watched while she entered the restaurant's back entrance. Then he walked through the front door and found a stool at the counter. By the time he picked up a breakfast menu, she was pouring coffee into his mug.

He noticed that the cheek her boyfriend had struck was still bright pink and that she had taken her hair down from the neat ponytail and tried to drape it over the left side of her face. She had also put on her apron and name tag.

Whitney.

When she noticed him staring at the name tag, she said, "I'm Whitney Poole."

He nodded. "Nice to meet you, Whitney. I'm Jeremy Arden."

"Hello, Jeremy."

He glanced down at the menu. "What do you recommend?"

She leaned across the counter and whispered, "That you eat at a better restaurant."

They both laughed, and then she said, "But if you have to eat here, the pancakes aren't bad."

"Pancakes it is."

He tried not to stare at her, but when she left to place his order, he inspected her narrow waist, her long, slender legs, and the way her trim hips swayed as she walked. He had a thing for pretty brunettes. Always had. Every important woman in his life had been a brunette and quite a few unimportant ones, too.

You're going to be important to me, Whitney Poole. Very important. You just don't know it yet.

"Yeah, sure, we thought it odd that Regina Bennett would kidnap two boys in one year, if she actually kidnapped all the other boys," George Bonner said. "We had no proof that she abducted either Blake Sherrod or Shane Douglas. Hell, we never had any proof that she kidnapped or killed any of the boys, except Jeremy Arden. And if it hadn't been for an anonymous phone call telling us where to look for Jeremy, he would have become just another statistic."

"An anonymous caller?" J.D. asked. "I thought I'd skimmed through the records, but that info didn't jump out at me."

"It should be in there somewhere," Bonner told him. "Somebody called the Hamilton County sheriff's office, but he or she didn't leave a name."

"The person who took the call couldn't identify the person's sex by their voice?"

"Apparently not. I remember him saying whoever called was whispering and if he had to make a guess, he'd say it was a woman because the voice wasn't as deep as most men's voices."

"Regina Bennett lived on a farm in Sale Creek with her aunt and uncle, right? Could it have been the aunt who called?"

"The aunt and uncle swore they knew nothing about Regina kidnapping the Arden kid, or any other kid, for that matter."

"How's that possible, if she lived with them?"

"She didn't actually live in the house with them," Bonner said. "She lived on the farm, but in a separate house. It was a neat little two-bedroom clapboard. One of the bedrooms was a real pretty nursery. We found Jeremy Arden in a blue baby bed. He was clean and well dressed and healthy and unharmed in any way."

"Physically, maybe."

"What?"

"I said Jeremy Arden might have been physically unharmed when y'all rescued him, but he was nearly three years old. He had been stolen from his mother, from his parents. That had to be traumatic for a toddler."

"Yes, I'm sure it was," Bonner agreed. "Hell, I know it was. He didn't talk. Not a word. And he didn't cry. Not when we found him. Not when we turned him over to his parents. He just stared at us with those big blue eyes."

"Were you able to question him? Later on, I mean," J.D. said.

"Once he'd been given a complete physical after the rescue, and social services were called in, he was questioned. But like I said, the kid didn't talk. Not then. And later, weeks later, when he'd been home with his parents for a while, he couldn't answer any of our questions."

"Couldn't?"

"His answer to every question was 'I don't know.' So we had nothing. The doctors seem to think that he would probably never remember any details, that his mind had blotted it all out."

"I guess that makes sense." J.D. had one final question about Jeremy Arden. "Did anyone ever talk to him when he was older, as a teenager or a young adult?"

"Not that I know of. Why do you ask?"

"Just curious if he ever did actually remember anything about the months he spent with Regina Bennett." J.D. paused, and then asked, "And as far as you know, Arden still lives here in Chattanooga?"

"He lives here now, but I think he's moved around a lot over the years. I haven't kept close tabs on him."

"Hmm . . . The aunt and uncle, Regina Bennett's aunt and uncle, do you think they really didn't know anything?"

"I think they were hiding something," Bonner said. "But we had no evidence against them, nothing concrete."

"And they're both dead now."

"Yeah."

"Did Regina have any other relatives? Siblings? Cousins?"

"No siblings. And the aunt and uncle didn't have any children. We checked, but couldn't find anyone who would admit being related to her. Nobody else lived on the farm, although there were day laborers who worked for the uncle."

"Was it one of the day laborers who raped Regina?"

"She didn't say who raped her. She claimed to have been forced to have sex." Bonner cleared his throat. "The way she told it, she was repeatedly raped. And the only information we could get out of the aunt and uncle was the fact that Regina gave birth at home, with the aid of a midwife who was a member of that lunatic church they all belonged to. They claim they had no idea who Cody Bennett's father was."

"The Holy Brethren Church," J.D. said. "I never heard of it before."

"They were a bunch of fundamentalist crazies. I don't think the church still exists, or if it does, they've gone underground."

"And there was no way to substantiate the fact that Regina was raped, right? I mean she's the one who told the doctors at Moccasin Bend that she'd been raped." J.D.

flipped through the copied files. "According to the records, Regina told the doctors that he—whoever he was—hurt her, that he forced her to have sex numerous times."

"She wouldn't name the guy. But we thought at the time that it was probably the uncle," Bonner said. "There were rumors about the Holy Brethren Church. Rumors that the elders in that church, which Regina's uncle Luther Chaney was, had the right to initiate any of the young women they chose."

"Did y'all follow up, try to prove—?"

"There was no point. The uncle died while the investigation was ongoing, less than a month after we rescued Jeremy Arden. Heart attack."

"And the aunt?"

"She sold the farm a few months later and moved away. We didn't keep track of her."

"Did she ever visit her niece at—?"

"I have no idea." Bonner cleared his throat. "Look, once we returned Jeremy Arden to his parents and Regina Bennett was locked up in Moccasin Bend for evaluation and we thoroughly searched the Bennett farm for bodies or any other evidence and found nothing, the Baby Blue kidnappings became a cold case. After Regina was apprehended, there were no more similar kidnappings, so we felt reasonably certain we had the right person."

"I understand. But now, if it turns out that the skeletons left with Jill Scott's and Debra Gregory's bodies belong to two of the kidnapped toddlers, your old cold case is going to be red hot again."

Audrey met Porter for Wednesday lunch at the Big River Grill & Brewing Works, as she did every week when they were both free. Since it was such a gorgeous early autumn day, they chose to sit outside beneath one of the huge red umbrellas. As always, Porter was immaculate, from his perfectly styled blond hair to his expensive suit and matching silk necktie and handkerchief stuffed precisely in his coat pocket. Occasionally, Audrey had the urge to muss his hair or spill something on his suit, but she never had. Not even in their more intimate moments had she dared to run her fingers through his hair. Of course, their intimate moments were never wild and passionate and hadn't gone beyond a few kisses. Audrey had never been a sexually passionate person, and she suspected that Porter hadn't, either. That was one reason they had seemed so well suited. But recently Audrey had realized that she wasn't being fair to Porter or to herself. He needed to be free to find someone else, someone who could truly love him. And she? Well, she just needed to be free. She hoped that Porter wouldn't get upset when she broached the subject of their not dating each other exclusively.

She liked Porter, for all his faults and idiosyncrasies, and they shared some common interests which they could enjoy together. Also, it was nice not to have to find a date for social occasions where a date was required. And being in a relationship kept her friends and acquaintances from constantly arranging blind dates. Why was it that married people—or those who wished they were married—couldn't believe that a woman could be happy single and living alone?

"You're awfully quiet," Porter said only moments after the waitress took their drink order.

"Sorry. I'm afraid I have a lot on my mind."

He studied her for a moment. "One of your patients or—?"

"Let's have lunch first," Audrey suggested. "Then we can talk."

He lifted an inquisitive brow. "Talk? That sounds serious."

The waitress returned with their iced teas. "Are you folks ready to order?"

Audrey didn't need to look at the menu. "I'd like the gorgonzola pear salad, please."

"Yes, ma'am." She turned to Porter. "And you, sir?"

"The low country shrimp and grits." And before the waitress could ask, he said, "No salad."

When they ate lunch at this particular restaurant, they always chose exactly what they had just ordered. Another thing they had in common—they were both creatures of habit and horribly predictable.

As soon as the waitress was out of earshot, Porter focused on Audrey, concern in his eyes and obvious tension in his neck and shoulders. "You aren't going to tell me that there's someone else, are you? Another man?"

"No, Porter, there is no one else, no other man."

Visibly relaxing, he smiled. "Then there's no reason to ruin a perfectly lovely lunch, is there?"

"No, no reason whatsoever."

Audrey listened as Porter talked, responding to his idle chitchat often enough so he didn't realize that, for the most part, she wasn't really listening. She was thinking about how a person could know something about herself and could understand why she was the way she was and still be unable to change. She was by nature a loving, caring person and quite emotional. In every aspect of her life, she was true to her nature, but when it came to romantic relationships, she guarded her emotions. She never truly gave herself, heart and soul, to another person, nor had she ever wanted that type of passion reciprocated. Oh, she knew all the textbook reasons. She and Hart had both gone through some minor counseling after Blake's disappearance and Enid's suicide. Garth had been opposed to their undergoing any type of therapy, calling it a bunch of crap. But in the end her father had taken advice from Geraldine and Willie, and months after Enid's suicide had allowed both children to see a therapist for a few weeks, just long enough to convince everyone that he'd done his job as a parent.

And of course, over the years, Audrey had psychoanalyzed herself more than once. *Physician, heal thyself!* Audrey groaned silently. A mental health therapist treating herself was as stupid as a lawyer defending himself.

She had commitment issues. Big-time. And her fear of being rejected and unloved colored every aspect of her life. And yes, it was all her father's fault, wasn't it? No, of course it wasn't. Sure, Wayne Sherrod had been a failure as a father. He had been and still was a cold, distant man who had instilled a sense of unworthiness in his only daughter. But she wasn't a child any longer. She was a grown woman. An intelligent, attractive, successful woman. And mentally, she understood that she had to own her problems and no longer blame anyone else. But emotionally, she often still felt like the lonely, unloved, and unwanted child she had believed herself to be.

No wonder she understood Hart so well and repeatedly forgave him.

While they ate, Porter continued to talk, the conversation ranging from the warm weather in late September to his purchase of tickets for the Chattanooga Symphony on Friday night.

"It's Rimsky-Korsakov's *Scheherazade,*" Porter said as he wiped the corners of his mouth with his napkin.

"Porter, I don't think I can make it this Friday night," she said.

"Why can't—?"

The waitress reappeared, asked if she could remove their plates, and inquired if they wanted dessert.

"No dessert," Porter told her. "But I'd like coffee, please. Cream. No sugar."

"And you, ma'am?" the waitress asked.

"Nothing for me, thanks."

Porter waited until the waitress left to prepare his coffee, then asked, "Does your not being free to attend the symphony with me on Friday night have anything to do with the talk you want us to have?"

He sounded upset. She thought he might be, but knowing him as she did, she felt certain he wouldn't make a scene. Nor would he beg her not to end their going-nowhere relationship.

She reached across the table and laid her hand over his. His gaze met hers, head-on.

"You're breaking up with me, aren't you?" He drew in a deep breath and released it on a soft moan, as if he were in pain.

"Porter, I'm very fond of you. We're great friends. But . . . that's all we are. Friends. Anything else just won't work for us."

"If you're referring to sex . . ." he said in a hushed tone, well aware that if he spoke louder, he might be overheard. "We haven't even given that a try, yet. And so far, our relationship has been quite satisfactory, or so I thought."

"Do you love me?" she asked point-blank.

His eyes widened with surprise. "I—I'm very fond of you."

"And I of you, but I don't love you. And if we haven't had sex by now, then I think that should tell us both something, don't you?"

"Then there is someone else, isn't there?" He jerked his hand away from hers. "Someone you want to—"

"No, Porter. I told you that there is no one else. I simply think we both deserve more from a relationship than being friends, than just being compatible. I've sensed that you want more from our relationship and I . . . well, I don't."

"I can wait."

"No, I don't want you to wait. I want you to be free to find someone else, someone who can give you what you deserve in a relationship."

Dear God, he looked as if he was going to cry. Did she actually mean that much to him? Could she have misjudged the depth of his feelings for her?

"Porter?"

He swallowed. "I'm quite all right."

He didn't look all right. He looked devastated.

The waitress returned with his coffee.

"I suppose we can still be friends, can't we?" he asked, his voice slightly unsteady.

"Of course, we can still be friends."

"And since neither of us is involved with anyone else—not yet—there's no reason why you can't go to the symphony with me Friday night, is there? Just as friends, of course." Forcing a fragile smile, he looked at her pleadingly.

She knew that a clean break would be best for both of them, but for the life of her, she couldn't say no to his request. "All right. Just as friends."

The deeper he dug into the Baby Blue cases, the more intrigued J.D. became with the complicated, convoluted story the files told. He was fascinated by Regina Bennett, mesmerized by the unsolved mystery of the missing toddlers who were never found, and puzzled by several aspects of the old case. He understood that after a certain amount of time, neither the FBI nor local law enforcement had enough manpower to continue working on seemingly unsolvable cases. And he didn't doubt everything humanly possible that could have been done more than two decades ago had been done.

No stone unturned. No question unasked. No lead not followed.

So why was it that his professional instincts urged him to find out more, to dig even deeper, to do his damnedest to unearth any still-buried secrets?

His gut told him that the DNA tests would prove the tiny

skeletons found with the two recent murder victims belonged to two of the Baby Blue toddlers. When the test results came in, then the old case would be reopened.

When J.D.'s cell phone rang, he answered immediately without checking caller ID.

"Don't forget to pick me up today," Zoe told him. "We're getting pizza on the way home and you're helping me with my geometry. I have a test tomorrow."

"I'm heading out in five minutes," he said. "I didn't forget about the pizza or the geometry test." He was lying, of course. He had forgotten. And he knew that Zoe knew he had.

As soon as he hung up, he gathered the documents, photos, and reports scattered on top of his desk, lifted a cardboard box from the floor, placed it in his chair, and stuffed everything into the box. After Zoe went to bed tonight, he intended to go over several files more thoroughly, especially the file on Regina Bennett. He wanted to know everything about her that the old information could reveal. Tomorrow morning at nine, he had an appointment—arranged by his superior—at Moccasin Bend Mental Health Institution, where Regina Bennett had undergone her initial evaluation and where she had spent the last twenty-three years of her life.

Chapter 13

Wayne Sherrod hadn't seen or talked to Steve Kelly in nearly fifteen years. When he'd made a few inquiries, he had learned the guy was divorced from his third wife, worked as a bartender, and lived at the Cedar Creek Mobile Home Park off Lee Highway. Steve's son Devin had been the boy abducted the year before Blake disappeared, and Wayne had gotten to know the man when he'd shown up at Enid's funeral and introduced himself. For several years, Wayne and Steve had been drinking buddies, both men single, grief stricken, and filled with rage. They had revealed more of themselves to each other during a few drunken binges than men would normally share.

"If I could kill that bitch over and over again, I'd do it," Steve had said when Regina Bennett had been arrested for kidnapping Jeremy Arden. "She killed my Devin and she killed your little Blake. You know she did. She killed our boys and God only knows what she did with their bodies."

Wayne had made a few illogical, irrational comments himself, threats that, like Steve, he had never carried out.

Anger and pain combined with too much liquor made a man say all sorts of crazy things.

As Wayne turned off into the Cedar Creek Mobile Home Park and drove slowly, searching for Steve's lot number, he asked himself what the hell he was doing there. It wasn't as if they had remained friends, as if he owed Steve anything. But then again, maybe he did. They'd seen each other through some pretty rough years . . . way back when. Maybe he owed it to Steve to tell him there was a possibility that two of the missing toddlers had been found. If the DNA tests proved the identities and the info leaked out, he'd hate for Steve to find out by reading it in the newspaper or hearing it on TV.

Maybe he had no right to reveal information that the CPD hadn't shared with the press, even if he believed Steve had a right to know. But in this case, he made the decision as a father who had lost a son and not as a former police officer.

He found Steve's trailer, an older model, but neatly painted and well maintained. After parking, he got out and walked up to the door and knocked. The door opened to reveal a tall, skinny redhead, probably around forty. She wore a pair of tight jeans and a halter top that revealed a lot of skin and several tattoos.

"Yeah?" she asked, scowling at Wayne.

"Steve around?"

"Who wants to know?" She studied Wayne as if trying to figure out if he was trustworthy.

"An old acquaintance."

She hesitated for a minute and then said, "Steve's not here."

"Know where I can find him?"

"Maybe."

"Look, I'm not here to cause trouble. I just need to talk to Steve."

"Are you a cop?"

"I used to be," he told her. "I'm retired."

"Why do you want to talk to him?"

"It's personal."

She glared at Wayne, sized him up, and grunted. "He's over at Callie's Café. You know where that is?"

Wayne nodded.

"He has breakfast with his brother there a couple of times a week. That's where you can probably find him this morning."

"Thanks."

Without another word, she slammed the door.

Wayne returned to his truck, hit Lee Highway, and backtracked, going southwest until he reached Shallowford Road where Callie's Café was located. As he got out and walked toward the entrance, he wondered if he'd recognize Steve or if Steve would recognize him. The last time they'd seen each other, they'd both been in their late forties.

After entering the café, a seat-yourself establishment, he glanced around, taking in the counter area first before scanning the booths to the right and the tables to the left. That's when he saw Steve sitting alone at a table near the front windows. He held a white coffee mug cradled in both hands. When Wayne approached the table, Steve glanced up, did a double take, and then grinned.

Steve set the mug on the table and stood. "As I live and breathe, if it's not Sergeant Wayne Sherrod." He stuck out his hand. "My God, man, it's good to see you."

Wayne shook his old drinking buddy's hand. Steve looked every day of his fifty-nine years, his face haggard and marred with deep lines caused more from hard living than the passing of time. His once light brown hair was now entirely gray, but he was still slim, actually almost skinny.

"Sit down. Have a cup of coffee with me." Steve indicated the chair across from his.

"Yeah, sure," Wayne said.

Steve snapped his fingers at a passing waitress and then ordered a refill and a fresh cup for Wayne. "Talk about a coincidence. Imagine after all these years, running into each other here."

The waitress poured their coffee and asked Wayne if he wanted a menu. "No, thanks," he replied. "Coffee's fine." He looked at Steve. "Actually, it's not a coincidence. I went by your place and a . . . uh . . . lady told me where I could find you."

Steve chuckled. "That would be Juanita. We've been shacking up for a couple of months now." He stared at Wayne, his gaze slightly puzzled. "Why'd you look me up after all these years?"

It was on the tip of Wayne's tongue to tell him the reason and then suddenly he realized that telling Steve about the toddler skeletons wasn't the only reason he'd come looking for him. For an instant, an insane thought had crossed his mind. What if Steve was acting out his old, liquor-induced threat and was killing Regina over and over again? Only it wasn't Regina he was killing, just women who looked like her. Or looked the way she had two decades ago.

"Remember how you used to say that you'd like to kill Regina Bennett over and over again?" Wayne said, keeping his voice low.

"I said a lot of things back then. But yeah, I remember."

"Still feel that way?"

Steve didn't respond immediately. He waited as if giving Wayne's question a lot of thought. "Yeah, I guess I do. Don't you?"

"Sometimes, maybe. When I let myself think about the past too much."

Just how crazy are you to think that Steve might have killed Jill Scott and Debra Gregory?

Steve was no more a killer than he was. And no way

would Steve have had any idea where Regina Bennett had hidden the toddlers' bodies.

Steve shrugged. "I don't see that it makes any difference one way or the other. Even if we'd both still like to punish her, we can't. That bitch is dead now. But if you ask me, she didn't suffer nearly enough for what she did."

"Maybe we don't know how much she suffered. How do you judge the suffering of an insane person?"

"You're getting awfully philosophical on me, aren't you, old friend? What's really going on? Why did you look me up after all these years?"

"I'm sharing this information with you only because you're Devin's father, just as the police shared it with me because I'm Blake's father." Wayne watched Steve closely as he said, "You've heard about the two Rocking Chair Murders, right?" Steve nodded. "What you don't know is that the bundle found in each woman's arms was not a doll. It was a toddler's skeleton. They're doing DNA tests on the skeletons now to see if the bodies belong to two of the Baby Blue boys."

Steve simply stared at Wayne, his face scrunched in a disbelieving frown. Finally, he breathed deep and hard. "You think there's a chance that those bodies . . . those skeletons belong to Devin and Blake? Is that it?"

"It's one theory. There is a possibility that they could be two of the missing toddlers, but not necessarily Blake and Devin. Of course, the odds are that the skeletons don't belong to any of the Baby Blue victims."

"My God! When will we know?"

"Soon," Wayne told him. "Maybe tomorrow. Early next week at the latest."

"But how? Why? What's the connection? If whoever killed those two women put the skeletons of a couple of Baby Blue boys in their arms, then that means the killer knows what Regina Bennett did with their bodies after she murdered them."

"The police have no idea, nor does the TBI, about any possible connection. They just don't have enough information. Not yet."

Steve took a hefty swig of coffee. "Do you ever wonder if there's even the slightest chance that maybe Blake isn't dead? I know I think about it sometimes. What if Devin's not dead? What if Regina didn't kill him? What if he's out there somewhere, a grown man, nearly thirty years old?"

Wayne sucked in a deep breath as pain ripped through his gut. And the pain was momentarily as fresh and agonizing as it had been twenty-five years ago when Blake had disappeared. Gradually, with each heartbeat, each passing second, the paralyzing pain subsided, leaving only an aching sadness.

Wayne finally managed to say, "Yeah, sure. I've wondered."

"If the DNA tests prove one of the bodies belongs to Blake, that settles it once and for all," Steve said. "No more wondering. No more hoping beyond hope that he's still alive." Steve paused for a moment and the two men stared at each other. "Do you want it to be Blake? Do you want to know for sure?"

"I don't know," Wayne admitted. "I honest to God don't know."

J.D. had spent the past couple of hours at Moccasin Bend. He had spoken to several doctors and nurses and various attendants. He couldn't find anyone who had worked at the facility twenty-three years ago who specifically remembered anything about Regina Bennett, other than her story had been front-page news for weeks after her arrest. Regina had spent nearly a quarter of a century confined at the Mental Health Institute after being ruled criminally insane. She had confessed to killing her toddler son, Cody. A mercy killing to end his suffering. And when the FBI had rescued Jeremy Arden, Regina had insisted that the toddler was her son, that he was her little Cody. Although she had rambled almost incoherently about people stealing Cody from her and that she had been forced to find him and bring him home again and again, she had never admitted smothering anyone except Cody. And she had adamantly refused to tell anyone where she had buried her child. Five minutes alone with the woman and anyone could see she was crazy. That had been the opinion of everyone who had worked on the case.

To this day, there was nothing but circumstantial evidence that Regina had killed the other five toddlers or that she had actually kidnapped them.

J.D. had made a request to see Regina's medical records. The TBI had used their subpoena power to compel the hospital to release copies of her files. He had been assured that the copies would be ready for him in twenty-four hours.

"Would it be possible for me to find out if Ms. Bennett had any visitors and who those visitors were?" J.D. asked.

"I see no reason why not," Ms. Milsaps, the office clerk said. "The visitor's log isn't confidential, and Dr. Lassiter has told us to cooperate fully with the TBI."

"What about the logs that go back a couple of decades? Do y'all still have those?"

"I'm not sure, but I believe our records as far back as the mid-seventies are now on computer files. I can check for you, if you'd like."

"Yes, please, thank you."

Half an hour later, J.D. had completed searching the files that listed each patient's visitors. Year, month, day, and hour. During her first year of confinement, Regina had not been allowed any visitors except for her lawyer, her aunt, and FBI agent George Bonner. After a couple of years, Bonner hadn't visited again, nor had her aunt.

Keith Lawson's mother and father had visited once, as had Chase Wilcox's mother and Shane Douglas's mother. Wayne Sherrod had come to see Regina twice, as had Devin Kelly's father, Steve. All these visits had been years ago, less than two years after Regina's confinement.

Bereaved parents pleading with a crazy woman to tell them if she had killed their child, and if she had, where she had buried the body.

After those first few years, there were no visitors. Not until last year, a few months before she died. Steve Kelly had visited her less than a week before her death. Why would Devin Kelly's father, after all that time, pay Regina another visit?

But even more curious were two other visitors who had come to Moccasin Bend, one on a weekly basis for several months.

Jeremy Arden had visited every other Saturday morning for two months and had spent between thirty minutes and an hour with Regina each time.

Why?

The other visitor's name puzzled J.D. There was no mention of him in any of the FBI records.

Corey Bennett.

"Ms. Milsaps." J.D. turned to the clerk who had been helping him search files containing the visitor's log. "Do you have any idea who Corey Bennett is?"

"Yes, I believe he's Ms. Bennett's nephew. I vaguely remember meeting him once when I was working on a Sunday afternoon." She pointed to the computer screen. "As you can see, he always visited her on Sunday afternoons and stayed several hours."

Nephew? But Regina didn't have any siblings, no known

relatives other than the now-deceased aunt and uncle. Or did she?

"Do you happen to remember anything about him? Hair color? Eye color? Age? Build?"

"If I recall correctly, he was average looking and he was young, I believe. I'm not sure, but perhaps in his late twenties or early thirties. He didn't have black hair. It was brown, I think, or possibly blond. I believe he had a mustache and wore glasses. But my memory isn't always reliable. I encounter so many people in just one day's time."

"Would you recognize him if you saw him again?"

"No, probably not."

"Do you have any record of his address or a phone number?"

"I doubt it, but I can check."

J.D. stood and stretched while he waited.

What difference did it make if Jeremy Arden had visited Regina several times? Maybe the young man had needed to confront the woman who had kidnapped him. Maybe he had found a way to forgive her for what she'd done.

The existence of a nephew no one knew about puzzled J.D. There was something off about that bit of info, but he couldn't quite put his finger on exactly what. A mysterious, unknown nephew appeared out of the blue only a few months before Regina died and began visiting her on a regular basis. Where had he been all those years? And why had he suddenly decided to visit his criminally insane aunt?

Ms. Milsaps cleared her throat. "Special Agent Cass?"

"Yes?"

"We don't have an address for Corey Bennett, but we have a phone number. I believe it's a cell number." She handed J.D. a Post-it Note on which she'd written down the number. "And there's something else."

"What?"

"It seems that Mr. Bennett paid for his aunt's funeral."

"He did? Which funeral home?"

"The Chattanooga Funeral Home, East Chapel, in East Chattanooga."

J.D. thanked her for her assistance, and by the time he reached his Camaro, parked in the area designated for visitors, he had already placed a call to the office requesting a records search for a man named Corey Bennett.

He waited for her.

Taking her from the café parking lot was not advisable. There were too many people in the general vicinity who might suspect something and try to interfere. He had been watching her and studying her routine for days now, although he had limited his visits to the restaurant so as not to arouse suspicion. And in case anyone actually remembered him and described him to the police, a few occasional meals at Callie's Café could be explained quite easily.

As she drove into the parking area outside her second-floor apartment, his heartbeat accelerated. Whenever he was this close to bringing her home again—home, where she belonged—the excitement became overwhelming. Just a few more minutes and she would be with him, and within an hour she would be with Cody again. Poor little Cody had missed her terribly. But they would soon be together again, and everything would be as it should be.

A mother should love her child and take care of him.

A mother should be with her child and never leave him.

She and Cody belonged together. Forever and always. All he was doing was making sure that happened, just as he had promised.

She got out of the car, locked it, and headed for the exterior stairs leading to the second level. That man she dated wasn't with her tonight. Good. He hated him. Hated that he had abused her.

He remained in the dark corner of the staircase, waiting and watching patiently. His pulse raced. His heartbeat roared in his ears. His muscles tensed with anticipation.

Her footsteps tapped softly against the metal stairs, her cushioned walking shoes muffling the sound.

She's close. So close.

As if sensing his presence, she paused at the top of the stairs and looked behind her. He pushed himself back against the wall and held his breath. Unless she took several more steps in his direction, she wouldn't be able to see him. From experience, he had learned that surprising her when she had her back to him made persuading her to go with him a lot easier.

She hurried toward her apartment door, inserted the key in the lock, and—

He pounced immediately, threw his right arm around her neck, and covered her face with the ether-soaked rag he held in his left hand. She emitted a startled squeak, but after only a token struggle, she slumped unconscious into his arms. He stuffed the rag into his pocket, lifted her off her feet, and carried her down the stairs and straight to his car. After glancing around to make sure they weren't being watched, he opened the back door and placed her on the seat.

The headlights of what appeared to be an SUV flashed brightly against the building as the vehicle pulled into the parking area. He hurried into the driver's seat of his car, started the engine, and backed out just as the SUV slid in beside him. He didn't look their way as he drove away. Slowly. Cautiously.

"We're going home," he told her. "I'm taking you to Cody."

Whitney Poole regained consciousness slowly, her head aching and her stomach queasy. Why was it pitch-black in her bedroom? She always kept a night-light burning in the bathroom and the door partially open. Had the power gone out? Was that why it was so dark? She felt around in the bed beside her and instantly realized three things: Travis wasn't with her, she wasn't in bed, and her wrists were bound to the arms of the chair she was sitting in.

Then it all came back to her, like a tidal wave hitting shore. She had left work, driven home, gotten out of her car, and walked up the stairs to her apartment. She had glanced up at her windows facing the parking area when she'd first arrived and noticed that there were no lights on. That had meant Travis wasn't there. Good riddance! She'd thought he loved her, but did a guy slap around a woman he really loved?

When she had reached the top of the stairs, she'd gotten one of those weird feelings, the kind that gave you cold chills. But she hadn't seen anybody, so she'd started to unlock her door when—!

Suddenly, Whitney screamed . . . and screamed . . . and screamed.

Once she stopped, her throat sore and her body trembling, she listened to the silence. Deadly silence.

"Where are you?" she asked.

No response.

"Damn it, where are you? Are you sitting over there somewhere watching me? Listening to me? Are you getting your cookies off knowing I'm scared shitless?"

She heard only the unbearable solitude.

She sat there, twisting her wrists, which were tied to the arms of what felt like a wooden chair, and straining to loosen the rope that bound her ankles together. When she struggled harder and harder trying to free herself, the chair moved, rocking back and forth, creaking eerily.

Oh, God! Oh, God!

The reality of her situation became immediately evident.

The man who had kidnapped her and brought her here—wherever here was—had done this before. Twice. She had read about it in the newspaper, had seen it on the TV news.

No, no. You can't be sure that it's the same guy.

It could be a coincidence.

It's not.

The Rocking Chair Killer had chosen her for his third victim.

Chapter 14

J.D. left the Chattanooga Funeral Home's East Chapel with the same type of vague description of Corey Bennett that Ms. Milsaps had given him the day before at Moccasin Bend. Average. Young. Probably early thirties at most. Blondish brown hair. Wore glasses. Had a mustache.

"He paid in cash," Mr. Scudder had said. "Not completely out of the ordinary, but unusual."

"Anything else you remember about him?"

"No, not really. He was quiet. Didn't say much. Seemed genuinely sad about his aunt's death." Mr. Scudder had shaken his head sympathetically. "He picked up the ashes himself. I do remember him saying that she grew up on a farm in Sale Creek and she would want to go back home."

Then just after J.D. had thanked him and had started to leave, Mr. Scudder had called, "Special Agent Cass?"

"Yes?"

"There were a couple of other things that I—that we all thought were rather peculiar."

"Exactly what were they?"

"Mr. Bennett brought a special container for his aunt's ashes."

"And that's unusual?"

"No, but the container was, well, rather unorthodox."

"What was it?"

"The container was a very small toy box," Mr. Scudder had said. "A toy box that was covered with vividly painted ABC letters and various characters from nursery rhymes."

Yeah, the container was rather unorthodox, to say the least. And rather ironic, considering Regina Bennett had been obsessed with toddlers, with little boys who bore a resemblance to her dead son.

"You said a couple of things," J.D. had reminded Mr. Scudder. "What was the other thing?"

"He requested that we allow him to place a small item in the casket with his aunt before the cremation."

"What item?"

"Well, I didn't see it, but Mr. Bennett said it was a doll that had been his aunt's favorite toy as a child."

"A doll?"

"Yes, he had it wrapped in a blue blanket. I saw the blanket, but of course, didn't unwrap it and look at the doll inside."

Good God almighty. Had this man actually put one of the toddler skeletons in the coffin with Regina Bennett? If so, they would never know, because whatever had been wrapped in the blanket had been cremated along with Regina.

As he drove away from the East Chapel and headed back to his office, J.D. went over the information he had so far obtained about Corey Bennett. According to the search results from the TBI inquiry, the telephone number Corey Bennett had given at Moccasin Bend had belonged to a disposable cell phone at that time. And the list of Corey Bennetts the TBI came up with proved that the name was actually fairly common and there were even a few female Corey Bennetts. There were a number of Corey Bennetts in the Chattanooga area, but so far, they hadn't found a link between anyone by that name and Regina Bennett, kidnapper and murderer.

The records on Regina showed that she had no siblings and no first cousins. And she was never married. So, how was it that she had a nephew?

J.D. intended to follow every possible lead, even if that meant personally interviewing every Corey Bennett in Chattanooga. But first, before going back to the field office, he needed to make a side trip just to satisfy his curiosity. And to put an end to a highly unlikely scenario that had popped into his head. What if there was some connection between the people who now owned the farm where Regina Bennett had lived and Corey Bennett?

Instead of following Moore Road to Ringgold Road, the route that would take him back to McCallie, J.D. headed west on I-24. At this time of day, without any traffic delays because of accidents or road construction, he would be in Sale Creek within thirty-five minutes.

Tam and Garth hadn't talked about Hart, about how he had shown up on her doorstep at two in the morning. They both knew that there was nothing to say. She suspected that Garth believed she still loved Hart, but he understood that she had no future with his nephew, that he was pure poison to her.

It had been business as usual, the two working together on the Rocking Chair Killer cases, and coming to one dead end after another. Frustration was mounting on a daily basis, from the DA's office and the mayor's office straight to the chief of police. Everyone wanted answers, but so far, all they had were more questions.

Tam rubbed her right temple trying to soothe a pounding

headache. It was tension, pure and simple. Ever since Hart's unexpected late-night visit, she'd been coiled so tight that with the least provocation, she would snap. Marcus had commented on how irritable she'd been ever since he came home and she had assured him that it was just the pressures of her job, the two murder cases they hadn't been able to solve.

Last night, after she and Marcus had made love, after she had faked her orgasm, she had lain in her husband's arms and prayed for God to erase every thought of Hart Roberts from her mind and from her heart.

Marcus had held her, kissed her forehead, and told her how much he loved her. Then he had startled her by saying, "Is now a good time to talk about the future, while we're both relaxed and happy?"

How little he knew. How easily she pretended.

"What about the future?" she had asked, not daring to look him in the eye.

"I'm heading fast toward forty and you just turned thirty-four. I've been thinking that if we intend to have children, we might want to consider getting started sooner rather than later."

When she hadn't immediately responded, he had cupped her chin and turned her around to face him.

She had forced a smile, one she prayed he wouldn't realize was as fake as her orgasm. "Yes, I think we should talk about having a baby, but not now. Not while I'm so involved with these murders." She had caressed his cheek. "I love you. You know that. And we'll talk about having children soon. I promise."

Marcus had accepted her response without question, agreeing that they would temporarily postpone the discussion about parenthood.

"Headache?" Garth's question snapped Tam out of her thoughts.

She glanced up at him. “Yeah.”

“Take some aspirin.”

“I did.”

“Take some more. We need to head out soon and I want you at your best.”

She eyed him inquisitively. “We’re heading out where?”

“To talk to a missing woman’s boyfriend, employer, and neighbors,” Garth told her.

“And we’re working a missing persons case because . . . ?” But she already knew. “He’s kidnapped another woman, hasn’t he?”

“Maybe. She fits the general description. Young, attractive, tall, and slender. Long, dark hair.”

“Damn!” The word escaped from between Tam’s clenched teeth. “Who is she?”

“Whitney Poole, twenty-four. She’s a waitress at Callie’s Café. Her boyfriend reported her missing after she didn’t come home last night or this morning. And her boss called her apartment looking for her because she didn’t show up for work this morning. No one has seen her since she left the café last night. The boyfriend has called every girlfriend she has, and none of them have seen her.”

“She’s been missing less than twenty-four hours, so I assume the reason we’re jumping on this is because she fits the profile for the Rocking Chair Killer’s other two victims.”

“We can’t afford to wait,” Garth said. “If our guy abducted Whitney Poole, then the sooner we investigate, the better our chances are of nabbing this guy. And if it turns out he didn’t take her or that maybe she’s not actually missing, I’d rather know we acted immediately than risk the possibility that she is his third victim.”

* * *

The young woman who opened the door when J.D. arrived at the old farmhouse that had once belonged to Luther and Dora Chaney smiled warmly.

"Hello."

"Hi." J.D. returned her smile. "Mrs. Gilliland?"

"Yes, I'm Allison Gilliland."

He showed her his badge and ID. "I'm Special Agent Cass with the Tennessee Bureau of Investigation. May I come in and talk to you?"

Her smile vanished, replaced by a speculative stare. "Yes, of course, please come in." She invited him inside and showed him to the living room.

On arrival, he had noted the new tan vinyl siding on the house and freshly painted white shutters. The yard was neatly mowed, the landscaping was filled with greenery, and yellow mums lined the walkway. Once inside, he noted that the interior of the house had been renovated; also, the old wooden floors had been refinished, the walls had been recently painted, and the décor was a combination of traditional and contemporary.

"Won't you sit down, Special Agent Cass." She indicated the sofa as she sat in a leather recliner in front of the big-screen TV. Once they were both seated, she asked, "What's this about?"

"It's about a woman named Regina Bennett."

"Oh. I see, but I'm afraid I don't understand."

"You know who Regina Bennett is or rather who she was?"

"Yes, of course I know. And I know that she once lived here, in this house and later on in the rental house on this farm. You said who she *was*—is she dead?"

"Yes, ma'am. She passed away while an inmate at Moccasin Bend earlier this year."

"I'm afraid I'm confused. I don't understand what—?"

"The TBI is trying to tie up some loose ends concerning Regina Bennett," J.D. said. "Ms. Bennett was cremated, and when her nephew picked up her ashes, he mentioned to the funeral director that he planned to return his aunt to the farm."

Allison Gilliland's gray eyes widened in surprise. "If you're asking if anyone came here to the farm and asked permission to scatter Regina Bennett's ashes, then the answer is no. But we own nearly a hundred acres, so it wouldn't be difficult for someone to have entered the property without our permission or our knowledge."

J.D. believed Allison. There was no reason she should lie to him. As far as he knew, neither she nor her husband had any connection to Regina Bennett or her relatives. Nor to the previous owners, who had bought the farm from Dora Chaney. Had he actually thought the mysterious Corey Bennett would have asked permission to scatter his aunt's ashes?

"Would you mind if I took a look around the property?"

"No, I don't mind, but just what do you think you'll find here?" she asked, standing when he did. "It's my understanding that the local authorities and the FBI covered every square foot of this farm years ago."

"I don't expect to find anything in particular. I thought that since I'm here and if you don't have any objections, I'd take the opportunity to just look around, maybe check out the house where Regina lived. Would that be possible?"

"You mean the rental house?"

"Does someone live there?"

"No, not now. The house is run down, and we haven't bothered putting any money into fixing it and renting it since we bought this property a couple of years ago after Mrs. McGregor died and her daughter put the farm up for sale."

"How long has it been since you've been in the other house?"

"Well, actually, not since shortly after we bought the property. Why?"

"No reason. Just curious."

As he walked out of the living room, a framed wedding photo of a happy young couple caught his eye. The bride was obviously Allison Gilliland. The husky young groom in the picture had green eyes, red hair, and freckles.

Mr. Gilliland didn't fit the description he'd been given of Corey Bennett.

Not until that moment did J.D. realize he had subconsciously been wondering if it was possible that the new owner of the old farm might be Regina's nephew.

"The house isn't locked," Allison told him as she walked with him onto the front porch. "It's about a quarter of a mile east of this house. If you follow the dirt road over there, it'll take you straight to it."

J.D. shook hands with the young woman, thanked her, and surveyed the landscape as he walked toward his Camaro. As she'd said, there were nearly a hundred acres, some of it still cultivated farmland, some of it wooded, and a couple of dozen acres that climbed into the hills. From the FBI report he'd read and reread, the hills were dotted with caves and a couple of springs ran through the property, one to the south and the other to the west of the farmhouse. Both houses had basements. Both basements had been thoroughly searched. And every cave in the hills that they had discovered had also been searched.

Any evidence left behind twenty-three years ago would now be long gone. Besides, if the investigators hadn't found anything, it was probably because there was nothing to find.

And you're not going to find anything today.

On the short drive to the rental house, J.D. noted the time on his wristwatch. Nearly eleven. He had noticed a pizza place on Dayton Pike on his drive there earlier. When he left, he could stop by for a quick lunch. Since he and Zoe had their first appointment scheduled with Dr. Sherrod that afternoon at four-thirty, it would be after six before they'd get a chance to eat dinner. He sure wasn't looking forward to this family-therapy thing. Hell, he'd rather walk through broken glass in his bare feet than talk about his feelings for a solid hour. His gut told him that somehow Audrey Sherrod would make whatever problems he and Zoe had all his fault. Two females against one male. Yeah, even if one of those females was the counselor.

J.D. pulled up in front of the small, ramshackle, clapboard cottage. Several windows were broken and had been boarded over with plywood. The front porch sagged on one end and the roof was in bad shape. A few scraggly, overgrown shrubs grew along the sides of the house, and knee-high weeds and patches of grass dotted what had probably once been a well-kept yard.

As he stepped up on the porch, the boards beneath his feet creaked, and when he looked down, he saw that several slats of the wooden floor had rotted and given way in places. The front door opened easily with just a turn of the knob, the rusty hinges groaning as J.D. entered the house. The small living room lay before him empty and bare and he could see through into a kitchen that looked the same. A musty, unlived-in scent filled the house, and shards of prenoon sunlight crept through the boarded windows and cast long shadows on the dirty wooden floor. Taking his time, he walked through the house, going from room to room and opening closet doors, searching for anything other than dust and grime and an overwhelming sense of desolation.

He stood in the center of what had once been the nursery and recalled the description of the room from George Bonner's report. In his mind's eye, J.D. pictured the baby bed, the Mother Goose rug, the Humpty-Dumpty night-light, the big Raggedy Andy doll on top of the small toy box.

Had it been that same toy box that Corey Bennett had taken to the Chattanooga Funeral Home?

His mind whirled with thoughts, with possibilities, with outlandish ideas, and even with a few solid theories. If Corey Bennett was not Regina's nephew, and all evidence pointed to that fact, then who was he? Why had he visited her at Moccasin Bend in the months before she died? Why had he paid for her funeral? And why had he asked the funeral home to place her ashes in a toy box, possibly the same toy box that had been in Cody Bennett's nursery?

Two possibilities came to mind, neither exactly logical. Either he was one of the toddlers she had abducted, whom for whatever reason she had not killed, or he was actually Cody Bennett.

But Cody Bennett was dead, wasn't he? Regina had admitted that she'd smothered him to put him out of his misery. However, the little boy's body had never been found.

And only one of the six missing toddlers had been rescued; only one was alive. Jeremy Arden. Could Corey Bennett and Jeremy Arden be the same person? Had Arden disguised himself and visited Regina under an assumed name? If he had, then why?

Audrey checked her appearance in the bathroom mirror as she applied a fresh coat of pink lipstick. Carnation Pink, her favorite shade, one she wore almost every day. She looked quite presentable in her navy blue linen jacket, pale beige tailored slacks, and light pink silk blouse. She didn't usually wear her mother's pearls except on special occasions, but for some reason, she had taken them from the wall safe that morning and put them on without asking herself why. Now she asked herself, and she didn't especially care for the honest truth.

J.D. Cass undermined her self-confidence. Wearing her mother's pearls reminded her that she was Norma Colton Sherrod's daughter, that she came from a long line of intelligent, well-bred steel magnolias. If she had any hope of actually doing her job and helping J.D. and Zoe, then she couldn't allow J.D.'s attitude toward her to affect her professionalism.

When Audrey returned to her office, she laid out a pad and pen, took a deep breath, and sat down to wait for her four-thirty appointment. She had told Donna that she could leave early as soon as she showed J.D. and his daughter into her office. Once the session ended, she would have to rush home and change clothes before Porter picked her up for their date. A date, she reminded herself, that really wasn't a date. Just two friends going to the symphony together. Had she made a mistake by agreeing to see Porter tonight? She had hoped to make a clean break, but instead she had given in to her empathetic feelings and decided it best to cushion her rejection by seeing him this one last time.

A soft knock on the closed door brought Audrey out of her thoughts. Donna opened the door and stuck her head in.

"Mr. Cass and his daughter are here," Donna said.

"Ask Mr. Cass to come in first. Tell Zoe that I'll talk to her privately in a few minutes."

When J.D. entered her office, he ran his gaze over her quickly, and as if he found nothing of any interest, he inquired, "Do I sit down or spread out on the couch?" The corners of his lips lifted in a devilish smile.

She suspected that most women found his smile irresistible and that he knew it. Well, she wasn't one of those women.

"Sit down, please." She indicated the two chairs facing each other on the opposite side of the room.

He waited until she sat before he did, then he looked right at her. "I thought this was going to be family counseling, that Zoe and I would do this together."

"It is family counseling and I will be talking to the two of you together," Audrey said. "But first, I want to speak to each of you privately."

He nodded.

"You and Zoe need to know that both of you will be required to attend every session together. It's going to take your working together to resolve your problems."

J.D. was no longer smiling. "Okay."

"Tell me why you think you need counseling and what you hope these sessions will achieve."

He huffed, glanced up at the ceiling, and gritted his teeth. "I think the why is obvious. I have a teenage daughter who, apparently, I can't control. She was used to doing whatever the hell she wanted to do when she lived with her mother, and she resents having to follow rules and regulations." J.D. paused for a minute, apparently waiting for Audrey to say something, and when she didn't, he continued. "What do I hope these sessions will achieve? I hope you can make Zoe understand that I'm her father, that I'm the adult, that I'm the one who makes the decisions. I want her to stop fighting me tooth and nail over every damn little thing."

Audrey wrote hurriedly, making notes as he talked. When he stopped talking, she glanced up from her notepad. After asking him half a dozen more questions, she showed him to the door and invited Zoe into her office.

"I'm so nervous," Zoe admitted. "I barely made it through the day at school. I kept thinking about this session and wondering if J.D. would find some excuse not to show up."

"There's no reason to be nervous." Audrey reached out and patted Zoe's arm. "And as you can see, your father didn't find an excuse to back out of coming here."

"Yeah, he's here, but he sure isn't happy about it and he looked downright pissed when he left your office a minute ago."

"Come over and sit down and we'll talk." Audrey led Zoe to the same two chairs that she and J.D. had occupied.

"Why don't you tell me why you think you and your father need therapy?"

Zoe's eyes rounded wide and she laughed. "You're kidding, right?"

"I think you need to tell me."

"Okay. I'll tell you, and it's not a pretty story. Before my mother died, she told me that the man I'd thought was my father, lousy bastard that he was, wasn't my father. Then she called J.D. and sprang the news on him that he had a kid he didn't know existed. She died and J.D. got stuck with me because nobody else wanted me. He's miserable and I'm miserable. He doesn't want a daughter and I don't want him for a father." Tears glistened in Zoe's beautiful dark eyes, eyes so much like her father's.

Audrey pulled tissues from the decorative box on the table between the two interview chairs and handed a tissue to Zoe. The young girl glared at Audrey's offering.

"I don't need it. Thanks, anyway," Zoe said.

Audrey stuffed the tissues into her jacket pocket. "What do you hope these counseling sessions with your father will accomplish?"

Zoe snorted. "I don't know. Maybe he'll lighten up a little. I'm sick and tired of him bossing me around and telling me how to run my life. I did just fine before he came along and tried to play Big Daddy. My mom didn't smother me the way he does. Sometimes I think he's mean to me because he hates having me around." Zoe cleared her throat. "He's a lousy father."

After a few more questions for Zoe, Audrey asked J.D. to join them, and as he entered the office, she pulled up a third chair and created a seating triangle. Once father and daughter were seated facing each other, Audrey took the chair at the peak of the triangle, placing herself in front of and between them.

Less than fifteen minutes into the session, J.D.'s phone rang. Mouthing a hurried apology, he rose from his chair, walked toward the windows, and took the call. Zoe glared at her father's back. Audrey felt the girl's anger and didn't blame her for being upset. She wasn't exactly pleased with J.D. herself. She had told him and Zoe to either turn off their cell phones or silence them during the session. J.D. had done neither.

From his end of the brief conversation, Audrey couldn't make out much, but enough to realize it was a business call.

"I have to go," J.D. said. "Sorry about this, but—"

"But something more important came up," Zoe said.

"We can reschedule," Audrey told them.

"Why bother? J.D. will just find another way to get out of it." Zoe glared at her father.

"Look, that was Sergeant Hudson," J.D. said. "Another young, dark-haired woman disappeared last night and all the evidence points to the Rocking Chair Killer being her abductor. We've got an eyewitness who may be able to give us a description of a man she saw outside the woman's apartment last night, a man who doesn't live there and wasn't visiting anyone who does live there."

"Go on, then," Zoe told him. "I'll call Reesa and see if her mom can come pick me up and let me spend the night."

"I can drop you by Reesa's on my way."

"Don't bother."

Father and daughter glared at each other.

"Zoe, why don't I drive you to Reesa's house?" Audrey suggested. "That will save your father some time, and I don't mind in the least."

"Is that okay with you?" Zoe dared J.D. to argue.

"That's fine, if Dr. Sherrod really doesn't mind." He glanced at Audrey. "Thanks."

As soon as J.D. left, Zoe looked at Audrey. "Yeah, I know. It's not his fault that he had to leave. I know he's a state cop, and when duty calls, he has to go."

Audrey draped her arm around Zoe's slender shoulders. "You know what? I have an idea. Why don't you come home with me instead of going to Reesa's? I'll fix dinner for us and then we'll watch a movie."

Her impromptu invitation to Zoe was totally unprofessional, but it wasn't the first time Audrey had allowed her emotions to overrule logic. If she had ever seen a girl in need of someone's undivided attention, it was Zoe Davidson. And yes, truth be told, Zoe's hunger to be loved and wanted reminded her far too much of how she had felt as a young girl, with a policeman father who readily used his job as an excuse to maintain an emotional barrier between them.

"You mean it?" Zoe's face brightened instantly. "You want me to come home with you?"

"I can't think of anything I'd enjoy more than the two of us getting better acquainted. As friends," Audrey hastily added. "Not as client and counselor. So, why don't you wait for me in the outer office while I finish up in here and we'll head out in about five minutes."

Audrey had two phone calls to make, one to Porter to break their date, and the other to J.D. to tell him he could pick up his daughter at her house later tonight. And in all honesty, she didn't know which call she dreaded more.

Chapter 15

Audrey had waited until she and Zoe had arrived at her home before she excused herself and went into the bedroom to phone Porter. When she had explained the situation, she had expected him to be disappointed, but had not been prepared for his anger or the accusation he had hurled at her.

"I don't appreciate your canceling at the last minute," he had told her. "And for no better reason than to baby-sit Special Agent Cass's teenage daughter. Why you would volunteer to—?"

"I thought I explained what happened."

"So you did, but it doesn't ring true. My God, you aren't interested in the man, are you? I wouldn't have thought a Neanderthal like Cass was your type, but then I suppose most women prefer the blatantly male, chest-beating Me-Tarzan-You-Jane type."

"Porter, you're being ridiculous." She had seen a side to Porter Bryant that she'd never seen before, not in the six months they had dated.

"For your sake, I hope I'm wrong. You have to know that

up against Holly Johnston, you don't stand a chance." He had slammed down the receiver.

Doing her best to put the unpleasant conversation with Porter out of her mind, Audrey had returned to the living room and suggested that Zoe might want to join her in the kitchen. They had prepared sandwiches and soup for their supper, and afterward, they had taken their bowls of chocolate ice cream and a plate of sugar cookies into the living room. Zoe had chosen *Overboard* from Audrey's DVD movie collection, a romantic comedy starring Kurt Russell and Goldie Hawn. And although Audrey tried to concentrate on the movie, she kept thinking about where J.D. was and what he was doing. Another young woman had disappeared, someone who fit the same profile as Jill Scott and Debra Gregory, a possible third victim of the Rocking Chair Killer.

We've got an eyewitness who may be able to give us a description of a man she saw outside the woman's apartment last night.

J.D.'s comment replayed over and over inside her head. If the eyewitness could identify the man who might have kidnapped this young woman, wouldn't that mean there was a good chance they could find him and rescue the woman before he killed her?

"I love this movie," Zoe said. "It's so funny."

Coming out of her thoughts, Audrey replied, "You've never seen *Overboard* before?"

"No, never." Zoe picked up another cookie from the plate on the coffee table and took a bite. "These are good. They're kind of cake and cookie. Where'd you get them? At the grocery store or one of the bakeries?"

"Actually, I made them," Audrey said. "Baking is sort of a hobby of mine, especially desserts."

"Dang, how about that? I never thought that somebody like you . . . you know, an elegant, sophisticated career woman, would waste her time cooking."

Audrey laughed, her response a combination of amusement and appreciation for Zoe's flattering description of her. She had never actually thought of herself as either elegant or sophisticated.

"A good friend's mother taught me how to cook," Audrey explained. "I used to spend a lot of time at their house, and Geraldine is the best cook in the world. She let us make the desserts every weekend. And in the past few years, I've taken two gourmet cooking classes."

"Could you teach me to make cookies like these?" Zoe stuffed the remainder of the cookie into her mouth and smiled at Audrey.

"I could. They're not difficult to make."

"That would be great," Zoe mumbled as she chewed and then swallowed. "When? I know you're probably busy tomorrow, but if you're not, maybe . . ." Zoe frowned. "I'm sorry. I shouldn't assume that because you've been so nice to me it means you'd want us to spend more time together."

Audrey understood only too well Zoe's desperate need to be loved and accepted, to be wanted. But it would be unprofessional for her to allow herself to become a mother substitute for Zoe. And it would be so easy for that to happen because of the rapport they shared.

You could always refer Zoe and J.D. to one of your colleagues for their family-counseling sessions.

"Actually, I have an appointment for a manicure and pedicure in the morning," Audrey said. "If your father thinks it's okay, then why don't I pick you up around nine-thirty and you can go with me. I think Jessica might fit you in for a manicure and pedicure. And then we can come back here and I'll give you your first cooking lesson. Sugar cookies à la Audrey."

They both laughed.

"After you make your first batch, we can call them sugar cookies à la Zoe."

Giggling, Zoe beamed with delight. "I've never had a manicure and pedicure or made cookies."

"Then, my dear Ms. Davidson, you're in for a real treat."

They watched the rest of the movie as they talked and giggled and finished off the plate of cookies. Zoe lay sideways on the sofa, her head resting on a decorative pillow she'd placed on the armrest. After she yawned, she said, "Excuse me."

Audrey checked her watch. Ten forty-eight.

Why hadn't J.D. called?

"Looks like your father has been delayed."

"Yeah, he's probably forgotten all about letting me come home with you. He gets pretty involved with his job, and nothing else seems to matter."

"My father was like that." The moment she spoke, Audrey realized she shouldn't have voiced her thoughts.

"Really?"

"He was a policeman, very dedicated to his job. Some men are like that." Audrey reached out, grasped Zoe's hand, and tugged her up into a sitting position. "Come on. I'll get you a pair of my pajamas. You can take a shower and sleep in my guest room tonight."

Zoe's mouth dropped wide open as she stared at Audrey. "But if J.D. comes by to pick me up—"

"I'm sure he will. Eventually. But we have no idea when that will be. There is no point in your staying up when it's obvious you're tired. You go take a shower and I'll see if I can get in touch with your father and tell him you're staying here tonight. Give me his cell number again."

Zoe recited the phone number and Audrey memorized it. Then she shooed Zoe off toward the guest room while she headed for her bedroom. Audrey went through her lingerie drawer and chose a pair of lavender and white striped cotton pajamas to loan Zoe.

"Thanks so much," Zoe said. "It's so nice of you to . . . well, thanks."

Audrey thought the fourteen-year-old looked like a small child on the verge of tears. She wanted nothing more than to put her arms around Zoe and comfort her, but she didn't think it the wisest thing to do. Zoe needed to be the one who reached out first before she would be willing to accept comfort from anyone.

Audrey retreated to the living room, and as soon as she heard the shower running, she picked up the phone and dialed J.D.'s number.

"Yeah, what's wrong?" his deep, aggravated voice demanded.

"Bad night?" Audrey asked, ignoring his rudeness.

"Sorry, but yeah, it's not such a good night."

"The eyewitness didn't pan out as you had hoped?"

"Something like that."

"I wouldn't have bothered you, but I wanted to catch you before you—"

"God damn it!" She heard his voice as if he was holding the phone away from him, but she couldn't make out anything else. Then suddenly, he said to her, "Look, Dr. Sherrod, tell Zoe I'll pick her up in about an hour. I've got to go."

"But—but—"

J.D. had hung up on her.

She huffed loudly. Dear God, how that man infuriated her. She had half a mind to call him back and tell him exactly what she thought of him.

Within minutes, her temper had cooled enough for her to admit that calling him back was a bad idea. Instead, she went through her bedroom and into the adjoining bath and drew a tub of warm water to which she added some scented bath salts. A few minutes later as she lay there, her body immersed in the soothing heat, she tried to erase J.D. Cass from her mind, not an easy task when his daughter was asleep in her guest bedroom. The man was, if not an uncaring father, at the very least an insensitive one.

So much like her own father.

Don't assume that the two men are identical.

Judging J.D. on such a short acquaintance wasn't fair to him. And if she intended to work with him and Zoe as their therapist, she had to find a way to give him the benefit of the doubt.

You can't continue to counsel them.

No, she couldn't. Not if she formed a personal friendship with Zoe, which she wanted to do. She wanted to help Zoe, and oddly enough she believed that being her friend was more important than being her therapist.

She remained in the tub—a place where she often did her best thinking—until the water turned tepid. After drying off and putting on her turquoise pajamas and matching robe, she removed the towel from her head, shook loose her shoulder-length hair, and used her fingers as a makeshift comb. As she entered the hall, she paused outside the guest room and peeked inside, where Zoe lay sprawled across the bed, the covers at her feet. Audrey tiptoed into the room and pulled the top sheet and blanket over the sleeping child.

Zoe was such a pretty girl. Actually, she was beautiful. She had J.D.'s dark eyes and hair and—

Audrey shook off the thought of how attractive J.D. Cass was and closed the guest room door behind her as she returned to the hallway.

After checking the time, she noted that J.D. should be arriving within the next twenty minutes. She turned on the TV, kept the sound low, and curled up on the sofa. The next thing she knew, the insistent doorbell chimes woke her. She jumped to her feet and hurried to the front door, peered through the viewfinder, and then quickly unlocked and opened the door. J.D. stood there, a five o'clock shadow darkening his face and a world-weary look in his black eyes.

"Sorry I'm so late," he told her. "It's been a hell of a night."

She stepped aside to allow him entrance. "Come on in. Zoe's asleep, so try to be quiet."

He gave her a puzzled look.

"It's nearly midnight," Audrey reminded him. "When I called you earlier, I tried to tell you that Zoe was staying the night and you didn't need to bother with picking her up."

"I apologize about earlier. But we were dealing with a situation. . . ." He glanced into the living room. "Would you mind if I sit down for a few minutes?"

She floated her arm through the air, indicating an invitation.

He slumped down on the sofa, reared back, and closed his eyes. Audrey sensed how tired he was and pure feminine instinct took over.

"Have you had anything to eat?" she asked.

He opened his eyes and stared at her. "What I could use right now is a good stiff drink."

"I don't think that's a good idea. You'll be driving home soon and—"

His rather sarcastic chuckle shut her up instantly.

"I don't think one beer would impair my ability to drive home safely," he told her.

"I'm afraid I don't have any beer."

"Why am I not surprised?"

"I have milk and cola and juice, or I could fix you hot tea or decaf coffee."

He scanned her from head to toe as he sat up straight on the sofa. "You're being awfully nice to me. Why? It's obvious that you personally dislike me and disapprove of me as a father."

"I don't know you well enough to like or dislike you," she told him, assuring herself that in this instance, a little white lie was acceptable. "As for my opinion of you as a father . . . I'll reserve judgment until after you and Zoe complete your family-counseling sessions."

"Very well said, Dr. Sherrod. I almost believe you."

"Believe what you want." She kept her head high and her gaze locked with his. He wasn't going to intimidate her with his swaggering masculinity.

"I wouldn't mind some coffee . . . if your offer is still good."

She nodded. "It is." When she turned to go into the kitchen, she paused, glanced over her shoulder, and asked, "Would you like a sandwich? Roast beef? Ham and cheese?"

He got up off the sofa and came toward her. "You have no idea how much I'd like a sandwich. I'm so hungry I could eat a horse. Ham and cheese sounds great."

When he suggested that he could make his own sandwich while she prepared the coffeemaker, she told him where to locate all the ingredients and supplies in the refrigerator and the pantry. They worked together seamlessly, avoiding conversation and direct eye contact. He took his sandwich and sat down at the kitchen table, and by the time he'd gobbled down the first bite, Audrey poured him a mug of steaming black decaf coffee.

He glanced up at her, smiled, and said, "Thank you."

After placing the coffeepot back on the warmer, she pulled out a chair and sat across from him. He ate heartily and quickly. When he washed down the last bite with coffee, he wiped his mouth with the back of his hand and looked at Audrey, catching her staring at him.

"Would you like another sandwich?" she asked.

"I could probably eat another one or even two more." He chuckled. "But no thanks. I need to be heading out and let you get to bed." He scooted back his chair and stood. "If you'll give me a call in the morning after Zoe gets up, I'll come by and pick her up."

"That won't be necessary. Zoe and I sort of made plans for tomorrow." Audrey stood and faced him. "I hope you don't mind, but I invited her to go with me and have her first manicure and pedicure, then lunch, and afterward I'm going to teach her how to make sugar cookies like the ones we had for dessert tonight."

J.D. narrowed his gaze and studied her closely as if he couldn't quite figure out what her ulterior motive was for befriending his daughter. After a long, tense pause, he grinned. "Wouldn't happen to have any of those sugar cookies left, would you?"

Surprised by his pleasant attitude, Audrey took a couple of seconds to respond to his question. "Oh, yes, as a matter of fact, I do." She went to the pantry, removed a sealed plastic container from the shelf, popped off the lid, and offered him his pick of the cookies layered inside the rectangular box.

He took a handful of cookies, popped a whole one in his mouth, and moaned. "Damn, that was good." He looked straight at her. "You made these?"

"Yes, I made them," she snapped her reply. "And I'll thank you not to act so surprised."

"Lady, I can't figure you out. You obviously dislike me and yet you go out of your way not only to be kind to my daughter, but to offer me a meal in the middle of the night. You project a cool, superior, lady-of-the-manor attitude and yet I find out you bake homemade cookies and plan to give my daughter a cooking lesson."

They stood there in Audrey's kitchen, she in her pajamas and robe and he with cookie crumbs stuck on the corner of his mouth, and stared at each other. He took a hesitant step toward her. Immobilized by the look in his dark eyes, she watched him approach as her pulse quickened. When he was close enough to touch her, he stopped.

"You—you have crumbs on your mouth," she blurted out and then felt foolish for her outburst.

The tension between them snapped and they both laughed as J.D. reached up and wiped his mouth again. "Gone?" he asked.

"All gone," she told him.

"Speaking of gone . . . I'd better leave. About tomorrow . . . Thanks for giving Zoe the opportunity to do some things with a woman, things a girl her age should be doing with her mother."

"I lost my mother when I was quite young, so I understand." Audrey cleared her throat. "I'll bring Zoe home tomorrow afternoon, probably with bright purple fingernails and toenails and hopefully with a batch of delicious sugar cookies to give you to soften the shock."

J.D. groaned. "Bright purple, huh?"

"I hear it's one of the 'in' colors for teenagers these days."

Smiling, he nodded, and then moved around Audrey and headed out of the kitchen. She followed him to the front door where he paused before leaving.

"Her name is Whitney Poole," J.D. said. "She's twenty-four, a waitress at Callie's Café, and the photo her boyfriend provided Garth and Tam pretty much cemented our fear that she's the Rocking Chair Killer's latest victim."

"Long dark hair, brown eyes, young, slender, and attractive?"

"Yeah, and she bears a more than slight resemblance to Jill Scott and Debra Gregory. Not twin or even sister resemblance, but familial."

"That poor girl."

J.D. snorted with disgust. "The boyfriend is a jerk. All her boss is worried about is being one waitress short this weekend. And our eyewitness—what a joke! A nearsighted old woman who was walking her dog last night and saw a man she didn't recognize outside Whitney's apartment."

"Did she give y'all a description?"

"Yeah. She said he was a medium-size man. But it was dark and he was in the shadows for the most part. She was certain he was a white male and young, but to her young is anyone under fifty."

Audrey laid her hand on J.D.'s arm. "I'm sorry. I know how frustrated you must be. You and Uncle Garth and Tam and everyone involved with these abductions and murders."

He nodded. "Thanks again. Tell Zoe I'll see her tomorrow."

"Good night, J.D."

"Good night, Audrey."

As soon as he left, she closed and locked the door as quickly as possible, shutting out J.D. Cass, the look in his dark brooding eyes, and the husky timbre of his deep voice.

Whitney was half out of her mind. Her arms and legs ached. She reeked of the smell of perspiration and her own urine. Bound as she was to the chair, she had been unable to do anything more than struggle against the ropes that kept her securely confined. During her repeated efforts to loosen the ropes, she had rocked the chair so furiously as she bucked back and forth that she had toppled the chair. She lay on the floor, her bloody, bruised wrists still attached to the chair's arms. Her attempts to free herself had failed, leaving her wrists burning as if the flesh had been eaten away by acid.

She had screamed, begging for help, until she was hoarse. She had wept like a baby as the hopelessness of her situation became all too apparent. And oddly enough, she had slept, for how long she didn't know.

A terrifying pitch blackness surrounded her.

Tensing her fingers in and out to relieve the stiffness, she cried out when the rope binding the wrist on which she lay cut deeper into her already raw flesh.

How long had she been there? Hours? Days?

Where was he? Why had he brought her here and left her?

Was that what he'd done with the other two women, left them alone day after day after day until he finally returned and smothered them?

Oh, God! Why didn't he come back now and go ahead and kill her? She didn't think she could bear this endless waiting and wondering.

Whitney's stomach lurched and the queasiness she had been feeling since she came out of a groggy sleep suddenly worsened. Sour bile rose up her throat and the bitter taste coated her tongue. Try as she might to control the nausea, she could not prevent herself from retching again and again until she vomited violently.

Lying there, surrounded by the sickening stench, she cried quietly, almost choking on her own gulping sobs.

And then she heard a noise.

Footsteps?

Had he finally come back? Would he hurt her? Torture her?

The newspapers and TV hadn't mentioned anything about the other two women being tortured, but that didn't mean anything. The police kept things like that under wraps, didn't they?

A dim, faraway light appeared. Whitney gasped, startled by the relief that spread through her. She could see above her head, her wrist tied to the chair and her arm hanging limply.

The footsteps came closer. And closer.

"What have you done to yourself?" a male voice asked.

"Please, let me go." Whitney twisted and turned, trying to catch a glimpse of her captor.

"I didn't mean to leave you alone for so long, but I'm here now and everything will be all right."

He sounded strangely kind, as if he genuinely cared about her.

Don't freak out, Whit. Don't piss him off.

"Help me, please. . . ."

"You've made an awful mess," he told her. "But nothing that a little soap and water won't fix."

She felt him beside her, there in the semidarkness, but all she could see were his arm and shoulder as he lifted her, chair and all, into an upright position.

"There, that's better." He caressed the back of her head, smoothing her tangled hair with his fingers.

She listened to his footsteps as he walked away and then she heard the sound of water pouring as if being transferred from one container into another.

He came up behind her. She held her breath.

A torrent of cold water splashed down over her head, spread out across her shoulders, and soaked her cotton blouse and jeans. She shivered, her body wet and cold. Her senses heightened by the unexpected, Whitney was momentarily distracted.

And then he said, "I can't bring Cody to you while you're like this. We will have to get you cleaned up and in dry clothes first."

Who's Cody? her mind asked, but she was too frightened to voice the question aloud.

Chapter 16

Tam had left Marcus sleeping when she crept out of bed and went into the bathroom to shower and get ready for work. Saturday was supposed to be an off day, but there was no such thing when she and her partner were working a new case. She hadn't slept worth a damn last night despite being exhausted and getting to bed well past midnight. The image of Whitney Poole kept popping into her sleep-deprived brain. Like Jill Scott and Debra Gregory, Whitney was a young woman with her whole life ahead of her, but unless they could find her in time, she would become another of the Rocking Chair Killer's victims.

Tam halfway understood crimes of passion when someone murdered out of hurt and anger and misguided love. She certainly understood killing to protect yourself or a loved one. But senseless murder, without rhyme or reason except in the murderer's deranged mind, was terrifying on so many levels, because the victims were random, leaving a large segment of the population vulnerable. In the Rocking Chair cases, it seemed that any young, attractive brunette who fit a general profile was at risk.

Usually on Saturdays, she and Marcus slept late, woke, and made love. And afterward, he always prepared his delicious Southwestern omelets for their brunch. But this morning, Tam didn't even have time to put on coffee. She'd pick up some at a fast food drive-through on her way to headquarters.

After sliding her Smith & Wesson semiautomatic into the hip holster, she put on her black blazer and headed for the door.

"Why didn't you wake me?"

The unexpected sound of her husband's voice startled her so that she gasped for breath before turning around and smiling at him. He was still wearing only his low-cut gray briefs, his smooth, muscular chest bare and his morning arousal more than evident. She knew that if she had awakened him earlier, he would have wanted to make love, and as much as she usually enjoyed sex with him, there just wasn't time for that this morning.

"I didn't see any reason for you not to sleep late just because I have to work today," she said.

"I'll forgive you for trying to sneak off if you'll give me a good-bye kiss."

She studied his sly, provocative smile and slowly, seductively sauntered toward him, lifted her arms up and around his neck, and then kissed him. When he deepened the kiss, she sighed and opened her mouth completely, her tongue joining his in exploration.

His big hands cupped her buttocks and lifted her up and against his erection. Tam ended the kiss somewhat regretfully, grasped his wrists, and yanked his hands off her butt. "I have to go to work. Save this for tonight."

Pursing his full lips into a mock pout, he frowned at her, but he let her go.

"I love you, Marcus Lovelady," Tam told him.

He grinned. "I love you, too."

Tam thought she caught a glimmer of sadness in Marcus's beautiful brown eyes, but it was gone so quickly that she wondered if she might have imagined it. Surely, he didn't doubt her love for him. Had she ever said or done anything that might make him doubt how much he meant to her?

"I'm sorry that I have to work today," she said.

"It's all right." He ran his hands up and down her arms. "You have a job to do, Officer Lovelady, an important job." He kissed her nose. "Have I told you lately how proud I am of you?"

"Oh, Marcus . . ."

He shoved her away from him. "Go to work, woman." When she turned to go, he swatted her on the behind.

She laughed, enjoying that one sweet moment of happiness, knowing it would be the last contented moment she would have all day today.

J.D. had slept like the dead—for four hours. He had set his alarm for six-thirty. When it woke him, he shut the damn thing off and lay in bed for a few minutes, his mind in chaos. His thoughts jumped from one thing to another, not concentrating fully on anything.

He needed to call George Bonner and run a few things past him, things like the existence of Corey Bennett, a man who claimed to be Regina Bennett's nephew.

Another young brunette was missing, presumed kidnapped by the Rocking Chair Killer. If they didn't find her within a week, her odds of coming out of this alive were probably nil.

Forcing himself to get out of bed, he headed straight for the bathroom. After taking a leak, he washed his hands and then drew warm water into the sink. As he lathered his face and shaved, J.D. planned his day. Call Bonner on his way to police headquarters to meet Tam and Garth. Call Zoe and tell her to have a good time with Audrey—with Dr. Sherrod—today. Call Holly and . . . And what? Make a fuck date for tonight? Why not?

Maybe you should spend some time with your daughter, even if it makes you both miserable.

The family-counseling session yesterday afternoon had barely gotten off the ground when he had received the call about Whitney Poole. Zoe had been pissed at him. And he'd gone down a couple of notches in Dr. Sherrod's opinion, although he suspected her opinion of him as a parent hadn't been all that high to begin with.

Audrey Sherrod had surprised him by taking such a motherly interest in Zoe. He'd never pegged her as the motherly type. She came across as cool, controlled, and unsympathetic to the weaknesses of mere mortals.

J.D. chuckled as he stepped under the hot shower. Why was it that he thought of Audrey as an elegant goddess made of cold marble? She was just a woman. Flesh and blood. *Mortal like the rest of us.* A woman with hopes and dreams and human needs. And emotional baggage.

I lost my mother when I was quite young, so I understand. Was that why she seemed to honestly care about Zoe, why she was being so damn nice to his kid? If Audrey was any other woman, he'd question her motives. It wouldn't be the first time in the past year that some woman had pretended to be interested in Zoe when all she really was interested in was luring J.D. into a relationship. He'd give Holly that much—she hadn't even pretended to like Zoe, let alone show an interest in her.

And Audrey Sherrod isn't interested in you, buddy boy. The lady doesn't even like you.

But she does like Zoe.

* * *

Half an hour later, J.D. washed down a sausage biscuit with black coffee, both purchased at McDonald's on Taft Highway, before he hit US-27 and headed south. As he'd gulped down his fast-food breakfast, he had wondered what Zoe and Audrey were having for breakfast that morning. No doubt something homemade and a damn sight more appetizing than what he'd eaten. It wasn't as if his biscuit hadn't been good or that it wasn't his usual fare, so why had the thought of a gourmet breakfast crossed his mind?

No reason. Just a wild thought.

Using his Bluetooth headset, J.D. placed a call to George Bonner. Too bad if Mayor Bonner usually slept in on Saturday mornings. Halfway expecting to get the former FBI agent's voice mail, J.D. was surprised when Bonner answered.

"I thought you'd be calling this morning," Bonner said.

"I take it that someone has already notified you about Whitney Poole."

"Chief Mullins got in touch with me last night."

"I'm on my way to meet up with Sergeant Hudson and Officer Lovelady. I'm tagging along while they follow up on a few leads."

Bonner chuckled. "Tagging along, huh? Playing backup and trying your damnedest not to take charge. I know how it is."

"I had planned to call you anyway," J.D. said. "Before Whitney Poole was abducted. You know I'm primarily working on the old Baby Blue cases, on the off chance that they turn out to be connected to the more recent murders."

"And you've found something you think we missed?"

"No, not that. But I have discovered something interesting."

"I'm all ears," Bonner said with a note of impatience in his voice.

"Did you know Regina Bennett had a nephew?"

"She didn't. Regina was an only child. She didn't have any siblings. And her aunt and uncle were childless. What makes you think she had a nephew?"

"Because he not only visited her every week the last few months of her life, but he paid for her funeral."

"Well, I'll be damned."

"The only problem is that, so far, I haven't been able to locate a Corey Bennett that is in any way connected to Regina."

"A mystery man," Bonner said. "Someone who doesn't exist. An alias, maybe?"

"Maybe," J.D. agreed.

"Got a description of this Corey Bennett?"

"A vague description. Young, white male, average size, blondish brown hair. Mustache and glasses. That's about it." J.D. paused to give Bonner a few minutes to assimilate the info. "Jeremy Arden visited Regina several times before she died. From his driver's license photo, he fits the same general description as the one of Corey Bennett, minus the glasses and mustache."

"You think they could be one and the same?" Bonner snorted. "Doesn't make sense. Why would Jeremy visit Regina as himself and as her nephew? And why would one of her victims pay for her funeral?"

"I have no idea. It was just a thought."

"No, it was more than a thought. You've got a theory. Let's hear it."

J.D. hesitated. "Not so much a theory as a hypothesis, and a completely unsubstantiated one at that."

"You're talking about a gut feeling, right?"

"Yeah, pretty much. What if while he was with Regina Bennett back when he was a toddler, Jeremy Arden formed an attachment to the woman, maybe even saw her as a mother figure. From what I've been able to learn about Arden, he's been pretty messed up emotionally most of his life."

"Hmm . . . go on. You're making a weird kind of sense."

"Let's say that he felt compelled to visit her, to see her, talk to her, so he came back to Chattanooga and reconnected emotionally with her before she died. Her death could have triggered something inside Arden, something that compelled him to reunite Regina with all the toddlers she put to sleep."

"This hypothesis of yours works only if it turns out that those skeletons belong to a couple of the Baby Blue toddlers," Bonner reminded him.

"And if they do, then we'll have a jump start on figuring out a connection. At this point, unless we can find Corey Bennett, nephew of Regina Bennett, then Jeremy Arden is our best bet. He's the only kidnapped toddler who lived to tell the tale, so to speak."

"Was he?"

"What?"

"Jeremy was the one kidnapped toddler we rescued, but the bodies of the other five were never found. And even if the skeletons left with Jill Scott and Debra Gregory turn out to be two of the Baby Blue toddlers, that doesn't mean Regina killed the other three. She confessed to only one murder—her son's."

"I subpoenaed Regina's medical records and I've gone through enough of them to tell that she contradicted herself quite often and baffled her doctors a great deal of the time. She seemed unaware that she had killed more than one child. The doctors assume that each time she killed one of the Baby Blue toddlers, she believed he was Cody."

"That was their opinion, and you know what they say about opinions."

"Yeah, yeah, everybody's got one."

"Why don't you concentrate on Whitney Poole for the

time being," Bonner suggested. "Once the DNA results come back on the skeletons, then that will be time enough to continue trying to connect the Baby Blue cases to the Rocking Chair Killer cases."

Zoe had surprised Audrey by choosing a very pretty pink nail polish when given the choice from among more than fifty colors. On their way to the salon/spa, they had dropped by the house Zoe shared with her father so that Zoe could change clothes. Then they had spent hours indulging themselves in hot stone pedicures and deluxe manicures. Lunch at Chili's, followed by a quick dash into Publix for cookie ingredients, rounded out their morning and early afternoon. They had chatted about a variety of subjects, everything from makeup and clothes to their favorite foods, music, TV programs, movies, and movie stars, and the classes Zoe liked and disliked at school.

But now that the last batch of cookies—two batches of sugar cookies and one of Zoe's dad's favorites, chocolate chip—were done, Audrey and Zoe settled down on the sofa in the living room, each with a bottle of Diet Dr Pepper. When Audrey kicked off her leather loafers, Zoe removed her Skechers and wiggled her sock-covered toes.

"Thanks for last night and today." Zoe brought her legs up, bending them at the knees and wrapping her arms around her upper calves. "Today was fun. I've never done anything like this." She shrugged. "You know, girl stuff. Getting a manicure and pedicure and baking cookies."

"Didn't you and your mother ever do girl stuff together?"

When Zoe frowned, Audrey wondered if perhaps she shouldn't have mentioned Zoe's mother.

"No. Mom and I didn't . . . You'd have to have known my mother to understand. It wasn't that she was a bad person. She wasn't. She was a good person, but she wasn't cut out to be a mother. She liked to have fun. You know, grown-up fun."

"If you'd rather not talk about her—"

"It's okay. I really appreciate your not playing counselor last night or today. I didn't feel like you were studying me and trying to figure out what makes me tick."

"If the question about your mother made you feel that way, then I apologize."

"It doesn't. Actually, I've kind of been wanting to talk to you about my mother and J.D. and me and what a mess my life is, but . . ." Zoe brought her arms up her legs, lifted them until her elbows rested on her knees, and then lowered her chin down on top of her clasped hands. "I sure drew the short straw when it came to parents. I mean, why is it that two people who shouldn't have ever had a kid, who never wanted to be parents, wound up as my mother and father?"

Audrey felt a sharp, sympathetic stab of pain and paused for a moment to consider how to answer Zoe's question.

"Oh, I know about sex and how J.D. got my mom pregnant." Zoe laughed, the sound hollow and sad. "That's not what I meant."

"I know what you meant. And I'm not sure I have an answer for you. Luck of the draw. Fate. Meant to be. Take your pick, but none of them seem a satisfactory reason." Audrey lifted her feet off the floor and folded her legs sideways as she relaxed her back on the sofa arm behind her. "My parents got a divorce when I was five and even now, sometimes, I wonder why they couldn't have stayed together, why I couldn't have been one of those kids whose parents spend their whole lives together."

"Yeah, fairy-tale stuff." Zoe sighed heavily, a faraway look in her eyes.

"My friend Tamara's parents are still married, still love each other and are very happy, so a few people do get that happily ever after."

"It must be nice. She's lucky, huh?"

"You know, Zoe, your dad might not win any father-of-the-year awards, but don't you think he's doing his best?"

Zoe looked right at Audrey. "I thought you didn't like him, and here you are defending him."

"I'm not defending him. And whether I like him or dislike him has nothing to do with—"

"Yeah, I guess he's doing the best he can. For a guy who got stuck with a kid he didn't want and didn't even know he had, he's done okay. I mean, he's providing room and board and he makes noises like a father even if he doesn't have any idea how to go about being a real dad."

"And what's a real dad like?"

"Humph. How should I know? You tell me."

"Oh, I'm not an expert on fathers, believe me."

"What's your dad like?"

"Oddly enough, Zoe, he's a lot like your dad." *Strong and brave and totally male. Dedicated to his job. Emotionally aloof. And he's never had any idea how to be a loving father to a daughter.*

"A real pain in the butt, huh?"

Zoe and Audrey laughed and kept on laughing until their sides hurt. And when the laughter subsided, they exchanged knowing smiles, each understanding the feelings of rejection and neglect the other had experienced.

While her father, in his role as chief of police, had made a statement to the media, Tam had stood beside Garth and J.D. and Hugh Nicholson, head of the CPD Major Crimes Division, and shared the frustration the others felt. In the span of less than a month, three young women had been abducted and two were now dead. With the resources of the entire police department, as well as the TBI, and with federal assistance, they were no closer to discovering the identity of the Rocking Chair Killer than they had been weeks ago. Her dad had fended off media questions with the skill of the politician he was destined to become, perhaps even a U.S. Congressman. Being his daughter, she could read even the subtle variances in his facial expressions, and where no one other than her mother might suspect, she knew that the burden of his office under such trying circumstances was taking a toll on him. Willie Mullins cared. He cared about what had happened to the two murdered women and he cared about the hell their families were experiencing. And he cared about Whitney Poole.

Once back at headquarters, J.D. placed his hand on the small of Tam's back as they entered the building. "You're worried about your father, aren't you?"

Apparently she wasn't as adept at hiding her feelings as her father was. "He's taking all the hits from the press, when we're the ones who aren't accomplishing anything. We've got zip. Nada. We have no idea who this guy is or why he's targeting young brunettes."

"Unless it turns out that he's somehow connected to the old Baby Blue cases," J.D. reminded her.

"And if he is, if the DNA tests confirm that the skeletons belong to a couple of Baby Blue toddlers, what does that give us? How does that help us find this guy?"

J.D. followed Tam into the office she shared with Sergeant Hudson, who had entered the PSC before they had and had gone straight to the bathroom.

"If the DNA test results confirm what we suspect, then that's another piece of a very intricate puzzle. We start putting those pieces together, one at a time, and you never know what even a partial picture might reveal."

Tam flopped down in the swivel chair behind her desk, leaned back, and cushioned the crown of her head with her cupped hands. "I didn't peg you for an optimist, Special Agent Cass."

J.D. grinned. "And I didn't peg you for a pessimist, Officer Lovelady."

"I'm not. Not usually. But seeing the way these cases are affecting my father, not to mention what it'll do to Audrey and her family if one of those skeletons turns out to be Blake, has put me in a negative frame of mind."

"All we need is one lucky break," J.D. reminded her. "Someone who saw something."

"Someone other than a seventy-year-old, nearsighted woman." Tam groaned as she sat up straight.

"This guy is human. He's made mistakes. We just have to find out what they are. Once we figure out how he's slipped up, then it's only a matter of time until we nab him."

"Well, I'd like to figure out what, if any, mistakes he's made before he kills Whitney Poole." Tam looked J.D. square in the eye. "If he stays true to form, then we have less than two weeks to connect the dots before he props her dead body up in a rocking chair and sticks a toddler's skeleton in her arms."

The phone on Garth's desk rang just as he entered the office. Without even glancing at Tam or J.D., he walked over and picked up the receiver.

Garth's face paled. "Why the hell didn't they notify us yesterday? Yeah, sure. But God damn it, Willie, this isn't just some case, is it?"

Garth was talking to her father? She and J.D. exchanged puzzled expressions.

"Yeah, I'll tell them." Garth gripped the phone with white-knuckled tension. "I agree. We don't want word of this leaking out until the families have been notified."

Tam rose to her feet. She and J.D. were so focused on Garth that when he hung up the phone, he couldn't help but feel them staring at him. He glanced from J.D. to Tam.

"What was that all about?" she asked.

Garth swallowed. "That was your dad. He just got a call

from Dr. Reynolds. It seems the DNA test results came back yesterday afternoon, but there was a mix-up about who was supposed to notify the chief."

Tam's heart beat so hard and fast that she thought it was going to jump out of her chest. "Tell us. What were the results?"

"The toddler skeletons' DNA matched the DNA for Keith Lawson and Chase Wilcox," Garth said.

"Oh, God!" Tam reached out and gripped Garth's tense shoulder.

"Keith and Chase were the first two, weren't they?" J.D. said. "The first two toddlers who came up missing. Possibly the first two of Regina Bennett's victims."

Garth dropped down into his chair, stared at the floor, and cursed a blue streak.

Chapter 17

All J.D. wanted to do was pick up his daughter and take her home. He'd considered calling and telling her he was sending a taxi to pick her up, but if he had, she would have asked him half a dozen questions. Questions he couldn't have answered over the phone. Once the initial shock had worn off, Garth Hudson had recovered quickly and explained that until Keith Lawson's and Chase Wilcox's families had been notified, the information was to be kept under wraps.

"Willie . . . the chief has given me"—he had looked at Tam—"us permission to tell Hart and Audrey. He'll speak to Wayne himself."

"I'll tell Audrey," Tam had volunteered.

Garth had nodded agreement. "First, we need to track down the Lawson and Wilcox families. If any of them still live in the area, we'll go see them personally. If not, well . . ." Garth had huffed. "It's not the kind of news you want to deliver over the phone.'"

J.D. had stayed at police headquarters long enough that his departure didn't look like a hasty getaway. But the sooner he picked up Zoe, the better. It was only a matter of time before Tam showed up to tell Audrey that the toddler skeletons had been positively identified.

Wanting to get in and out quickly and be gone before Tam arrived, J.D. tapped his foot nervously after he rang the doorbell. He hadn't expected Zoe to open the door.

"Hi." She smiled at him, something she seldom did. "Come on in."

"Where's Dr. Sherrod?" he asked as he stepped over the threshold.

"In the kitchen. The peach cobbler we made is ready to come out of the oven, so she asked me to see who was at the door."

"Peach cobbler? I thought you were making cookies."

"We made sugar cookies," Zoe said. "And some of your favorite, too—chocolate chip. But Audrey said I can take those home with me."

"That's nice. And speaking of going home, are you about ready? We don't want you overstaying your welcome, do we?"

Zoe stared at him as if he were speaking a foreign language that she didn't understand. But before Zoe could respond, Audrey came out of the kitchen—a floral apron tied around her waist—and had apparently heard what he'd just said.

"Zoe certainly hasn't overstayed her welcome." There was a hard glint in Audrey's eyes, telling him plainly that she didn't approve of his comment. "We've had fun today. I enjoyed her company a great deal."

The expression on Zoe's face when she looked at Audrey Sherrod bordered on hero worship.

When Zoe turned to him, she smiled tentatively. "See, you were wrong. We don't have to rush off. Come on in, J.D. We—Audrey and I—cooked supper and everything's ready. We were just waiting for you."

J.D. forced a smile, not wanting Zoe to realize how badly he wanted them to leave. "You cooked, huh?"

Audrey walked over and draped her arm around Zoe's shoulders. "Your daughter seems to have a natural talent for it. She made the peach cobbler all by herself."

Zoe beamed with pride. "I did, but Audrey talked me through the whole process. And it was pretty easy."

"That's great. I'm glad you've had such a good time with Dr. Sherrod, and I appreciate—"

"Zoe, why don't you check on the potatoes," Audrey said. "They should be just about ready."

Without a moment's hesitation, Zoe whirled around and headed into the kitchen. The minute she was out of earshot, Audrey attacked.

"So help me, if you hurt that child's feelings by refusing to stay and eat dinner—the dinner she worked so hard this afternoon to prepare for you—I won't be held responsible for what I'll do to you."

J.D. didn't know whether to laugh or feel insulted. He tried not to grin. Audrey Sherrod had retaliated like a mama bear defending her cub.

"I'm sorry." J.D. huffed in frustration. "I don't want to hurt Zoe's feelings, and unfortunately, I seem to do just that quite often. I had no idea you two prepared a meal together and—"

"A meal your daughter prepared for you." Audrey glared at him. "Are you such an insensitive moron that you don't understand the significance?"

Had she just called him an insensitive moron? The cool, dignified Dr. Sherrod? He chuckled. She didn't. When their gazes met and locked, he realized that she was furious. Furious with him.

"You're right," J.D. admitted. "I can be an insensitive moron and I have been with Zoe on numerous occasions, but in my defense, I had a good reason this evening for wanting to get her out of here as soon as possible."

When he noted the puzzled look on Audrey's face, he groaned. Now, she'd want him to explain.

"The potatoes are ready . . . I think," Zoe called out from the kitchen doorway. "What do I do next? I've never creamed potatoes before."

J.D. inclined his head toward the kitchen. "You'd better go show her how."

"Be right there," Audrey told Zoe before she said to J.D., "After dinner, you and I are going to talk. Alone."

Lucky for J.D., Tam showed up just as they were finishing dinner. He was complimenting the chefs on the delicious meal when the doorbell rang. Audrey lifted her napkin from her lap, folded it, and placed it on the table; then she got up and went to the door.

J.D. downed the last bite of scrumptious cobbler before saying to Zoe, "Why don't you and I clear the table and then clean up in the kitchen?"

"Absolutely." Zoe stood and began stacking the dirty dishes.

As soon as Tam walked into Audrey's home, she saw that she had company. If she was surprised by seeing J.D. and Zoe clearing away the dining table, she hid it well.

"I didn't know you'd have dinner guests," Tam said.

"It's all right. We're finished," Audrey told her. "Zoe wanted to surprise her father, so I helped her prepare dinner for him."

Tam's brows rose as she widened her eyes in a just-what's-really-going-on-here appraisal of the situation. "Oh, I see." But it was obvious that she didn't.

"Where's Marcus?" Audrey asked.

"This isn't exactly a social call." Tam grasped Audrey's hands.

Audrey's face paled.

"Come on, Zoe, let's go in the kitchen and get started on cleanup," J.D. said.

Zoe did as he requested and carried a handful of dirty dishes into the kitchen. Once J.D. closed the door, she turned and faced him.

"Want to tell me what's going on?"

"Officer Lovelady needed to talk to Dr. Sherrod privately. They're close friends and—"

"I heard her say that this wasn't a social call," Zoe told him.

Damn! "Look, honey, this is none of your business."

When Zoe stared at him, her eyes filled with hurt, he cursed himself for not being more tactful. "Zoe . . ."

She spun around, carried the dishes across the room, and lowered them into the sink. He followed her, and when he placed his hand on her shoulder, she shrugged his hand off and refused to look at him.

"I should have put that more diplomatically," he said. "It's not any of your business because it's a police matter, and the only reason I know what Officer Lovelady is telling Audrey—Dr. Sherrod—is because it concerns me as a TBI agent. Do you understand?"

She lifted her head and glanced over her shoulder, a fine mist of tears in her eyes. She nodded.

J.D. wanted to grab his little girl, wrap her in his arms, and banish the hurt he had inflicted. Audrey had been right. He was an insensitive moron.

"Dinner was delicious," he said. "I enjoyed every bite, especially the peach cobbler. I appreciate all the hard work you did preparing the meal."

"I had fun and so did Audrey. She's great, J.D. And you know what? She likes me. She really likes me."

"And you like her, too, don't you?"

"Yeah, I do. A lot." She searched his face as she asked, "Is what Officer Lovelady has to tell Audrey bad news?"

"Sort of."

"Then she'll be sad."

"Probably."

"I wish I could help her," Zoe said. "Maybe I could stay over again tonight and be here for her."

"I don't think that's a good idea."

"Why? Because you think I'm not grown-up enough to understand what it's like to be unhappy and need a friend who cares about me?"

"Tamara—Officer Lovelady—is Audrey's friend," J.D. tried to explain. "And Audrey also has a father and an uncle and a brother. If she needs somebody, she's got family."

Zoe snorted. "So she has family. Big whoop-de-do. Why aren't any of them here? Where's her father? Where are her brother and her uncle? I didn't see anybody out there with her except her friend. And I'm her friend, too. She said so."

"Zoe, honey, you don't understand."

She glared at him, anger turning her brown eyes black. "Don't tell me that I don't understand. The guy I thought was my father was never around. He left and never looked back. And my mother was too busy having a good time to be bothered with a little kid. Do you know how many different people she left me with while she went out and partied? I slept on sofas and pallets in washrooms and even in a cardboard box behind some friend of hers's trailer." She took a deep breath, got a second wind, and lit into him with a vengeance. "And then there's you, J.D. My father. My real father, one of the many, many guys who screwed Carrie Davidson, and the poor sucker whose condom must have had a hole in it. God, I'll bet you prayed real hard when we were waiting for those DNA results that I wasn't your kid."

J.D. wished he could deny her accusation, but he couldn't, not without lying to her. "Zoe, I—I . . . I'm trying, you know."

When he couldn't bring himself to lie to Zoe, she knew she'd been right. "Yeah, sure. You're trying to be a dad, trying to take care of me, trying to love me. But you don't love me. You hate me. And I don't blame you. Who could love a messed-up, unlovable girl like me?"

"Oh, God, Zoe." When he reached out for her, she screamed at him.

"Don't touch me! And don't you dare feel sorry for me."

The kitchen door swung open and Audrey rushed into the room, swept past J.D. without even a sideways glance, and went straight to Zoe.

"We could hear y'all arguing." Standing in the doorway, Tamara Lovelady scowled at J.D.

Audrey put her arm around Zoe and walked her past J.D. and Tam, who closed the kitchen door and continued glaring at J.D.

"What the hell's going on?" Tam asked.

"My daughter and I had an argument."

"That's not what I meant." She marched over to J.D., got right up in his face, and asked, "What are you doing here? What's your daughter doing here?"

"It's a long story."

"I've got plenty of time."

J.D. gave her the condensed version, and when he finished explaining, he added, "I need to apologize to Aud—Dr. Sherrod—and take Zoe home."

"You didn't ask how Audrey took the news about the DNA results on the skeletons."

"With her usual dignified composure, I'm sure."

Tam's mouth gaped. "You son of a bitch. You have no idea. You don't know the first thing about Audrey, and yet you assume because she doesn't go off the deep end, she's unemotional. Nothing could be further from the truth. That woman in there"—she flung out her arm to indicate the other room—"is the most loving, caring, tenderhearted person I know. I would have thought you would realize that by the way she's treated your daughter."

Okay, he gave up. Every time he opened his mouth, he said the wrong thing. Tam Lovelady was the third female who had chewed his ass out this evening.

What does that tell you, buddy boy?

"It's already been pointed out to me that I'm an insensitive moron."

"Who am I to disagree," Tam said. "Look, I'm heading out. Audrey insisted. Just as I was about to leave, we heard the explosion in here."

"I am sorry about that."

"Apologize to Audrey. Better yet, apologize to your daughter."

"You accused me of judging Audrey when I really don't know her, but aren't you doing the same thing now, judging me without really knowing me or the situation with my daughter?"

Tam shrugged. "Why don't you give them a few minutes so that Audrey can talk to her?" She glanced at the stack of dirty dishes and cooking utensils. "Looks like you've got plenty to do in here until they're ready to talk to you."

J.D. groaned. "Yeah, looks like I do."

Wayne left Willie and Geraldine's home and drove straight to the neat brick house on Meadowhill Lane. Grace stood in the doorway, love and concern etched on her pretty features. He got out of the Silverado and walked into the arms of the woman waiting for him.

She kissed his cheek and asked softly, "How bad is it?"

He hugged her close and then pulled back and took her hand in his. "The DNA results came in." There was no easy way to say this, no way to cushion the blow. "The bodies belong to Keith Lawson and Chase Wilcox."

Grace gasped inaudibly, an involuntary indrawn breath, as she squeezed Wayne's hand. They both knew those names as well as they knew their own. The names of all the missing toddlers were forever branded on their hearts and minds.

"Then—then she did kill them, didn't she? Regina Bennett murdered . . ." Grace swallowed the tears caught in her throat. "All these years . . . hoping, praying, trying to hold on to the possibility, no matter how faint, that Shane . . ." She reached up and cradled Wayne's face with her open palms. "And Blake. They're dead, too, aren't they? That's what this means, that your son and my son are both dead."

Wayne pulled Grace back into his arms and held her as she cried.

Cry for me, honey. Cry until there are no tears left.

Garth sat alone in his office, the lights out, the only illumination coming from the one-bulb lamp on his desk. Saturday night used to be his night to howl and occasionally still was, despite him being past fifty now. He'd never been handsome, never had the kind of looks that drew women to him like moths to a flame. But he'd done all right with the fair sex. Hell, he'd been married four times, hadn't he? And he'd gotten his fair share of pussy. He sure as hell had never had to pay for it, although there had been a few times when he'd been in the mood for something special that he'd handed over some cold hard cash.

That's what he needed tonight. A woman who'd give him what he wanted—a few hours to forget about the past. All he had to do was drag his sorry ass out of there and head over to his favorite bar. The owner, Peggy Ann, was a lady who had never turned him away, not in the fifteen years he'd known her. More than once, she had put him up at her place overnight and let him sleep it off after he'd gotten totally wasted. If he drowned his sorrows tonight, he'd pay for it tomorrow, of course, but better to face reality with a bitch of a hangover than to go slowly out of his mind tonight. And that's what would happen if he stayed sober.

He had thought that it was long over, buried in the past so deep that it could never resurface. God damn it all, Blake and Enid had been gone for twenty-five years. Regina Bennett had been apprehended more than two decades ago and had spent the rest of her life in the nuthouse. They had all dealt with what had happened and moved on, he and Wayne and Hart and Audrey, each in their own way.

Why was this happening? Why, dear God, why?

Hadn't enough lives been destroyed? Hadn't everyone involved paid more than enough in pain and suffering and guilt? God, the guilt!

If any one of them had done something different in the past, would Blake still be alive? Would Enid? If he could go back to that day, the day Blake had gone missing, what could he change, what would he do differently?

Stop doing this to yourself!

Garth stood, slipped on his jacket, and turned off the lamp.

He'd have to tell Hart, but not tonight. Tomorrow would be soon enough. He had to find a way to help the boy, to prevent him from going off the deep end. He had spent years trying to keep his nephew clean and sober, but now he wondered if maybe . . . if getting drunk and staying drunk or getting high was the only way Hart could cope . . .

What about the other Baby Blue toddlers? How would their parents deal with the truth? Two families would soon learn the fate of their missing children. And once the information became public knowledge, what then?

If they didn't find the Rocking Chair Killer and stop him,

it was only a matter of time, wasn't it, before the bodies of the other missing toddlers showed up?

Keith Lawson's parents would have to be told. A quick search had revealed that the couple had divorced years ago; each had remarried and had children with their new mates. He still lived in the Chattanooga area. She lived in Knoxville.

Chase Wilcox's mother had died three years ago. His father now lived with his daughter in Nashville. She had been born after Chase had disappeared. Chase's brother, Blaine, five years older, was a detective with the Nashville PD.

As soon as Willie told Wayne about the DNA results, his former brother-in-law would go straight to Grace Douglas, was probably with her now. Wayne thought Garth didn't know about Grace. And Garth had never said any different. He figured Wayne's relationship with Shane Douglas's mother was a private matter between the two of them. Hell, he didn't give a rat's ass who Wayne was screwing. It wasn't as if he was being unfaithful to Enid.

Garth breathed in the night air as he left the station and walked across the road to the parking lot. The arthritis in his knees ached something awful tonight. Damn, getting old was the pits.

As he headed for his car, he thought about Audrey. Tam had told her by now. She knew about the DNA results. Knew the skeletons belonged to the first two Baby Blue toddlers. But Garth didn't have to worry about Audrey. Wayne's daughter was strong. She always had been, even as a little kid.

She'd be okay.

As long as she didn't remember. As long as the old nightmares didn't return.

Why was Enid screaming? Why was Hart crying? What was Uncle Garth doing here?

"Hart? Hart, what's wrong?" Audrey asked her step-brother.

He didn't answer. His tear-filled eyes stared straight ahead as he continued sobbing softly.

"Where's Daddy? I want my daddy." Audrey ran out of the house and into the backyard.

Something was wrong. Horribly wrong.

Enid cried a lot, but not like that, not screaming her head off. And Hart. Why did he look so funny, his eyes all blank and spooky, as if he was scared to death?

Something had happened to Blake.

Something terrible.

Poor Daddy. He loved Blake so very, very much.

Audrey felt strong hands grip her shoulders. "Daddy?" But the hands that turned her around did not belong to her father.

"Uncle Garth?"

He smoothed the flyaway tendrils of her waist-length hair out of her face and wiped the tears from her cheeks with his fingertips. "It's all right, Audrey. Don't be afraid."

"What happened to Blake?"

"Blake's gone," Uncle Garth said. "Do you hear me, Audrey, he's gone. Somebody came into the house while you and Hart were playing outside and Enid was asleep, and that person stole him. Your brother has been kidnapped."

"Kidnapped?"

"Yeah, sweetie, that's what happened."

"Daddy?"

"I've called your father. He's on his way home now." Uncle Garth squeezed her shoulders. "I need for you to be a big girl and not bother anybody. Your daddy doesn't need you bothering him. I'll look after you and Hart. I'm not going to let anybody ask you and Hart a lot of questions that will upset y'all. I'll protect you, both of you. Just do what I tell you to do. Do you understand?"

She nodded. "Yes, Uncle Garth."

"And if you need to talk to somebody about what happened today, you talk to me, okay?" He searched her eyes as if trying to decide whether or not she understood. "Losing Blake . . . it's going to kill your daddy and Enid." The last sentence he'd said almost as an afterthought.

Enid's anguished screams and mournful weeping replayed itself over and over again in Audrey's mind as she huddled near the fence in the backyard. The sirens wailed as police cars surrounded the house and an ambulance pulled into the driveway right behind Uncle Garth's car. Curious neighbors lined the street and peered over the fence. Audrey squatted on her knees and curled up as small and tight as humanly possible, hoping no one could see her.

Blake was gone.

Uncle Garth said someone had stolen her baby brother.

Audrey woke with a start and realized she'd been dreaming.

She didn't turn on a light, didn't get out of bed, didn't even glance at the bedside clock. For years after Blake's disappearance, she had been plagued with terrifying nightmares that often made no sense whatsoever. Occasionally, she simply relived that day or part of it, remembering bits and pieces. But the feelings were always the same. A strange mixture of sadness and fear. Even now, she still wasn't sure why memories of that day evoked a sense of fear deep inside her. The only reasonable explanation was that being a child herself, she had been afraid that she, too, might be abducted, that Blake's fate might become her fate.

If only her father had allowed her and Hart to stay in therapy longer than a few weeks. If they could have received, at the very least, some type of ongoing grief counseling, perhaps their lives would be different now. Of course, hindsight was twenty/twenty.

But Daddy and Uncle Garth had done what they thought was best at the time. Big, strong He-Men types sucked it up and went on. They didn't want or need some "headshrinker" asking them about their feelings. Neither of them made allowances for the fact that she and Hart were children who had been traumatized by the abduction of their baby brother. An abduction that took place while they were supposed to be taking care of their brother.

J.D. Cass was the same kind of man, cut from the same cloth as her father and uncle. He alternated between bulldozing over his daughter and neglecting her. He didn't know the first thing about being a good parent.

She believed Zoe had been right when she'd said, "My father doesn't love me and he sure doesn't want me."

Didn't J.D. have any idea how lucky he was to have a beautiful, smart, amazing daughter like Zoe? How many parents who had lost a child would gladly swap places with J.D.? Charlie and Mary Nell Scott would. Debra Gregory's mother would.

And what about Keith Lawson's parents? And Chase Wilcox's?

"And Daddy," she said aloud. Her father would give up anything and everything if he could have Blake back. He'd swap her for his son in a heartbeat.

Damn, Audrey, let it go. What is, is.

She had to stop comparing J.D. to her father. It wasn't fair to J.D. to make him pay for her father's sins.

J.D. had apologized to Zoe. And he had apologized to her.

Her father had never apologized to her for anything he'd ever said or done. Not even when he had accused her of wishing Blake dead, all the while knowing it wasn't true.

And J.D. had agreed to family counseling, hadn't he? That alone should prove he was different.

Audrey groaned. Monday she would have to refer J.D. and Zoe to one of her colleagues for family counseling now that she was personally involved with Zoe. And heaven help her, she was involved with J.D., too.

Chapter 18

J.D. had immersed himself in work, leaving the situation with Zoe as it was. He had apologized to her and she had accepted his apology, but nothing had really changed between them. Things weren't any better, but thank God, they didn't seem to be any worse. His job was something he understood and could for the most part control, unlike his daughter. It seemed that the harder he tried to be a good father, the more he screwed up. Why was it that Audrey Sherrod, unmarried and childless, seemed to instantly connect with Zoe, where he, her own father, had no idea how to deal with a teenage girl? Maybe that was it—Zoe was a girl and Audrey was a girl. Girls understood one another. Or it could be as simple as Audrey's knowledge and experience as a mental health therapist giving her an edge. Or could the fact that Audrey had lost her own mother when she was just a kid be the reason she had been able to form an instant bond with Zoe?

Audrey had phoned him on Monday to tell him that she had set up a five o'clock Friday afternoon appointment with Dr. Sally Woodruff.

"I've known Sally for years and I respect her as a person

and as a therapist," Audrey had said. "She and her husband Jim are friends as well as colleagues. I've always thought of Sally as my professional mentor."

J.D. had felt relieved that he wouldn't have to sit through counseling sessions week after week and have Audrey judge him as a father and as a human being and find him lacking on both counts. "I'm okay with the switch in counselors, but how do you think Zoe will take this news?"

"Actually, I spoke to Zoe first, and after I explained my reasons for handing y'all over to another counselor, she understood. She says that she's fine with having Sally as her counselor."

"She is? I'm amazed."

"Why? Because your daughter reacted in a rational manner and didn't throw a hissy fit?"

"Yeah, something like that."

"Perhaps if you would explain things to her first, before issuing orders, you might get a more positive reaction."

He had come close to losing his temper and telling Dr. Sherrod exactly what she could do with her advice. Instead, he had grunted and said, "Anything else you want to say to me?"

"Only one other thing—Zoe and I would like your permission for me to become an unofficial big sister to her. I've worked with the Big Brothers Big Sisters organization in the past and I've been a big sister to several young girls. But this time I wouldn't be going through the regular channels, just doing this on my own. Zoe needs a strong female role model in her life. I think it would help her tremendously. And it's something both Zoe and I—"

"You have my permission."

He had replied instantly. After all, how could he possibly object? Zoe did need a strong female role model, someone she could admire and emulate, someone who really cared about her, someone who understood her. And Dr. Audrey

Sherrod was the ideal person, seemingly the only person who fulfilled all the requirements. Besides that, apparently she was eager to take on the problems of an unhappy, often angry and rebellious teenager.

During the past four days since Audrey's phone call, she had eaten lunch with Zoe at school on Tuesday and again today. Zoe was supposed to spend the evening with Audrey tonight so that she could help Zoe with a class project. J.D. had no idea what the project was because his daughter had not bothered to share that information with him. But then, he could have asked her about it, which he hadn't done.

As he zipped in and out of heavy traffic, trying not to be late for his morning meeting with Tamara Lovelady, J.D. turned his thoughts from his personal life to his professional life. But before he'd had a chance to focus on the crossover cases—Baby Blue kidnappings and Rocking Chair Murders—his phone rang.

He answered on the second ring. "Special Agent Cass."

"Well, hello, Special Agent Cass." Holly Johnston's sultry voice held a tinge of amusement. "I haven't heard from you in a while."

"I've been busy. You know what's been going on."

"I know what the DA knows. The Rocking Chair Murders have become even more bizarre now that we know those skeletons belong to a couple of the little boys kidnapped all those years ago. It's just plain weird."

"That it is."

"I didn't call to talk business," she admitted. "I thought you might be free tonight. I could sure use some of your special brand of TLC." Her sexy sigh told him just how much she wanted him.

"Tonight's not good for me." *Why the hell not?* Zoe would be at Audrey's house until ten. That would give him plenty of time for some R&R with the gorgeous ADA.

"Tomorrow night, then?"

"Maybe. Let me get back to you first thing in the morning."

"If I didn't know better, I'd think you've found yourself another playmate," Holly said. "If you have, just say so and don't waste my time."

"At present, you're my one and only playmate," he assured her.

Holly laughed. "Then call me in the morning, but if you think I'll wait around for you, think again. If you're too busy tomorrow night . . ."

Did she think it would bother him if she had sex with another guy? He didn't give a damn if she screwed a dozen other guys. "I understand. You're a popular girl, and if I prefer not to come running when you snap your fingers, you'll find someone else who will."

"Is that what you think I'm doing, snapping my fingers?"

"Maybe."

"Sorry. I guess I forgot who I was talking to, didn't I? If you're free tomorrow night, call me in the morning, and if I don't hear from you by noon, I'll consider our mutually satisfying relationship over. How's that?"

Did she just issue him an ultimatum? "Sounds about right to me."

"God, I'm glad I didn't fall in love with you," Holly told him, an angry edge to her voice. "But I hope I'm around when you finally fall, and you will. One of these days, you'll fall hard, and some woman will have you eating out of the palm of her hand."

The idea of him being pussy-whipped by some unknown woman out there somewhere amused J.D. He hadn't meant to laugh, knowing it would only piss Holly off more than she already was, but he did.

"Don't hold your breath," he told her. "Not even my ex had that kind of power over me."

"Maybe that's why your marriage imploded."

"Maybe. Or maybe it was because she found somebody else." Some guy who had been able to give her what he couldn't. Erin had wanted a man who would worship at her feet, a guy who'd sit around adoring her from daylight to dark. He wasn't that type of guy. Never had been. Never would be.

Holly reversed gears and, breathing heavily, proceeded to remind him of all of the little bedroom tricks that she knew he enjoyed.

Her vivid descriptions aroused him. A man would have to be dead not to respond to such erotic promises. But oddly enough, he wasn't thinking about Holly, about her big tits, her rounded butt, or her talented mouth. No, damn it to hell, the woman who came to mind was the tall, slender, aloof Dr. Sherrod.

J.D. grimaced. How stupid was he? He wasn't interested in Audrey Sherrod, not in that way. Hell, he didn't even like the woman, and she certainly didn't like him. That was one road he would never travel. No way.

"My father thinks that Garth and I should consider handing over the Rocking Chair Killer cases to another team," Tam explained to J.D. shortly after he entered the office she shared with Garth. "He believes that all of us, him included, are too personally connected to the Baby Blue kidnappings to remain objective."

"What do you think?"

"Honestly?" She shrugged. "I don't know. I'd like to think that despite the current investigation overlapping with the old cold cases, we can do our jobs effectively without allowing our emotional connection to one of the missing toddlers to cloud our judgment."

"You'll be walking a tightrope," J.D. said. "Especially

Garth, since that missing toddler was his nephew." He glanced through the open door. "Where is Garth?"

"Talking to Dad, trying to persuade him not to replace us."

"Hmm . . . Your family and the Sherrod family have been friends for a long time, huh?"

"As long as I can remember," Tam said. "My dad and Wayne went through the academy together. And Audrey's mom and mine were college friends, which considering their vastly different backgrounds seems implausible. My mother never knew her father, and her mother worked two jobs to support them, so for the most part my mom was raised by her grandmother. My mother grew up very poor whereas Norma Colton grew up with the proverbial silver spoon in her mouth."

"Audrey's mother came from money?" He should have known. Despite being the daughter of a retired police sergeant, she had an air of superiority that often came with being filthy rich.

"Oh, yes. Norma came from old Chattanooga royalty." Frowning, Tam shook her head and snorted. "Audrey's grandparents disowned Norma when she married Wayne Sherrod. Audrey never met her mother's parents, and even after Norma and Wayne divorced, she didn't try to mend any fences with them. Then when she died, her parents didn't come forward and acknowledge Audrey as their grandchild. Of course, that was years ago. Mr. and Mrs. Colton are both dead now."

"Interesting."

Tam eyed him suspiciously. "Why all the interest in Audrey?"

"I don't think I initially asked you about Audrey," he told her. "I believe I asked if your family and the Sherrod family had been close for a long time."

"So you did. My mistake."

Tam's close scrutiny bothered J.D. It was as if she were trying to read his mind. "Shall we exchange information about the case we're working on?" he asked, hurriedly changing the subject and getting back to business.

Tam rose from her desk. "It's about time for my morning break. I'm getting a Coke and some crackers out of the machine. Want anything?"

"Nothing, thanks."

She left him sitting there for only a few minutes. When she returned, she was munching on cheese and wheat crackers. She placed the open cola can on a colorful ceramic coaster before sitting down in the brown swivel chair behind her desk.

After chewing and swallowing and taking a sip of the Coke, she said, "Talk. I can listen and eat at the same time."

J.D. went over some basic info about the Baby Blue kidnapping cases and then tossed out a couple of the hypotheses he had discussed with George Bonner.

"Let me get this straight," Tam said. "You think it's possible that Jeremy Arden or one of the other kidnapped toddlers who somehow survived could be our killer?"

"It's a thought. We know that Jeremy Arden has been back in Chattanooga for a while now and that he visited Regina Bennett several times before she died."

"Why do you suspect Jeremy and not the unknown nephew?"

"Maybe Jeremy Arden and the nephew are one and the same."

"Oh . . ." Tam considered the possibility. "That would be a reasonable assumption if only one of them, either Arden or the nephew, had visited Regina Bennett, not both of them."

"Maybe only one of them did, but using two different names and possibly a disguise of some type when he visited as Corey Bennett."

"Why would he do that?" Tam asked.

"Who knows, maybe to throw suspicion off himself if anyone started snooping around trying to find out who had visited Regina."

"Okay, that's possible, but the idea that maybe one of the other Baby Blue toddlers survived isn't feasible. We know now that the first two missing boys are dead and the sixth boy was rescued. That leaves three possible survivors." Tam scrutinized him with a surely-you-don't-believe-this-is-true expression on her face. "There is no reason why Regina Bennett would have kept one of those little boys alive, not if she thought each one of them was her son Cody."

"Probably not," J.D. agreed. "Like I told you, I'm just tossing out possibilities. Anything and everything that might help us to discover who our Rocking Chair Killer is."

"Until a better choice becomes available, my money would be on Corey Bennett, whoever he is."

"Yeah, whoever he is."

"You don't think he exists, do you?"

"I think he exists, but I don't think he goes by the name of Corey Bennett."

"Was he ever Corey Bennett?" Tam asked.

"I'm not sure, but if he was, that means he was in some way related to Regina. Brother, cousin, uncle, nephew, or son."

"Son? But—but I thought Cody was her only child."

"The only child we know about," J.D. said.

"How could she have hidden a second child? When the FBI arrested her and rescued Jeremy Arden, there was no other child with her or with her aunt and uncle."

"And there's no record of Regina having any siblings or an uncle or a cousin or a son by the name of Corey. But it isn't out of the realm of possibility that she had another child, that he lived with her during the years when she killed Cody and the other toddlers."

"If that were true, then where was he when the FBI arrived at the farm that day?" Tam asked. "What did she do with him? And where has he been all these years?"

"I don't have the answers," J.D. admitted. "All I have are a few unsubstantiated scenarios and a lot of questions. Maybe Corey Bennett is Regina's other son. Maybe he's Jeremy Arden. Maybe he's really her nephew. Maybe Jeremy Arden is our Rocking Chair Killer, or it's possible, if there really is a Corey Bennett, he's our guy."

Tam dropped the two remaining crackers in the garbage, took a sip from the can of cola, and then said, "I'll agree that either is possible. But the idea that one of the other toddlers survived and is now killing Regina Bennett over and over again is a little far-fetched."

J.D.'s brow wrinkled. He knew Tam was right. "Okay, here's another scenario, a more probable one, but one you're not going to like and are going to refuse to consider."

"Try me."

"Okay. What if the killer is a member of one of the Baby Blue toddlers' families?"

She stared at him, her expression telling him plainly that she wasn't certain she'd heard him correctly, and if she had, she didn't quite grasp his insinuation.

"Each little boy had a mother and a father. Some of them had siblings. They had aunts and uncles and cousins," J.D. said. "Let's say that this guy named Corey Bennett had nothing to do with the murders; then our description of him is meaningless as far as a description of our killer goes."

"You think a relative of one of the Baby Blue victims is our killer?"

"It's worth looking into." J.D. leaned forward and gazed straight into Tam's big brown eyes. "Actually, I've gone over the list of close relatives for each boy, and I've narrowed the list down to the most likely."

"How did you narrow the list down? What criteria did you use?"

"Personal histories. I looked closely at members of each immediate family. A few people stood out, people with personal issues that tagged them as mentally or emotionally unstable."

J.D. noted the slight tremble in Tam's hand as she lifted the Coke to her mouth, and he didn't miss the way her jaw tensed after she swallowed.

When she didn't speak, J.D. said, "Jeremy Arden heads the list, of course. Devin Kelly's father, Steve Kelly, hasn't been able to hold down a steady job since his son disappeared. He has a drinking problem. He's been arrested numerous times for disorderly conduct. He's been married and divorced—"

"None of those personal problems make Mr. Kelly a serial killer," Tam said in the man's defense.

"I agree. No more than the fact that Sergeant Garth Hudson has a reputation as a hard-drinking womanizer who has been married and divorced four times and—"

"Stop right there. That sounds too much like an accusation against my partner."

"I'm not accusing anyone of anything," J.D. told her. "I'm just naming relatives who, for one reason or another, have lived problematic lives. Jeremy Arden, Steve Kelly, Garth Hudson, and his nephew, Hart Roberts." When J.D. noticed Tam's eyes widen and her mouth form a shocked oval, he quickly added, "Arden heads my list, but Hart Roberts runs a close second."

"You don't know what you're talking about." Tam jumped to her feet, her angry gaze damning J.D. for his opinion. "Hart is one of the gentlest souls you'll ever meet. The very idea that he might be a killer is the most idiotic thing I've ever heard. And whatever you do, don't you dare mention this to Garth."

"I realize Hart Roberts is Garth's nephew and Audrey Sherrod's stepbrother, but neither fact rules him out as a possible suspect."

"I refuse to listen to another word."

"I'm sorry." J.D. rose to his feet. "I thought it was our job to go over every possibility. If you can't simply look at the facts and accept that—"

"Damn it, you might as well accuse Wayne or even Audrey. You're talking about people I know, people who are no more capable of cold-blooded murder than I am."

"Look, I really am sorry. I should have taken your personal relationship with the family into consideration before shooting off my mouth. Besides, that scenario is just one of several. Take your pick from the others and let's pursue these one at a time. How does that sound?"

Tam drew in and then released a deep breath. "Okay." She nodded. "When Garth comes in, we'll talk to him, but you will not mention Hart's name. Understand? We'll start with Jeremy Arden and Corey Bennett and see where that investigation leads us." She glared at J.D. "Agreed?"

"Agreed."

Breaking a nail was no big deal. But when Audrey pried open an uncooperative file drawer and jammed her index finger in the process, it was the final straw. From the time she awoke that morning—after another of those nightmarish dreams about the day Blake disappeared—one thing after another had gone wrong. She had burned her toast, accidentally dropped her toothbrush into the toilet, spent fifteen wasted minutes looking for her misplaced keychain, and had, in her rush to leave the house, bumped her hip against the antique mahogany commode in the entrance hall.

The French-manicured acrylic nail on her right index finger broke off to the quick. Cursing as pain radiated from her severed nail up her finger and into her hand, Audrey grabbed a Kleenex from the box on her desk and managed to stop the bleeding quickly. She rushed into the bathroom, ran cool water over her entire hand, and with her left hand reached in the cabinet above the sink and removed a bottle of peroxide and a box of Band-Aids. Once she had cleaned the wound and stuck a Band-Aid over the end of her finger, she returned to her office.

Since she had strong-armed Hart into meeting her for lunch today, she would have to wait until after work to get her nail repaired.

Damn! She couldn't go after work because she was picking up Zoe for dinner at her house so that they could begin work on her science project. She had an hour and a half between appointments today. If her manicurist could see her immediately, she could still have lunch with Hart, but only if they changed restaurants and ate somewhere near the spa.

She phoned Jessica Smith and explained the situation. "Of course, Dr. Sherrod," Jessica said. "No problem. It won't take long to put on a new nail."

She dialed Hart's cell number and got his voice mail. "Hart, it's Audrey. Change of plans. Meet me at the Beauty and Rest Day Spa. I have a fingernail emergency." She laughed. "We can grab a bite at the Sandwich Shoppe next door to the spa."

On the short drive from her office to the spa, Audrey noticed a silver Lotus similar to Porter's in the heavy traffic behind her. But it probably wasn't Porter. He usually ate lunch downtown. Dismissing him from her thoughts, she fixated on her less-than-stellar morning. Adding to the other minor catastrophes, Donna had taken the day off for a root canal, one patient had canceled at the last minute, and Mrs. Fredericks had gone into one of her hysterical crying jags and thrown up on the floor, barely missing Audrey's black-and-white Manolo Blahnik slingback pumps.

God in heaven, Audrey! Emergency nail appointments to fix a broken acrylic nail. Concern about a pair of shoes, albeit an expensive pair that just happened to be one of her favorites. She certainly sounded like a pampered piece of fluff, didn't she?

Okay, so sue me, I'm a woman who likes to look good and appreciates fine things.

She needed to concentrate on what she was going to say to Hart. Since she'd learned the identity of the toddler skeletons found with the two murder victims, Audrey had seen her uncle Garth and they had discussed the situation. She had also spoken to her father on the phone, a succinct conversation that had been difficult for both of them. But Hart had not returned her phone calls, and Garth had told her that he was spending most of his time in his room.

"I've tried to talk to him, but he's dealing with this by pulling back and keeping to himself," Garth had said.

And then, like a minor miracle, Hart had phoned her yesterday. "I'm sorry I've been avoiding you. I just wasn't ready to talk to you or anybody else, not even Uncle Garth. But I know you won't believe I'm okay unless you see me in person, so, how about lunch tomorrow?"

Audrey pulled into the strip mall parking lot, three spaces down from the spa and directly in front of the sandwich shop. When she entered Beauty and Rest Day Spa, the receptionist welcomed her warmly.

Within minutes, she was seated in front of Jessica, who carefully removed the Band-Aid and frowned when she saw the ripped nail. "You know putting on a new nail will make it look good, but the pain won't go away completely until the skin heals."

"I know, but I'm vain enough to want the nail to look great and I'll just suffer the pain." Audrey smiled. "I really appreciate your working me in so quickly. Are you missing your lunch break because of this?"

"I'll grab a bite later," Jessica assured her. "Besides, you're going to give me a big tip, one that will cover the price of my lunch."

They looked at each other and smiled.

Jessica was a pretty young woman with brown eyes and a thick mane of long, dark hair that she kept confined to a ponytail while she worked. Audrey had never seen her wearing anything except jeans and a Beauty and Rest Day Spa T-shirt, the jeans revealing slender legs and hips and the T-shirt accentuating her high, full breasts.

Working quickly, Jessica put on the new nail and had just begun the paint job when Audrey glanced at the open doorway as a man entered the room.

"Hart?"

"Hi, sis."

"What are you doing here?"

"I thought I'd take a look at where you women get beautified," he said as his gaze settled on Jessica. "Hi there. I'm Hart Roberts, Audrey's brother."

He flashed his million-dollar smile and Jessica melted right before their eyes. "Oh. Hi, Hart." Jessica's cheeks flushed.

Merciful Lord! Jessica was smitten. Audrey had seen it happen too many times. Her stepbrother could be lethally charming, and few women could resist his blond good looks.

Please, don't hit on her, Audrey wanted to shout. *Leave her alone. She's young and sweet and innocent and you're no good for her.*

As if sensing Audrey's disapproval, Hart glanced away from Jessica and said, "Want me to go on over to the Sandwich Shoppe and order for us?"

"That would be great, thanks."

"What do you want?"

"Half a club sandwich and a cup of whatever their soup of the day is. And iced tea." When he hesitated, giving Jessica a complete once-over, Audrey cleared her throat. "I'll be there in five minutes, tops."

Hart grinned, winked at Jessica, and sauntered casually toward the door.

When he was out of earshot, Jessica said, "Your brother is gorgeous. He's not married, is he?"

For half a second, Audrey considered lying. "No, he's not married, but . . ."

"But?"

"Nothing. It's just that Hart's thirty-three, so he's a little old for you. If I remember correctly, you're twenty-two, right?"

"I'll be twenty-two next month," Jessica admitted. "I guess he is a little too old for me."

Hart didn't mean to break hearts right and left, but he did. He changed girlfriends as often as Audrey changed the sheets on her bed. Liking women wasn't a crime, but using them, as he used drugs and booze, to ease the deep ache inside him was a crime. A moral crime.

Audrey left Jessica a big tip and a word of advice. "If my brother asks you out, say no."

As she exited the spa and turned to her right, she caught a glimpse of a familiar car in her peripheral vision. Another silver Lotus Exige identical to Porter Bryant's cherished sports car. Of course, it couldn't be Porter's car. It was probably the same car she'd seen in her rearview mirror on the drive from her office to the spa. She couldn't think of any reason Porter would be parked at this strip mall.

Bracing herself for lunch with her brother, telling herself that she would not warn him about flirting with young girls, Audrey was caught off guard when someone came up behind her and grabbed her arm.

She whirled around, uncertain and slightly alarmed, and then heaved with relief when she saw the man's face. "Porter!"

"I thought that was you," he said. "Meeting someone for lunch in an out-of-the-way place? It wouldn't happen to be J.D. Cass, would it?"

A cautious knot formed in the pit of Audrey's stomach when she noticed the strangely accusatory look in Porter's eyes and felt his hand on her arm tighten painfully.

She jerked loose from his tenacious hold. "I'm having lunch with Hart, if it's any of your business."

Porter's smile sent off alarm bells inside Audrey.

My God, you're being silly. Porter Bryant is not dangerous.

"I'm glad to hear that," he told her. "I'd hate to see you get mixed up with a man like Cass."

"I appreciate your concern, but I can assure you that I'm not involved with Special Agent Cass. However, if I were, I'm quite capable of taking care of myself."

"I apologize if I overstepped with my concern." Porter looked at her longingly. "It's just that I care a great deal and wouldn't want you to get hurt."

Sensing the sincerity of his apology, Audrey leaned over and kissed his cheek. "Apology accepted. Take care, Porter. I'm sorry, but I have to run. Hart's waiting for me at the Sandwich Shoppe."

"Yes, of course. Go."

Audrey didn't glance back as she entered the restaurant. When she saw Hart at a window-side table, she hurried toward him and did her best to ignore the slightly uneasy feeling in the pit of her stomach. Surely, Porter Bryant wasn't stalking her.

Chapter 19

"Was that Porter Bryant you were talking to?" Hart asked when Audrey sat down at the table in the Sandwich Shoppe.

"Yes, it was Porter."

Hart examined her face closely. "What's wrong? Did Porter say something that upset you?"

Her stepbrother knew her too well and had apparently noted some nuance in her expression that hinted she was slightly unnerved. "No, not really. It's just he showed up out of nowhere and startled me."

"Do you think he followed you here?"

Audrey shook her head. "No, I don't think so. But . . . We've agreed not to see each other anymore. Our last date was supposed to have been this past Friday night, but something came up and I had to cancel."

"Another man?" The corners of Hart's mouth curved in a barely discernable smile.

"No. Certainly not."

"Maybe Porter isn't ready to end things. Could be he thinks there is another man and he followed you today to see who you were meeting."

Audrey released an agitated breath. "He did ask who I was meeting for lunch. For some reason, he thought my lunch date was with Special Agent Cass and he warned me not to become involved with J.D."

"He warned you? I don't like the sound of that." Hart rose halfway as he said, "I think maybe I'd better have a talk with Porter."

"No, you will not." Audrey laid her hand on Hart's arm and motioned for him to sit back down. He looked her in the eyes and saw that she meant what she'd said. "I can handle Porter. I don't need my brother socking him in the nose."

They both laughed, which eased the tension that had coiled tighter and tighter inside Audrey since the moment Porter had grabbed her arm outside the restaurant.

"Let's order, if you haven't already," Audrey suggested. "And forget all about Porter Bryant."

Hart motioned to the waitress, an attractive young blond who giggled the entire time she was taking their order. The girl looked to be about twenty, but that didn't stop Hart from flirting outrageously with her the moment he realized she couldn't take her eyes off him. As soon as she left to place their order with the cook, Hart watched her walk away, obviously appreciating the view of her slim hips and small, inverted heart–shaped derrière.

Audrey snapped her fingers and Hart turned to face her, his slightly wicked grin telling her that he knew she didn't approve of his interest in the waitress.

"You're shameless," she told him. "First Jessica and now our waitress, who is just barely legal. She could be eighteen, certainly not a day over twenty."

"Ah, come on, sis. All I was doing was flirting a little." When he noted that she was still frowning, he added, "I flirt a little, but most of the time, that's all. If I ask a woman out, I don't lead her on. I tell her, up front, that I'm not into anything serious, that I'm a recovering alcoholic and addict, and for her not to get any ideas about being the one who's going to save me from myself."

"Oh, Hart." Audrey reached across the table and laid her hand over his.

"I'm not a complete asshole, you know. But I do like the ladies. I always have." He gave her hand a gentle squeeze. "You didn't want to see me to discuss my love life."

The waitress brought their glasses of sweet iced tea, but when Hart didn't pay any attention to her, she didn't tarry.

"I thought we should talk about the DNA results, about the Baby Blue toddlers . . . about Blake." *About the fact that I'm having nightmares again and I'm sure you are, too.*

"What's there to talk about?" Hart asked.

"The fact that after all these years, two of the toddlers have been found."

"Yeah, both of them dead."

"If the Rocking Chair Killer murders Whitney Poole before the police can find her, then there's a good possibility that another toddler skeleton will show up. What if . . . ?" She paused, her thoughts almost unbearable.

"What if the next corpse is Blake's?" Hart finished for her.

"For years, I've hoped and prayed for a miracle, that somehow Blake was still alive, that he wasn't one of Regina Bennett's victims," Audrey said. "I know how illogical that sounds."

"Don't you think that Dad has held on to the hope that Blake's alive? And God knows that I'd give anything . . ." Hart swallowed. "And Uncle Garth . . . We'd all like for Blake to be alive and well and for him to come home to us, but it's not going to happen. You have to know that Blake's dead. He's been dead for twenty-five years."

Biting down on her bottom lip, Audrey nodded. "I know. In my mind, I know." She laid her hand in the center of her chest. "But in my heart . . . If, God forbid, another toddler corpse shows up and it turns out to be Blake, it could bring closure for all of us. But I don't know how Dad will react. I have absolutely no idea what my father thinks or feels or . . . God, Hart, I don't know my own father. I don't think I ever did."

The waitress returned with their lunch order—sandwiches, soup, chips, pickles, and a fruit cup for Audrey and a slice of apple pie for Hart.

Suddenly the very thought of eating tightened Audrey's throat. She wasn't sure she could swallow a bite. Hart bit off a huge chunk of his steak and cheese sandwich, apparently not having a problem eating.

Audrey took a sip of tea. "I've been having nightmares again."

He lifted his head and stared at her. "Since when?"

"Since the first Rocking Chair Murder."

"I thought . . . I mean, it's been years, hasn't it, since you dreamed about Blake, about that day?"

"You'd think that after all these years, the dreams wouldn't still be so vivid, as if it had all happened only yesterday."

"Are the dreams just like they used to be?"

"Pretty much. Parts of the dreams are exactly the way I remember that day, but other parts are all mixed up and don't make a lot of sense. But that's the way dreams are. Dreams and nightmares." She forced out her question quickly. "Do you still have nightmares, too?"

Hart stopped eating. He became very still and very quiet. Then he inhaled a deep breath and exhaled slowly.

"Hell, sis, my whole life is a freaking nightmare. Awake or asleep, Blake haunts me. Inside my head, I've relived that day over and over again. If only, huh?" He picked up his sandwich and began eating again.

"It wasn't your fault," she told him. "And it wasn't my

fault. It wasn't anybody's fault. We were a couple of kids who shouldn't have been given the responsibility of looking after our baby brother. It wasn't Enid's fault because she was sick or my dad's fault because he was at work. Or Uncle Garth's fault because he couldn't find Blake."

Hart didn't respond. Audrey understood. After all, what else was there to say?

J.D. spent most of the day with Tam and Garth, who were still in charge of the Rocking Chair Killer cases. They had gone over the basic facts again, reread the eyewitness accounts, and discussed the forensic reports on the evidence found at each dump site. And now that they had irrefutable proof that the murder cases were somehow connected to the old Baby Blue kidnapping cases, even Garth reluctantly agreed that one of J.D.'s hypotheses about the killer's identity could be valid.

"If we could just figure out which, if any, of your scenarios is the right one," Tam said. "We could bring Jeremy Arden in for questioning, but unless he chooses to talk to us, we have nothing that we can use to hold him."

"Yeah, and if he's our guy, bringing him in would alert him to the fact that we're suspicious," Garth said. "Why not tail him first, see where he goes, who he spends time with, what he does?"

"Putting Arden under surveillance is a good idea," J.D. agreed. "But not just Arden."

Garth snorted. "Humph. You want to put a tail on me and Wayne and Hart and Steve Kelly, too? Do you honest to God think one of us is the Rocking Chair Killer?"

J.D. glared at Tam. Obviously Officer Lovelady had shared his comments about how any one of them, under certain circumstances, could be a suspect.

"Shit!" J.D. mumbled under his breath. "No, I don't actually think you or Wayne Sherrod is the killer. Steve Kelly is another matter. He's probably not our guy, but I wouldn't rule him out completely. And your nephew . . . I know you don't even want to consider the possibility that he—"

"Damn right I don't," Garth said. "Hart's a little screwed up, but he's not crazy. And there's no way he's a serial killer."

"Yeah, that's what Tam said." J.D. appraised the way Garth and his partner shared quick, cryptic glances and then deliberately avoided eye contact. Despite their vehement denials that Hart Roberts shouldn't even be considered as a suspect, did Tam and Garth actually have some doubts? Did they know something about Hart that they weren't sharing, something that could incriminate him?

When the silence dragged on for several minutes, those minutes seeming much longer than they actually were, Garth cleared his throat and tossed out a comment.

"You know, there's one possibility that we haven't considered."

"What's that?" J.D. asked.

"Maybe there isn't a connection between the Baby Blue cases and the Rocking Chair cases," Garth said.

J.D. could tell by Tam's puzzled expression that she was as surprised by her partner's remark as J.D. was.

"There's a connection," Tam said. "We have the DNA results and we've compared photos of the three kidnapped women to photos of Regina Bennett, and the resemblance is obvious."

"Yeah, all three women fit the same general profile. Young, attractive, long dark hair and brown eyes," Garth said. "I agree that our guy is abducting women who resemble one another, that he's targeting a specific type. But the fact that, years ago, Regina Bennett fit that profile doesn't mean that there's a connection between our victims and Regina."

"Are you forgetting about the toddler skeletons? About

the DNA tests that prove they belong to two of the Baby Blue toddlers?" J.D. asked.

"No, I haven't forgotten," Garth assured him. "But what if our killer somehow came across where Regina Bennett or somebody else had hidden the bodies? What if there's another explanation for why he put those toddlers in his victims' arms?"

"You're not making any sense," Tam told him. "What you're suggesting is too far-fetched to be believable. Why are you trying so hard to come up with another—?" She stopped midsentence as if suddenly understanding the reason behind Garth's absurd explanation.

Tam turned and walked toward the door. "I need a break. I'm going to take a walk."

Garth dropped down into the chair behind his desk. Then he reached up and rubbed the back of his neck.

J.D. rested his open palms on top of Garth's desk and leaned forward to look the other man right in the eye. "If you're so sure that there is no way your nephew could be our killer, then why make up some outlandish story about how the two cases might not be connected when you know damn well that they are?"

Garth Hudson glared at J.D. "Go fuck yourself, Cass. You're way out of line."

Audrey had purposefully not mentioned Dawson Cummings and had instead waited for Zoe to bring up the subject of the young man she had been bound and determined to date despite her father's objections.

"I think maybe J.D. was right about Dawson," Zoe said while sharing dinner with Audrey Thursday evening.

Without so much as batting an eyelash, Audrey asked, "How's that?"

"Well, he hasn't called me or tried to get in touch since he was arrested. And he hasn't answered any of my calls or text messages."

"And how does that make you feel?" Audrey asked.

Zoe laughed. "You sounded like a therapist just then and not a big sister."

"Sorry. Force of habit."

"It makes me feel stupid for ever thinking he cared about me," Zoe admitted. "And it makes me not care if I ever see him again."

"Hmm . . ." Audrey thought it best to be noncommittal about the subject of Dawson Cummings. Zoe was a smart girl who had made a good decision all on her own. "Ice cream for dessert? I have Turtle Tracks and plain vanilla."

"None for me, thanks."

"Maybe later, when we finish with your science project."

"Sounds good. Maybe J.D. can join us when he picks me up. Would you believe vanilla is his favorite?"

"Is it?"

She couldn't be Zoe's big sister without a certain amount of contact with J.D., but she could keep that contact to a minimum. She didn't have to invite him for dinner or even for coffee—or ice cream—when he dropped Zoe off and picked her up. As a matter of fact, in the future, she would probably rearrange her schedule so that she could pick Zoe up at school and then drive her home later and thus avoid even seeing J.D. on most occasions.

Providing Zoe with a pleasant domestic atmosphere, teaching her how to cook, and helping her realize her own potential as a young woman did not require Audrey and J.D. to interact on a personal level.

"Do you like my father?" Zoe asked.

The question took Audrey off guard. "What?"

"I don't mean do you have a thing for him. I just meant you don't dislike him, do you? Sometimes, I'm not sure about you two."

"I barely know your father," Audrey said. No way was she going to admit to Zoe that there were moments when she detested J.D. and other times when she liked him a little too much. "And no, of course, I don't dislike him."

"J.D.'s not a ladies' man," Zoe said. "Oh, he likes women and he . . . well . . . he has sex and all that." Zoe giggled. "Don't look at me that way. I'm fourteen, not four. I know when J.D. goes over to Holly Johnston's apartment, they do a lot more than hold hands."

"I'm not sure your father's love life is an appropriate subject for us to discuss."

"We're just talking in general terms," Zoe told her. "Nothing specific. Not that I know anything specific. Since I've been living with him, he's dated less than half a dozen women. Five, I think. Five in a little over a year isn't very many. And he's had an ongoing thing with only two. There was some woman named Denise back in Memphis when I first went to live with him, and for the past few months, it's been Holly." Zoe huffed loudly. "Holly's an A-Number-One bitch, if you ask me. And before you say anything, Holly doesn't like me any more than I like her."

"If your father is in a serious relationship with Holly, then you may have to find a way to get along with her."

Zoe snickered. "Serious relationship? J.D.? You've got to be kidding. You just wait and see if Dr. Woodruff doesn't come to the conclusion during our sessions that he's got commitment issues."

Audrey smiled. "Have you been psychoanalyzing your father, young lady?"

"He's not so hard to figure out. He had a bad marriage. Got burned. Enjoys being a loner. The last thing he ever wanted was a kid messing up his bachelor life." Zoe stood, stacked her soup bowl onto her plate, and carried them over to the sink.

Audrey cleared the rest of the table, and together she and

Zoe loaded the dishwasher. "I think your father is trying, but he just doesn't know how to be an instant father." She laid her hand on Zoe's shoulder. "You haven't exactly been helping him, you know."

"Yeah, I know. But it's not easy when it's obvious that he'd rather I didn't exist."

"Oh, I don't think that's true. Actually, I think he loves you, but he just doesn't know it yet."

"He doesn't love me. He just sees me as an obligation. He's not a bad man. He's got his principles and all. If he didn't, he'd have turned me over to social services and washed his hands of me."

"Then we agree that J.D. has some good qualities," Audrey said. "And I'm sure these sessions with Sally Woodruff will benefit you and your father. Given time, I think y'all will be able to build a solid father/daughter relationship."

"You're an optimist," Zoe told her.

Audrey draped her arm around Zoe's shoulders. "I try to be. Like right now, I'm optimistic in believing I'll be able to help you with this science project. The truth of the matter is that I'll probably do more observing than actually helping. I don't think a girl with your IQ needs anybody to help her with a simple science project."

Zoe looked at Audrey with affection. "You're very smart yourself, Dr. Sherrod. You saw right through my fabrication."

"Zoe, you don't need excuses to spend time with me. I'm here for you whenever you need me. And that includes our just hanging out together."

Zoe's smile widened, so bright and honest and filled with gratitude.

When J.D. got home a little after seven, he tossed a frozen meal in the microwave, heated it for five minutes, and then wolfed it down with a beer before he settled in to work for a while. An hour later, just as his vision began to blur and he wondered if he might need bifocals soon, his phone rang. At first glance, he didn't immediately recognize the name and number, and then it hit him—Cara Oliver—she was Zoe's friend Jacy's aunt, the woman who had chaperoned the girls' trip to the mall.

"Hello," J.D. said.

"Hi, J.D., this is Cara Oliver. I hope I'm not disturbing you, not interrupting anything important."

"Not a thing."

"How's Zoe?"

"She's fine."

"I wanted to apologize again about—"

"No need," J.D. assured her. "What happened wasn't your fault."

"Nevertheless, I feel guilty. Jacy's parents grounded her for a month, but I imagine Zoe's already told you about that."

No, Zoe hadn't told him. But then, his daughter spoke to him only when he spoke to her. "Actually, she hasn't mentioned it."

"Oh, well, I'm sure she will." Cara hesitated, as if she was considering what she was going to say next. "The other reason that I called . . . other than to apologize is . . . well . . . I was hoping you might want to go out for dinner. Sometime soon. I'm sure you're busy tomorrow night—"

"As a matter of fact, I am." *I'll be giving Holly a goodbye fuck.* "But how about Saturday night?"

"Saturday night would be great."

They chatted for ten more minutes. Small talk, which J.D. hated. But women in general seemed to feel it was necessary, especially pre, during, and post the first couple of dates. Cara gave him her address and the directions to get from his house to hers and told him how much she was looking forward to their date. And then J.D. sat back on the sofa and smiled. It was great the way women had no problem taking the lead and inviting a man out for dinner. If he recalled correctly, Holly also had been the one to make the first move. Holly, who was on her way out. And Cara, who was on her way in. An old saying came to mind: *There are always more fish in the sea.*

His relationship with Holly had pretty much run its course, and they both knew it. She had become a little too demanding to suit him. And although he appreciated her unique talents in the bedroom and admired her barracuda lawyer's mind, Holly wasn't the kind of woman he needed in his life. In the future, any woman he dated more than a couple of times had to not only be sexy, attractive, and agreeable to a no-strings-attached affair, but had to like his kid.

J.D. checked his watch. Eight twenty. He was supposed to pick up Zoe before ten, but since the drive from his house on Signal Mountain to Audrey's town house in downtown Chattanooga would take about fifteen minutes, there was no reason for him to head out now.

What the hell. It wouldn't make any difference if he showed up a little early, would it? He might actually be able to help Zoe and Audrey finish up Zoe's school project.

Maybe he should shave and change his shirt. He had a heavy five o'clock shadow and his button-down was wrinkled.

What was the matter with him? He was just going to pick up Zoe, so who cared if his shirt was wrinkled and he needed a shave?

J.D. grabbed his jacket, flung it over his shoulder, and headed out the door.

Since traffic wasn't bad, he found himself in front of Audrey's town house on Second Street twelve minutes later.

The fashionable and expensive Walnut Hill townhomes were within walking distance of numerous restaurants and tourist attractions, including the Walnut Street Walking Bridge, the Hunter Art Museum, and the Art District, as well as the Riverwalk. After parking his Camaro and getting out, he wondered if he should think of an excuse for showing up more than an hour early.

"I had dinner downtown." "I worked late and came straight here." "I thought maybe y'all would finish up early."

By the time he reached Audrey's front porch, he had decided that if neither she nor Zoe mentioned how early he was, then neither would he. When he walked up the steps, the porch light came on, thanks to a motion sensor. As he approached the front door, he noticed a long, white rectangular box braced against the right side of the black iron railing that ran along both sides of the porch and down the front steps. He studied the box more carefully, then picked it up and saw the emblem of a local florist attached to the mauve ribbon circling the box. Someone, probably Porter Bryant, had left a bouquet for Audrey. Why leave it on her porch instead of delivering it in person? A lover's surprise?

The last time J.D. had bought flowers for a woman had been for his senior high school prom date.

With florist box in hand, he rang the door and waited.

Audrey opened the door and glanced from his face to the box.

Before she got the wrong idea, he said. "They're not from me. I found them propped up against the porch railing."

"Please, come in. Zoe and I were about to dip up some ice cream."

"Then y'all are finished with the . . . er . . . project?"

"A science project," Audrey whispered. "And all I did was watch her work and give her a little praise, which is all she really needed."

"Thanks."

Okay, so he should know more about Zoe's schoolwork, but short of giving her the third degree on a daily basis, he wasn't likely to learn one damn thing about it. It wasn't as if Zoe volunteered any information.

After J.D. entered the small foyer, Audrey closed and locked the door and then took the florist box from him. Keeping her voice low and soft, she told him, "Zoe's project required a great deal of research. She finished the research tonight and we compared her findings. This weekend she'll write the paper. And in case you'd like to know, the topic is Design Considerations for Solar Cell–Powered Homes."

"That's a ninth-grade project? Things sure have changed since I was in ninth grade."

"The hope is that each generation will be smarter than the one before." Audrey smiled. "I assume you know that your daughter has a brilliant mind."

"God only knows where she would have gotten it," J.D. joked. "Carrie wasn't the sharpest tool in the shed, and I'm sure no genius."

Ignoring his self-criticism, Audrey said, "Zoe's in the kitchen. Come on back and join us. I understand vanilla is your favorite ice cream flavor, and it just so happens that I have a half gallon of vanilla."

"Lead the way." J.D. fell into step behind her.

When she opened the kitchen door, Zoe looked up from where she stood at the counter busily dipping ice cream into a crystal bowl. "You're early," she told him as she dug the scoop back into the container.

"Audrey said you're finished with your research for the science project. Solar power, huh? An interesting subject."

Zoe stared at J.D. and for half a second he saw genuine pleasure in her eyes. His daughter had been pleased that he actually knew not only what kind of school project she'd been researching, but knew the topic. And then realization dawned and that glimmer of pleasure disappeared.

"Audrey told you, didn't she?" Zoe glanced away and focused on putting ice cream in a second bowl.

"Zoe, would you please dip up some vanilla for your dad?" Audrey walked over beside Zoe and laid the florist box on the counter by the sink.

"Sure." Zoe glanced at the box. "I know he didn't bring you flowers, so who are they from?"

"I guess I'll have to open them to find out."

Audrey slipped the mauve ribbon off the box and lifted the lid. J.D. looked over her shoulder as she picked up the small card lying near the long stems of a dozen red roses. When she read the card, the muscles in her face tensed.

"Who are they from?" Zoe asked again as she placed the Turtle Tracks ice cream in the freezer and removed the carton of vanilla.

"Porter Bryant." Audrey crushed the card in half and held it tightly in her clenched fist.

Zoe didn't notice, but J.D. did, and he sensed that Audrey was not only displeased and annoyed, but slightly unnerved.

"A dozen roses," Zoe said. "How romantic. I don't think I've heard you mention him. Is he your boyfriend or something?"

"No. Porter and I dated for a while. We are . . . were friends."

Audrey dropped the crumpled notecard back into the florist box and left the box on the counter. "J.D., would you like chocolate sauce or nuts or whipped cream on your ice cream?" She removed another crystal dessert bowl from an upper cupboard and set it on the counter.

"No, thanks. I'll take it plain."

"Are red roses your favorite?" Zoe removed the lid from the carton of ice cream.

"No, actually, they aren't." Almost as an afterthought, speaking more to herself than anyone else, she said, "I've always loved white gardenias."

"I like daisies," Zoe said as she dipped into the vanilla ice cream. "And lilies and carnations. But I guess I like roses, too. But not red ones. Pink. That's my favorite color."

While Audrey and Zoe were busy discussing flowers, J.D. reached down inside the florist box, picked up the wrinkled notecard, and unfolded it. He read the message quickly and then dropped the card back into the box.

If you don't give us a second chance, you will regret it.
Love,
Porter

Well, I'll be damned.

Just what did the message mean? Was the guy begging for a second chance or . . . ?

Whatever was going on between Audrey and her former boyfriend was certainly none of his business. He had no intention of becoming involved in her personal life. But it was obvious that she didn't want anything to do with the man or his flowers; and the accompanying note had rattled her usually composed demeanor. Had Porter Bryant been harassing her?

J.D. hadn't been aware that she'd broken up with the ADA, but why should he have known? She didn't know any details about his love life. They didn't have the type of relationship where they shared that kind of personal information. Apparently Audrey had been the one who had ended the relationship with Bryant, and he was having a problem letting her go.

Not that it was anything to him one way or the other, but he was glad, for her sake, that she'd dumped Bryant. There was something a little too smooth and slick about his appearance and something a little too superior and condescending about his attitude. A guy like that wouldn't take kindly to being told to "hit the road, Jack." Maybe the flowers and the note were just his way of trying to woo Audrey back into his arms.

But so help me God, if I find out that he's actually threatening her, I'll have a man-to-man come-to-Jesus talk with the son of a bitch.

Chapter 20

"Are you sure you want to do this?" Grace Douglas asked Wayne.

Keeping his eyes glued to the road ahead, he replied, "I'm sure."

"What will happen if anyone finds out that you've shared confidential information with Steve Kelly?"

"I've shared the same information with you," he reminded her.

"And I've told no one, not even Lance. And you have no idea how much I want to tell my son. But I would never betray your trust. Are you sure you can trust Steve Kelly?"

Wayne didn't respond immediately; instead, he mulled over her question. Could he trust Steve? Hell if he knew. But he did know one thing for sure—Steve Kelly had a right to know about the DNA results on the two toddler skeletons. Sooner or later, the police would have to release that information to the press about the toddler skeletons and the DNA results. Steve needed to be told beforehand so the news wouldn't catch him off guard. He needed to be prepared for the possibility that if Whitney Poole became the Rocking

Chair Killer's third victim, when her body was discovered, she would probably be holding a tiny skeleton. And since the first two victims had been holding the first two Baby Blue toddlers, then the odds were that the next toddler skeleton would belong to Devin Kelly.

"You didn't have to come with me," Wayne told Grace.

"I didn't want you to have to do this alone."

He didn't reply. He couldn't. If he did, he might cry. And damn it, Wayne Sherrod didn't cry. Not in front of anyone, not even the woman who loved him.

Grace understood him better than anyone and accepted him as he was, warts and all. He was a lucky bastard. Not many men got a third chance at happiness. Yeah, damn straight. Grace made him happy. And he hoped he made her happy. He tried, did the best he could. What had begun as a friendship cemented with their mutual grief had gradually grown into love, and now, he couldn't imagine his life without her.

They rode along in silence until they reached the turn-off for the Cedar Creek Mobile Home Park. Then Wayne said, "If you change your mind, you can always wait in the car."

As he pulled to a stop, Grace reached over and laid her hand on his arm. "Is there some reason you don't want me to go in with you?"

Wayne tensed. "He's living with some woman. A pretty rough customer. I'm not sure . . . Hell, you know what I'm trying to say. She's a different kind of woman than you are, and I wouldn't want you to be offended by—"

"Oh, I see." Grace leaned over and kissed his cheek. "Wayne Sherrod, you are, without a doubt, an old-fashioned gentleman. You're the type who still divides women into two categories, ladies and whores."

Wayne cleared his throat, but didn't look at Grace.

She laughed. "Considering the fact that you and I have been fornicating like crazy for a number of years—"

He turned, grasped her shoulders, and looked right at her. "You, Grace Douglas, are a lady through and through."

Grace smiled at him; then apparently something caught her eye as she glanced over his shoulder.

"What is it?" he asked.

"It's Steve Kelly," Grace told him. "Or I think it is. A man just opened the door to his trailer and is standing there looking at us."

By the time Wayne got out, rounded the truck's hood, and opened the door for Grace, Steve had walked out into the small yard at the side of his trailer. He stood there and waited for them.

Steve inspected Grace from head to toe. "I see you brought somebody with you."

"This is Grace Douglas," Wayne said. "Her son Shane was the fifth Baby Blue toddler."

Steve's gaze softened. "Ma'am." He nodded and then turned toward his trailer. "Y'all come on in." After opening the door and stepping aside on the small attached porch, he glanced back and looked from Grace to Wayne. "Juanita's not here. She . . . uh . . . reconciled with an old boyfriend."

Wayne breathed a little easier knowing that Grace wouldn't have to meet the skanky Juanita.

Steve's trailer was as neat inside as it was outside, even if the furniture was old and worn, as were the appliances in the kitchen. He indicated for Wayne and Grace to sit on the sofa. After they sat, he settled into the ratty leather recliner.

"When you called, you said you had some information about the Baby Blue kidnapping cases." Steve stared at Wayne. "I figure it's not good news."

"The DNA from the two toddler skeletons found with Jill Scott and Debra Gregory belonged to Keith Lawson and Chase Wilcox."

Grace slipped her hand over Wayne's and entwined her fingers with his.

Steve didn't say anything. Moisture glazed his eyes.

"The CPD and the TBI are pretty sure that the Rocking Chair Killer abducted Whitney Poole," Wayne finally said, breaking the silence. "If he has her . . . if he kills her . . . and poses her in a rocking chair with a toddler skeleton in her arms, then . . ."

"Then that toddler could be Devin." Steve closed his eyes. "He was the third child who disappeared. Whitney Poole is the third woman."

"The information about the DNA results hasn't been released to the press. Not yet. I thought you had a right to know now, to be prepared, just in case."

Steve looked at Grace. "Your son was the fifth little boy that she kidnapped, wasn't he?"

"Yes." Grace clenched her teeth tightly and Wayne knew she was fighting back tears.

"That woman did more than just kill our little boys," Steve said. "She destroyed so many lives. If you ask me, she got off way too easy just being confined to a mental hospital for life." He dropped his clasped hands between his knees and looked down at the floor. "I went to see her, you know."

"We all went to see her," Grace said. "You and Wayne and I and Chase Wilcox's mother and Keith Lawson's parents. We all wanted her to tell us if she had taken our babies . . . if she had killed them."

"I'm not talking about more than twenty years ago. I went to see the bitch about a week before she died."

"Why would you do that?" Wayne asked. "What possible reason—?"

"It was Devin's birthday. He would have been twenty-nine. All I could think about was that damn crazy bitch and how she was alive and Devin was dead and . . ."

Grace stood, walked over to Steve, and knelt in front of him. "Steve." She spoke his name in a soft whisper.

He looked up at her. "I wanted to kill her," he said. "I

wanted to strangle her with my bare hands. After all these years, I still wanted—" He squinched his eyes tightly shut. Tears squirted out from the closed lids and dampened his face.

Grace took his big clasped hands and covered them with her own much smaller hands. "I understand. Wayne and I both understand. We've felt what you've felt."

Steve opened his eyes, but couldn't speak. Grace released him and rose to her feet. Wayne came up behind her and slid his arm around her waist. They were three kindred souls, each a parent who had lost a child to the same madwoman's senseless actions.

The Hideaway was a bar. It wasn't an upscale, urban white-collar hangout or a redneck roadhouse watering hole, but something in between. Hart knew that this was the kind of place he should avoid, a place where beer flowed like water and a guy could easily score a hit in the men's room. So far, he had been able to withstand temptation because he hadn't come here tonight looking for a fix. He'd come here to meet Jessica Smith, the long-legged, dark-eyed manicurist that Audrey had warned him to stay away from.

He had considered listening to his sister's advice. She was right about him being too old and too worldly for a kid like Jessica. But when he thought about Jessica, how she had responded to him, all giggles and fluttering eyelashes, he'd done what he knew he shouldn't do. He'd called the spa and asked to speak to her.

She'd been the one who suggested they hook up at seven-thirty, here at the Hideaway. The girl couldn't be all that sweet and innocent if she frequented places like this. His big sister had to realize that not all women—young or old—had her high moral standards. Some women liked sex for the sake of sex, with or without love being involved. Just as many women as men enjoyed an occasional walk on the wild side.

It might be good for Audrey if just once she would come down off her high horse and wallow in the mud with the rest of the peasants.

Hart laughed at the thought of his sister literally wallowing in mud. Even as a kid, Audrey had been fastidious. Her room had always been neat and clean, nothing out of place. She had ironed her clothes and his, too, and reminded him to comb his hair and brush his teeth.

And God, she was a chronic hand washer. She kept both hand sanitizer and lotion in her purse and in her car. A bottle of liquid soap and a bottle of lotion were by every sink in her house and office.

He loved Audrey. Even though they weren't biological siblings, they had bonded as brother and sister during the first year of their parents' marriage. In all the years since Blake's death, no matter what he did or how many times he screwed up, she had never deserted him. He owed her, owed her more than he could ever repay.

Maybe he should have listened to her and not gotten in touch with Jessica.

"Hey there," a female voice said. "I'm not late, am I?"

The minute he looked at Jessica Smith, any second thoughts he'd had disappeared instantly. The girl looked good enough to eat. She had freed that mane of dark hair so that it hung around her shoulders in thick curls, the ends almost reaching the tips of her high, firm boobs. Boobs that obviously needed no assistance from a bra in order to stand at attention. The silky red top she wore clung to her body and did nothing to hide her erect nipples. And damn if she didn't look like she'd been melted and poured into her black jeans.

"No, ma'am, you're right on time." Hart slid his arm around her slender waist.

"I'm starving," she told him as she cuddled against his side. "This place has some great burgers."

"Let's find a table and we'll order dinner."

"Burgers, fries, and beer for me."

"You are over twenty-one, right?"

When she giggled, he wondered if maybe she wasn't legal drinking age, but she assured him she was.

"I'm twenty-two. Almost."

As they searched for a table in the crowded bar, Hart caught a glimpse of someone he recognized sitting alone at a table near the dance floor. When Jessica noticed him staring at the man, she punched him gently in the ribs.

"Somebody you know?" she asked.

"Yeah, a . . . uh . . . fellow recovering alcoholic and addict." He should have told Jessica the truth about himself before he asked her out. But better now than later.

"Oh, somebody you just see at meetings, or are you two buddies?" Jessica asked, seeming unfazed by his admission.

He stopped, turned, and looked at her. "Did you already know about me?"

"That you've had problems with alcohol and drugs? That you haven't been out of rehab for long? Yeah, I knew. I'm your sister's manicurist. She's mentioned you and I asked around. People talk."

"And you don't care about—?"

"You're clean now, aren't you?"

"Yeah."

She shrugged. "Then who cares? It's not like we're getting married or anything. This is just a date. Two people grabbing a burger and getting acquainted." When he smiled, she continued talking. "And just so you know, I don't have sex on a first date. Kissing is okay for tonight. And heavy petting on a second date isn't out of the question."

"And sex on date three?"

"Sometimes. It just depends on how much I like you and how persuasive you can be."

Hart smiled. He liked Jessica Smith. There was a lot more to her than just perky tits and a pretty face. And if things went well tonight, maybe there would be a second date and possibly a third. It had been quite a while since he'd thought about actually dating a girl long enough to get to know her and even longer since he'd actually cared about someone.

As for love—there had been only one girl.

"Want to ask your friend to join us?" Jessica asked.

"Nah, let him find his own date."

The lullaby replayed itself inside her head, the melody and lyrics, once sweet and familiar, now bitter and terrifying.

Hush, little baby, don't you cry . . .

She was alone. Lost in the darkness. Only a glimmer of faraway light in the pitch blackness. Her heartbeat the lone sound in the unbearable solitude. Sometimes she thought she heard insects crawling all around her, on the floor, on the walls, on the ceiling. But she couldn't see the floor or the walls or the ceiling. Her world had shrunk to the size of one chair. A rocking chair.

She had stopped struggling, stopped fighting against the degrading confinement, stopped pretending that there was some way she could escape. She had become reconciled to her fate. Oddly enough, she had reached the point where she feared living far more than dying. Living like this, strapped to a chair, her feet bound, unable to do more than wiggle her toes and fingers and twist her head from side to side was unendurable. But endure it she must. Until he killed her. And he would kill her.

But far worse than being bound to the damn rocking chair or even knowing her captor would eventually end her life were those moments when he laid the tiny bundle in her arms, the body of a little child wrapped in a blanket. The skeleton of a toddler, just bones, baby teeth, and wisps of blond hair.

Poor baby. Poor little dead baby.

When he killed her, when she became his next victim, would anybody remember her name?

"I'm Whitney Poole!" she screamed. "I'm Whitney Poole and I don't want to die! I want to live! I want somebody to find me and get me out of this horrible place!"

Her voice echoed in the stillness. The room where he kept her had to be large and empty to create such an echo.

"I'm Whitney Poole," she murmured softly as tears trickled down her cheeks. "I'm Whitney Poole. Please, somebody remember my name."

Chapter 21

J.D. dropped Zoe off at Audrey's town house Saturday night and remained in his car until he saw Audrey open the door and usher his daughter inside her home.

"Tell Audrey I appreciate her looking after you tonight," J.D. had said on their drive into downtown Chattanooga. "I'm not sure what time I'll be back by to pick you up. I'll try to make it before midnight. But if not, Audrey told you that you're welcome to spend the night, right?"

Zoe had given him a disapproving look.

"You aren't going to stay long enough to even say hi to Audrey," she had whined, more than just a little unhappy with him.

"Cara lives in Ooltewah. It'll take me half an hour to get there, and our dinner reservations are for seven. It's our first date and I don't want to keep the lady waiting."

"It'll take you twenty minutes to get there the way you drive," Zoe had told him. "And it's not even six o'clock. You have plenty of time. You just can't be bothered."

"I'm not arguing with you about this." During the one-hour family counseling session yesterday—with Dr. Sally

Woodruff—he'd had one of those lightbulb moments. He couldn't remember exactly what Dr. Woodruff had said that triggered the realization that by arguing with his daughter to make her understand his point of view, he was actually facilitating her rebellious attitude. She was not one of his peers or a superior whose approval he needed. She was, despite being fourteen or maybe because of it, a child. His child. He was the adult.

"It's very discourteous to just drop me off. Aren't you always preaching to me about the importance of good manners?" Zoe had glared daggers at him.

When he hadn't responded, she had crossed her arms over her chest and pouted all the way to downtown.

He watched while Zoe disappeared into the house. Audrey lifted her hand and waved at him. He waved back and then drove off, heading for West Fourth. Focusing straight ahead, he tried to forget that he'd left his daughter, once again, mad as hell at him. And he didn't want to think about the displeased look Audrey had given him. Or had he imagined that her expression denoted disapproval? She hadn't actually been frowning at him, but she certainly hadn't been smiling.

As he merged onto I-24 East, Audrey's image flashed through his mind. That undecipherable expression on her face. Her shoulder-length chestnut brown hair, tucked behind her ears, shimmering in the late-evening sunlight. Loose-fitting lounge pants in some weird shade of green clung to her hips, and the matching top, the neckline encrusted with some type of beading, hung in loose pleats over her breasts.

J.D. growled. What the hell was wrong with him?

Stop thinking about Audrey. Stop worrying about Zoe.

He had a date with a gorgeous babe tonight. Possibly the first of many dates.

* * *

Audrey had allowed Zoe to grumble and complain about her father's lack of manners, but she hadn't made any negative comments. J.D. had his faults—everyone did—but it was better if she kept any negative opinions about his character to herself. It was in Zoe's best interest to point out her father's good qualities.

"I'm sure your dad didn't mean to be rude," Audrey had said. "It's a first date for him with Ms. Oliver, and he wants to make a good impression by showing up early."

"You know what? I didn't have any idea he'd split up with Holly last night until he told me this morning that he had a date with Jacy's aunt."

The man certainly didn't waste any time, did he? He'd seen Holly Johnston last night, and tonight he had a date with Cara Oliver. Out with the old and in with the new.

"I should have figured that Holly's days were numbered. She was getting a little clingy, and if there's one thing J.D. hates, it's clingy."

During dinner Audrey had tried to steer the conversation away from J.D. Cass and his personal life. The less she knew, the better. She wasn't the least bit interested in learning more about the man. He was Zoe's father and a colleague of Tam's and Uncle Garth's. Those were her only connections to J.D. As far as she was concerned, they were merely acquaintances and nothing more, certainly not friends.

Curling up on the sofa together after dinner, Audrey and Zoe watched one of the two movies Audrey had rented, each a lighthearted comedy that she thought appropriate for someone Zoe's age. As it turned out, the one Zoe chose for them to watch was a real dud, so they had started talking about halfway through and even though the movie was still playing, they pretty much ignored it.

"I like Dr. Woodruff," Zoe said. "She's not you, of course, but she's okay."

"Sally is a nice person and an excellent counselor. She also raised three daughters, so she understands teenage girls better than anyone I know."

"I think J.D. liked her okay. It's hard to tell with him. He's not always easy to read. Sometimes, he says one thing when I'm sure he's actually thinking the opposite."

"Maybe you should stop second-guessing him and take him at his word."

"Maybe. It's just I wish . . ." Zoe ran her tongue over the edge of her teeth.

"What do you wish?"

Zoe shook her head, the movement bouncing her glistening, shoulder-length black hair. "I wish I had a real family. You know, a mom and dad and a brother or sister. I can only imagine how great it would be to be normal."

"I used to wish for the same thing," Audrey admitted. "First my parents divorced when I was five, and then my mother was killed in an accident when I was six. My dad remarried and for a while I thought maybe, just maybe . . . At least I got a couple of brothers out of Dad's second marriage."

"Your little brother was kidnapped, wasn't he?"

"Yes, Blake was abducted when he was two and was never found."

"I'm sorry." Zoe reached over and rubbed Audrey's arm. "I didn't mean to make you sad."

"It's okay. You and I are friends, aren't we? That means we can share sad moments."

"Sometimes when I think about my mom, I get sad. She wasn't an ideal mother or anything, but in her own way she loved me. When she told me she had cancer, I was scared to death. For her. For me. Weird thing is that if she hadn't known she was dying, she'd have never told me about J.D. I'd have spent the rest of my life not knowing who my real father was." Zoe looked at Audrey. "Why aren't you and your dad close?"

Audrey hesitated, uncertain what to say, considering just how honest she should be. "When my brother Blake was kidnapped, my dad changed. And then my stepmother took her own life and things got worse. He never recovered from losing his son and his wife."

"But he still had you and your other brother."

"My stepbrother," Audrey said. "But it wasn't the same for Dad. Blake was special."

"I think you're special. I wish my dad could see just how special you are."

"Oh, Zoe . . ." Audrey realized she had to handle this situation with kid gloves. "I think you're pretty special, too. As for your father . . ." She cleared her throat. "Your father and I aren't . . . we're just acquaintances. You and I are friends. Your father and I are connected only through you. Do you understand what I'm trying to say?"

"Don't you think my dad is hot?"

"Ah . . . oh . . . er," Audrey sputtered and then laughed. "I think your father is a very attractive man, but—"

"You could ask him out, you know. Jacy's aunt did. She called him up and asked him. Women do that all the time, don't they, ask guys out."

"Zoe, I'm not going to ask your father for a date."

"I could ask him for you."

"No. You will do no such thing."

"I'll bet he'd say yes."

"Zoe!"

"Oh, all right. I won't ask him," Zoe promised. "But you know what? I think a daughter should have the right to give a thumbs up or a thumbs down to the women her father dates. Believe me, I'd have given a thumbs down to Holly Johnston."

"And what about Ms. Oliver?"

"Hmm . . . I'm not sure. A possible thumbs up. I like Jacy's aunt all right, but she's not you. I'd much rather my dad was dating you."

"That's not going to happen."

Not now. Not ever

Porter checked his wristwatch. 10:50 P.M. He parked his car across the street from Audrey's town house. He had driven by earlier that evening and then returned a few hours later. He had circled the block half a dozen times before leaving. This was his third trip.

Audrey hadn't phoned him, hadn't e-mailed or sent him a text since he'd left the roses on her porch last night. He had been so sure she would get in touch, if for no other reason, at least to thank him.

Their relationship had been progressing nicely, their going from friendly acquaintances to good friends over a period of months. Lovers would have been the next logical step. He had done everything right. He had been patient and understanding, not rushing her, allowing her all the time she needed. He had studied her likes and dislikes and made them his own. He had learned how to be the perfect mate for Audrey Sherrod.

From the time he was a child, he had set goals for himself and done whatever was necessary to achieve those goals. He had allowed no one to get in his way and nothing to steer him in the wrong direction. Even as a little boy, he had been aware that in order to survive, he had to reinvent himself. He had plotted and planned. He had learned to fit in, to project whatever image was needed at the time, to become whoever and whatever each person in his life required.

His mother, Lynn Porter Bryant, had wanted him to be

her beautiful little angel, sweet and obedient and adoring. He never disappointed her, and she died when he was twenty-five, never knowing who he really was.

His father, Morris Bryant, a wealthy attorney, had wanted him to be smart and successful, to make him proud by following in his footsteps. He had become a lawyer to please the old man. On Porter's last visit home to Lexington before his dad died, Morris had told him that he needed to find a good woman and settle down.

His father would have approved of Audrey, as his mother would have. She was the type of woman who would make the ideal wife. He had been so sure of her, so certain that he had executed his plans without fault, so convinced that, like every other goal he had ever set, making Audrey his mate was a fait accompli.

So what had gone wrong?

Why had she rejected him?

I want you to be free to find someone else, someone who can give you what you deserve in a relationship.

When she had asked him if he loved her, he should have lied and said yes. He should have gotten down on one knee right then and there, professed his undying love, and asked her to marry him.

Perhaps it wasn't too late.

She had said there was no one else. If that was true, then there was still hope, still a possibility that he could change her mind.

But what if she was lying to him?

He couldn't be certain, of course, but he suspected that their relationship had begun to change when Audrey met J.D. Cass. He had never thought a man like that would interest Audrey. Cass might be intelligent enough to get by in his job, but Cass was more brawn than brains, a guy with a lot of rough edges. Some women liked that type. Holly Johnston certainly did. But surely not a refined, dignified lady such as Audrey.

But what other reason would Audrey have to spend so much time with Cass and his teenage daughter? It was one thing for her to work with them as a counselor, but why become personally involved?

He had watched the TBI agent drop off his daughter at Audrey's town house earlier that evening, but hadn't seen him return. Was the girl staying the night? When he spoke to Audrey again, he didn't want an audience. He wanted them to be alone, just the two of them. It would be so much easier to persuade her, to bring her around to his way of thinking, if no one interfered.

In his peripheral vision, Porter caught a glimpse of Cass's red Camaro as he passed by. Porter slid down in the seat, hoping Cass hadn't noticed him, and watched while the TBI agent pulled up in front of Audrey's home.

He would wait until Cass picked up his daughter and left before he put his plan into action.

J.D. parked his car, killed the engine, and sat there outside Audrey's house. He was back from his date before midnight—a whole damn hour before midnight. Zoe was too perceptive not to figure out that his showing up this early meant that the big date had been a royal flop. And he couldn't count on his daughter not making some snide comment about him not getting any tonight.

Not that he had expected sex on his first date with Cara. Or with any woman, for that matter. And damn it, his sex life was not something he ever wanted to discuss with his daughter, and it sure as hell was none of Audrey Sherrod's business.

What had promised to be a pleasant evening with an attractive woman, and had actually started out that way, had gradually gone downhill. Even though he had arrived at Cara's a little early, she'd been ready and waiting, wearing an incredible, hugged-every-curve purple silk dress and matching spike heels. She had looked so luscious that he'd quickly dismissed a niggling thought—most women would have kept him waiting. Did that mean Cara was overeager?

On the drive to the restaurant, she hadn't taken her eyes off him, and that alone had made him uncomfortable, as had the way she had clung to his arm when the maitre d' showed them to their table. But what had really thrown him for a loop was when she had asked him to order for her.

"I'm sure I'll love whatever you choose for me."

His first thought at that comment had been, *Are you for real?*

Not once in his life had he ever dared to choose his date's meal. In his experience, women in general would have considered doing such a thing an insult.

He had ordered salad, steak, and baked potato for both of them. And when Cara had cuddled up against him where they sat in the plush booth, he'd run his index finger under his collar, loosening his tie. From that point on, one red flag after another had popped up. *Warning. Danger. Fanatically possessive female attaching herself to you.*

Cara had seemed completely unaware of his discomfort. Even when he had mentioned that people were staring at them, she hadn't taken the hint.

"They're just jealous, darling."

Wanting to put an end to the date as soon as possible, he hadn't ordered dessert. Unfortunately, Cara had decided his rush to leave the restaurant was because he wanted her for dessert. Needless to say, she'd been disappointed when he took her home, walked her to her door, and said good night.

"But don't you want to come in?" She had rubbed herself against him.

"I'm afraid I can't," he'd told her. "I promised Zoe I'd pick her up by eleven."

All the way from Ooltewah to downtown Chattanooga, J.D. had cursed himself for a fool. He should have suggested lunch instead of dinner when Cara had called him. A mistake he wouldn't make again in the future. God help him, if he'd had any forewarning that Cara would assume that one date would give her any proprietary rights over him, he'd have run like hell before instead of after the date.

Damn it, he couldn't sit out here in his car for the next hour. *Might as well go on in and take your medicine like a good boy.*

When he rang the doorbell, Audrey opened the front door and smiled pleasantly. "Well, hi there. We weren't expecting you this early. Actually, Zoe has already put on her pajamas. She seemed to think she'd be spending the night."

"I don't know why she'd think that." J.D. grumbled the words quietly as he ran his gaze over Audrey, noticing that she was wearing tan silk pajamas, her initials monogrammed on the breast pocket.

"Oh, I think you know." Audrey's smile widened. "Did your date end after a good-night kiss at the door?"

"Something like that."

"Smart lady."

"No, smart man. I got invited in, Dr. Sherrod. I chose not to accept."

Audrey laughed. Damn her, she laughed. He had the oddest urge to grab her and shake her. But as he stood there looking at her, at those big hazel eyes and those smiling lips, another even stranger urge hit him.

Don't be an idiot twice in one night.

"Tell Zoe to grab her overnight bag and we'll hit the road so you can go to bed," J.D. said.

"There's no reason to rush off. Come on in and—"

"Oh my God!" Zoe cried out from the living room.

J.D. and Audrey shared startled gazes and then together they rushed from the foyer into the living room. Staring wide-eyed at the television, Zoe hung halfway between standing and sitting, her rounded eyes glued to the TV. With her mouth still gaping, she flopped back onto the sofa.

"What's the matter?" Audrey asked.

"Zoe?" J.D. asked simultaneously.

"Look." Zoe pointed to the television. "And listen." She grabbed the remote control from the coffee table and increased the volume. "That guy just said that those dolls found with the Rocking Chair Killer's victims weren't dolls at all. They were skeletons of real babies."

J.D. glanced at the TV as the nightly news anchor, James Paul Dill, narrated while a series of old photographs flashed across the screen.

"Two of these skeletons have been identified through DNA testing," Dill said. "It has been confirmed that they are both Baby Blue toddlers who were kidnapped more than two decades ago and have been identified as Keith Lawson and Chase Wilcox."

Photos of two golden-haired, blue-eyed toddlers appeared on the screen.

J.D. heard Audrey's indrawn breath and barely resisted the urge to reach for her, instinct urging him to offer support and comfort.

"Did you authorize this information to be released to the press?" She looked at him, demanding an answer.

"No, of course not. Chief Mullins would be the one to make any announcement about the Rocking Chair Killer, and I would have been informed if he planned a press conference. That means somebody leaked classified information."

One by one, photos of the six missing toddlers presumed kidnapped by Regina Bennett appeared on the screen as the news anchor identified each by name. When Blake Sherrod's photo came up, Audrey swayed slightly. J.D. reached over and grasped her arm to steady her. As if suddenly realizing that J.D. had touched her, Audrey pulled away from him.

"Apparently there is a connection between the Baby Blue kidnappings and the Rocking Chair Killer," Dill told the TV audience. "It has been confirmed that the Tennessee Bureau of Investigation will be questioning several persons of interest as early as Monday morning."

"Where the hell did this guy get his info?" If J.D. found out who had leaked the information, he would personally see to it that he or she lost his or her job. "Whoever confirmed this info has to work for either the CPD or the TBI."

"Our sources were able to obtain the names of the persons of interest," Dill continued, a self-satisfied expression on his TV-pretty face. "The TBI will be speaking to Jeremy Arden, the Baby Blue toddler who was rescued from his kidnapper twenty-four years ago. And they are searching for a man named Corey Bennett, believed to be the nephew of Regina Bennett, the Baby Blue kidnapper."

"She has a nephew?" Audrey stared at J.D.

He nodded. "Yeah." J.D. glanced at Zoe. "Why don't you turn that damn thing off? I think we've heard enough." He knew that the next name on the persons-of-interest list—the list he had compiled—would make Audrey despise him.

"The third person of interest is Hart Roberts, stepson of former police detective Wayne Sherrod. Roberts is also the nephew of Sergeant Garth Hudson, one of the lead detectives on the Rocking Chair Murder cases. Roberts's half brother was the fourth toddler kidnapped in a series of abductions that began twenty-eight years ago and ended with the arrest of Regina Bennett five years later."

Audrey turned so quickly that her shoulder brushed J.D.'s arm. She glared at him, anger and shock and disappointment apparent in her expression.

"Why would you think that Hart could be involved in any

way with those women's murders?" She sucked in a shaky breath. When he reached out to her, she backed away from him. "And don't you dare try to deny that you're the one who put together that persons-of-interest list for the TBI."

"That's all it is, damn it, just a persons-of-interest list. It doesn't mean—"

"It means that my brother, who is a recovering alcoholic and addict, who has been emotionally fragile since Blake disappeared and his mother committed suicide, is now going to be hounded by the press because people will suspect him of murder."

"I'm sorry," J.D. said. "This information was not supposed to go outside the TBI and the CPD."

"Sorry isn't good enough. Damn you, J.D.!"

"Audrey, please listen to me. Try to understand."

Zoe tugged on his arm. "Come on, J.D. I think it's time you and I went home."

He glanced at his daughter and noticed that she had her overnight case in her hand. "Yeah, I think you're right."

Before J.D. could make his escape, Audrey's phone rang.

"We'll let ourselves out," Zoe told Audrey, who cast Zoe a you-and-I-are-okay look.

The last thing J.D. heard on their way out the door was Audrey saying, "Yes, Tam, please come over as soon as you can."

Chapter 22

Eileen Campbell came straight from morning church services to her antique shop in East Ridge. Sunday afternoon was a prime time for shoppers, and she made a habit of arriving early to get everything ready before opening time at one o'clock. Taking pride in the shop she had owned with her late husband since the early days of their marriage more than twenty years ago, she didn't leave even the smallest detail to employees. She owned a third of the store's contents, and the remaining two-thirds belonged to people who rented booths from her. Although the items displayed in half a dozen of the rental booths didn't quite meet her high standards, being more or less junk, she was smart enough to know that some customers actually liked junk.

The long straps of her shoulder bag slid down her arm as she clutched the paper sack containing her lunch—a sandwich, pickles, and an apple—with her left hand. Holding her keychain in her right hand, she approached the double front doors, inserted the key, and unlocked her shop. She hurried inside, closed and locked the door behind her, and flipped on the light switches lined up along the wall at the entrance.

One by one, the fluorescent lights came on, brightening the dark interior.

Eileen walked around the L-shaped counter that contained the cash register and credit card box as well as stacks of flyers advertising special sales for today. After hiding her purse and lunch sack under the counter and removing her lightweight jacket, she went straight to the utility closet and removed the vacuum cleaner. She vacuumed first and then swept any areas where the vacuum didn't maneuver easily. While she dusted—only her own For Sale items—she checked to make sure no one had disturbed the way in which she had arranged each booth. The correct display was of the utmost importance if you wanted to catch an antiquer's eye.

As she passed by Susan Cornelius's booth, she caught a glimpse of something odd in her peripheral vision. It took a couple of seconds for her brain to register what she'd seen. Merciful Lord, there was someone sitting in one of the antique rocking chairs!

Eileen's heartbeat accelerated as she stopped, turned around, and stared at the unwelcome visitor. How on earth had someone gotten inside the store? She kept the front and back doors locked. And in all the years she had been in business, she'd had only two break-ins, and those had been years ago before she put stickers on the doors and windows and a sign out front stating that the business was protected by a security system. Actually, it wasn't. No way was she going to pay for the system when more than one person had assured her that having the signs and stickers would be enough to warn off potential burglars.

Should she actually confront the person, or should she walk away and hurry back to the front desk where she could call the police? If only she had put her cell phone in her pocket instead of leaving it in her purse, she could make the call immediately.

"Whoever you are, you should know that I've already

called the police and they're on their way here now," Eileen lied.

No response.

Seeing the back of the person's head—long, dark hair—as well as the narrow slope of the shoulders and slenderness of the waist, Eileen decided that the figure sitting in the rocking chair belonged to a woman. Armed with that belief, she ventured toward Susan Cornelius's booth.

Hesitantly, Eileen made her way around to the front of the booth. Preparing to meet the intruder face-to-face, she picked up an antique brass bed warmer propped against the side of a small walnut bookcase. As Eileen opened her mouth to demand the person get out of the rocking chair and explain what she was doing inside the shop, the words died on her lips and a shrill scream erupted from her throat. The bed warmer fell from Eileen's hand and hit the rug-covered concrete floor with a loud thud.

Sitting there, utterly still and quite obviously dead, an attractive young woman stared sightlessly straight ahead.

"Merciful Lord, merciful Lord." Eileen wrung her hands together as she turned and ran up the aisle between the booths, heading straight for the telephone to call the police.

J.D. was now number one on his daughter's shit list. She had not said two words to him since they left Audrey's house last night. When he had tried to talk to her that morning, she had clamped her mouth shut and glared at him as if he were a monster. He had called Audrey several times, using her home number, her office number, and her cell number. Each time, the call had gone immediately to voice mail. He didn't know if she wasn't answering any calls or just not answering his. Damn it, both Zoe and Audrey were blaming him for something that wasn't his fault. He hadn't been the one to leak the information to the press.

No, but you're the one who put Audrey's stepbrother on your persons-of-interest list.

But no matter how he figured things, there was no denying that Hart Roberts *was* a person of interest. Did J.D. suspect him of being the Rocking Chair Killer? He had no proof of any kind against the man. There was no reason to suspect Roberts of a crime. But J.D.'s gut told him that he couldn't overlook the possibility that Roberts was involved simply because he was Audrey's brother.

Jeremy Arden was a more likely suspect, but J.D. would lay odds that the mysterious Corey Bennett would turn out to be their killer. This guy's true identity was the problem. No one by that name in the Chattanooga area had any connection to Regina Bennett or her aunt and uncle. And if he was their killer, he wouldn't be traveling long distances to kidnap his victims, kill them, and then disappear. No, their killer would probably be living somewhere within a fifty-mile radius. J.D. would bet his pension on it.

He couldn't rule out the possibility that Corey Bennett might be an alias for either Roberts or Arden.

If he thought it would do any good, he'd try calling Audrey again.

Better to wait and give her time to cool off. Eventually her brain would override her emotions. Once she had a chance to think things through logically, she would understand.

And if she didn't understand?

What difference did it make? It wasn't as if he and Audrey were involved. Hell, they weren't even friends. She and Zoe were friends, and he knew that Audrey wouldn't penalize Zoe for anything she thought he had done wrong.

J.D. poured himself a fourth cup of coffee and sat down at the kitchen table where he'd left his cereal bowl and juice glass from breakfast. Just as he picked up the Sunday paper and stared at the Rocking Chair/Baby Blue headlines on the front page, groaning as he started rereading the article, his phone rang.

For the second time today, his boss was calling. The first time had been at seven o'clock. They had discussed who the possible leak was and how they could smoke the person out into the open. Heads would roll if Phil Hayes found out that someone under his command was the culprit. Identifying the leak wouldn't be easy and might prove impossible.

"It had damn well better be someone at the CPD," Phil had said. "I'd rather this be Willie Mullins's headache instead of mine. But the bottom line is that we're all taking fire from the press and looking like we're trying to hide information the public should know."

J.D. answered the phone on the third ring. "What now? More bad news?"

"You could say that. Whitney Poole has shown up."

"Dead, I assume."

"You assume correctly."

"When and where?" J.D. asked.

"Less than an hour ago. She's sitting in a rocking chair inside an antique store. And yeah, she's holding a blanket-wrapped toddler skeleton."

"Son of a bitch."

"You're not very popular with Sergeant Hudson or Officer Lovelady," Phil told him. "But they don't have any choice but to work with you. I told Willie this morning that if they can't be even halfway objective, then he needs to pull them and assign the Rocking Chair Killer cases to another team."

"They're not going to hand over their cases willingly. And I can't blame either of them for being pissed at me. After all, Hudson is Hart Roberts's uncle and Tam Lovelady is Audrey Sherrod's best friend."

"You didn't do a damn thing wrong. When you placed Hart Roberts on the persons-of-interest list, you were just doing your job."

"Try explaining that to them." *Try explaining it to Audrey.*

"You don't owe them an explanation," Phil told him. "You just continue doing your job and try to ignore their hostility. It won't be the first time you've worked with people you've pissed off."

"Where's the antique store?"

"East Ridge. Slater Road. The whole street is lined with antique shops. The one you're looking for is called One Man's Treasure."

"I'm on my way."

"One more thing—there may be a witness."

"A witness to what?"

"To our guy putting the body inside the antique store."

"I hope this supposed eyewitness is more helpful than the last one was."

Garth avoided J.D. as if he had the plague. That suited J.D. just fine. Considering the fact that both he and Sergeant Hudson had reputations as hotheads, it was best if they didn't wind up in a confrontation, possibly even a physical altercation. If Garth threw the first punch, there was no way J.D. would turn the other cheek or simply walk away. It wasn't in his nature. Maturity had taught him not to start a fight, the way he'd occasionally done when he was younger, but he sure as hell wouldn't walk away from a fight the other guy started.

Tam had met him when he first arrived on the scene at One Man's Treasure. "You're not to go anywhere near Sergeant Hudson. You'll deal strictly with me. Understand? Those are the chief's orders."

"I'm surprised you're speaking to me."

"Either I work with you or Dad . . . the chief will have to take Garth and me off the Rocking Chair Killer cases," Tam had admitted.

In the past half hour, J.D. had done his best to stay out of the way of the experts while police and civilian specialists investigated the crime scene. He spoke with the officers first on the scene, had a few words with ME Pete Tipton, and inspected Whitney Poole's body sitting serenely in the antique rocking chair. A toddler skeleton, wrapped securely in a blue blanket, rested in Whitney's arms. Mother and child. Posed almost identically to the previous two victims.

"Do you want to speak to Eileen Campbell?" Tam asked.

"Who?"

"The owner of the antique shop?"

"Not now. Maybe later."

"A window at the back was smashed," Tam said. "We figure he broke the glass, reached inside, and opened it. Then he crawled in and unlocked the door from the inside."

"Why didn't the security system go off?"

"She doesn't have a security system. Just stickers and a sign claiming she does."

"How would he know that?"

"Maybe he took a chance. If the alarm went off, he could have made a run for it and been gone before the police arrived."

"Maybe."

J.D. glanced around at the crowd gathered just beyond the yellow crime scene tape. Reporters and curiosity seekers. Passersby. People who had intended to shop for antiques that afternoon. What were the odds that the killer was among the onlookers, blending in without being noticed?

"What about the witness?" J.D. asked.

"What about him?" Tam's hard gaze told J.D. her attitude toward him hadn't softened in the least.

"Who is he? Where is he?"

"He's a vagrant," Tam replied. "An old wino who was sleeping it off behind the row of antique stores along this street. His name is . . ." She paused to refer to her notes. "Henry O'Neal. Fifty-seven. No permanent address."

"Just what did Henry see?"

"He saw a car pull away from behind One Man's Treasure. Henry was asleep in a bed he'd made from discarded boxes at the back of the store next door. And no, he can't ID the car, except that it looked like an 'older-model big car.' His exact words." Tam crossed her arms over her chest. "He has no idea what time it was. He said it was dark."

"Did he see the man driving the car?"

"A glimpse. He couldn't even give us a description."

"Then there's no point in my questioning him, is there?"

"Probably not. You can read Officer Grissom's report and my report. We both questioned Henry." Tam frowned, twisting her mouth and glancing up and down, as if she was considering her next words carefully. "He did see something else."

That comment got J.D.'s undivided attention. "What did he see?"

"A bumper sticker on the back of the car. He said it glowed in the dark."

J.D. groaned. "Why couldn't he have seen the license plate, too?"

"He says it was too dark."

"Anything unusual about the bumper sticker, other than it glowed in the dark?"

"It was a pro-life sticker that read 'Smile! Your mother chose life!'"

"The sticker could have been there when he bought the car."

Tam nodded. "It could have been."

"But you don't think so. You think the killer chose the sticker and put it on the car himself. 'Smile! Your mother chose life!' is a unique way of saying she didn't kill you, so be happy."

"Your mother didn't kill you the way Cody Bennett's mother killed him, the way she killed him again and again by taking the lives of other little boys."

"I get it." J.D. cleared his throat. "I have some photos in the car that I want the uniformed officers to take a look at and then walk around through the crowd to see if anyone looks familiar. And I think I'll show the same photos to Henry O'Neal."

"I want to see the photos first," Tam said.

"Sure. But I can tell you now that you're not going to like the fact that one of the photos is of Hart Roberts."

Tam glared at him.

When she didn't say anything, he added, "The other photo is of Jeremy Arden."

"Go get the photographs. I'll have a couple of our officers take them and look through the crowd. But I can promise you that if Hart is out there, it's only because he's interested in the fact there's been another body discovered, along with a child's skeleton that could be his brother, Blake."

"I understand," J.D. told her. "Look, for what it's worth, I don't think Hart Roberts is our killer, but if I didn't even consider him as a possible person of interest, I wouldn't be doing my job."

"I know," Tam said reluctantly before turning and walking away.

When her doorbell rang at seven twenty that evening, the last person Audrey expected to find on her doorstep was J.D. Cass. For a split second she thought about slamming the door in his face.

"If you're here to tell me that Whitney Poole is dead, I already know."

"I figured you did since you have an in with the CPD. Plus the fact that every reporter in the state showed up at the crime scene."

"Then what do you want?" she asked.

"May I come in?"

Reluctantly, Audrey stepped aside so he could enter. Once he was inside, she closed the door, turned to him, and crossed her arms over her chest.

"Why are you here?"

"I thought we should talk."

"I have nothing to say to you."

"Well, I have a few things to say to you."

"Please say them as quickly as possible and then leave."

"You're pissed at the wrong person."

Clenching her teeth and scrunching her face into an angry frown, she glared at him, and then after a hasty in-drawn and released breath, she said, "No, I think I am, as you so eloquently put it, *pissed* at the right person."

J.D. groaned.

She could tell that he was frustrated by her refusal to see things from his point of view. "If that's all—"

"No, by God, that's not all."

She stepped back, afraid that he was going to grab her.

"I'd like to shake some sense into that pretty head of yours." He growled the words.

"Don't you dare touch me."

He huffed angrily. "I wouldn't touch you with a ten-foot pole."

Sensing she was on the verge of tears, Audrey swallowed several times, hoping to control her emotions. "Will you please say whatever it is you came here to say."

"I will be interviewing your stepbrother tomorrow. I wanted to be the one to tell you."

"I see. All right, you've told me."

"I'm also interviewing Jeremy Arden. And we're continuing our search for Corey Bennett."

"Leaving no stone unturned."

"That's right. Damn it, Audrey, you're a retired policeman's daughter, the niece of a CPD detective. You know that if I didn't consider every possibility, didn't question anyone who might know anything about these murders, I wouldn't be doing my job. Interviewing your stepbrother could easily eliminate him from the persons-of-interest list altogether."

Audrey knew J.D. was right. He *was* just doing his job. But Hart was her brother and she knew he wasn't a killer. There was no way Hart could tell the TBI anything about the murders. Couldn't J.D. see that? No, of course not. J.D. didn't know Hart the way she did. To him, her stepbrother was simply a guy with emotional problems who had been in various kinds of trouble most of his life.

"I understand that you're just doing your job," Audrey said. "What I don't understand is why you thought it necessary to come here and try to explain yourself to me."

He didn't respond at first. He stood there and stared at her. And then he said, "Damn if I know."

Without another word, he turned around, opened the door, and left.

Audrey released a pent-up breath and closed her eyes as they filled with tears. She hated J.D. Cass. Hated him, hated him, hated him.

No, you don't hate him. And that's why you're so upset.

Chapter 23

J.D hadn't slept worth a damn. And it was more than concern about the seemingly unsolvable Rocking Chair Murders that had kept him awake. For the life of him, he couldn't get Audrey Sherrod off his mind, not last night and not this morning. For a smart woman, she sure as hell was acting stupid. She'd said she understood that by interviewing her stepbrother, he was just doing his job. And he understood that she loved and trusted Hart Roberts, that as his stepsister, she was extremely protective of her emotionally unbalanced sibling. Roberts was a borderline crazy who had been in and out of rehab numerous times, and since his teen years, he'd been in trouble with the law time and again. From what J.D. could find out about Roberts, the guy was a ticking time bomb who could explode at any moment.

Maybe he'd already exploded. Maybe that last screw in his mind had come loose and he was kidnapping and killing Regina Bennett look-alikes. For an unbalanced mind, it wouldn't be so far-fetched to seek a sick kind of revenge against the woman he believed had kidnapped and murdered his baby brother.

But how would Hart Roberts know where Regina had hidden the toddlers' bodies?

He wouldn't. Not unless there had been some type of communication between Regina and him. And there was no evidence whatsoever that the two had ever met or communicated in any way.

Unless Hart Roberts was the mysterious Corey Bennett.

But that was unlikely, wasn't it?

After spending the better part of the morning doing some reinterviewing in the field, he was finally on his way back to the office. First thing this morning, he had talked to Ms. Milsaps and several other Moccasin Bend employees. Then he had gone from the mental hospital to the Chattanooga Funeral Home's East Chapel and spoken again to Mr. Scudder, the funeral director. His last stop had been at Callie's Café, where he had spoken to the manager again. He had shown all of them photos of both Hart Roberts and Jeremy Arden.

"I recognize Mr. Arden," Ms. Milsaps had said. "But not the other man."

"You've never seen him?" J.D. had pointed directly to Hart's photo.

"No, I don't think so. But . . . Well, Mr. Arden and this man are very similar in looks, don't you think? And Corey Bennett, as best I can recall, is also fair, blond and has a similar look."

"I thought you said Corey Bennett had brown hair."

"Light brown, I believe I said. You know, the kind of hair that's a shade between blond and light brown. Just like Mr. Arden and this other man."

J.D. had studied the photos. The resemblance between Jeremy Arden and Hart Roberts was entirely superficial. Blue eyes, brownish blond hair, medium height and build. Both of them were the pretty-boy type. He could see where the two men could easily be mistaken for each other if seen only from a distance or if someone was trying to recall their face from a past meeting.

A couple of the Moccasin Bend employees recognized Jeremy Arden's photo and vaguely remembered he had visited a patient there. But no one recognized Hart Roberts.

Mr. Scudder had taken his time looking at the photos, then shaken his head and said, "I don't think either of these men is Corey Bennett, although they do fit the description I gave you, don't they. And I suppose if you added glasses and a mustache . . ."

"Do you remember anything else about Corey Bennett, anything at all, even something you'd consider completely insignificant?"

Mr. Scudder had thought quite seriously for several minutes. "No, nothing. Well, maybe. I did think it odd that a man wearing an expensive suit and sporting an obvious professional manicure would be in need of a haircut."

"What do you mean exactly?"

"His hair was rather shaggy and hung down over his collar. Come to think of it, at the time, I wondered if perhaps he was bald or balding and was wearing a wig."

One by one the pieces fell into place. Shaggy hair that could have been a wig. A mustache. And eyeglasses. The three items combined suggested a disguise, a disguise that would hide the man's true identity.

But the expensive suit and the professional manicure revealed a man who could afford both. Neither Jeremy Arden nor Hart Roberts had any money to speak of. Roberts didn't even have a job.

J.D.'s phone rang. He checked caller ID and groaned. It was Cara Oliver again. The woman had called a dozen times since Saturday night. She'd left a voice-mail message each time. If he didn't answer her calls or return them, maybe she'd take the hint that he was not interested in her.

Ignoring the call, he checked the time on the dashboard clock. Eleven twenty. He had asked the CPD to find Henry O'Neal and escort him to the TBI office for further questioning. O'Neal was probably there now, waiting on him. Running a few miles over the speed limit, J.D. headed toward McCallie Avenue.

When he arrived at the State Office Building, Suite 650, he found a uniformed officer standing watch over a seated Henry O'Neal inside J.D.'s office. Hard living and heavy boozing had aged O'Neal beyond his fifty-seven years. Apparently someone had gotten their witness some coffee because he cupped a mug between his shaky hands and barely managed to put the mug to his lips without spilling the contents.

When J.D. entered, the young officer nodded and introduced himself as Tom Bonds. O'Neal looked up through bloodshot eyes, his face a craggy mass of deep lines and heavy wrinkles.

"Thanks for coming in, Mr. O'Neal," J.D. said as he walked over and propped his hip against the edge of his desk.

"Don't know why you want to talk to me again. I told you and them other cops yesterday what I saw. I can't tell you no more today than I could then."

"I understand. We won't keep you long, but I'd appreciate it if you'd take another look at the photographs I showed you. Only this time picture both men with longer, slightly darker hair, perhaps with a mustache and wearing glasses."

O'Neal gulped down another hefty swig of black coffee, shook his head, and said, "I can't help you none. I told you that. I didn't see the guy's face."

J.D. picked up a file folder from his desk, opened it, and removed duplicates of the photos of Jeremy Arden and Hart Roberts. "Take another look anyway." He held the photos in front of O'Neal.

After looking over each picture for a few seconds, he grunted. "It could have been either of them. I don't know. It might not have been. It was dark. I didn't see his face."

"But you're sure the driver was a man?"

"Yeah, I'm pretty sure."

J.D. tossed the photos down on his desk. "What about the car?"

"It wasn't a new car. It was one of them big old cars, a Lincoln maybe." O'Neal finished off his coffee and held up the mug. "I wouldn't mind another cup. And maybe something to go with it. A doughnut or a sandwich or—"

J.D. glanced at the uniformed officer. "Get Mr. O'Neal another cup of coffee, would you?"

With an offended look on his face, Officer Bonds took the mug from O'Neal and did as J.D had requested.

"Tell me more about the car," J.D. said.

O'Neal shrugged. "Not much to tell. Like I said, it was probably an older-model Lincoln or Cadillac. Light color. Maybe white. And it was dirty; the tires were caked with dried mud like he'd been driving it off road."

"You said it was an old Lincoln or Cadillac. Which was it?"

"Not sure, but I think it was a Lincoln."

"How old? Ten years old or older?"

"Older. One of them big jobs from the eighties."

Just as J.D. suspected, Henry O'Neal had seen a lot more than he'd realized, at least about the car if not about the driver.

"You saw the bumper sticker, but not the car tag, right?" J.D. asked.

"That's right. The sticker glowed in the dark."

"Think real hard, Mr. O'Neal. You saw the car drive away, so why if you were bedded down behind the antique stores, didn't you see the car when it arrived?"

"I don't know."

"Think about it."

"I was asleep."

"You were drunk."

O'Neal nodded. "I—I didn't see the car or the man driving it until he drove off, but I might have heard something before then."

"What did you hear?"

"Doors opening and closing. Car doors, I think. And I might've heard glass breaking. I'm not sure. Like you said, I was drunk. I was bedded down all snug and warm. I didn't want to be bothered. As long as nobody messed with me, it wasn't nothing to me what they was doing."

J.D. continued questioning him while O'Neal downed a second cup of coffee, but within half an hour, J.D. knew he'd gotten all the information he was going to get. Less than he'd hoped, but more than he'd gotten yesterday.

The info he had acquired today added up, one detail at a time. Assuming that the driver of the old car Henry O'Neal had seen late Saturday night or early Sunday morning was their killer, then they knew he either owned, had access to, or had stolen an older-model vehicle, possibly a white eighties-model Lincoln. It could be a piece of old junk that he'd bought for practically nothing. Or it could be a restored classic. But just how many cars fitting that description were still on the road? Especially one with a pro-life, glow-in-the-dark bumper sticker?

The tires were caked with dried mud like he'd been driving it off road. Off road. Out in the country? Possibly on a farm in Sale Creek?

J.D. was forming another hypothesis, one that put the killer on the farm where Regina Bennett had lived with her aunt and uncle. Was there a place on those hundred acres where he had kept Jill Scott, Debra Gregory, and Whitney Poole captive? Was there an area that the FBI had somehow missed in their thorough searches more than two decades ago, a place where Regina Bennett had hidden away the bodies of her son and five other little boys?

What were the odds that, without any real evidence to support his possibly far-fetched scenario, he could persuade a judge to issue a search warrant for the hundred acres and all the structures on the farm?

Slim to none.

J.D. picked up the phone and enlisted some help. A sketch artist could create pictures of Jeremy Arden and Hart Roberts each with long, blondish brown hair, a mustache, and glasses.

A quick check should reveal if either man or a family member owned an older-model Lincoln. Local antique car clubs might know of a car that fit the description. If the car was registered, had a tag, and was insured, they would be able to track it. And it wouldn't hurt to check out any cars that Regina Bennett or her aunt and her uncle had owned.

At one-thirty, Jeremy Arden and Hart Roberts arrived at the TBI office, along with their own small entourage comprising of two lawyers, Sergeant Garth Hudson, Officer Tamara Lovelady, and retired Sergeant Wayne Sherrod. Once all the introductions were made, Garth took Jeremy and his lawyer into his office and closed the door.

"This is an informal interview," J.D. said. "Nothing more."

"Nevertheless, my client prefers to have legal representation," the lawyer, who had introduced himself as Edward Gates, informed J.D.

"Do you wear glasses, Mr. Arden?"

"No."

"Contacts?"

"No?"

"Do you own a pair of glasses?"

"Sunglasses."

"Prescription?"

"No."

"Do you own a car, Mr. Arden?" J.D. asked.

"No. I have a motorcycle."

"Have you ever been back to the farm where Regina Bennett kept you after she kidnapped you?"

Jeremy shifted uncomfortably in his seat. "No. Why would I want to go back there?"

J.D. let his gaze drift casually over Jeremy, from his blond hair to his faded jeans and worn corduroy jacket to his scuffed leather boots.

"Why did you visit Regina Bennett in Moccasin Bend several times shortly before her death?"

Jeremy's facial muscles tensed. He turned, leaned over, and whispered something to his lawyer. They talked quietly for a couple of minutes. J.D. looked at Jeremy's small, slender hands and his thin fingers. A couple of his nails were chipped, one broken into the quick, and there was what looked like grease under one thumbnail. J.D.'s guess was this guy had never had a professional manicure in his life.

"I wanted to see her, talk to her, to come face-to-face with the woman who had kidnapped me. I guess you could call it an unhealthy fascination," Jeremy said. "Every time I went to see her, she called me Cody. She was nuts and I knew that, but . . . I kept remembering things. Like her singing to me. And her rocking me."

"Just how much do you remember?"

"Not a lot. And to be honest, I'm not sure if any of the memories are real."

"Are we about through here, Special Agent Cass?" Edward Gates asked.

"Just a few more questions." He focused on Arden. "Did you know any of the Rocking Chair Killer's victims?"

"What?" Arden's face paled.

"Did you, for instance, know Whitney Poole?"

Arden swallowed hard, then conversed with his lawyer again before answering. "I saw her a few times when I ate at the café where she worked."

"Did you ever talk to her? Flirt with her?"

"Yeah, a couple of times, but I didn't kidnap her and I didn't kill her. I liked her. I'd been trying to work up the courage to ask her out when she disappeared."

"So, it's just a fluke, just a weird coincidence that you were interested in dating one of the Rocking Chair Killer's victims. You, Jeremy Arden, the one and only Baby Blue toddler who was rescued."

Arden became visibly upset. Sweat dotted his upper lip and his breathing quickened as he stood quickly and wrung his hands together.

Arden's lawyer intervened, calmed him down, and from then until the end of the interview consulted on every answer Arden gave.

J.D. continued the questioning, keeping his voice even and his attitude friendly. Jeremy was highly agitated and a few times he got rattled again and looked like a scared rabbit caught in a hunter's snare.

"If I were to ask you where you were and what you were doing on the nights when our three victims were killed and each one's body staged in a rocking chair with a toddler's skeleton in her arms, could you tell me? Would you have an alibi for all three nights?"

"I don't know. Probably not. I live alone. I don't have any friends. And no girlfriend."

After a half-hour interview, J.D. opened the office door, thanked Jeremy Arden for his cooperation, and walked him outside where Hart Roberts was waiting. Roberts was alone except for Tam Lovelady and his lawyer. Roberts and Arden glanced at each other, nodded, and then Arden left with his lawyer.

"I'm ready for you now, Mr. Roberts."

"I'd like to speak to you first," Tam said.

"All right." J.D. glanced from Hart Roberts to his lawyer, a fortysomething brunette who looked vaguely familiar. "Why don't you two wait in my office."

"I hope you don't intend to keep us waiting much longer, Special Agent Cass," the lady lawyer said.

And then J.D. remembered where he'd met her and who she was. "This shouldn't take long, should it, Officer Lovelady?"

"A few minutes," Tam replied.

J.D. smiled at the lawyer he had met briefly a couple of months ago when Holly had dragged him off to some social function she simply couldn't miss. Kim Miner was a friend of Holly's, actually more than a friend. Holly considered the woman her mentor and had patterned herself after the lawyer known in legal circles as the Barracuda Bitch. The lady didn't work cheap, which immediately made J.D. wonder who was paying her bill.

"If y'all will go on in, I'll be with you shortly." J.D. kept his fake smile in place and as soon as Roberts and his lawyer entered his office, J.D. turned to Tam. "Did Garth leave?"

"Wayne took him outside to try to cool him off," Tam said. "Keeping Hart waiting while you interviewed Jeremy Arden gave Garth plenty of time to work up a head of steam. I'm just glad Wayne was here."

"And just why is Wayne Sherrod here?" J.D. asked. "As a matter of fact, why are you and Garth here?"

"Garth is Hart's uncle. He's here for moral support, as is Wayne."

"And you?"

"I'm a friend of the family."

"So, what was it you wanted to talk to me about?" J.D. asked.

"I know you've done your homework, that you've learned

a great deal about Hart, about his problems with the law, with drugs and alcohol and that he's had emotional issues since he was a kid." Tam paused, reached out, grasped J.D.'s arm, and said, "Hart Roberts is not your killer."

"I'm not accusing him of anything. You know what this is. Just an informal interview."

"If you push him too hard, he—he could break. Emotionally." She squeezed J.D.'s arm. "I'm asking you to be careful when you question him. Please."

J.D. realized that Tam Lovelady cared about Hart Roberts, cared a hell of a lot. Maybe even loved him. More than as a friend's brother?

Tam removed her hand from J.D.'s arm.

"Okay. Don't worry. I'll take it easy," J.D. said, then turned around, went into his office, and closed the door.

For the next twenty-five minutes, he went over most of the same questions with Hart Roberts that he'd asked Jeremy Arden. Roberts said he did own a car, but not an older-model Lincoln. J.D. knew the car he mentioned—an eight-year-old Toyota—was actually registered to his uncle. More questioning revealed that Roberts didn't wear glasses or contacts, but like Arden did own nonprescription sunglasses. He had eaten at Callie's Café several times but couldn't remember ever seeing Whitney Poole, and he said he'd never met either of the other victims.

"Did you ever have any type of contact with Regina Bennett?" J.D. had asked.

"God, no!"

"You never visited her at Moccasin Bend or—"

"Hell, no." Roberts had laughed then, laughed too hard and too long. Finally, he controlled himself and added, "I'm afraid if I ever visited that place, they'd keep me."

Later, when asked about an alibi for the nights of the three murders, he'd smirked at J.D. "I'm sure my uncle can give me an alibi. I live with him, but then you know that, don't you."

When the interview concluded, Tam was waiting for Roberts and Ms. Miner, but Garth Hudson and Wayne Sherrod were nowhere to be seen.

J.D. sat down in the swivel chair behind his desk and immediately began going over both interviews. His gut instincts told him that Audrey's stepbrother was hiding something. But was it something about the Rocking Chair Murders? The man had been more than just normally nervous, and yet he'd been cocky and belligerent at times. J.D. had done his best to ask all the questions he needed to ask without unduly upsetting Roberts, but the guy had been upset before being asked the first question. And although J.D. had done nothing more than casually glance at Roberts's clothes and hands, he'd jumped up and demanded to know why J.D. was inspecting him. Ms. Miner had spoken to him and urged him to be seated again.

"You get a manicure often, Mr. Roberts?"

He had lifted his hands and shown them to J.D. "I've gotten a few. This one was a gift from a manicurist I'm sort of dating. I can give you her name and number if you—"

"No, thanks." J.D. had looked him over from head to toe. "Nice suit. Expensive. Looks new."

"It is."

"You always dress this way?"

"No, I don't, but my lawyer"—he had glanced at Kim Miner—"advised me to wear a suit and tie today. So I wore the new suit my sister bought me for a recent job interview."

Audrey had bought him a suit. She was probably paying Kim Miner's exorbitant fees, too. And Garth, Wayne Sherrod, and Tam had accompanied Roberts, acting as his backup team. With so many people in his corner, helping him, supporting him, loving him, why hadn't Roberts been able to get his act together? Why was he, at thirty-three, still such a screwup?

After the interview, Tam had been waiting when J.D. walked Hart and his lawyer to the door. Apparently, Wayne Sherrod had persuaded Garth to go back to police headquarters, which suited J.D. just fine. He didn't want a confrontation with Hart Roberts's uncle.

With Audrey's uncle.

J.D. would have liked to believe that out there somewhere was a man using the name Corey Bennett, a man who fit the same general description of both Jeremy Arden and Hart Roberts. He didn't want to believe that Roberts could possibly be the Rocking Chair Killer. But after today's interviews, he knew without a doubt that he couldn't eliminate either man from his persons-of-interest list. Not yet.

The office door swung open and hit the doorjamb with a bang. J.D. glanced up from behind his desk at the man standing just inside his office. Sergeant Garth Hudson glared at J.D., his facial features stretched tight with anger.

J.D. rose from his chair and faced the other man.

"You don't want to make an enemy out of me, Cass," Garth told him. "Leave my nephew alone and we'll pretend today's interview never happened."

"What are you so afraid of?" J.D. asked. "Do you think if I keep digging, I'm going to find out that Hart Roberts is somehow connected to the murders?"

"Damn you, Cass. I'm warning you. Hart is in no way connected to the murders."

"If that's true, then why are you so bent out of shape about my interviewing him?"

"I've given you fair warning. Leave Hart alone or you'll regret it."

Chapter 24

Hart had used the interview with TBI Special Agent Cass as an excuse to get rip-roaring drunk Monday night. He barely remembered the fight he'd gotten into with some biker who'd come on to Jessica. Uncle Garth had bailed him out of jail this morning and reminded him that what he'd done would keep him front and center on Cass's radar. Once again, his uncle had rescued him. Once again, he had disappointed the man who'd been like a father to him.

"I'm sorry," he'd said. "I know my apologies aren't worth much, but—"

"Save the apologies. Show me that you're sorry, prove it to me."

"How?"

"Audrey's waiting outside in her car to take you to a meeting," Garth had told him. "Go with her and do whatever she tells you to do. If she says go to half a dozen meetings a day, you go. If she says you go back into rehab, you go. If she says jump off the Walnut Street Bridge, you jump."

"Okay, okay, I get the idea. Audrey is the boss."

And so he'd gone to the meeting, and afterward, Audrey

had picked him up and was now issuing him a list of dos and don'ts. "You're going to, at the very least, one meeting a day. You're staying out of bars. You're going to the employment office and tell them you want a job. You will go to whatever job interviews they send you on, and you're going to work, I don't care if it's sweeping floors or washing dishes."

"Yes, ma'am." He saluted her.

"This isn't funny." She shot him a condemning glare.

"Sorry. I know it's not funny, but lighten up, will you?"

"Do you have any idea how serious it is to be questioned by the TBI? I know you are not involved in any way with the Rocking Chair Murders, but my God, Hart, why give J.D. Cass more ammunition against you?"

Audrey was right. She was always right. Getting drunk and winding up in jail had been a stupid mistake, one more in a long line of stupid mistakes.

"Why don't you just give up on me?" he asked her.

"Damn it, Hart, stop feeling sorry for yourself."

"Hell, sis, it seems to be the only thing I'm good at."

She cast him a sidelong glance and released a heavy, exasperated breath. "One other thing—don't see Jessica Smith again. She's a sweet kid, and if you continue seeing her, she'll wind up getting hurt."

Hart wanted to protest, wanted to tell Audrey that she had no say-so in who he dated, but he couldn't deny that she was right. He had a history of breaking hearts. "Yeah, you're right. I need to stick to one-night stands with women who know the score."

"Then you'll end things with Jessica as soon as possible?"

"There really isn't much to end. We've had two dates and a good-night kiss."

"Good," Audrey said, then continued with instructions for how he was going to live his life for the immediate future.

"I'll drop you at the employment office. Take a cab home. I've arranged for your sponsor to check in on you several times each day for the next week or so. Garth can't baby-sit you, and neither can I. But if you need either of us—"

"You'll come wipe my nose and change my dirty diaper."

She didn't respond to his flippant comment or even glance his way. He couldn't blame her. Hell, he wouldn't blame her if she washed her hands of him completely. But that wasn't Audrey's style. No, she was loyal and steadfast and forgiving. And a natural-born caretaker. She should have gotten married and had kids. She'd make a great mother.

"I don't know what I'd do without you," Hart admitted. "You and Uncle Garth. I'd be dead by now if you two hadn't taken care of me all these years."

"We love you, you know that." She kept her gaze fixed on the road. "You're family. You're my brother."

"Lucky me. Unlucky you."

Unlucky Blake, too. If I'd been taking care of him the way I was supposed to, he'd still be alive and all our lives would be so different. So very, very different . . .

J.D. had debated what to do about Garth Hudson's threat. *Leave Hart alone or you'll regret it.* Had the warning been nothing more than an uncle's concern for his nephew, an angry outburst from a man with a reputation as a hothead? J.D. understood only too well how a man could lose his cool and say something he shouldn't. He'd done it more than once himself. But the deciding factor had been obvious—could Sergeant Hudson continue as the senior investigating officer on the Rocking Chair Killer cases and remain objective? J.D. didn't think so. But when he had spoken to his boss late yesterday, Phil had suggested waiting.

"Let's see how things play out over the next few days.

Hudson may have cooled off by now. If he's uncooperative and causes any problems for you, then I'll personally talk to Willie Mullins."

A face-to-face with Garth today had been avoided, partly because Garth had been too busy bailing his nephew out of lockup. Apparently Hart Roberts had gotten drunk and wound up in a brawl with another customer at a local dive. From everything J.D. had learned about Roberts, the man seemed to live his life as if he was on a suicide mission. If there was a wrong choice to be made, the guy made it.

Deciding to work alone in his office all morning, J.D. had come up with the answers to several questions concerning recently acquired information. After lunch, he had gathered up all the info and gone to CPD headquarters. He had to admit that when he found Tam alone in the office she shared with Garth, he had been relieved.

Tam was on the phone when he walked in. She glanced up and motioned for him to take a seat.

"He just walked in," she said. "Yeah, I'll fill him in." She paused to listen. "Okay. Call me when you're on your way and I'll meet you there." She hung up the phone and turned to J.D. "That was Garth."

J.D. nodded.

"He picked up Whitney Poole's mother from the airport and dropped her off at the Holiday Inn. She lives in Detroit. According to the mom, she and Whitney hadn't seen each other in nearly four years. Whitney and her stepfather didn't get along."

"Hmm . . . Still, it had to be hard for the mother to learn her daughter had been murdered."

"I'm sure it is hard for her. No matter what, there's a bond between a parent and child, right?"

J.D. nodded. What could he say? *I'm still trying to bond with my child.*

"Do you have a few minutes or will you be leaving soon?" he asked.

"I'm all yours until Garth calls back." She looked at J.D. then and said, "I guess you know about Hart, don't you?"

"Yeah, I heard."

"Garth's going by his place to check on Hart before he comes back here."

Then where are y'all going? he wanted to ask, but didn't. Instead he told her why he was there. "I did some checking about that glow-in-the-dark 'Smile! Your mother chose life!' bumper sticker, and I'm afraid what I found out won't help us much. They sell them on the Internet at dozens of sites. It seems that one is a popular sticker. Several churches in Hamilton County even ordered them by the hundreds to distribute to their parishioners."

"Meaning tracing that one particular bumper sticker is highly unlikely."

"Yeah, that's pretty much a dead end," J.D. told her. "But we had better luck with the eighties white Lincoln."

Tam's eyes brightened with interest. "Tell me."

"I did a cross-check. Eighties white Lincoln with the names of the Rocking Chair Killer's victims, their parents and siblings as well as with the names of the parents and siblings of all the Baby Blue toddlers."

"And?"

"And nothing."

Tam narrowed her gaze and frowned. "Then what?"

"I ran a cross-check with the names Regina Bennett, Corey Bennett, and Luther and Dora Chaney."

"The aunt and uncle?" Tam's eyes again brightened with interest.

"Bingo. Luther Chaney owned a white 1980 Lincoln Town Car." J.D. couldn't help smiling. "He bought it used in '82, but there is no record of the car ever being sold again."

"The uncle died not long after Regina Bennett was arrested, more than twenty-three years ago, so that must mean the aunt kept the car. So, where is the aunt now?"

"Dead," J.D. said. "Dora Chaney passed away a couple of years ago. Not long after her husband died, she left Sale Creek, moved to Bristol, and remarried. I've put out queries up that way to find out if anyone remembers her and if her second husband is still alive. If we can trace what happened to that old Lincoln, it could lead us straight to our killer."

"We should get so lucky."

"Who'd think an old wino getting a glimpse of a car the night Whitney Poole's body was placed in the antique store could actually be the one bit of info that might crack this case wide open."

J.D. parked his Camaro, sat in the car for a couple of minutes, and then made himself get out and walk toward the town house. This was the last place on earth he wanted to be, but it seemed he couldn't stay away. Audrey Sherrod was the last person he wanted to see. What made matters even worse was that he suspected Zoe had purposely arranged this little scenario.

"Please, Daddy, you have to stop by Audrey's and get my notebook. My geometry homework is in it and I have to finish it tonight."

Audrey had picked Zoe up from school that afternoon and they had gone shopping for a Halloween costume for Zoe. All the kids at Baylor dressed in costume for the holiday, but since it was only early October, he hadn't seen the necessity for them to shop so early.

"All the great costumes will be gone," Zoe had whined. "Besides, if we don't find what I want, Audrey says we can make the outfit ourselves. She knows how to sew. Her friend Tam's mom taught her."

J.D. had reluctantly agreed to go by Audrey's and pick up the notebook, but he had cautioned Zoe, "Don't let this happen again. Understood?"

"Yes, sir. Understood."

He rang the doorbell and waited. And waited. He rang the bell again. Audrey was at home, or she was supposed to be. He had told Zoe to call her and tell her he was dropping by and why. Just as he rang the doorbell for the third time, he heard a woman scream.

"Audrey! Audrey!" He rang the bell repeatedly and then pounded on the door.

Just as he was about to look for another way in, possibly break out a window, the door opened and Audrey practically threw Zoe's notebook at him. But he didn't pay much attention to the notebook; he was too concerned about Audrey's appearance. Her face was flushed. Long, mussed tendrils of her hair had escaped from their usual neat confinement, one curling at chin level and the other down the back of her neck. It was obvious she'd been crying. And she had that half-dazed look a person has during those first few minutes after awakening.

"Are you okay?" he asked. "I heard you scream."

"I'm fine," she replied curtly.

"No, you're not. What's wrong?"

When she tried to close the door in his face, he grasped the edge of the door and stuck his foot over the threshold. She didn't try to stop him as he shoved open the door completely and moved toward her.

"Would you please just take Zoe's notebook and leave."

"Not until you tell me why you screamed."

She closed her eyes and heaved a heavy, resigned sigh.

J.D. closed the door behind him, and then turned back to Audrey. "You look like you could use a stiff drink."

"Drinking doesn't solve a person's problems, and it certainly doesn't chase away nightmares."

"Is that why you screamed, you had a nightmare? It's a little early for bedtime, isn't it?" He glanced at his watch—8:35 P.M.—for emphasis.

"It's been a long day. I didn't sleep well last night and I dozed off on the sofa." She frowned. "Why am I telling you this? It's none of your business."

"Don't you recommend talking through your problems, Dr. Sherrod?" He was trying to lighten the mood, but noting her deepening frown, he accepted the fact that she was in no mood for levity. "That must have been some nightmare."

"If I wanted to talk about my nightmares, it certainly wouldn't be with you."

Audrey crossed her arms over her chest, the action bringing his attention to her breasts. She wasn't wearing a bra underneath that soft, velvety pullover.

"Why not? I'm here. And I'm willing to listen." He did his best to keep his gaze at eye level, despite the temptation to take another look at her braless breasts.

"You're not leaving until I open up a vein and bleed all over you, are you?"

J.D.'s lips twitched as he tried not to smile. "You certainly have a dramatic way of expressing yourself, Dr. Sherrod."

"Will you please stop calling me Dr. Sherrod."

"Are we back on a first-name basis?"

"You really are insufferable, aren't you?"

J.D. slid Zoe's notebook under his arm. "Flattery will get you nowhere with me, Dr. Sher—Audrey."

She grumbled something unintelligible under her breath. "I had a nightmare about the day my brother Blake disappeared. There, are you satisfied?"

"What made you scream?"

"The nightmare," she said, leaving off the obvious "you idiot" at the end of her sentence.

"What about the nightmare was so terrifying?"

"I don't know. I don't remember exactly. I never remember—"

"You've had the dream before?"

"All my life," she admitted. "Almost every night for months after Blake disappeared, I had nightmares about that day. And then gradually I had them less often, until by the time I was a teenager, I seldom dreamed about it. But now, since these Rocking Chair Murders have taken place, the nightmares have returned."

"It must be hell to relive that day over and over again," J.D. said. "I'm sorry. I had no idea. You probably went through therapy, maybe even hypnosis and whatever else you could do to try to figure out what terrifies you about the dreams."

"It's not always the same dream," she told him. "And I don't always wake up screaming. Just sometimes. And yes, I've been through counseling."

"Ever wonder if you might have seen the person who took your little brother, that you actually witnessed what happened and your conscious mind blocked it out?"

She stared at him as if an extra head had suddenly sprouted from his shoulder. "That's not possible. Afterward, yes, my memory was fuzzy, but later on, it all came back. Now I remember that day in detail. So does Hart. Neither of us saw who took Blake. We had no idea he was even gone until Hart went to check on him and found him missing."

"It was just a thought. Sorry I mentioned it."

"Don't you think I wish I had seen her, that I could have given the police a description of her? If I could have, then maybe Blake would have been the toddler the FBI rescued and Jeremy Arden would never have been kidnapped."

"Look, how about I get you that stiff drink and—"

"No, thanks. I'm okay now. Really. Just take Zoe's notebook and go."

"If you're sure."

"I'm sure."

When he turned and opened the front door, she called to him, "J.D.?"

"Yeah?" He glanced back at her.

She looked as if she wanted to tell him something, but thought better of it and simply said, "Good night."

"Good night, Audrey."

If she'd been any other woman on earth, he wouldn't have left. He would have reached out, grabbed her, and kissed her. God knew he wanted to, and only God knew why.

But he didn't kiss her. He didn't stay. Common sense kicked in just in the nick of time, reminding him that he and Audrey didn't even like each other.

Chapter 25

J.D. had kept tabs on Jeremy Arden and Hart Roberts for the past few days. Not that he could tail them 24/7 or that he'd been able to persuade his boss or Chief Mullins to assign officers for surveillance. But the deeper he had dug into Arden's and Roberts's pasts, the more dirt he had dug up on each man. Both were addicts, supposedly recovering addicts. Neither had held a steady job for more than six months at a time. Neither had been married or involved in a long-term relationship. Roberts had been in trouble with the law most of his life, even as a teenager, but had been rescued by his uncle Garth again and again. Apparently Roberts wouldn't have survived without the support of his uncle and his stepsister. If not for them, he would have been one of the unfortunate misfits who slipped through the cracks of society and wound up dead in an alley somewhere. Jeremy Arden had somehow managed to survive on his own since he was eighteen, moving from one town to another, one job to another, one woman to another. And it had been that series of women who had provided him with temporary love and support.

Both men were takers, users, never seeing beyond their own needs.

If either had been his brother or nephew, J.D. would have cut him off years ago and allowed him to sink or swim on his own. Tough love, that's what J.D. believed in. Nobody deserved an endless supply of second chances. There was only so much you could do for somebody who wouldn't help himself.

Sure, he could understand how you'd want to stand by a family member, especially one who had emotional or mental problems. But good God, there was a limit, wasn't there? Apparently, Garth and Audrey didn't think so, because they hadn't given up on Hart, or if they had, they chose to continue being caretakers of a man not worth the lead to shoot him.

J.D. didn't have much sympathy for either Arden or Roberts. Correction, make that no sympathy. But he figured Arden had more reason to be unbalanced than Roberts did. After all, Jeremy Arden had been one of the Baby Blue toddlers, the last one, the only one rescued from certain death. Who knew what that experience had done to him? But Hart Roberts hadn't been a victim. His younger brother Blake had been. So what excuse did he have for his behavior? Unless you considered the possible hereditary instability that his mother could have passed on to him. From what little he'd been able to find out about Wayne Sherrod's second wife, J.D. surmised that the lady had suffered from mental problems all her life.

All the digging into the past coupled with gut instinct brought J.D. full circle, back to his original conclusions. Unless there was some unseen wild card in the mix, the Rocking Chair Killer was more than likely one of the Baby Blue toddlers or a family member of one of the kidnap victims or someone closely related to Regina Bennett. He had all but eliminated the victims' family members except for Hart Roberts. But there was absolutely no evidence linking Roberts to Regina Bennett or to the three recent murders. Of course, that didn't mean he wasn't guilty. As for surviving Baby Blue toddlers—as far as anyone knew, Jeremy Arden was the only one. And there *was* evidence linking Arden to Regina Bennett. He had visited her in the mental hospital more than once. As a little boy, he had lived with the woman for months and perhaps had formed an attachment to her.

But neither Arden nor Roberts was the most likely suspect. That dubious honor went to the mysterious Corey Bennett. The name might be fake, but the man was real. The only question: Who was he? Was he really Jeremy Arden or possibly Hart Roberts? His general description fit both men, since they were similar in height, build, and coloring. Or was he someone else entirely, a third man, a third person of interest? And was he actually related to Regina Bennett? Could he be her nephew? If so, why was there no record of him, just as there had been no record of Cody Bennett except for his hospital records? The only people who would have known of another child's existence—a nephew, a younger brother, or even another child—were all dead. Regina Bennett and her aunt Dora and uncle Luther.

J.D. had begun searching for anyone who would admit to having belonged to the now-defunct Holy Brethren Church in Sale Creek and the surrounding area. If another Bennett child existed, there was a possibility that someone in the fundamentalist church would have seen the boy.

When he had searched the records on Dora Chaney's life after she'd left Sale Creek more than two decades ago, he had discovered her second husband was Frank Elmore, a widower with two daughters, both grown and no longer living at home when he married Dora. J.D. had seen Frank's obituary and a copy of his death certificate. He'd passed away last year. Neither of his daughters lived in Bristol, but J.D. was searching for both women on the off chance either would know something about Luther Chaney's old Lincoln or about a man named Corey Bennett.

J.D.'s conversation with the Bristol, Tennessee, police department hadn't borne fruit, not yet, but Chief Tully had been cooperative and promised he'd make some discreet inquiries about Frank Elmore's second wife.

J.D.'s phone rang. He eyed the caller ID. Even though Cara hadn't called again since Wednesday and this was Friday, he wanted to make sure before he answered.

"Yeah, hi, Phil. What's up?" J.D. didn't think his boss would be calling him while he was en route to pick up Zoe for their family-counseling session unless it was something important.

"I just got off the phone with Chief Mullins," Phil Hayes said. "The DNA test results on the toddler skeleton found with Whitney Poole identified the child as Devin Kelly."

"Which means that the third toddler Regina Bennett kidnapped was found with the Rocking Chair Killer's third victim."

"Not a coincidence."

"Damn straight. No way was it a coincidence. This guy is putting the two sets of victims together in chronological order. He's returning the Baby Blue toddlers in the exact order in which they were abducted."

"It would seem so," Phil agreed. "That's an odd choice of words—returning the toddlers in the exact order in which they were abducted."

"But that's what he's doing, isn't it? Whether it's his intention or not, he's giving those little boys back to their families."

"Son of a bitch. You're right."

* * *

Audrey sat alone in the dark. Only the faint glimmer of moonlight mingling with the streetlight's glow allowed her to see shapes and shadows in her living room. Tam had stopped by earlier to tell her the news. The toddler found with Whitney Poole was Devin Kelly, the third little boy Regina Bennett had kidnapped.

"Marcus and I are going to Mom and Dad's for dinner tonight," Tam had said. "Come with us, please. You don't need to be alone."

She had begged off, telling her best friend a little white lie. "I'm expecting Hart and Uncle Garth later."

Neither Garth nor Hart had called her. She hadn't expected them to call. Her uncle knew that Tam would bring her the news in person. Besides, she was not his first priority. He would have to tell Hart about the DNA results and then deal with whatever fallout resulted. Hart would probably get drunk again or possibly get high. After all these years, she knew her stepbrother well enough to know that he would use any excuse to justify doing exactly what he wanted to do. It wasn't that she didn't understand the reasons that drove Hart on a path of self-destruction. She was plagued by those same demons, and yet she had managed to live a reasonably normal life.

Hart's emotional fragility combined with his mental instability created a man who lived on the edge, always a hairsbreadth from falling into the abyss. If his life had been different from childhood to the present day, he would be a different person. If not completely normal, at least normal enough to function in the real world without relying on alcohol and drugs to dull the pain inside him. If Blake hadn't been abducted . . . If Enid hadn't committed suicide . . . If, if, if . . . if only.

Damn the if onlys. Damn the wishing and hoping and

praying that things could have been different for both of them.

She should have gone with Tam tonight. Should have spent the evening with friends, with people who cared about her. But as she so often did, Audrey chose to be alone, chose to shut herself off from everyone else.

There were times when, even in the presence of others, she felt alone. Isolated. On the outside looking in to a life that could never be hers.

Oh, that's the way to handle things. Feel sorry for yourself. Sit here in the dark, crying and wallowing in self-pity.

She needed to get up, go to the kitchen, and find a bite to eat. She had skipped dinner and her stomach was now growling to remind her. *Eat first, then a long, hot soak in the tub, read a paperback novel, and go to bed early.*

Audrey didn't need someone else to console her, someone to pet and pamper her, someone to hold her and tell her everything would be all right. She was entirely self-sufficient and had been since childhood. Early on, she had learned not to rely on others because they would let you down again and again.

Lost in thought, she didn't hear the doorbell at first, but as the ring repeated several times, she realized that someone was at her front door. Who on earth? She wasn't expecting anybody. Dear God, she hoped it wasn't Porter. She had not seen or heard from him since he'd left the bouquet on her porch.

Forcing her legs into motion, she got up and went into the foyer. After peering through the peephole and recognizing her guests, she unlocked and opened the door.

Zoe Davidson breezed in, holding two pizza boxes in front of her. Her father followed, a six-pack of Cokes in one hand and a brown paper sack in the other.

"I hope you haven't eaten," Zoe said. "We'd have been

here earlier, but we ran a little late with Dr. Woodruff and then we had to order the pizza and stop by the mini-mart to get the Cokes and candy."

What were they doing there? Had she forgotten that J.D. was dropping off Zoe tonight? She glanced from a chattering Zoe, who headed straight toward the kitchen, to a silent J.D.

He lifted his shoulders in a don't-ask-me shrug, then said, "This was all Zoe's idea. She overheard me on the phone talking to my boss about the DNA tests results on toddler number three, and she immediately decided that you'd need us . . . need her tonight."

Before Audrey could reply, Zoe paused in the kitchen doorway, glanced back, and barked orders. "Come on, you two. I'm starving. I haven't had anything to eat since lunch today."

"Madam Bossy Butt is in charge," J.D. said. "We'd better do as she says or it'll be off with our heads."

When J.D. smiled, Audrey returned the smile instantly. Not a forced smile, but one that had formed with absolutely no effort whatsoever. She really didn't understand her reaction.

J.D. motioned for her to go first and when they reached the kitchen, he held the door open for her. Zoe had placed the pizza boxes on the counter and was filling three tall glasses with ice cubes. J.D. set the six-pack beside the glasses and tossed the brown sack on the table.

"The plates are in the upper right-hand cabinet," Zoe told J.D. and he immediately reached up and opened the cupboard.

Audrey finally managed to speak. "I can get the plates."

"You sit down," Zoe told her. "Dad and I are here to take care of you tonight. We'll do everything. You relax and enjoy being waited on hand and foot."

Audrey stared at Zoe, not quite believing what was happening. When she glanced at J.D., he pulled out a chair for her and indicated for her to sit. Slightly dazed, she did as she'd been told. J.D. eased her chair forward. His fingertips lightly brushed her shoulders. A shiver of awareness shot through her and her body instantly stiffened in response.

Zoe set the filled glasses on the table, one by one. "We've got Meat-Supreme and chicken spinach. Which do you prefer?"

"Oh, chicken spinach, definitely," Audrey said.

Zoe grinned from ear to ear as she looked triumphantly at her father. "See, I told you she'd like my favorite pizza."

J.D. shrugged good-naturedly. "You girls are welcome to it. That means the entire Meat-Supreme is mine."

They all three laughed.

Within minutes, Audrey was sharing dinner with Zoe and J.D. as if it were the most natural thing in the world, as if it were an everyday occurrence. The topics of DNA testing, Baby Blue toddlers, and the Rocking Chair Killer weren't even mentioned, as if by telepathic agreement the three of them had made a pact. Instead Zoe told them about her school day, no doubt embellishing certain details purely for entertainment value. Oddly enough, Zoe made everything sound amusing, everything from a description of several funny-looking students and a couple of weird teachers to a tale about two guys almost coming to blows over a certain girl in the dining hall. By the time they finished eating, stacked the dishes in the dishwasher, and took the candy bag and their refilled glasses of Coke into the living room, Audrey had temporarily forgotten why she'd been so down in the dumps earlier.

"*Ghost Whisperer* is on tonight." Zoe picked up the remote as she sat on the floor and placed her glass and the candy bag between her spread legs. "It's only five after eight, so we won't have missed much." She clicked on the TV, laid the remote aside, and pulled a candy bar from the sack.

Audrey and J.D. sat on the sofa, one of them on each end. They placed their glasses on coasters atop the coffee table.

"We've got Hershey's bars with and without almonds, Mars bars, Three Musketeers, Mounds, Reese's cups, and Snickers," Zoe said. "What'll it be?"

"Snickers," J.D. replied.

Zoe tossed her dad a candy bar. "You, Audrey?"

"Oh, I don't know. A plain old Hershey's bar, I guess."

Zoe handed the candy bar to Audrey. "I like mine with almonds." She held up her candy bar and smiled.

They drank cola, devoured candy bars—one each for Zoe and Audrey and two for J.D.—and watched TV for the next hour. With each passing moment, Audrey relaxed more and more, feeling oddly content with J.D. Cass sitting only a few feet away from her.

During the nine o'clock commercial break, Zoe jumped up and excused herself to go to the bathroom. Once she was out of earshot, J.D. placed his arm across the back of the sofa and turned to Audrey. She looked at him and smiled.

"Thanks," he said.

"For what?"

"For letting Zoe play mother hen tonight. For not tossing me out of here on my ass. For being such a good friend to my daughter. For—"

"I get the picture. But I'm the one who should be thanking you and Zoe. I was in an awful funk, suffering from the terminal poor-old-Audrey syndrome, before you two showed up on my doorstep."

"Bearing gifts," he reminded her. "We didn't show up empty-handed."

"Indeed you didn't."

"I wasn't sure what your reaction would be," he confessed. "I tried to talk her out of it, told her I'd be the last person you'd want to see tonight, but Zoe insisted. I've learned that my daughter can be very stubborn, and when it comes to doing what she thinks is right, she's very persuasive at getting her own way."

"Like father, like daughter."

J.D. grinned. "You think so?"

"I know so. She's a lot more like you than you realize," Audrey said. "And it's far more than the obvious physical resemblance, as great as that is."

"You've worked a few minor miracles with my daughter," J.D. told her. "You've been good for her. I don't think I've told you how much I appreciate all you've done."

"It's been my pleasure. I genuinely like Zoe. She's a very special young lady. You should be proud to be her father."

J.D.'s smile vanished. "I haven't been much of a father to her. My parenting skills need a lot of improvement. Maybe you can work a few minor miracles with me, too."

Audrey held her breath as she stared into J.D.'s black eyes. "I—I—"

"*Medium* is on," Zoe said as she returned to the living room and resumed her position on the floor in front of the TV. "Since J.D. won't let me date until I'm fifteen—"

"Sixteen for single dating," he told her. "Fifteen for double dates . . . maybe."

Zoe snorted. "Fifteen for double-dating is definite. We agreed. Anyway, until I turn fifteen, I'll be watching a lot of TV on Friday nights. Good thing two of my favorite shows are on then."

Audrey glanced at J.D. "So you and Zoe have agreed on when she can date. That's a giant step in the right direction. I assume Sally helped y'all—"

"Sort of," Zoe said. "When we discussed it today during our session, I asked her how old you were when you started dating and she told me—fifteen for double dates and sixteen for single dates."

Audrey and J.D. exchanged glances, then he leaned over and said so quietly that only she could hear him, "I can't think of anyone I'd rather Zoe choose as a role model."

Speechless for several moments, her gaze locked with J.D.'s, she finally said, "Thank you."

Chapter 26

Somer Ellis enjoyed her part-time job as a salesclerk at Belk in Hamilton Place Mall. There were so many pluses, the least of which was receiving an employee discount. Being a clotheshorse was one of her worst vices. But being a people person made dealing with the general public less of a hassle than it could have been if she were an introvert. And working in the children's department was a real bonus because she loved kids. Once she completed her studies and earned her bachelor of arts degree from UTC next spring, she would start job hunting. With a degree in advertising, she looked forward to finding just the right niche for her specific talents. Luckily, Quint had a good job as an assistant manager with First Tennessee Bank, and his future looked bright, so they weren't dependent upon her salary to pay their bills. What she earned was extra that went into a savings account for the future. They wanted to go to Hawaii in a few years, for the honeymoon they hadn't been able to afford two years ago when they'd gotten married. Then after their dream vacation, they wanted to start a family. But they had plenty of time. Quint was only twenty-seven, and she had just turned twenty-five in July.

Monday afternoons were usually slow, and today was no exception. Time dragged by when she wasn't busy. She checked her watch. Almost one o'clock. As soon as Gwen returned from her lunch break, she could head for the food court.

When an attractive man came up to the counter with a boxed blue baby shawl in his hand, she smiled and asked, "May I help you, sir?"

"Yes, please." He laid the box on the counter.

"Would you like it gift-wrapped?"

"No, that won't be necessary." He possessed an incredibly appealing smile.

"There's no extra charge, and I'd be more than happy to—"

"My wife prefers wrapping gifts herself." He removed his wallet from the inside pocket of his jacket.

"Oh, of course. I understand perfectly. I'm the same way myself." As she rang up his order and took the cash payment, she continued chatting.

"I assume that you and your wife have a friend or relative expecting a baby boy soon," Somer said.

"A relative," he replied, but didn't elaborate.

"I love kids."

"Do you have children?"

"Not yet, but Quint and I—Quint's my husband—want children someday, at least two. Do you and your wife have children?"

"No, not yet," he replied.

When she handed him the Belk sack containing his purchase, he smiled, nodded, and thanked her. She watched as he walked away. *What a nice man. And so good looking.* Not that she was interested, of course, since she was married.

Besides, he wasn't actually her type. She'd never been attracted to blondes.

What an unbelievable coincidence that he would find her here, of all places. Talk about hiding in plain sight. She had acted as if she didn't know him, which was what she always did whenever he found her. And he always played along, pretending they were strangers when they both knew better.

He had thought he'd found her last week, had been almost certain, but after seeing her here today, he realized he'd been mistaken. The other woman had looked so much like her that if he hadn't come face-to-face with her today, he might have taken the wrong mother home to Cody.

She must have known he was buying the blue blanket for Cody, but she'd asked about gift wrapping all the same. Playing the game by her rules, at least for now, he had pretended to have a wife and she had pretended to have a husband, some man she called Quint.

He paused far enough away so that she wouldn't notice him, but close enough so that he could watch her, inconspicuously, of course. She was so pretty. Still. Time had been good to her. She didn't look any older now than when he'd been a child.

Closing his eyes for only a moment, he let the memories wash over him in soft, sweet waves. He could see her smiling, hear her crooning quietly, the words of the lullaby forever imprinted on his brain. He could almost feel her arms around him, holding him with such tenderness.

He took in a quiet breath and released it on an easy sigh. He and Cody missed her. She shouldn't have left them. Didn't she know how much they needed her? He would bring her home soon and reunite her with Cody, reunite mother and son forever. Just as he had promised he would do.

After one final look at Regina, he clutched the bag containing the blue baby blanket in his hand and then turned and walked out of the store. Once in the mall parking lot, he checked his wristwatch. He had less than an hour to drive across town.

Wayne pulled in behind the line of parked vehicles, and by the time he had emerged from his truck and rounded the hood to get to the other side, another vehicle pulled in behind him. He didn't immediately recognize the driver, but as soon as he had opened the passenger door and helped Grace out onto the road, Porter Bryant emerged from his sporty Lotus. Wayne had met the guy once when Bryant had been with Audrey, and he hadn't liked the smooth pretty boy one damn bit. Of course, he had kept his opinion to himself. His daughter neither wanted nor needed his advice on men. While Wayne slid his arm around Grace's waist, Porter walked past them, nodded, and continued toward the small crowd gradually assembling at the gravesite.

"Are you sure you want to do this?" Wayne asked Grace.

"I'm sure." She reached up and caressed his cheek. "We both need to be here today . . . for Steve Kelly and his ex-wife. They lost a son just as you and I each did. No one else knows what they're going through the way we do. No one else can truly sympathize. They're burying a child twenty-six years after they lost him."

As he led Grace closer to the congregating group of mourners, he recognized several people. Garth and Hart were both there. He had expected his former brother-in-law, but not his stepson. Porter Bryant had spotted Audrey and was making a beeline for her. From the expression on his daughter's face, he figured she was none too happy to see Bryant. She was probably wondering, just as Wayne was, why the ADA was there.

"We should speak to Steve," Grace said. "Let him know we're here."

Wayne nodded.

Off in the distance, the distinct roar of a motorcycle rumbled through the stillness, as did traffic noises coming from Highway 153. Overhead, thickening gray clouds obscured the afternoon sun, and a chilly October breeze murmured sadly. Unless he missed his guess, it would be raining before nightfall.

When they approached Steve, Wayne noticed the woman at his side, a woman he hadn't seen in twenty-six years. Not since the summer Devin Kelly had been abducted. Sheri was still a damn fine-looking woman, her hair still blond and her figure still slender. A man about Wayne's age—tall, broad shouldered, and bald—stood beside Steve's ex-wife, his arm draped lovingly around her shoulders.

Two young, pretty girls flanked Steve Kelly, and both had tears in their eyes. Wayne couldn't remember their names, but he knew they were Steve's daughters, the elder about twenty, from his second marriage, and the younger about fifteen, from his third marriage.

After the introductions were made—Sheri was now married to the man at her side, William Dodson—Grace and Sheri hugged each other, and Wayne shook hands with Dodson and then grasped Steve's hand tightly before he patted him on the back. Steve's girls were Shiloh and Brandi.

Music began playing, soft piano music, no doubt taped. And then a trio of female voices blended together to sing a hymn that Wayne remembered from his childhood—"Does Jesus Care?"

The funeral director asked that the immediate family be seated in the two rows of chairs beneath the protective canopy that covered the open grave and the tiny blue casket resting in a sling above the freshly excavated earth. Sheri Dodson wept. Steve's big shoulders trembled.

Grace held on to Wayne for dear life. "I'm okay," she assured him. But he knew she wasn't.

She was thinking about her son Shane, about how she would feel today if she was burying his tiny skeleton more than two decades after a madwoman had killed him. God knew he was thinking about Blake. If the Rocking Chair Killer struck again, would he place Blake in his victim's arms and leave them posed and waiting to be found?

Audrey's gaze connected with her father's for a brief moment and she recognized the pain in his eyes, a pain refreshed by recent events. Even after all the years of emotional separation, she longed to go to him and put her arms around him and tell him she loved him. As a trained therapist, she understood a child's need to love and be loved by his or her parents, a need that remained a constant throughout life. So often a boy, once a man, judged all women by his own mother and in the same way, a girl, be she six or sixty, compared all men to her father. Had she been doing that all these years, comparing every man she met to Wayne Sherrod? Was that why, at thirty-four, she had never made a commitment? Of course, logic told her that it was a huge part of the reason she had no desire to ever marry. Marriages like Geraldine and Willie Mullins's were the exception instead of the rule. People divorced one another at the drop of a hat, for insignificant, often stupid reasons. She didn't want to risk a marriage that would become just another divorce statistic.

When her father averted his gaze, Audrey glanced at the woman leaning so trustingly against him. Grace Douglas was a lovely lady, although not looking her best today. Her eyes were bloodshot and her pale, porcelain complexion blotchy from crying. Audrey had learned about Grace through Tam, who had found out about Wayne's romantic relationship with the woman from Geraldine.

"Mom says they've been seeing each other for years," Tam had told Audrey a couple of years ago. "It started out as friendship and gradually turned into love. Mom and Dad like Grace. They think she's good for your father."

The fact that her father had never even introduced her to the most important woman in his life hadn't surprised Audrey.

Slowly moving farther back into the small crowd, Audrey wished she hadn't come there today to the graveside service for Devin Kelly. It wasn't as if either of the little boy's parents or anyone else in the Kelly family knew her. And her father quite obviously didn't need her comfort and support. He had Grace Douglas for that. And even Hart didn't need her, not when he had Uncle Garth.

Why was Hart there? Whatever his reasons for wanting or needing to be there, Garth should have talked him out of coming. But then again, when had anyone ever been able to dissuade Hart from doing what he wanted to do?

She supposed her stepbrother was there for the same reason she was—because there was a connection between Devin Kelly and Blake. Both were Baby Blue toddlers, both victims of a madwoman, both little boys missing for more than two decades. And now Devin Kelly had come home.

Would Blake be next?

As the minister began speaking, his voice strong and yet somehow soft at the same time, Audrey glanced at the people gathered there at the cemetery. Most of them, she didn't know. She caught a glimpse of Porter Bryant and hoped he wouldn't approach her again. She had deliberately avoided him since his arrival. Thankfully, he now stood halfway turned in the opposite direction, his gaze fixed on the tiny blue casket. Had the district attorney's office sent him as their representative? Probably. That was the only possible explanation for why he was there.

Audrey bowed her head and closed her eyes as the minister prayed.

"Merciful Lord, comfort the bereaved today. Look down upon little Devin's mother and father, his stepfather and his sisters, and give them peace, knowing that their loved one is safe in Your arms. Let them know that he has been with You all these years and let that knowledge afford them the closure in their lives they so desperately need."

Closure. Yes, that's what the Kelly family needed. It's what her family needed. Her father, her uncle, her brother. Knowing Blake's fate could bring them closure, couldn't it? Being able to place his remains in a little coffin and have a long-overdue memorial service could give them all peace.

But would it?

Nothing could change the past. Nothing would bring Blake back to them. Nothing would alter the fact that Enid had killed herself. Closure wouldn't miraculously heal broken hearts, wouldn't transform Hart into a mentally and emotionally stable man, wouldn't alter her father's feelings for her.

When the minister said "amen," Audrey opened her eyes and looked down at her feet. The female trio sang again. "Just a Closer Walk with Thee."

In an effort to hold the tears at bay, she let her gaze wander again, glancing at her father and Grace Douglas, at her brother and uncle, at Porter, at Devin Kelly's mother weeping, her heart breaking, the pain of her loss as fresh as it had been all those years ago.

And then she saw Jeremy Arden, whom she had met only once. Strange that he would attend Devin Kelly's funeral. But then again, maybe he needed to be there. But for the grace of God, Devin's fate would have been his, almost had been his.

The minister spoke again, his comments gradually veering away from the tragedy of Devin's untimely death as a young child to a preacher's oratory on sin, death, and eternal damnation. *Repent now, before it's too late* seemed to be every clergyman's mantra. Somehow, it seemed totally inappropriate at Devin Kelly's funeral service. He'd been a sweet, innocent, without-sin toddler.

The tears she had managed to control began to slowly fill her eyes. She would not give in to her emotions. Not now. Not today. She had cried too many tears for a past that couldn't be altered, for a little brother no doubt long dead, for her father and Enid and Uncle Garth and Hart. And yes, for the little girl she had once been, a little girl who to this very day wondered if she could have done something to save her baby brother.

As the tears cascaded down her cheeks, Audrey straightened her shoulders and knotted her hands into loose fists. And then suddenly, someone came up beside her, reached down, unfolded her right fist, and entwined his large fingers with her smaller ones. She stared down at the hand holding hers and then allowed her gaze to travel up his long, muscular arm, over his neck and jaw to his face.

J.D. Cass!

He squeezed her hand as he fixed his gaze on her. And before she knew what was happening, he produced a crisp white handkerchief and gently wiped the tears from her cheeks. Her breath caught in her throat.

When J.D. offered her his handkerchief, she took it. And when he continued to hold her hand, she held on to him, grateful for his presence.

Thankfully, the service concluded after one final song—"Jesus Loves Me"—that brought tears to almost everyone's eyes. Once the small crowd began to disperse, J.D. slipped his arm around Audrey's waist. She didn't withdraw from him; instead she accepted his support.

Without either saying a word to the other, J.D. walked her

to her SUV. When she unlocked and opened the door, she turned to him.

"You know that Blake will be next," she said.

He nodded. "If our killer abducts another woman, which he will if we can't stop him, then yes, Blake will be the next toddler to reappear."

"And my family will go through a funeral service and say a final farewell, just the way the Kelly family did today."

He didn't reply, just gave her a sympathetic look.

"Did you come here today because you're involved with the murder cases?" she asked.

"Partly," he told her. "And I knew you would be here and thought you might need a big strong shoulder to cry on." His lips curved upward into an almost smile.

"Thanks."

"You're welcome. It's the least I could do for you, considering all you've done for Zoe and me."

"Tell Zoe hi and that we're still on for tomorrow night."

"I'll tell her."

J.D. waited until she was securely inside the Enclave before he closed the door and walked away. Audrey's heart pounded frantically as she watched him, her gaze fixed on his broad shoulders.

Her right hand, the hand he had held so tenderly, tingled with the memory of his touch.

No, no, no! Not J.D. Cass. Not now. Not ever.

Chapter 27

Tam had known Garth Hudson most of her life. She had seen him happy and sad, drunk and sober, kind and cruel, but she had never seen him so fiercely driven. He was obsessed with finding the Rocking Chair Killer. If he didn't need to check on Hart from time to time, she doubted Garth would have gone home at all this entire week. He had practically been living in their office for the past few days. Garth's unrest, agitation, and anxiety had worsened progressively since Devin Kelly's funeral on Monday. And even though his animosity toward J.D. was palpable, Garth had managed to control it, at least enough so that the two men could work together.

When she arrived at headquarters that Friday morning, she found Garth bleary eyed, slightly unkempt, and in bad need of a shave.

"My God, go home and take a shower and change clothes," she told him. "You look like holy hell."

He glared at her, his expression haggard and pained. "I don't have time."

"Make time."

"Later. Cass is picking me up in fifteen minutes."

"Why? Where are wc going?"

"*We* aren't going anywhere," he told her. "I'm going with Special Agent Cass to Johnson City. The sheriff up there has arranged for us to talk to Dora Chaney's stepdaughter. It seems she moved from Bristol to Johnson City when she got married."

"Dora Chaney, Regina Bennett's aunt?"

"One and the same."

"And why am I not going?"

"Because you're staying here and working on every possible lead we have. Maybe our guy bought blue baby blankets in bulk. If he did—"

"Get real. We've already agreed that we can't track down every blue baby blanket purchase on the off chance that someone in one of the local stores might remember the person who bought the blankets. He could have ordered them online for all we know."

Garth frowned. "You can sift through all the evidence again, just in case we've missed something."

"What could we have missed when there's practically no evidence? Even the dirt samples off our three victims' shoes told us nothing more than that it was the same type of dirt on all three. And big surprise, the specific composition is in dirt found in most rural areas in and around Chattanooga. Besides that, if going over everything again and again could shed any light on these cases, you'd have already found something. You've been driving yourself to the brink of exhaustion this week."

"Damn it, Tam, think outside the box. There has to be some way to find this guy." Garth slammed his fist down on his desk. "We have to find him before he kills again."

She placed her hand on Garth's shoulder. He tensed; then

he shrugged off her hand and looked right at her. "I need somebody close by, just in case . . . If Hart were to . . . I know I can trust you to take care of him."

Tam's pulse quickened at the mention of Hart's name. "I thought you said he's been doing all right since Devin Kelly's funeral."

"He has been, but . . ." Garth huffed. "Damn. You know it doesn't take much for him to dive off the deep end."

"Okay. I'll stay here without any more arguments." She looked at him sympathetically. He knew that she and Audrey were the only two people on earth who loved Hart half as much as he did. "Why don't you go to the restroom, use your electric razor, and at least wash your face and comb your hair before J.D. gets here."

Garth grunted. "Yeah, I guess I can do that much." He opened a bottom desk drawer, grabbed his electric razor pouch, and headed out the door; then he paused and glanced over his shoulder. "Thanks, Tam."

She nodded.

Would it ever come to an end, Garth's compulsive need to take care of Hart? Wasn't there a time when no matter how much you loved someone, you just had to give up?

That's what you did, didn't you? You gave up on Hart.

But what else could she have done? She'd been eighteen and pregnant. And she'd known there was no way seventeen-year-old Hart could have taken on the responsibility of a wife and child, not when he couldn't even take care of himself.

"Knock, knock," a man's voice called from the open doorway.

Tam snapped around and saw J.D. standing there, his fist tapping lightly on the door frame.

"I knocked a couple of times, but you didn't hear me," he told her. "You seemed a million miles away. Everything okay?"

No, everything wasn't okay, but she could hardly explain

herself to J.D. "Sure, everything's fine. I'm keeping the home fires burning today while you and my partner track down a possible lead."

"So you're not going with us?"

"Apparently not. It seems I'm needed here."

"Hmm . . ."

"Do you think this woman, Dora Chaney's stepdaughter, might know something about Corey Bennett?"

"Since the few former Holy Brethren Church members we were able to locate claim they never heard of a child named Corey Bennett, then I'm hoping the stepdaughter might know something. And it's possible she might remember something about Luther Chaney's old Lincoln. I figure Dora must have kept the car because there's no record of it ever being sold and no record of a car tag purchased for it after Luther's death."

"The license plate on the car now was probably stolen off another car," Tam said.

"More than likely."

"You're counting on this woman knowing an awful lot, aren't you?"

"I'm hoping she does. And doing a little praying, too."

Tam grasped J.D.'s arm and tugged him closer as she said quietly, "Listen, look after Garth, will you? I've never seen him like this. He always works his butt off on a case, gives it his all, but this time, it's different. It's like he's obsessed with finding this guy."

"It's personal for him," J.D. said. "The odds are his nephew Blake will be the next toddler to show up."

"I don't think Garth wants that to happen. I think he's afraid of what it might do to Hart." She noted the quizzical glint in J.D.'s eyes and hastily added, "Audrey thinks knowing for sure that Blake is dead, being able to bury him, will give the whole family closure. But Garth doesn't agree. He thinks it will simply do even more to reopen all the old wounds. He's concerned about how he and Hart and Wayne and even Audrey will deal with having to relive that horrible time in their lives."

Before J.D. could respond, Garth reappeared, his hair neatly combed, his face freshly shaved, and a look of steely determination in his eyes. "You ready?" Garth asked.

"Yeah, I'm ready," J.D. replied.

As the two men headed out the door, Tam said, "Call me and let me know what happens."

"Sure thing," J.D. said.

And then they were gone, off to Johnson City. Tam was definitely going to do a lot of hoping and praying, too, just as J.D. was.

Frankie Jo Rogers, nee Elmore, stood six feet tall in her work boots and grimy overalls, which hung loosely on her lean, rawboned body. When J.D. introduced himself and Garth, she off wiped her large, work-worn hands on a rag hanging from her pocket, stuffed the rag back in her pocket, and shook hands with each of them.

"What can I do for you gentlemen?" she asked.

A no-nonsense, busy woman who didn't have time for the type of pleasantries many Southern women would have believed essential for good manners, Frankie Jo didn't ask them to take a seat or offer them refreshments. Then again, doing either would have required they leave the barn where Mrs. Rogers had been working on a yellow and green John Deere tractor.

"I believe Sheriff Tully got in touch with you," J.D. said.

She nodded. "Yep, he did."

"Then you know we'd like to ask you some questions about your stepmother, Dora Chaney . . . Dora Elmore."

"Me and her didn't cotton to each other," Frankie Jo admitted. "She weren't no bad woman, just odd. Not sure what the old man ever saw in her, except maybe she was a good cook, kept a clean house, and he was lonely after Mama died."

"How did your father meet her?" Garth asked.

"Not really sure. I think a mutual friend introduced them. I wasn't living at home at the time. Me and Butch had done got married and moved down here to Johnson City."

If this big, rough-hewn, blunt-spoken woman couldn't tell them what they needed to know about Dora Chaney Elmore, then they weren't likely to find anyone else who could. Frank Elmore's elder daughter, Jewel, had died five years ago, leaving Frankie Jo the only one who might be able to help them.

"I know this may seem like a peculiar question, but do you remember if Dora owned a car, one she had before she married your father?" J.D. studied Frankie Jo closely as her brow wrinkled and she sucked in her cheeks while she mulled over the question.

"Humph! My daddy bought her a spanking-new Ford Taurus as a wedding present, and she still insisted on keeping that old Lincoln. Daddy wanted her to sell it, but she wouldn't. I think he was jealous because the car had belonged to Dora's first husband. You know how men are." She glanced from J.D. to Garth, a wide grin on her weathered face.

"Do you happen to remember what color the car was?" J.D. already knew the answer, but needed confirmation.

"White," she said.

"What ever happened to that old white Lincoln?" Garth asked.

Frankie Jo chuckled. "After Dora died, Daddy sold it to some guy for scrap."

"Who'd he sell it to?" J.D. asked.

"Got no idea. Just some guy. He paid Daddy cash for that old heap. It had been parked for a good many years. The thing wouldn't even run. The guy had to tow it."

"When exactly did your father sell the car?"

"I'm not sure exactly. I don't know the details, but I do remember Daddy saying that he gave the money he got off the sale to the church building fund."

"What church? What religion?" Was it possible that some branch of the Holy Brethren Church still existed, that Frank Elmore had been a member?

"Baptist," Frankie Jo told them. "My folks been good God-fearing Baptists as far back as anybody can remember."

Whoever had bought the 1980 white Lincoln—for scrap—had undoubtedly had some work done on it, enough to keep it running. But why hadn't a car without a valid license plate or insurance been stopped by law enforcement? Luck? What other explanation could there be?

Maybe the only time he used the car was when he disposed of a body.

"Was Dora Baptist, too?" Garth asked.

"I guess she was. She went to church with Daddy every time the doors opened."

"Did Dora have any family that you knew of, anyone you ever met?" J.D. wondered if she knew about Regina Bennett.

"Nobody except that crazy bitch niece of hers, the one who killed all them little boys." The left side of her mouth hitched upward in a smirk. "You didn't think I knew about that, huh? I'll give Dora that much, she didn't lie to Daddy about it. Told him up front before they got married."

"Did Dora ever mention anyone else, a nephew perhaps?"

"Oh, now that you mention it, there was that kid, but he wasn't her nephew."

J.D.'s pulse rate quickened. "What kid?"

"Her first husband's son," Frankie Jo said. "He was just a little boy. I don't know how old. He could have been a big six-year-old or a small ten-year-old. I just saw him the one time."

"What?" J.D. and Garth spoke at the same time.

Frankie Jo laughed, the sound a deep rumble coming from her chest and exploding when she released it. "She didn't tell me any details about the child, of course, but Daddy did. Seems the first husband, that Chaney guy, fathered a bastard child, and old Dora took the boy in. But Daddy drew the line at raising the little bastard. He told Dora right off that she'd have to get rid of the kid."

"And did she?"

"Sure did."

"Do you know what happened to the child?"

"I ain't sure. Daddy said some rich couple adopted him. Seems when the boy left, Dora come by some money, more than twenty thousand."

"You wouldn't happen to know the name of the couple who adopted the boy or where they were from?" It was unlikely that she knew, but for a split second J.D. hoped she did.

"Got no idea. Sorry."

"Do you recall the boy's name?" Garth asked.

"Hmm . . . I only saw him once. Cute kid. Blond, blue-eyed. Right pretty for a boy. Maybe too pretty. I believe she called him by a double name, but for the life of me I can't remember. Something Ray, I think."

"Could it have been Corey Ray?" J.D. held his breath.

"Could've been. Sounds right, but I can't say for sure. Why? Is there some reason this kid is important?"

J.D. glanced at Garth before answering. "Yes, ma'am, he could be. You wouldn't happen to know who the boy's mother was?"

She shook her head. "Nope. I'm pretty sure Daddy never knew. Could be Dora didn't even know."

Dora Chaney had known, all right, just as J.D. believed he

knew the mother's identity. What he was thinking was downright repulsive—that Luther Chaney had raped his niece, Regina, and gotten her pregnant, not once but twice, producing two sons—Cody and Corey Bennett.

Frankie Jo propped her rough, chapped hands on her hips. "Well, you gonna tell me or not why this boy is so all-fired important?"

"He's important because it's possible that he grew up to become a killer."

"Two killers in the same family, huh?" Frankie Jo let out a long, low whistle.

Consumed with work, J.D. ran late picking up Zoe after school, which made them late for their Friday afternoon family-therapy session. Of course she was upset with him, even though he'd apologized and asked her to understand that sometimes his job had to come first. But since he couldn't share the details about his cases, especially about the conversation with Frankie Jo Rogers, with his fourteen-year-old daughter, he'd had to accept her anger and hostility.

"It's rude to keep people waiting," she had told him as soon as she got in the car, and then she'd pouted all the way to Dr. Woodruff's office.

To make matters worse, his mind had kept wandering during the session, a fact that didn't escape either Zoe's or their counselor's notice. When Dr. Woodruff asked to speak to him privately after the session ended, he prepared himself for a verbal thrashing.

"Look, I apologize for missing a few beats here and there," J.D. told her. "But there were things that happened today on the cases I'm dealing with, things that I can't simply dismiss from my mind."

"You don't need to apologize to me, J.D.," Sally Woodruff said. "You need to apologize to Zoe. You let her down today.

She's made remarkable improvement in a very short period of time, due in great part to—"

"To Audrey Sherrod." J.D. knew better than anyone else the miracles that Audrey had performed with his daughter. Since spending time with Audrey, Zoe had, in many ways, become a different person.

"Yes, I think Audrey is most definitely a positive influence on Zoe, but I was going to say due in great part to your showing her that you're willing to work at improving your father-and-daughter relationship."

"And today, I dropped the ball, huh?"

"Something like that." Dr. Woodruff smiled tolerantly. "I understand that your job is important to you and that you're involved in a very high-profile case, but for the one hour that you're here with Zoe, you need to learn to focus solely on your daughter and your relationship with her. Can you do that?"

"Yes, ma'am, I can." He looked her square in the eye. "And I will."

They went straight from their therapy session to Audrey's home. The minute they arrived, Zoe rushed straight into the house, hugged Audrey, and disappeared down the hall. She dumped her book bag on the floor, went into the powder room, and slammed the door.

Audrey glared at him questioningly.

"She's upset with me," J.D. said.

"Do you have time to tell me what happened or are you in a hurry? If you have a date tonight—"

"I don't." J.D. closed the front door behind him. "I had planned to drop Zoe by here and go back to work, but . . ." He blew out a perplexed huff. "I take one step forward with her and then two steps back. I'm trying, God knows I'm trying, but Zoe won't cut me any slack. I'm no good at this father-and-daughter stuff."

Audrey's nonjudgmental expression changed instantly to one of annoyance.

"Don't look at me that way," he told her.

"What way?" She tilted up her chin and gave him a disapproving glare.

"Like you're as disappointed in me as Zoe is. But damn it, Audrey, it's not my fault that we got a break in the case today, maybe a halfway decent lead, and I had my mind on what it could mean instead of on Zoe during our session with Dr. Woodruff."

"If it's not your fault, whose fault is it?"

"Huh?"

"I said if it's not—"

"I know what you said," he told her. "But didn't you hear what I said? My mind was on work because for the first time since Jill Scott showed up dead with a child's skeleton in her arms, we've got a lead that may pay off."

"I heard you. And I hope whatever happened today will help you find and stop the killer. I understand how important your job is to you. My father's job was always more important to him than my mother was, than I was." She broke eye contact and cleared her throat. "Is it too much to ask that you give your undivided attention to Zoe for one hour each week? I don't think that's asking for very much, and yet you don't seem to be able to give your daughter even that."

"I should have known," J.D. grumbled.

"What?"

"That you'd see things exactly the way Dr. Woodruff does and that you'd be sympathetic to Zoe."

"Did you honestly think I'd tell you Zoe was being unreasonable and she shouldn't have reacted the way she did?"

"Hell, I don't know what I was thinking."

"There's no need for you to curse at me."

"I'm not cursing at you." He wanted to grab Audrey and shake her. "It's just that I can't deal with Zoe right now. I need to go back to the office tonight and I was hoping you'd look after her for me."

"I'd be more than happy to look after Zoe."

"Thanks." He wished he could make her understand.

"You're quite welcome. I enjoy spending time with Zoe."

J.D. clenched his teeth. What difference did it make whether or not Audrey understood him?

Hell if I know, but it does.

"Look, tell her that I'm sorry. Tell her . . . tell her not to give up on me, that I'm doing the best I can and that I'm going to keep trying to do better."

When he opened the door and stepped out onto the front porch, Audrey followed him. "J.D.?"

"Yeah?" He glanced back at her.

"I'll tell her."

"Okay, thanks again."

"You really meant it, didn't you, that you're going to keep trying to do better?"

"Yeah, I meant it. Zoe's turning out to be a pretty great kid and she deserves a halfway decent father, which I haven't been."

"If you don't finish up at the office until really late tonight, why not let Zoe stay here. And when you leave the office, if . . . if you need somebody to talk to, you could stop by. I'm a good listener."

"I may take you up on both offers."

A really crazy thought went through J.D.'s mind.

I need Audrey as much as Zoe does.

He tromped down the sidewalk toward his Camaro, all the while thinking, *You're an idiot, Cass, a certifiable idiot!*

Chapter 28

"Is he gone?" Zoe asked as she walked up beside Audrey where she stood in the open doorway watching J.D.'s Camaro until all she could see were the red taillights.

After she closed the front door, she turned and smiled at Zoe. "He went back to work. They got an important lead of some sort today on the Rocking Chair Killer case, and right now, his job requires his full attention."

"When doesn't it?" Zoe frowned.

Audrey put her arm around Zoe's shoulders and gave her a commiserating hug. "His job is very important to him, and this case he's working on involves people's lives, you know. It's not as if your dad is out there wheeling and dealing in the business world in order to make tons of money or working a regular nine-to-five job that he can forget about when he leaves the office."

Zoe pulled away and stared up at Audrey. "Are you defending him?"

Audrey smiled. "I'm cutting him some slack."

Zoe grinned. "His words, not yours. I guess he said that I'm not doing that, not cutting him some slack."

Audrey nodded. "He said some other things, too." Audrey inclined her head toward the kitchen. "Let's put together a big salad and warm up some leftover lasagna. And while we're preparing supper, I'll tell you what your dad said."

Once again, Audrey chose preparing a meal together as a means of normalizing an evening for Zoe. The easy, relaxed atmosphere of working together in the kitchen was just what both she and Zoe needed tonight.

Audrey flipped on the overhead lights in the kitchen and assigned Zoe the task of making the salad. The lasagna was left over from two nights ago, but should still be good, especially if she added some fresh cheese and allowed it to warm slowly in the oven for about twenty minutes instead of popping it into the microwave.

Zoe removed the salad ingredients from the refrigerator and cupboard and placed everything on the counter. "So, tell me, what did my dad say?"

Audrey set the oven temperature to 300 degrees. "He said to tell you that he's sorry."

"Yeah, sure."

"I believe him."

"Do you really?"

Audrey nodded.

"Why?" Zoe asked. "Therapist intuition?"

"Yes, that and simple human instinct. I think I know your father well enough to believe he means what he says. And it's the very fact that he's not all that good at diplomacy, at pretending one thing while he feels something else, that tells me he's sincere in wanting to be a better father."

"Did he say that he wants to be a better father?"

"He did," Audrey assured her. "He told me to ask you not to give up on him, that he's doing the best he can and that he's going to keep trying to do better."

Zoe's mouth dropped open and her hands stilled in the

middle of slicing a tomato. "So, I guess you think I shouldn't give up on him, huh?"

"What do you want to do?"

"You know what I want. I want a real family. A mom and dad and a brother and sister and we all love each other and spend loads of time together and . . ." Zoe snorted softly. "Well, that's really stupid, isn't it?"

"No, I don't think it's stupid at all. It's what every child wants, even when that child is an adult. It's what I always wanted."

Zoe laid the paring knife on the chopping block beside the tomato slices. "Life sucks, doesn't it?"

"Yes, sometimes it does. But just because we don't have an ideal family doesn't mean we can't be grateful for what we do have. You have a father who is trying to make things work for the two of you. Who knows, if you don't give up on him, you might find yourself with a father who genuinely loves you and wants to spend loads of time with you. You could have a strong father-and-daughter relationship. And it's possible that someday, he'll get married and give you a brother or sister."

"So, what you're really saying is that J.D. and I have to cut each other some slack if I want him to be a real father to me."

Audrey smiled. "It would definitely be a step in the right direction."

Zoe picked up the knife and finished slicing the tomato while Audrey removed a loaf of French bread from the pantry and cut off several pieces.

"I told you that J.D. was married once, didn't I," Zoe said.

"Hmm . . ."

"Her name was Erin. He never talks about her. They've been divorced for years and years." Zoe took the small, firm cucumber to the sink, rinsed it, and then laid it on the cutting board. "He's not dating Holly Johnston anymore, you know."

"Is that right?"

"He had that one date with Jacy's aunt Cara, but it must not have worked out because he hasn't seen her again." Zoe sliced and diced the cucumber and added it to the salad bowl. "You broke up with that Porter guy, didn't you? You didn't decide to give him a second chance, did you? I mean, he was practically stalking you for a while."

Audrey removed a stick of butter from the refrigerator and spread the butter on the bread. "I believe Porter may have finally realized our relationship is over. I haven't heard from him in a while."

The oven buzzer dinged, informing Audrey that the oven had reached the proper temperature.

"So, if J.D. were to ask you out on a date, would you go?" Zoe asked.

Audrey almost dropped the casserole dish as she opened the oven door and placed it inside. "Zoe, your father and I aren't even friends. I've tried to explain this to you before. Our only real connection is you."

"So, is that a no?"

"What?"

"If J.D. asked you out on a date, would you say no?"

"It's highly unlikely that your father will ask me out on a date."

Zoe wiped her hands on the kitchen towel, crossed her arms over her chest, and studied Audrey. "You're being deliberately evasive, Dr. Sherrod. You'll feel much better if you're honest with me and with yourself." The corners of Zoe's mouth twitched and then her lips spread into a wide smile.

"My God, do I sound that sanctimonious?"

"No, of course not. I was laying it on a little thick." Zoe's smiling eyes fixed on Audrey's. "I guess you know that if I could have my pick, I'd choose you for my mother."

Audrey's heart skipped a beat. Emotion caught in her

throat. *Oh, Zoe, Zoe . . .* "Thank you. I believe that's the nicest compliment anyone has ever paid me."

The old wooden church, built in the late eighteen hundreds, had stood vacant for a couple of decades. The back side of the roof had rotted and caved in years ago, leaving a gaping hole that allowed rain and snow to enter the sanctuary and aid in the slow, steady dilapidation of the pulpit, the altar, the baptismal font, and the once-sturdy wooden benches. Long abandoned and all but forgotten in the woods on the hillside, the former meeting place for the Holy Brethren held malevolent secrets that had been known by only a few.

He parked the white Lincoln behind the church, picked up the shopping bag, got out, and entered through a back door. Streaks of jagged lightning shot through the night sky; shortly after, a rumble of thunder echoed in the distance. Using a small flashlight to assist him in the moonlit darkness, he made his way carefully to the half-open door in the vestibule that led to the basement. The precariously unsteady wooden stairs creaked ominously with each step he took. When his feet touched the solid floor, he released a relieved breath. The concrete block walls surrounding him wept with moisture. Mustiness, mildew, and decay created a stale, odorous air.

He took me to the church and made me go with him down into the basement. He knew that no one could hear me down there, no one could hear my cries and pleas. My screams.

Shivering as Regina's voice echoed in his head, he paused and took several deep, calming breaths.

I was only sixteen the first time. He had been so good to me. I trusted him. I never thought he would hurt me.

If Luther Chaney wasn't already dead, he would kill him for what he'd done. His actions had not only turned a fragile young girl into a woman capable of murdering her own child, but his cruelty to his niece had destroyed other lives as well.

Cody's life.

My life.

My first baby was born dead. I had a miscarriage when I was barely four months pregnant. He told me that it was punishment for my sins.

The sin had been his, all his, never hers. Even later on, when she had smothered Cody, the sin had not been hers. She had done only what she believed in her mother's heart was the right thing.

When the doctors told me Cody had leukemia, he said that, too, was punishment for my sins. I was bad. He wouldn't have done those things to me if I hadn't been such a bad person.

He shone the flashlight's beam against the wall of deteriorating wooden shelves. Five shelves reached from floor to ceiling, effectively covering both the wall and the camouflaged single door in the center.

There is a secret door behind the shelves in the basement that leads to a large room used only by the church elders. My uncle was one of the elders. He took me to that room. He made me undress. He touched me. He did terrible things to me.

When he reached the back wall, he slid his fingers behind the middle shelf and pushed. The shelf creaked as the door behind it opened into the vast darkness. Putting his shoulder into it, he shoved the door wide open and entered the room where Regina had been repeatedly raped and tortured by her uncle decades ago.

Promise me that you'll go there and find Cody. I want him to be with me in heaven. Put him in my arms so I can hold him forever.

He had promised her, and he would keep his word. When

she died, he had taken Cody to her and placed him in the coffin with her. And later, he had strewn their combined ashes around the small cottage where she had lived with her sons.

In an effort to fulfill his promise completely, he had reunited Cody with Regina three more times, allowing her to hold him and rock him and sing to him. And in the end, to release him from his pain as he released her from her pain.

His footsteps on the hard-packed earth echoed in the cavernous room as he walked toward the cradle. Yesterday, he had removed Cody from the wooden box where Regina had placed him for safekeeping until she could return. He had laid him in the large, wooden cradle, his body filling the bed from head to foot.

"I've brought you a new blanket, Cody," he said as he shone the light down on the sleeping child. "I'm going to bring Mommy home so we won't be so lonely. She'll rock you and sing to you. You'll like that, won't you?"

He removed the blue baby shawl from the shopping bag, and making sure not to awaken Cody, he carefully removed the tattered blanket covering his little body and replaced it with the pretty new shawl.

"I'm going to bring her home to us tonight. I know where she is now. I saw her and talked to her on Monday. It'll be nice to have her back with us, where she belongs, won't it?"

Audrey had offered Zoe a choice of pajamas or a gown. But she had declined. As if she had known she would wind up spending the night, Zoe had pulled out an oversized sleep shirt from her backpack.

"I came prepared. Just in case." Zoe had shrugged. "J.D.'s been fostering me off on you a lot and I figured you'd tell him to let me stay here tonight if he worked late."

Less than half an hour ago, she had checked on Zoe and

found her fast asleep, her MP3 player resting on her chest and one arm hanging off the side of the bed. Audrey had quietly entered the room, placed the MP3 player on the nightstand, and gently lifted Zoe's arm back onto the bed.

If she had any sense at all, she would go to bed. It was past midnight and she was sleepy. Why was she waiting up for a man who probably either had already gone home or was spending the night in his office?

She had replayed those last few moments with J.D. over and over again. "*If you don't finish up at the office until really late tonight, why not let Zoe stay here.*" Why hadn't she left it at that? Why had she felt prompted to add, "*And when you leave the office, if you need somebody to talk to, you could stop by. I'm a good listener.*"

Good grief, Audrey, what if he misunderstood your offer? You were being kind. You were being your usual empathic self, right? You make a living listening to people, helping them sort through their problems and deal with their emotions.

"I may take you up on both offers," he had told her before leaving.

He had taken her up on the offer to let Zoe spend the night. A little before eleven, he had called Zoe. After their brief conversation, she had turned to Audrey and said, "I'm sleeping over tonight."

Apparently, he hadn't taken Audrey up on the second offer. Oddly enough, she wasn't sure if she was relieved or disappointed.

You are relieved. Do you hear me? You are relieved.

Then why hadn't she gone to bed?

Audrey walked through the house, turned off all the lights, set the security alarm, closed Zoe's bedroom door, and went into her own room. After washing her face and brushing her teeth, she slipped into a pair of peach pajamas and removed the pins from her hair. She shook her head and then combed her fingers through her hair from scalp to blunt-cut ends.

Just as she removed the throw pillows from her bed and turned down the covers, the doorbell rang. Her heart stopped for a split second and when she began to breathe again, her pulse raced wildly. Without taking time to put on house slippers or a robe, she ran through the house, turned on the overhead light in the foyer, quickly disarmed the alarm, and peered through the peephole.

She opened the door and stood aside to allow J.D. to enter, which he did hurriedly.

"It's really cold out there," he said. "It's only October and it's already dropping down in the thirties some nights."

"Would you like something hot to drink? Herbal tea? Hot chocolate?"

He looked at her then, surveying her from head to toe. "Did I wake you?"

"No, I wasn't asleep."

When he kept looking at her, she realized she wasn't wearing a robe and that the pajamas she wore were made of thin, wispy silk. "I should put on a robe." She glanced down at her bare feet. "And some house slippers."

"No need to on my account," he told her. "You look fine just the way you are."

"I . . . uh . . . I didn't think you'd be back tonight."

"You invited me, if I remember correctly."

"Well, yes, I did, but I—I—"

"You what? Wish you hadn't?"

"No, of course not. It's just that I assumed . . . It is after midnight."

He rubbed the back of his neck, the gesture indicating weariness. "Yeah, it was damn inconsiderate of me to show up so late and assume I'd be welcome."

"You are welcome." She huffed to release the tension that

had coiled tightly inside her. "Let's not argue. Take off your coat and go sit down in the living room. I'll fix us both some tea—"

"Make mine hot chocolate," he told her as he shrugged out of his coat.

"Two hot chocolates coming up."

She made it to the kitchen door before glancing over her shoulder. She watched J.D. as he tossed his jacket on the back of the tapestry-upholstered accent chair. And then he turned on a table lamp, removed his gun holster, and placed it on the coffee table.

Once in the kitchen, working quickly, she mixed cocoa powder and sugar and placed the mixture into two large mugs before pouring milk into a saucepan to heat on the stove.

Vanilla. Geraldine always added vanilla to the milk before pouring it over the cocoa-and-sugar mix. Tam's mother was Audrey's domestic role model.

Just as she opened the cupboard where she kept her spices and flavorings, she sensed someone come up behind her. She held her breath, knowing it was J.D. and realizing that she hadn't heard him enter the kitchen because she'd been so focused on preparing the hot cocoa, wanting it to be perfect for him.

"Need some help?" he asked, his breath warm against her neck.

She clutched the bottle of pure vanilla flavoring in her hand as she turned around to face him. When she did, her breasts brushed against his chest.

Oh God . . . oh God . . .

"I . . . no, thanks. I don't need—" She looked up into his black eyes and there was no doubt in her mind what he intended to do.

"You don't need what?" He lowered his head.

"I don't need any help." Instinctively, her body swayed

closer to his and she tilted her face upward, bringing her lips into contact with his.

Whether she kissed him or he kissed her, she didn't know. Lips touched. Mouths opened. Tongues explored.

Audrey grasped his shoulders for support, trapping the bottle of vanilla between her half-open palm and his body.

J.D. grabbed her butt and pressed her hard against him.

A spewing, splattering sound behind them brought Audrey out of the sensual haze. She suddenly realized two things—that she wanted to have sex with J.D. and that the milk in the saucepan had boiled over onto the stove.

"The milk," she said as she pulled backward and away from him. She set the vanilla aside and then picked up an oven mitt, grabbed the saucepan handle, and removed the overflowing hot milk from the stove.

"It was my fault," he said. "I'll help you clean it up."

"No, please." She gestured with her hands. "Go back in the living room. I'll take care of everything in here."

He looked at her, uncertainty in his dark eyes. "Are you sure?"

She nodded. "I'm sure. Now, go. Please, J.D."

She was grateful that he didn't insist on helping her. The moment he left the kitchen, she began cleaning the stovetop. And all the while she kept asking herself what the hell had happened. Had she kissed him? Had he kissed her? Did it matter? No, not really. What mattered was how quickly the kiss had gotten out of hand, going from lips touching to tongues plunging and aroused bodies straining for closer contact.

How could she go into the living room and face him? What if he expected her to invite him to stay the night? What if he thought she wanted him to make love to her? What if she had misunderstood and he really didn't want her?

Damn it, Audrey, stop analyzing this thing to death. It is what it is. You and J.D. kissed. You both got hot and bothered. That's as far as it went, as far as it's going to go.

Ten minutes later, with the stovetop cleaned and two mugs of hot cocoa in her hands, Audrey exited the kitchen and walked into the living room. *Just act as if nothing happened. Be calm and cool and friendly. But not too friendly. You can do this. Be brave.*

She stopped and stared at the man lying on her sofa, his head propped up on the sofa arm and his feet dangling off the opposite arm. After placing the mugs on coasters atop the coffee table, she inspected him closely and realized that he was sound asleep.

He must be exhausted to have gone to sleep that fast.

There was no need to wake him, no reason he couldn't sleep on her sofa. After a quick trip to the hall linen closet, she returned to the living room with a pillow and a blanket. She gently lifted his head and slid the pillow underneath before she covered him with the blanket. And then without giving any thought to what she was doing, acting purely on feminine instinct, she reached down and caressed his rough cheek. When he mumbled and stirred ever so slightly, she jerked her hand away.

Don't be a fool, Audrey.

She turned off the table lamp, reset the security alarm, and went to her room. Sometime before three o'clock, she finally dozed off, her mind filled with images of the man sleeping on her sofa.

Chapter 29

Somer Ellis's head hurt. Maybe she should get up and take a couple of aspirin. But she was so sleepy she didn't want to move. She could wake Quint and ask him to get the aspirin for her. He wouldn't mind. He loved doing things for her. And she loved him for always being so kind and considerate.

"Quint," she mumbled his name in her half-awake/half-asleep state.

He didn't answer. Maybe she hadn't actually called his name out loud.

Was she still asleep and dreaming?

She tried to turn over and found that she couldn't. And when she struggled to lift her arm, intending to throw it around Quint and cuddle against his back, she discovered her arm wouldn't move.

Her eyes flew open.

Darkness.

A pale light somewhere behind her was too weak to illuminate the room, but enough to show that she hadn't awakened in complete darkness. She couldn't see anything in her bedroom, but she knew where everything was. The chest, the dresser, the nightstands. But she didn't see even the shadows of any furniture.

She tried again to move her arms and suddenly realized that she could lift her elbows only an inch or so, but no higher because her wrists were tied to something. Flexing her fingers, she felt beneath them and found a hard, solid surface, which she gripped tightly.

Her wrists were bound to the arms of a wooden chair.

I'm dreaming. I'm having a nightmare.

Wake up, Somer, damn it, wake up.

All she had to do was wake up, kick off the covers, and get out of bed.

Do it now!

She tried to lift her feet and found she couldn't—her ankles were tied together.

Wake up, wake up.

She danced her toes against the hard surface beneath her feet and found it cold and slightly damp. When she took a deep breath, the smell of mustiness and rot filled her nostrils. She struggled with the ropes on her wrists and ankles and suddenly the chair she sat in began moving, rocking back and forth, back and forth.

This isn't real. You're having a nightmare. Don't be afraid. You'll wake up soon and tell Quint about it and you'll both laugh about how real nightmares can seem.

"Quint," she said out loud. The single word echoed in the room.

Somer shivered. She was cold. Had Quint hogged the covers again and left her shivering without even a sheet to cover her?

"Quint?" she called to him repeatedly. "Quint . . . Quint . . ." Her voice grew louder. "Why won't you answer me?"

Because you're dreaming and he can't hear you. You need to wake up now, Somer.

Please, God, let me wake up!

After endless minutes of agony, trying to force herself to awaken, Somer finally admitted the horrifying truth—she was awake. This was no nightmare. She was bound to a chair in a dark room. And she was alone.

But how did I get here?

What is the last thing you remember? she asked herself.

She had left work around nine fifteen, shortly after Belk closed. She and several of the other salesclerks had walked out together, said good night, and headed toward their parked vehicles.

When she approached her dark red Acura, she didn't pay much attention to the old Lincoln parked beside her. But as she opened her car door, she felt someone behind her. She turned instantly, preparing to fight off an attacker, but the man smiled at her in a nonthreatening way, the way a child would smile at his mother.

"I hope I didn't frighten you," he said.

"I'm afraid you did." She forced a smile, hoping she projected confidence and not fear.

"You don't remember me?" he asked, a hopeful expression on his handsome face.

He did look familiar. Somer racked her brain trying to remember and at the same time uneasiness gnawed at her gut. She wanted him to go away so that she could slide safely into her car. Keeping her gaze fixed on his face, she suddenly recalled where she'd seen him before tonight. At work. Earlier that week. He was the good-looking blonde who had bought the blue baby blanket. But tonight he was wearing glasses.

"Of course, you bought the blue baby shawl on Tuesday," she said, then corrected herself, "No, on Monday."

His smile faded slowly. "It was for Cody. His old one was in pretty bad shape. I think he likes the new one."

"That's nice." She sensed something horribly wrong. Hadn't he told her on Monday that it was a gift that his wife wanted to wrap personally? "I really have to go now. I'm glad Cody likes the blanket."

Get away from him, her survival instincts told her. *Get away from him now.*

Moving as fast as possible, she turned around and got in her car. When she realized that he hadn't tried to stop her, a feeling of intense relief washed over her and she grasped the door handle. But her relief was short-lived when he reached inside the car, grabbed her shoulders, and hauled her out of the car.

Fight him!

But before she could do more than mentally prepare for battle, he yanked a rag from his pocket and shoved the smelly cloth over her nose.

No, no, no . . .

Somer shivered as the memory of what had happened exploded in her mind and explained why she wasn't at home in her bed sleeping alongside her husband. The handsome blond man who had purchased a blue baby blanket on Monday had come back to the mall tonight, waited outside in the parking lot until she had reached her car, and then he had kidnapped her.

In no particular order, questions zipped through her mind at lightning speed. How had he known which car was hers? Why hadn't she called out to her coworkers before they drove away? Why had he abducted her? Why had he tied her to a rocking chair? Where was she? How could she free herself? What did Quint think had happened to her when she hadn't come home? Was Quint out looking for her? Had he called the police? What was her kidnapper going to do to her?

* * *

"What are you doing here?" Zoe asked.

J.D. woke instantly at the sound of his daughter's voice and shot straight up, knocking the blanket off and onto the floor. For a split second he thought he was at home in his own bed, but quickly realized he was on Audrey Sherrod's sofa and that was the reason he ached all over, from neck to hips. He swung his legs off the sofa, rubbed the back of his neck, grunted, and then cleared his throat.

"I must have fallen asleep," he said. "Audrey was fixing us some hot chocolate and I sat down for a couple of minutes and . . ." *Holy hell!* He glanced at the pillow lying against the sofa arm and down at the blanket on the floor.

"Why did you come back here? You'd already called and told me to spend the night."

J.D. leaned over, propped his elbows on his thighs, and lowered his head so that he could rub his temples. "I came back to talk to Audrey."

"Really? About me?"

"Actually, no."

"About what? The case you're working on?"

"In a way. I needed to talk to a grown-up, someone I don't work with, someone who could listen and be objective. Audrey offered to listen if I needed to talk, and I accepted her offer." *And that's all there was to it. Yeah, right. What about that kiss? You can't forget the kiss. And it's damn sure Audrey won't have forgotten.*

"Apparently you didn't do much talking," Zoe said.

"Huh?" J.D. couldn't bring himself to look at his daughter. Did she suspect that he had kissed Audrey?

"Well, if you fell asleep, you couldn't have talked much."

"Yeah, right. No, we didn't talk much."

Zoe glanced back at the hallway leading to the two bedrooms. "Is she still asleep?"

J.D. nodded. "As far as I know."

What time was it? He twisted his wristwatch around so he could see the face. 8:48 A.M.

"Maybe you and I should gather up our stuff and head home, let Audrey sleep in," J.D. suggested.

"Aren't you going to work today?"

"Yeah, I am." He stood up and stretched, then glanced at his daughter and saw the disappointed expression on her face. "Hey, we can stop by McDonald's for a Big Breakfast on the way home. How does that sound?"

"Okay, I guess," Zoe said. "But I was looking forward to one of Audrey's cheese and sausage omelets."

J.D.'s stomach growled. Zoe laughed. He grinned.

"Good morning," Audrey said.

J.D. and Zoe whirled around at the sound of her voice.

"Morning," Zoe replied. "Looks like we all slept late."

J.D. swallowed hard as he stared at Audrey, who stood in the arched entrance to the living room. She looked as fresh as a daisy in her long-sleeved white cotton shirt and slim-fitting dark jeans. She had pulled her hair away from her face, secured it on each side with small gold barrettes, and left the length hanging loosely against her shoulders.

Audrey looked right at him, her expression blank, giving away nothing of what she might or might not be thinking and feeling.

"Ah . . . uh, Zoe and I were planning to leave and let you sleep in," he told her.

"J.D.'s going to take me to McD's for breakfast," Zoe said. "Before he takes me home and goes back to work."

"Why don't you both stay here for breakfast?" Audrey glanced from Zoe to J.D. "Unless you're in a big hurry to leave."

What did she mean by that?

Did she think he was running away before she could confront him about the kiss they'd shared?

"I think we've imposed on your hospitality long enough as it is." J.D.'s gaze remained fixed on Audrey's face.

"It's no imposition. I invited you."

A flicker of emotion shot through Audrey's expressionless green- and gold-flecked brown eyes. Exactly what was she saying? Was she telling him that she had not only invited him to come over last night if he needed someone to talk to, but that she had also invited him to kiss her?

"Come on, J.D. Let's stay for breakfast, please."

How could he resist the hopeful look on his daughter's face?

An hour later, Zoe scooted back her chair from the kitchen table, jumped to her feet, picked up her plate, silverware, and glass, and placed them in the dishwasher. "I'm going to get dressed," she said as she exited the room.

J.D. and Audrey sat in silence for a couple of minutes, then she asked, "More coffee?"

"No, thanks."

"Another scone?" She held up the basket filled with savory butter-and-chive scones.

He rubbed his stomach. "I couldn't eat another bite." He smiled. "I see why Zoe preferred breakfast here to eating fast food, even though the McD's Big Breakfast is a favorite of hers."

"Since you're going to work today, you could let Zoe stay here. I can run her home to pick up a change of clothes and—"

"No, you don't have to do that. I'm going home to shower, shave, and change clothes anyway. And I certainly don't expect you to baby-sit Zoe again. She's old enough to spend the day at home without me. I'm sure you've got better things to do with your day than—"

"Stop right there," she told him in no uncertain terms. "I

don't baby-sit Zoe. And I know she's old enough to be left alone during the day. I happen to enjoy your daughter's company. I thought you understood that she and I have become friends."

"I'm sorry. I didn't mean to imply—"

"If you spent a little more time with her, took the trouble to get to know her better, you might realize—"

"It always comes back to this, doesn't it?" He slid his chair from the table and stood. "Every time we have a conversation, you find a way to remind me what a lousy father I am and take it upon yourself to advise me about my lack of parenting skills. It's becoming a case of beating a dead horse, don't you think?"

He stood over her, glaring at her as she rose slowly to her feet and faced him. She looked at him without saying a word, as if his retaliation had rendered her speechless.

"I don't want us to argue every time we're together," he told her. "But that's all we seem to do. Except for a few minutes last night."

They both knew he was referring to the kiss.

"I don't know why that happened or how it happened," she said. "It was a mistake . . . wasn't it?"

"Was it?"

Zoe called out from the living room, "J.D., your phone's ringing."

He released a pent-up breath. "Grab it for me, will you?"

Audrey stepped back and began clearing the table and loading the dishwasher. J.D. met Zoe as she entered the kitchen and handed him his cell phone. Not bothering to check the caller ID, he answered on what was probably the fifth or sixth ring.

"Special Agent Cass."

"J.D., it's Tam Lovelady."

"Yeah, what is it?"

"I received a call from headquarters an hour or so ago,"

Tam said. "They contacted me about a woman whose husband reported her missing. She didn't come home after work last night."

"What's special about her?"

"She's in her early twenties and attractive. She has long, dark hair and brown eyes. Sound familiar?"

"How long has she been missing?"

"Her husband called in this morning around one o'clock. It seems when she didn't come home from work last night, he contacted every friend he knew of, called her parents, and drove the route she usually takes coming home from work. That's when he found her car, a late-model Acura, the driver's side door open, parked at Hamilton Place Mall, where she works."

"What time did she get off from work?"

"At nine."

"That time of night, there should have been a lot of people around the area. Maybe somebody saw something."

"I agree. I've contacted the Belk manager and he's calling the other employees who worked last night and is asking them to come in this morning and speak to us. Garth and I are heading that way now. I—we thought you might want to join us."

"I do," J.D. said. "I'll be there as soon as I can."

He pocketed his phone and turned to Audrey as he rubbed his chin. "Any chance you have an electric razor? I really [illegible]ahe quick shave."

"[illegible] the a lady's razor, but yes, I have one." She laid her hand on his arm. "He's kidnapped another woman, hasn't he?"

"We think so. A woman who fits the general description of his other victims. She didn't come home from work last night."

* * *

J.D. sat in on the interviews, but left the questioning to Tam and Garth. For all intents and purposes, the Rocking Chair Killer cases were theirs. And even though they had no proof that Somer Ellis had been kidnapped by the man who had abducted and murdered Jill Scott, Debra Gregory, and Whitney Poole, his gut instinct told him that it had been the same guy.

One by one, they questioned the employees who had left work with Somer last night. So far, each of them had said the last they saw of Somer, she'd been walking toward her car.

"She was parked a little farther back than I was," one of the women had said. "When I drove off, she was almost to her car, I think."

"Did you see anybody else around?" Garth had asked.

She had shaken her head. "No, no one."

Alice Finch entered the manager's office, glanced around the room at the two police officers, the TBI agent, and then her boss. J.D. guessed her to be a well-preserved sixty, her makeup flawless, her short platinum hair stiff with hair spray, her body slender and her clothes no doubt Belk's top-of-the-line merchandise.

"Sit down, please, Alice," the manager said and then he introduced Tam, Garth, and J.D. "They want to ask you a few questions about Somer, about when y'all left work last night."

"Has something happened to Somer?" Alice inquired, genuine concern in her voice.

"Somer Ellis has disappeared," Tam said. "She didn't go home last night. Her husband contacted the police early this morning to report her missing."

"Oh, dear. This is awful. If I'd had any idea . . . if I'd thought for one minute . . . but she seemed to know him and—"

"Please, Mrs. Finch, slow down." Tam sat in the armchair

identical to the one Alice settled into, both chairs facing the manager's desk. "Start over, at the beginning from when you left work last night."

Alice nodded. "I said good night to everyone, including Somer, and we all walked into the parking lot, going to our vehicles. Somer was parked a little farther away than the rest of us. She works a short shift on Friday evenings and I suppose she parked as close as she could." Alice took a deep breath. "I noticed a car parked next to hers, the only one nearby. I didn't think anything about it. I mean, it is a parking lot and sometimes people leave cars there all night."

"We understand," Tam assured her.

"Do you remember what model car you saw parked next to—?" Garth asked.

Alice cut him off with an instant reply. "A big white car. An older model. A Lincoln, I believe. I'm not very good with makes and models, but I do know an older car from a newer one."

Garth glanced at J.D. Their gazes locked as they processed the information. Each knew there now could be little doubt that the Rocking Chair Killer had abducted Somer Ellis.

"Did you see anyone inside the car?" Tam continued her questioning.

"No," Alice said. "He wasn't in the car when I saw him."

"You saw him?" The words came out before J.D. realized he had spoken.

"It was when I was driving away," Alice explained. "I noticed there was a man standing between that older-model car and Somer's car. They were talking. She was smiling. I thought she knew him. She didn't act like anything was wrong."

They had a witness. Alice Finch had seen the Rocking Chair Killer.

"Mrs. Finch, can you describe the man you saw?" Tam leaned forward, closer to Alice.

"Well, it was after nine last night, so it was dark, and Somer wasn't parked under one of the security lights."

J.D.'s hopes sank like a lead balloon. Once again they had a witness who could no more ID the killer than the two previous witnesses could.

"Then you didn't see his face," Tam said. "You can't describe him."

"Of course I can describe him. He was medium height and build and had light hair. I caught just a glimpse of him, but I could tell he was young. And I remember thinking he was quite good looking. That made me wonder if perhaps Somer was cheating on her husband, that this man might be her boyfriend."

"If you saw him again, do you think you could identify him?" Garth asked.

"Pick him out of a lineup, you mean?" Alice asked.

"Yes, ma'am." Garth moved in behind Tam's chair.

"Probably not. Not positively. But you know, I did think he looked familiar. I thought I'd seen him before."

"Any idea where?"

"I'm not certain, but I think he may have been a customer. Not mine, but Somer's."

"Does Somer work in the men's department?" Tam asked.

"No, she works in the children's department."

J.D. wanted to ask the next question, but waited, certain that Tam would ask it for him.

"The children's department, does that include infant and toddler items such as baby blankets and shawls?" Tam asked.

"Yes, of course."

Tam turned to the store manager. "I need to see Somer Ellis's sales records for the past two months, starting with this past week."

Chapter 30

The sketch artist had drawn a picture of the person Alice Finch had described. But since she had caught only a quick glimpse of the man's face, the results had shown a rather generic likeness, one that could have fit a great many young, handsome, fair-haired men who wore glasses. But no mustache. They had asked Alice about the mustache and she had been certain that the man she saw had been clean-shaven.

The man in the sketch bore a vague resemblance to Hart Roberts as well as Jeremy Arden. The face also possessed the same sexiness women saw in Matthew McConaughey and, decades ago, in Paul Newman. Bottom line—the sketch was all but useless in identifying their killer. There were too many good-looking blond guys who fit the same general description. After the sketch artist had completed the picture, J.D. had shown Alice photos of both Hart Roberts and Jeremy Arden and asked her if she could ID either man. She had taken her time studying each photo before answering.

"It might have been either one of them," she'd said. "But I can't be sure."

So they were back to square one in positively identifying their killer.

J.D. continued to do his best to keep tabs on Roberts's and Arden's movements, but he was only one guy and couldn't be in several places at once. He'd tried to convince Tam to put a tail on both men, but she had told him they didn't have any evidence against Hart, certainly nothing to warrant tailing him 24/7. And the same held true for Jeremy Arden.

So J.D. had focused on what he could do on his own, which included tracking down the guy who had bought Luther Chaney's old Lincoln for parts and scrap metal and searching for any records of the adoption of a little boy named Corey Bennett. So far, no solid results on the adoption records. But he was waiting on a court order that would allow him partial access to sealed adoption records for the year that Frankie Jo Rogers had told them Dora Chaney had sold her husband's illegitimate child for twenty thousand dollars.

Ever since Somer Ellis had disappeared, three days ago, the local and state media, as well as nationwide TV, had crucified both the CPD and the TBI for their inability to stop the Rocking Chair Killer. From the mayor and DA to Chief Mullins, orders had been issued to make these cases the police department's top priority. And J.D.'s boss had relayed word for word his conversation with the TBI director, who was none too pleased with the unfavorable publicity the state bureau was receiving. J.D. hadn't enjoyed getting his ass chewed out, but it had been worth it because now the director was involved and his influence could open doors that would otherwise be closed. Subtle pressure could persuade judges to issue court orders and light a fire under everyone even indirectly involved with the crossover Baby Blue and Rocking Chair cases.

J.D. hadn't taken a day off in a couple of weeks, nor had

Garth Hudson. And Tam had been working practically around the clock ever since Somer Ellis's kidnapping. He wasn't sure what he would have done without Audrey's help. If she hadn't offered to look after Zoe, he would have had little choice but to hire some unknown baby-sitter for nighttime duty, which Zoe would have hated.

"Let Zoe pack a bag and move in with me, temporarily," Audrey had told him Saturday evening. "It will make things easier all the way around, for Zoe and for you."

Audrey had been right, of course, and any reluctance he'd felt had been only because having Zoe living with her meant daily contact with Audrey. He didn't have time to analyze the kiss they'd shared. But he knew one thing for sure, that kiss had been a one-time-only thing. He had no intention of getting involved with a woman who had Trouble with a capital *T* stamped on her forehead. A guy would be a fool to think he could have a casual fling with Audrey Sherrod. She was the type who'd get under a man's skin, in his blood, and could make a guy forget all the reasons he had sworn off committed relationships for the rest of his life.

J.D.'s phone rang, effectively snapping him out of his now daily keep-Audrey-at-arm's-length rationalizations. He didn't recognize the caller's ID.

"Special Agent Cass."

"Yeah, this here's Eugene Vann Jr. up in Erwin."

Erwin, Tennessee, was a small town south of Johnson City. J.D. gripped the phone tightly. "Yes, sir, Mr. Vann, what can I do for you?"

"Ain't what you can do for me, it's what I can do for you."

"Is that right? Just what can you do for me?"

"I can tell you what happened to that 1980 white Lincoln you state boys have been looking for."

J.D. smiled. "I'm listening, Mr. Vann."

"Well, I bought me an old Lincoln from a man named Frank Elmore a couple years back intending to scrap the car and sell whatever parts I could. But my wife took a liking to the car so I fixed it up a little for her. Had a new engine put in and had it painted, and that sure did tickle her pink."

"I assume your wife doesn't still have the car, is that right?"

"That's right. I had a guy offer me twice what the darn thing was worth before I even got a chance to buy a car tag," Eugene said. "So I sold it to him and halved the money with Patsy. Had to give her half to smooth over her ruffled feathers. She was powerfully fond of that old car."

"Who bought the old Lincoln?" J.D. asked.

"Figured you'd ask."

"Yeah?"

Eugene chuckled. "His name was Corey Bennett."

J.D. hadn't doubted it for a second, had known who it would be even before Eugene said the name. "Can you give me a description of this guy?"

"Sure can. Young, good-looking fellow. Light hair, blue eyes. About five-ten, slender."

"If you saw this man again, would you recognize him?"

"Yep, I probably would."

J.D.'s gut tightened. He didn't want to get excited over the possibility that they might finally have an eyewitness who had seen Corey Bennett face-to-face and believed he could ID him.

"You don't happen to have a fax machine or a computer, do you, Mr. Vann?"

"Ain't got no fax machine, but I got a computer. Do all my bookkeeping on the computer."

"I'd like to send you a couple of photos and see if you might be able to identify either man as Corey Bennett."

"You do that, Special Agent Cass, and I'll call you back as soon as I take a look at them pictures." Eugene cleared his throat. "Mind if I ask you a question?"

"You can ask, but I can't promise I can answer you."

"Fair enough. What I want to know is why you state boys are so all-fired interested in that old Lincoln?"

"We're interested because there's a possibility this car is being used for illegal purposes." J.D. kept the response as honest and yet as vague as possible.

"We get the state, country, and world news up here in Erwin, too, you know," Eugene said. "You state boys and the Chattanooga police are looking for that Rocking Chair Killer, so it don't take no rocket scientist to put two and two together and come up with four."

"Whatever you think you know, I'd appreciate it if you kept it to yourself for the time being. And the TBI director and Chattanooga chief of police would appreciate it."

"Mum's the word. I can keep my mouth shut."

"Thanks, Mr. Vann." J.D. brought up the photo of Hart Roberts on his computer screen. "Give me your e-mail address and I'll get those photos to you right away."

Eugene Vann recited his e-mail address, assured J.D. that he wouldn't breathe a word to anybody about the old Lincoln, and promised to call him back as soon as he'd taken a good look at the photos.

Audrey had awakened with a headache that morning. So far, neither coffee nor aspirin had helped very much, and it was now nearly noon. After dropping Zoe at Baylor, she had come to the office early and tried to take care of some backlogged paperwork that Donna had been pestering her to do.

"It's not like you to get behind," Donna had told her. "It's this Baby Blue and Rocking Chair mess that's got you all tied up in knots, isn't it? That and a certain TBI agent who could most definitely eat crackers in my bed any time he wanted to."

"J.D. Cass has nothing to do with—" She had stopped abruptly, knowing her denial was a lie. "Okay, so maybe I'm confused about J.D. A part of me cannot stand the man, but another part of me, the crazy, stupid, I'm-an-idiot part of me, finds him attractive on some elemental, primitive level."

Donna had laughed. "Yeah, I know what you mean. He's definitely the type that makes you wonder what it would be like to be his woman."

Leave it to Donna to bluntly state the obvious.

Audrey's feelings about J.D. confused her. And being conflicted about her feelings right now only added to the emotional pressure she had been experiencing since the first skeleton had been identified as a Baby Blue toddler. Nightmares that she had conquered years ago had returned to haunt her, dreams about the day that Blake had disappeared. Sometimes the nightmares seemed as accurate as her memories of that long-ago day; and yet sometimes they made no sense at all because they were about things that hadn't happened.

Because of her mixed emotions about J.D. and the reoccurrence of the nightmares, Audrey had spent several restless nights lately.

When Mr. Dwyer, her 11:30 A.M. client, left a few minutes after 12:30, Audrey opened the middle desk drawer, removed a bottle of aspirin, and dumped two tablets in her palm. Just as she got up, intending to retrieve a bottled water from the mini-fridge, Donna knocked, called Audrey's name, and cracked open the door.

"I'm heading out for lunch." Donna inclined her head backward, the gesture indicating the outer office. "You've got a visitor."

J.D.?

As if hearing Audrey's unspoken question, Donna shook her head. "It's Porter Bryant."

Audrey groaned quietly. What was he doing here? Didn't she have enough problems without having to deal with Porter today?

"Thanks, Donna. You go on to lunch."

"Are you sure?" Donna asked.

"I'm sure." Audrey forced a smile as she walked toward the door between her private office and the outer office waiting area.

Porter looked as he always did—immaculate. A gray pinstriped suit, silver shirt, and dark red tie. Spit-polished shoes. Manicured nails. His hundred-dollar haircut kept neatly styled with hair spray.

"Hello, Audrey." He held out a single red rose.

Go away, Porter, please.

She had hoped that since she hadn't heard from him in a while, his unnerving pursuit of her had been a short-term obsession.

She took the rose and laid it on Donna's desk. "Why are you here, Porter?"

"I miss you." He took a tentative step toward her.

She stood her ground. "Please don't do this."

"How about lunch? I have to eat. You have to eat. Just two friends sharing a meal. What do you say?"

If she thought he actually meant what he'd said—just two friends sharing a meal—she might have accepted the offer. But she had no intention of giving Porter any false hopes about their relationship. The easiest excuse was a lie. "I'm sorry, but I already have lunch plans."

"With Special Agent Cass?"

"Who I'm meeting for lunch is really none of your business," she said. "But no, I'm not meeting J.D. for lunch."

"Another man? I had no idea you had become so popular with the opposite sex. You're certainly not the type. That's what attracted me in the first place—the fact that I wouldn't have to compete with anyone else for your favors."

"If you were trying to be insulting, you succeeded." Audrey sensed a strange vibe coming from Porter, something she hadn't felt in the first few months they'd been dating and something she had ignored until she ended their going-nowhere relationship.

"I would never insult you, darling. I adore you. You must know that."

"Porter, you have to stop this. Do you hear me? If you don't stop—"

He grabbed her upper arms and shook her. She yanked out of his firm hold and glared at him. A rush of pure fear-induced adrenaline pumped through her system.

"What is the matter with you? Have you lost your mind?" Despite being rattled by Porter's unexpected actions, Audrey didn't back down; instead, she confronted him with her bold attitude. "If you don't stop harassing me, I'll have no choice but to take out a restraining order against you."

"You wouldn't do that."

"Yes, I would. I thought I knew you, but the Porter Bryant I knew would never stalk a woman. This is insanity. You have to see that."

He stood perfectly still. His eyes misted. The pulse in his neck throbbed when he clenched his teeth.

After a few silent, intense moments, he cleared his throat and said, "I thought you were the one. I thought you, of all people, would understand. But apparently I was wrong about you, about us."

"Yes, you were wrong," she told him, not completely sure what he was talking about, but it didn't matter as long as he accepted the fact that there was no "us" now or ever.

"I'm sorry. I was so sure," he said, his expression one of complete puzzlement. "I can assure you that I will not bother you again with my unwanted attention."

"Thank you, Porter." On the verge of mentally sighing with relief, she held her breath, sensing he had something else to say.

Staring at her, his blue eyes bright and moist, he said, "Why you would prefer J.D. Cass to me, I don't understand.

I am superior to him in every way. I have more money, I'm more intelligent and have more class in my pinky than he does in his entire body."

Before Audrey could respond, Porter snapped around, squared his shoulders, and left Audrey's office without a backward glance.

Several minutes later, certain that he was gone and wouldn't return, she slumped down in one of the waiting-area chairs and finally breathed that mental sigh of relief.

J.D. answered his phone after the first ring. "Cass here."

"Yeah, this here is Eugene Vann."

"Yes, sir, Mr. Vann. Have you taken a good look at the photos I e-mailed you?" *Please, God, please, let him ID either Roberts or Arden as the guy who bought the old Lincoln.*

"Sure have. Took my time, just like you said. I wanted to make sure before I called you."

"And?"

"And I can't say for certain."

J.D. felt like a tire gone suddenly flat. "You don't recognize either man?"

"Didn't say that. I just said I couldn't be certain, at least not about one of 'em."

"What do you mean?"

"The picture you got labeled Number One. I don't think it's him. Got the same coloring and all, same look about him, but it ain't him."

Hart Roberts's photo was labeled #1.

"What about the other photo?" J.D. asked.

"Well, there's where I'm not sure. Could be him. He sure looks more like the fellow I remember than the other guy. But there's something different about him. Could just be the picture, I guess, but there's something not quite the same.

Can't put my finger on it. It's like this guy maybe could be a brother to the man I sold the Lincoln to instead of being him."

"Then the resemblance is strong enough that they could be mistaken for brothers?"

"Yeah, that's what I said. If I saw the man in person, I might be able to say for sure. I thought I could ID him from a picture, but I wouldn't want to swear when I ain't a hundred percent sure."

"I understand. Thank you, Mr. Vann. I appreciate your help."

"Any time, Special Agent Cass, any time. I'm a God-fearing, law-abiding citizen and I'm proud to do my part to help out you state boys."

After the phone call ended, J.D. sat at his desk, his thoughts centered on the best way to use the information. No positive ID that would stand up in court. Nothing that would warrant arresting Jeremy Arden or putting the man in a lineup.

Eugene Vann couldn't be sure that Arden was the man who had bought the old Lincoln from him, but he'd been sure it was not Hart Roberts. Was Jeremy Arden also using the name Corey Bennett? If so, did that mean that Luther Chaney's illegitimate child wasn't Corey Bennett, that whoever the boy was he had nothing to do with the Rocking Chair Murders?

If he eliminated Hart Roberts and concentrated only on keeping tabs on Jeremy Arden and locating Luther Chaney's bastard son, could he be certain that one of them was the man who had already murdered three women and abducted a fourth? Yes, definitely yes, his gut instinct told him. It had to be one or the other, didn't it?

But what if your gut instinct is wrong?

Chapter 31

Jeremy had needed a fix last night. Had needed one bad. But he hadn't been able to score, so he'd settled for getting pass-out drunk. The thoughts that had driven him to drink last night had returned this morning, as strong and tormenting as ever.

He couldn't get her off his mind.

Regina Bennett wouldn't die.

No matter how many times he mentally killed her, she kept coming back. Again and again.

Damn you! Get out of my head. Go away and never come back.

Sitting on the side of the bed, he moaned as his stomach rumbled. He was going to throw up again.

Within minutes, he was hanging over the commode, groaning and puking. He knew better than to drink so damn much of the hard stuff. It wasn't as if this hadn't happened to him before more than once. He deserved what he got, even if he was suffering from alcohol poisoning.

Merciful God, he felt like shit.

Fumbling from the toilet to the sink, nearly falling into

the wall, Jeremy managed to turn on the faucets and splash cold water on his face.

He had to get hold of himself, had to find a way to separate fact from fiction. His muddled brain kept messing him up, kept telling him things that weren't true.

Or were they?

He stared at himself in the mirror. "Regina Bennett is dead."

That's right. She's dead. And you didn't kill her. She died in Moccasin Bend.

But what about the other one?

What other one?

Jeremy beat on his head with his fists.

Damn it, you know, you know. The other Regina. The one rocking Cody in her arms.

Hush, little baby, don't say a word, Mama's going to buy you a mocking bird. He could hear her singing to him, her voice soft and sweet, her arms tender and caring.

No! She was a monster. She stole me from my real mother. She thought I was Cody. She was going to kill me.

And that's why I have to make her go away. Again and again.

Every time she reappears, I have to get rid of her. I have to make her stop tormenting me. I have to make her get out of my head. If I don't, I'll go crazy.

Jeremy laughed hysterically.

"I'm already freaking crazy," he said aloud as he dropped to his knees on the bathroom floor. "God help me."

J.D. had been living off coffee and fast food, sleeping no more than four hours at night, and hadn't seen his daughter in five days. He'd been living and breathing the Rocking Chair Killer cases, determined to find the son of a bitch before he killed Somer Ellis. As best he could, he had coordinated his efforts—the TBI's efforts—with Garth and Tam and the CPD. Garth had continued to set aside any hostility he'd felt toward J.D. in order for them to work together to solve this case. Garth Hudson was the only person who was even more determined than J.D. to find their killer before he could kill again.

Armed with Eugene Vann's "could be him" ID of Jeremy Arden as the man who had called himself Corey Bennett, J.D. had at least gotten the CPD to put an around-the-clock tail on the guy. So far—nothing. If he had kidnapped Somer Ellis and was keeping her under lock and key somewhere, he hadn't checked on her in several days. Of course, she might already be dead. But if she was, why hadn't her body shown up?

Then again, maybe Arden wasn't their guy. Maybe Hart Roberts was, despite Eugene Vann's certainty that he wasn't the man who had bought the old Lincoln. Or maybe the real Corey Bennett, Regina Bennett's son, a second child fathered by her uncle, was out there somewhere, a man living under another identity. A judge had finally issued the court order that allowed the TBI to search the sealed birth records, starting with the state of Tennessee, of every male child adopted the year that Dora Chaney married Frank Elmore. If there was a record of Corey Bennett or any child with the last name of either Bennett or Chaney, it was only a matter of time before the TBI secured the information.

J.D. parked the Camaro, killed the engine, and sat there for a few minutes. He had spoken to Zoe once every day, usually at night before her bedtime. Their conversations had been succinct, as if for both of them the daily call was a mere formality. He was trying to be a good dad; she was trying to be the kind of daughter she thought he wanted.

He hadn't seen or spoken to Audrey since Saturday evening. But despite being consumed with the Rocking Chair Killer cases, he had thought quite a bit about her, far more than he should have. At the oddest moments, her pretty face would pop into his mind. Her soft pink mouth curving into a smile. Her smooth, slender neck inviting his touch. Her green- and gold-flecked brown eyes gazing at him with a combination of curiosity and longing.

If you need a woman, there are a lot less dangerous choices. You know damn well that Audrey Sherrod is off-limits. And you know all the reasons why she is.

When Zoe had called and asked him if he could take time from his busy schedule to at least stop by and have dinner with her, why hadn't he told her he couldn't make it? Why had he instantly said, "What time?"

Because he missed his daughter? Sure, that was part of it. Oddly enough, he did miss Zoe. He'd sort of gotten used to having her around. He had been alone most of his life and had convinced himself he liked it that way. J.D. Cass was a loner, a guy who didn't want or need anyone else.

He barely remembered his mother, and his sister Julia had no memory of her at all since she'd left them high and dry when Julia was barely a year old. Sometimes he thought he could remember her laughter, and other times he was sure he remembered the sound of her crying. But what he remembered most about his childhood was their old man. Jed Cass had been a man's man in every sense of the word. Hard as nails. Unemotional but not uncaring. As long as their dad lived, he and Julia had known they could count on him. He'd never once told them he loved them, but he had shown them every day of his life. J.D. had been just shy of nineteen when the old man had died. A freak accident. After an ice storm had downed power lines, Jed Cass, along with the utility company's other electricians, had worked around the clock. On his way home, driving up Fifth Street that freezing-cold February morning, his father had been killed. An enormous overhanging limb from one of the many oak trees that lined the street had broken off from the weight of the ice, hit his truck, and crushed the cab down on him, breaking his neck and killing him instantly.

J.D. had dropped out of college and gotten a job so he could support himself and Julia. Eventually, he'd earned a degree by attending night classes, after going through the academy and being hired by the Memphis PD. He supposed that in some ways, he'd been as much a father to Julia as he had a big brother. So why was it that he couldn't make that father-and-daughter connection with his own daughter?

Julia had been easy. He had loved her always, from the first moment he saw her. She had such a sweet disposition, and never once had she defied him. Zoe wasn't easy. He hadn't loved her instantly. And God knew no one would ever call her sweet. She was far too much like him in every way. And he'd be damned if she didn't defy him every chance she got, although he had to admit that since Audrey had come into their lives, Zoe's behavior had greatly improved.

So get your sorry ass out of the car and go have supper with your daughter. For Zoe's sake, you can spend a couple of hours in Audrey Sherrod's company without her managing to put a ring through your nose.

Now where the hell had that thought come from? What made him think Audrey wanted to put a ring through his nose?

Because it was the women whose strength came wrapped in gentleness who were dangerous to men. Steel magnolias. Velvet steamrollers. Both descriptions fit Audrey. He didn't know how to deal with that type of woman. He had always steered clear of them.

Even his ex-wife had been a tough, in-your-face bitch. That type he knew how to handle. Since his divorce, it had been strictly love 'em and leave 'em. If he'd been smarter, that's what he would have done with Erin. Marrying her had been a huge mistake. But he'd been young and stupid.

Now he was no longer young, and he wasn't going to do anything stupid. He could handle his attraction to Audrey.

Zoe had helped Audrey put a beef roast and vegetables in the Crock-Pot before they left that morning. All they'd had to do was prepare a green salad and pop some store-bought rolls into the oven for dinner. She would have preferred not to see J.D. again so soon, not until she had gotten any foolish notions about him out of her mind. But Zoe wanted to see her father. And Audrey believed that whether he knew it or not, J.D. needed to see his daughter.

She had stayed in the kitchen and let Zoe answer the door and spend some one-on-one time with her father before dinner. When Zoe and J.D. had entered the kitchen, he had nodded, said hello, and thanked her for inviting him to dinner.

"Something sure smells good," he'd said.

During dinner, Audrey managed to keep a pleasant smile in place and held up her end of the conversation. Zoe took the lead by telling J.D. about school, this new boy she liked, and an upcoming field trip tomorrow.

"This boy you keep talking about—?" J.D. asked.

"Noah Brady," Zoe said.

"Yeah, about this Noah Brady—?"

For a second time, Zoe cut J.D. off midsentence. "You'll approve of him. He's fifteen. He doesn't have a car or a driver's license, of course. He doesn't drink or smoke or do drugs. His dad's a banker and his mother is a professor at UTC."

"He's fifteen, huh?" J.D.'s lips twitched. "Sounds about right."

"So, you don't have any objection to our going to a movie together, do you? Maybe this weekend?"

"I'd take Zoe and Noah's mom would bring him; we'd drop the kids off and then pick them up when the movie's over," Audrey explained.

"Sounds as if you two already have this all worked out." He looked at Audrey. "I trust your judgment. If you think it's okay, then—"

Jumping to her feet, Zoe shoved back her chair and hurled herself at J.D. Audrey couldn't help laughing at the shocked look on his face when Zoe actually hugged him.

Pulling back and smiling at her father, Zoe said, "Thank you, thank you, thank you. I promise I'll behave myself and not get into any trouble."

J.D. cleared his throat and then grinned, but he didn't say anything. Audrey suspected that despite evidence to the contrary, J.D. Cass was not an uncaring, insensitive brute.

"May I be excused?" Zoe asked Audrey. "I want to call Noah and tell him that we're definitely on for Saturday night."

"Go call him," Audrey said. "And I'll double-check with his mother in the morning to coordinate—"

Zoe ran out of the kitchen before Audrey finished her sentence, leaving Audrey and J.D. alone. For several minutes, neither of them spoke, but when the tension grew unbearable, Audrey asked if he'd care for dessert.

"Just cookies, I'm afraid," she told him.

He patted his stomach. "Nothing for me, thanks. I couldn't eat another bite."

"Coffee or hot tea or—?"

"No coffee. I've probably drunk enough coffee lately to fill the Tennessee River."

"I know y'all are working around the clock," Audrey said. "Tam's been living on Cokes and potato chips." Audrey paused, considered what she wanted to say, and then said it. "She told me that you're not really looking at Hart as a suspect now. I'm glad you know my stepbrother isn't a killer."

"He was never a suspect."

"A person of interest, then." Audrey got up and began clearing the table.

"He's still a person of interest, but not the focus of our investigation." J.D. rose to his feet and immediately assisted Audrey by stacking his and Zoe's plates and carrying them to the sink. "I'm sure Tam told you that we've got more information to work with now than we've had at any other time since Jill Scott was abducted and murdered."

"Yes, she mentioned it. Just in general terms. Nothing confidential. And Tam says Uncle Garth is like a man obsessed. She's never seen him so crazed with finding a killer. Part of what's riding him so hard is probably knowing that if or when this man kills again, the child he places in Somer Ellis's arms will be Blake."

"Yeah, I'm afraid that's inevitable. Your brother was the fourth Baby Blue toddler and Somer is the fourth kidnap victim."

"How close are you—the TBI and the CPD—to finding him?"

"Closer than we were, but not nearly close enough. Time's running out."

Audrey nodded and then glanced away, not wanting him to see the tears in her eyes. If he tried to comfort her, if he touched her even in the most innocent way, she wasn't sure how she might react.

For the next five minutes, they worked side by side, clearing the table, loading the dishwasher, and cleaning up in the kitchen. And then, as they were going into the living room, what she had dreaded most happened. He placed his hand on the small of her back as he followed her from one room to the other. The moment he touched her, she froze. When she stopped unexpectedly, the action brought his chest in direct contact with her back.

"Audrey?" His voice was low and deep, his mouth close to her ear.

"J.D., please—"

Zoe burst into the room, all but jumping up and down

with excitement. "It's all set. Saturday night. And we even agreed on the movie we want to see. Isn't that fabulous? Oh, and guess what? He said no Dutch treat. This is a real date and he believes the guy should always pay on a real date."

"He's a smart boy," J.D. said. "Seems somebody's teaching him the right way to treat a lady."

Audrey managed to make her legs move forward so that she could walk away from J.D.

"Supper was great, as was the company," J.D. said. "I hate to eat and run, but—"

Zoe whined, "Ah, J.D., don't go yet." Then she smiled. "Sorry. I know you're working on a very important case and you're trying to find a murderer before he kills again. You should get back to work."

"Who are you, young lady?" J.D. asked playfully. "And what have you done with my daughter Zoe?"

Zoe laughed. Audrey smiled.

J.D. put his arm around Zoe's shoulders and said, "I'll call you tomorrow, and after your big Saturday night date, I'll want a full report."

"Come on, I'll walk you out," Zoe said. "And as for a full report . . . well, you don't want to hear any of the mushy stuff, I'm sure."

Audrey heard him say, "There had better not be any mushy stuff going on," as he and Zoe headed outside onto the porch.

She hadn't intended to eavesdrop when she passed the front door on her way into the hall. But she couldn't help overhearing Zoe say, "I'm worried about Audrey. She's been having nightmares. I've heard her crying a couple of nights and this morning early, I heard her screaming. She says it's just bad dreams about the day her little brother disappeared. I wish we could do something to help her."

"Just be as good a friend to her as she's been to you," J.D. said.

"I'll try."

Audrey hurried down the hall before Zoe could come back inside and catch her listening to what was supposed to be a private conversation.

Chapter 32

Hart pumped into the woman lying beneath him, his thrusts increasing with the urgency of an impending climax. She clutched his shoulders, digging her nails into his flesh. The pain sent him over the edge. As the aftershocks rippled through him, she shivered, whimpered, and then cried out as she came. Falling off her and onto his side, Hart opened his eyes and stared up at the ceiling. He had just had mind-blowing sex with a woman whose name he couldn't remember. Iyana? India? No, it was Imani.

When she curled up against him and danced her long, red nails over his chest, he glanced at her. Imani was pretty, with short, curly black hair, sparkling brown eyes, and skin the color of smooth caramel. He had noticed her immediately and picked her up in the bar because she reminded him of Tamara. And from the moment he had stripped her naked and laid her down in his bed, he had made love not to Imani, but to Tam. Always Tam.

Hart rolled out of bed and removed the condom on his way to the bathroom. After taking a piss and quickly washing his genitals, he returned to the bedroom, picked up his discarded jeans from the floor, and slipped into them.

Imani sat up in bed, her melon-sized breasts revealed as the sheet dropped to her waist. "Playtime over?" she asked.

"Yeah, for tonight," he told her as he gathered up her panties and knee-length sweater dress. "Here, sugar—" He tossed the clothes to her. "Get dressed and I'll take you home. Or back to the bar, if that's where you want to go."

"Who's Tam?" she asked as she flung back the sheet and stood.

"What?"

"You called me Tam a couple of times." Imani went into the bathroom. "Who is she?" she called to him. "Your ex?"

"Yeah," Hart said.

"Want to talk about it, tell me what she did to break your heart?" Imani came out of the bathroom wearing her bikini panties. She reached down on the floor and picked up her bra.

"No."

"Suit yourself." She hooked her front-closure bra and pulled her dress over her head. "And the night's still young, so you can take me back to the bar. Who knows, I might find a guy who can remember my name when he's fucking me."

"Look, I'm sorry, okay? But you got your cookies off, didn't you? What more were you expecting?"

"You're a real shit, you know that, don't you?" She slipped into her spike heels, walked over to Hart, and gave him the finger. "I'll call a cab. You'll pay for it."

"Sure, whatever you want."

Hart escorted Imani out of his bedroom and into the living room, and she retrieved her purse from the floor where she had dropped it earlier.

The front door swung open and his uncle Garth tromped into the house. He stopped dead still and looked from the empty beer bottles on the coffee table to Hart and then to the sultry woman at his side.

"God damn it, Hart, what's this?" Garth demanded.

"By this, are you talking about me? If you are, then 'this' is a woman," Imani said. "And 'this' is leaving just as soon as Hart calls me a cab."

"You got a cell phone with you?" Garth asked.

"In my purse," she replied.

Garth jerked his wallet from his pocket, opened it, took out a fifty, and handed it to Imani. "Get out and call yourself a cab."

"Who the hell do you think you are?" She snarled the question.

"I'm the man who's going to toss your ass out onto the sidewalk if you don't get out now," Garth told her.

"Some friend you've got." Imani flashed Hart an angry glare, gave Garth the finger, and headed for the door.

As soon as the door slammed shut, Hart was left alone to face his uncle's wrath. "Yes, I picked her up in a bar. And yes, I had a few beers and I drove when I shouldn't have. But I promise you that—"

"Shut the hell up!" Garth yelled at him. "You know damn well what's about to happen. How can you bring home some spicy piece of ass and get drunk and maybe say or do—?"

"Booze and sex help me forget," Hart said. "You know that. You've used both for as long as I've known you for the same reasons."

"I won't deny it, but damn it, boy, you need to pull yourself together. We've got trouble heading our way." Garth removed his jacket, but left his shoulder holster in place. "If we can't find our killer in time to stop him from murdering Somer Ellis, then she's going to show up in a rocking chair somewhere with a toddler's skeleton in her arms. And we both know who that toddler is going to be, don't we?"

Hart followed Garth into the kitchen and watched while

his uncle removed a box of leftover Chinese takeout and a water bottle from the refrigerator.

"Is there any chance y'all can stop him before it's too late?" Hart asked.

Garth set the water bottle on the table and then dumped the leftovers onto a plate and stuck the plate in the microwave. "If we're lucky, real goddamn lucky, it could happen."

"At least I'm no longer a suspect." Hart snorted. "Ironic, huh, that Special Agent Cass thought I might be the Rocking Chair Killer."

"You're not a murderer. It's not in you to deliberately harm another human being." Garth removed the plate from the microwave, set it on the small kitchen table, and then pulled out a chair.

Hart sat down at the table opposite his uncle. "What'll happen if he kills Somer Ellis and another Baby Blue toddler shows up?"

Garth wolfed down several huge bites of chicken-fried rice and chugalugged the water. He looked at Hart. "We hang in there together, as a family, you and me and Audrey and Wayne."

"That's a given," Hart said. "But that wasn't what I was talking about."

"I know. Try not to worry. I'll figure out something. There has to be some sort of reasonable explanation," Garth said. "But I can't deal with work, with our problem, and take care of you all at the same time. I need you to straighten up and fly right until this is all over, one way or another. Can you do that, boy? Tell me you can. I want to hear you say the words."

Garth reached across the table and patted Hart's cheek as if he were still a child. He supposed in many ways, he hadn't grown up . . . and never would.

"I can do it, Uncle Garth. I swear I can."

* * *

"Hush, little baby, don't you cry."

Somer's quavering voice echoed in the hushed stillness as she sang the old lullaby. She remembered a few of the words, enough to please her captor; the rest of the words, she made up and repeated them again and again.

When he left her alone, she went out of her mind, waiting and wondering, longing to be rescued, praying for life. But now she knew who had abducted her and the fate that awaited her, the same fate that had ended three other lives. Why was he prolonging her agony? Why didn't he just smother her and end the torment the way he had with those other women she had heard about on the TV news?

If by some miracle she could escape or if she was rescued, she would be able to identify him. She had seen his face. Awake or asleep, his image never left her mind.

Had the other women he had kidnapped and murdered known who he was, had he showed them his face, or had he hidden himself from them?

When he was there in the dark room with her, she couldn't begin to describe the terror she experienced. The first time he had placed Cody in her arms, she had screamed hysterically. Even now, after holding the tiny skeleton in her arms many times, she couldn't bring herself to look down again at the "child." He had once been someone's little boy. His parents had loved him and were perhaps still mourning his loss. Did they suspect his fate or did they still live in hopes that he was alive and would one day come home to them?

When his hand smoothed down over her head from crown to nape, she shuddered. She hated the feel of his hands, despised the sound of his voice, and felt nauseous smelling the faint hint of his expensive cologne. Each time he touched her, always with the utmost gentleness, she wondered if it was the touch of death, if this time, he would end her life.

"He loves it when you sing to him," he told her. "And so do I. Keep singing so Cody won't cry anymore."

He stood behind her, his hand on her shoulder. "If that looking glass gets broke . . ." Her voice cracked with emotion. She gasped for air. Tears filled her eyes. He moved to the side of the rocking chair, reached out and fingered the dampness on her cheek. "Don't cry, Mommy. Don't you cry, too. Cody's going to be all right. God will take care of him. You'll be with him forever. I promised you, didn't I, and I would never break my promise."

She gulped several times, swallowing her fear, doing her best to believe that God would take care of her, too.

Are you there, God? Can you hear me? Do you care?

With a courage forged of pity and resolve, Somer rocked back and forth, humming the old Southern lullaby generations of women had crooned to their babies. *Poor little baby.* She cradled the shawl-wrapped skeleton. *Somebody's baby. I don't know who you are, little boy, but one day very soon, you will be going home. Your mommy and daddy will be able to say a final good-bye to you.*

Somer tried not to think about her own fate, although she knew the odds of ever leaving this dark, dank room were not good. It would take a miracle for anyone to find her, and she wasn't sure she believed in miracles or in a loving, benevolent God.

The question of why bad things happened to good people had become far more than just a philosophical one.

What had she ever done to deserve this? What had the sweet, innocent child she held in her arms ever done to deserve death at the hands of a madwoman?

Spending time with his mother and brother always gave him a feeling of deep and abiding peace. His sweetest memories were of standing beside his mother's rocking chair as she sang to Cody. For so many years after he was taken from her, he dreamed about her and Cody. But when he had shared his dreams with anyone else, he had been told he was simply having nightmares, that none of it had ever happened. And eventually, he had believed what he was told and had almost forgotten about his mother and his brother.

Two years ago he had begun searching for the truth about his biological parents. What he had unearthed had changed his life forever. He had known the first time he visited Regina Bennett at Moccasin Bend that she held the answers to all his questions. Regina, Cody's mother. And his mother, too.

Coming out of the old, ramshackle church, he stood on solid ground and gazed up at the night sky. Twinkling like minuscule Christmas lights thrown onto a black canopy, stars glimmered from far, far away. The crisp autumn wind rustled through the treetops in the surrounding woods.

Regina's voice came to him. He could hear the last thing she'd ever said to him, could feel her hand clutching his and her eyes pleading.

Promise me that you'll go there and find Cody. I want him to be with me in heaven. Put him in my arms so I can hold him forever.

He breathed in the night air, cool and fresh there on the country hillside, far from the city and its dirtiness. Once he fulfilled his promise to his mother, she and Cody could rest in peace, their souls joined forever in heaven. And then he would be free to live the life he had been destined to lead without being weighed down by nightmares from his childhood.

Rest tonight, Mommy. Tomorrow night, I'll come back one final time. I'll place Cody in your arms and you'll be with him forever and ever.

* * *

J.D. wiped the shaving cream off his face and splashed warm water over his smooth cheeks. He had come home after midnight last night and had fallen fast asleep. His alarm had gone off at six. He had showered and just now shaved. He was meeting with Tam and Garth at police headquarters at eight that morning.

As he walked barefoot into the bedroom, wearing only his boxers, he heard his cell phone ringing. Where the hell had he put his phone? Was it still attached to his belt? No, he distinctly remembered taking it off his belt and laying it down somewhere. He checked the nightstand. Wasn't there. He glanced around the floor on either side of the bed. Not there.

The phone stopped ringing. J.D. cursed under his breath as he stomped around in his bedroom searching for his phone.

And then it rang again.

He stopped, listened, and followed the sound.

Squatting on his haunches, he ran his hand under the right side of his bed until his hand encountered his phone. How the hell had it gotten under there?

"Special Agent Cass," he answered.

"Good morning," his boss, Phil Hayes, said. "Are you at home?"

"Yeah. I'm meeting Sergeant Hudson and Officer Lovelady at eight."

"Well, you're going to have some mighty interesting news to share with them," Phil told him.

"I am?"

"You are."

"And what news would that be?"

"I have some information that's going to blow your mind if it turns out to be what I think it is."

"Damn it, Phil, stop dragging this out and tell me."

"Those adoption records you were so interested in . . . Seems like that court order has paid off. In spades."

"We've found Corey Bennett."

"Yep. A nine-year-old boy named Corey Bennett was adopted the year Dora Chaney married Frank Elmore. It was a private adoption, and as you already know, the adoptive parents, through their lawyer, paid Dora Chaney twenty thousand dollars."

"Who were the adoptive parents? Have you got a name for me?"

"The adoptive parents were a well-to-do Lexington, Kentucky, couple, both in their mid-fifties at the time of the adoption," Phil said. "He was a lawyer and she was an interior designer. Their son followed in the old man's footsteps and became a lawyer. Morris and Lynn Bryant are dead now, and before you ask, both passed away of natural causes."

"Morris and Lynn Bryant?" J.D.'s mind whirled with the information. "My God!"

"Blondish brown hair, blue eyes, medium height and build. Pretty-boy good-looking. Last name of Bryant. Ring any bells?"

"Porter Bryant is Corey Bennett!"

Chapter 33

Driving like the proverbial bat out of hell, J.D. arrived at police headquarters twenty minutes after he got off the phone with Phil Hayes. But before leaving home, he'd called Tam and told her that they had found Corey Bennett and he'd fill her and Garth in on the details as soon as they met. Phil had told him that he would contact Chief Mullins.

"I want you to do something for me," J.D. had told Phil.

"Okay, what do you need?"

"Have Chief Mullins station an officer outside Audrey Sherrod's town house and follow her if she leaves home today. Tell him this needs to be a discreet operation."

"You think Porter Bryant is a danger to—?"

"Possibly. Bryant and Dr. Sherrod dated for a while. When she broke things off with him, he came damn near close to stalking her for a while. I don't want to take any chances."

"Is this personal for you, J.D.?"

"In a way."

"I'll see to it immediately."

J.D. parked his Camaro, got out, dashed across the road,

and hurried into the police station. Tam met him moments after he entered and offered him a cup of coffee.

"I figured by the way you sounded when you called that you wouldn't take time even for coffee this morning," she said.

He accepted the mug and walked with her into Garth's office, where the sergeant waited at his desk.

"Close the door," J.D. told her.

Tam closed the door. "What's going on? You said that you know who Corey Bennett is. Does that mean he's using an alias?"

J.D. set his coffee mug on Tam's desk and turned to face the CPD investigators. "If he'd had a birth certificate, which he didn't, the information would have read Corey Ray Bennett. Mother, Regina Bennett. Father, unknown. But he didn't have a birth certificate, just as his brother Cody didn't have one. It seems the Bennett boys were twins."

"Twins? Then Regina Bennett really did have another son," Tam said.

"What happened to Corey?" Garth asked. "Where is he now?"

"A better question is who is he now." J.D. glanced from Tam to Garth.

"Don't tell me he's someone we know," Tam guessed.

"When Corey Bennett was eight years old, Luther Chaney died, Regina was admitted to Moccasin Bend, and Dora Chaney moved away and remarried less than a year later. She took Corey—more than likely her husband's son—with her to Bristol, but the new husband wouldn't allow her to keep the boy, so she sold him."

"This is old information, Cass," Garth grumbled.

"The boy was adopted by a well-to-do Lexington, Kentucky, couple. Morris and Lynn Bryant." J.D. waited, allowing the surname to sink into their minds.

"Morris and Lynn Bryant." Tam repeated the names a

couple of times. Her eyes widened in shock. "You can't mean that . . ." She gulped. "My God, is Porter Bryant—?"

"Porter Bryant is Corey Bennett?" Garth shot up out of his chair.

"One and the same." When J.D. saw Garth reach for his phone, he quickly said, "Audrey's safe. She has protection. Phil Hayes took care of it for me."

Garth visibly relaxed, but frustration and anger stamped tension lines on his face. "Think of all the time you've wasted suspecting Hart." Garth mumbled several obscenities. "And apparently you were dead wrong about Jeremy Arden, too. And all along the real killer was right under your nose."

"He was right under our noses, too," Tam pointed out to her partner. "How could J.D. have known? How could anyone have known? Porter Bryant certainly seems normal. He's hardly the type you'd suspect of being a serial killer. My God, I've socialized with the man for months. My best friend dated him." Tam groaned. "Oh, God, how is Audrey going to feel when she finds out?"

"Audrey's feelings aren't important at the moment," J.D. said. "What's important is putting a surveillance team on Bryant ASAP. If he is our killer—"

"What do you mean *if* he's our killer?" Garth asked.

"Just because he's Regina Bennett's son and fits the general description of our killer and the man who purchased the 1980s Lincoln from Eugene Vann doesn't mean he's the Rocking Chair Killer."

"You're right," Tam said. "We have no proof whatsoever."

"That's why we're going to watch him twenty-four/seven. If he abducted Somer Ellis, sooner or later, he'll go to wherever he's keeping her. And when he does, we'll follow him."

"What if he's already killed her?"

"We'll work under the assumption that he hasn't," J.D. said.

"We can haul Bryant's ass in here and beat the truth out of him." Garth spat the words through clenched teeth.

"That's emotion talking," J.D. told him. "Not logic."

"The last thing we want is for him to have any idea that we suspect him." Tam watched her partner closely, waiting for his reply. J.D. figured she'd seen Garth Hudson's temper get the best of him on more than one occasion.

Garth grunted. "Yeah, yeah, you're right."

"As soon as Chief Mullins and SAC Hayes arrive, I want us to have a plan of action to present to them so that we can implement it without any delays. The sooner we start keeping tabs on Porter Bryant's every move, the sooner we may find Somer Ellis and capture the Rocking Chair Killer."

"Commander Nicholson will want to have a predeployment briefing before the surveillance is started," Tam reminded them.

"Right," J.D. said. "Call Hugh and ask him to join us."

Porter had a standing Saturday-morning appointment for a manicure and a monthly appointment with his hair stylist. Today was the Saturday for both. He was a man who appreciated the finer things in life, thanks to his parents, Morris and Lynn Bryant. Lynn had been a meticulous lady in every aspect of her life, from the furnishings in her beautiful home to her impeccable personal appearance. Her fastidiousness had rubbed off on him, as had his father's love of the law. From the age of twelve, he had known he would one day make Morris proud of him by becoming a lawyer. The Bryants had adored him, had treated him as if he were their own, had given him everything money could buy. And he had loved them and appreciated the life they had given him.

He still missed them.

Losing his father had been difficult, but when he had lost

his mother, he had been devastated. Lynn Bryant had been his ideal woman. Elegant, attractive, intelligent. When he met Audrey Sherrod, he had immediately perceived a similarity between her and his mother and had mistakenly assumed she would make him the perfect mate.

He had been so certain. But he had been wrong.

Of course, he knew that there was someone out there, someone with his mother's sterling qualities who would be proud to be Mrs. Porter Bryant.

He checked his Rolex. 3:38 P.M.

Enjoying the view of downtown from his penthouse apartment, Porter poured himself another glass of Chablis Premier Cru, a twelve-year-old vintage. He appreciated the steely edge to the light, crisp, fruity wine.

Despite not yet having found the right woman, Porter enjoyed his life. By thirty, he had accomplished a great deal and was already an ADA. By the time he was forty, perhaps he would be the DA or even a young congressman or senator. Or there might be a judgeship in his future.

But for now, he was satisfied.

Or he would be once he had kept his promise to Regina Bennett.

He never would have found her again if not for his mother. After his father's death, he had discovered documents his mother had stored away in her safety deposit box, documents that told his life story. Adoption papers. Newspaper clippings. Letters from Regina, addressed to My Sweet Corey, mailed to him over the years in care of Dora Chaney. Apparently, Dora had forwarded the letters to Lynn.

He had been barely nine when the woman he had thought of as his grandmother had handed him over to strangers. He had been too young to understand why she had done such an unforgivable thing, just as he'd been too young to understand why his mother had disappeared months before that. Dora

Chaney had told him that his mother didn't want him any longer and neither did she.

Over the years, those first nine years of his life had gradually slipped into the recesses of his subconscious, coming alive only occasionally in his dreams. What he had remembered at odd times was the sound of a woman's voice singing.

Hush, little baby, don't you cry.

And there had been times when he had looked at himself in the mirror and had seen two identical images staring back at him. The ghost of his twin brother, Cody. He had never forgotten his brother.

When he had discovered that Regina Bennett, the woman accused of being the Baby Blue kidnapper, was his biological mother, he had felt compelled to go and see her. But he could hardly visit a convicted murderess as ADA Porter Bryant. However, Regina's "nephew" Corey could visit her. It had taken very little in the way of a disguise to hide his true identity.

Looking back on that first meeting with Regina, he recalled the instant recognition. He had known her the moment he saw her, and the memories of his life with her and his brother resurfaced gradually over the next few months, more and more with each visit.

Despite who she was and what she had done, Regina Bennett had given birth to him. She had loved him. Dora Chaney had lied when she'd told him his mother didn't want him. And when Regina had asked only one thing of him, he had felt compelled to keep the promise he had made her.

Promise me that you'll go there and find Cody. I want him to be with me in heaven. Put him in my arms so I can hold him forever.

* * *

Somer Ellis kissed her husband. His lips were warm and moist and gentle. She loved Quint. Being his wife made her so happy. Their life together wasn't perfect, but it was good and held the promise of a bright future.

Today was a glorious day. Springtime warm, the sun shimmering, the birds singing outside her bedroom window, a soft breeze blowing the curtains and sweeping inside with sweet, fresh air.

She stretched languidly as she lay in Quint's arms, completely content.

"I love you." Quint nuzzled her neck.

She turned into his arms and smiled at him. "I love you, too."

"Let's not wait to go to Hawaii," he said. "Let's go now. We'll take our savings and if that's not enough, we'll put the rest on a credit card. Life's too short to waste dreaming about the things we want to do."

"*Yes, Quint, yes, life is too short. . . .*"

Somer's eyelids flew open. A silent cry screamed inside her head when she realized that she had been dreaming. She wasn't at home safe in Quint's arms. She was still strapped to this damn rocking chair, alone in the darkness, waiting for her captor, wondering if, when he came back the next time, he would kill her.

The 24/7 surveillance paid off sooner rather than later. Having no idea that anyone knew his true identity and suspected him of being the Rocking Chair Killer, Porter left his home that Saturday evening, not realizing his every move was being watched.

When he headed north from downtown Chattanooga, taking US-27, in his pursuit of Corey Bennett/Porter Bryant,

J.D. suspected the guy was on his way to Sale Creek. The minute Bryant had left his penthouse and gotten behind the wheel of his expensive Lotus Exige—a $65,000 sports car—J.D. had eased the nondescript black Chevy Impala into the traffic, keeping at least two car lengths behind him. Another unmarked car that had been parked a block from the penthouse and was driven by TBI agent Will Brannock fell in behind J.D. By the time he passed the Soddy-Daisy/Sequoia exit, two more unmarked cars, both driven by county deputies, had joined the team, the four men keeping in radio contact as they followed Porter Bryant.

The CPD, TBI, and Hamilton County sheriff's department were working together as a team. A vast number of personnel had been assigned as a precautionary measure: intelligence, homicide, fugitive, and narcotics investigators.

As soon as the silver Lotus exited onto TN-29 N toward Dayton, J.D. knew he'd guessed right. Porter was headed for Sale Creek, probably the old Chaney farmstead. The Hamilton County sheriff's department was providing more backup, as was the CPD, including their SWAT team. But everyone involved knew the importance of keeping a safe distance behind the suspect. Tam and Garth were bringing up the rear.

Garth Hudson was a hothead and this case was personal for him. The last thing J.D. needed was for the veteran officer to go off half cocked and blow this entire operation. If he didn't trust Tam to keep Garth under control, he would have excluded them from the unit.

Excitement coursed through Porter's body, following the flow of his blood and affecting every nerve ending. Tonight he would completely fulfill his promise to Regina Bennett, his birth mother. Tonight she and Cody would be together eternally. In only a few hours, it would all be over and he would be free to continue his life, move forward, and forever put the past behind him.

Once she had gone to be with Cody, he would miss her, of course. How sad to think that he would never hear her sing again, never stand beside her and watch her rocking Cody and soothing his cries. How many nights as a young child had he stood and watched her lavish love and attention on his twin brother? How many times had he wished he and Cody could trade places so that he could be the center of their mother's world? He hadn't understood back then that Cody had been dying.

He gripped the steering wheel, his palms damp inside his stylish driving gloves, as he veered off the highway and onto Leggett Road. His heartbeat hummed inside his head. He met a couple of oncoming cars, each dimming its lights as it approached, and he noticed several sets of headlights behind him.

Mile after mile zipped by quickly as he increased the Lotus's speed without even realizing what he was doing. Driving faster than he intended, he almost missed the turnoff that would take him past the old Chaney farmhouse and eventually carry him to the dirt road leading deep into the woods.

J.D. slowed down when he saw the silver Lotus turn off on the winding road that led to the Chaney farmhouse and beyond to the next farm and then looped back and around to rejoin the county road. He waited a few minutes before he turned and followed. He had to be careful not to alert Porter that he was being tailed.

No streetlights illuminated the old country lane, only the three-quarter moon. A dense, pervasive darkness surrounded him, turning the fields and wooded areas on either side of the road into black, shadowy blurs. The vibratory murmur of the Impala's engine and the whirl of tires on the rutted pavement droned in his ears as he managed to keep the Lotus in sight and still remain a discreet distance behind the sports car. Adrenaline pumped through J.D.'s system, preparing him for whatever lay ahead, as he reminded himself that Somer Ellis's life might well depend on what he did tonight.

When he saw the entrance to the old Chaney farm, he expected Porter to turn off, and when he didn't, J.D. slowed the Impala to a crawl. Where was Porter going? J.D. had been so sure that Corey Bennett would be returning home, that somewhere on that hundred-acre tract, he was keeping his victims near wherever Regina Bennett had stored the Baby Blue toddlers' bodies.

"He's gone past the farm," J.D. informed the unit as he crept along a safe distance behind the Lotus. "He's turning off onto what looks like a dirt road going into an open field."

Farmland always had dirt pathways for equipment and workers. But there were no hiding places out in the open.

"I'm turning off my headlights and following him."

Porter parked the Lotus at the edge of the open field, a cluster of high grass and wild shrubs hiding it from the view of passersby. He picked up a flashlight from the floorboard, got out, locked the car, and hiked into the woods, taking the gravel path that led up and into the hills. Within minutes, the crumbling old church came into view. Moonlight reflected off the broken windowpanes. Taking his time, mentally preparing himself for the monumental task facing him, he made his way to the back of the building. As he passed by the old Lincoln, he stopped and opened the trunk. After stuffing the small bright blue flashlight into his pocket, he removed the folded quilt near the extra tire and jack and spread it out inside the trunk, preparing a bed for Regina and Cody.

Leaving the trunk open, he entered the church and crept down the wooden stairs into the basement. The stairs creaked with each step he took. After tonight, he wouldn't come back to this church ever again. Like Regina and Cody, it, too, would become nothing more than a part of his past. And after tonight, he would have no need for the old Lincoln. He knew exactly what to do with it. Less than half a mile behind the church, there was a deep ravine, a fitting burial place for Luther Chaney's car.

J.D. parked the Impala just off the road, and notified the others that he would be on foot from here on out as he followed the suspect into the woods. Surprised to find a gravel path wide enough to accommodate a vehicle, he veered off onto the grassy shoulder to prevent his footsteps from crunching on the rocks. In the distance, he caught a glimpse of Porter as he disappeared behind the hulk of an old wooden building. What the hell was it? Why hadn't the FBI discovered this place twenty-three years ago when they had searched the Chaney farm and the surrounding area?

As J.D. drew closer and was able to see the structure more clearly in the moonlight, he realized that it was the ruins of a church.

Maybe the FBI had discovered the church years ago and found nothing suspicious inside the building. Or maybe they had somehow missed it. He couldn't recall any mention of a church in the old files about the Baby Blue toddlers.

His voice little more than a whisper, he gave the others directions. He told them he was going into the building to investigate and ordered them to approach the area silently.

Chapter 34

Somer heard his footsteps.

She had suspected for a while now that she was underground, possibly in a basement or a storm shelter. He was coming down creaky stairs, which meant she had only a few precious moments to prepare herself. There was no reason to think that this time would be any different than the other times, no reason to believe that her life might end tonight.

Why hadn't she paid more attention to the news on TV and in the *Chattanooga Times Free Press* about the Rocking Chair Killer? If only she could remember the timeline between when he abducted his victims and when they were found dead, their bodies sitting in a rocking chair, a toddler's skeleton in their lap. Had it been a week? Ten days? Two weeks? God, why couldn't she remember?

Was she destined to share the same fate as those other three women, women whose names she couldn't recall?

Of course she was.

Tonight?

Please, God, please, give me more time. I don't want to die. I want to go home to Quint. I want that vacation in

Hawaii. I want to be a mother. I want to grow old with Quint and live to see our grandchildren.

Suddenly, a dim light flickered softly behind her.

He came up behind the rocking chair.

Every muscle in her body tensed.

"I'm back, Mommy. I'll bring Cody to you. He needs your arms around him. He's missed you. We've both missed you."

He reached out and untied her raw, bloody wrists. Even knowing her attempts to escape were futile, she still occasionally struggled against the ropes that bound her to the chair.

"Don't try to get up. Sit still and I'll put Cody in your arms."

No, no, not yet. This wasn't the usual sequence of events. He hadn't allowed her to use the slop jar. He hadn't asked her if she was hungry, hadn't offered to let her wash herself.

"Didn't you bring me something to eat?" she asked.

"You don't need to eat tonight," he told her. "Cody must come first. That's what you always told me. Cody needs you. Can't you hear him crying?"

"Please, let me wash off—"

"No!" He screamed the word.

"Just my hands. Please." She rose halfway up in the chair. "You don't want—"

"Hush now. You mustn't upset yourself." He clutched her shoulders and forced her down into the rocker. "Everything is as it should be. You can trust me to keep my promise. I'm a good boy, aren't I, Mommy? Isn't that what you've always told me? 'You're such a good boy, Corey. You know Mommy loves you, but Cody has to come first because he's very sick.' "

Tell him what he wants to hear, what he desperately needs to hear. Buy yourself some time. Don't give up. Don't you dare give up.

"I—I do love you . . . just as much as I love Cody."

When he stroked her hair, she shivered involuntarily, knowing the gentle hands touching her belonged to a killer. "And I love you, too," he told her. "That's why I'm going to keep my promise."

"What—what promise?"

He leaned down behind her and kissed her forehead. She gasped. He had never kissed her before tonight. There was nothing sensual in his touch, only a tender affection.

"Do you want me to promise you again?" he asked. "Do you want to hear me say the words, to swear to you that I will fulfill my promise?"

She nodded. "Yes, please . . . Corey . . ."

He moved away from the chair.

She held her breath.

She had tried getting away from him in the past and only wound up flat on her face on the floor and then dragged back and tied to the chair. There was no point in trying again, was there?

Tonight was the night. He was going to kill her. She knew it as surely as she knew he was insane.

"Open your arms," he instructed. Coming from behind the chair, he lifted the blanket-wrapped bundle over her head and placed it in her arms.

Don't look down.

She accepted the dead child, cradled it gently, and without any prompting, she began singing softly, crooning to a toddler who had been dead for many years.

He stood beside the chair as he always did and listened to her sing.

"He's still crying. He won't stop because he's in so much pain." Her captor bent and picked up something from the floor and then handed it to her. "Do what you have to do, Mommy. Do what's best for Cody so he won't suffer anymore."

She grasped the small baby pillow he had placed in her

hand, but she couldn't move, could barely breathe. Her entire body stiffened. He reached down, took her hand holding the pillow, and laid it over the skeleton's little face.

"You know it's the right thing to do, the only thing that will end Cody's pain and suffering."

Her hand moved of its own volition. She pressed the pillow down on the skull and held it there.

In her mind, she was screaming. Screaming loud enough to be heard for miles away.

J.D. followed the sound of voices. A man talking. A woman singing. The open door to the basement hung precariously on rusted hinges. He paused at the top of the stairs and shone his flashlight over the rickety wooden steps.

Will Brannock stood behind J.D. in the church's vestibule, his Glock drawn and ready. J.D. motioned to him, letting Will know that he was going down into the basement, and then signaled for him to wait there. Will nodded agreement. Knowing instinctively that the steps would moan under his weight, J.D. placed his foot on the first rung. Only a soft, barely audible moan followed. One by one, slowly and cautiously, he began his descent. Halfway down, the steps creaked. He stopped. Waited. He could hear Porter talking, apparently still unaware that he and his captive were not alone. The woman kept singing, her voice actually growing louder.

When J.D. reached the end of the stairs and his feet touched the concrete floor of the basement, he found the area totally dark except for a dim glow against the back wall. Light from a lone lantern cast a pale light into the darkness. After turning off his flashlight, he moved toward what appeared to be a door in the wall, a door situated between two shelves that had been pushed aside.

As he made his way across the room, he pulled his Smith &

Wesson 9mm from its hip holster before he reached the gaping entrance to what appeared to be a secret room.

"He's at peace now," the male voice said. Porter Bryant's voice, oddly soft and kind.

J.D. slipped quietly through the doorway and into the large, semidark area, hidden behind the shelving. He paused when he saw Porter standing behind a figure in a rocking chair, her long, dark hair cascading over her shoulders. Porter reached down and lifted something over the woman's head. It took J.D. a few seconds to figure out that the small square object Porter held was a pillow.

The woman continued singing, the words vaguely familiar to J.D. The song was a lullaby, about diamond rings turning brass and mocking birds that wouldn't sing.

"You can stop singing now, Mommy," Porter said. "Cody can't hear you anymore. He's gone to heaven."

He had called the woman *Mommy*. Did he actually believe his captive was Regina Bennett? Was Porter that far gone that he couldn't tell the difference between reality and fantasy?

The woman that J.D. assumed was Somer Ellis stopped singing.

"Now, I'm going to keep my promise. Tonight, you will be with Cody. You will be able to hold him in your arms forever."

Porter brought the pillow down very slowly over the woman's head. "I love you, Mommy."

The woman in the rocking chair struggled. She lifted her hands in an effort to fight, her muffled screams filtered through the pillow.

Porter was trying to suffocate her.

J.D. had to act fast.

"Move away from her," J.D. said.

Porter drew in a sharp, startled breath. His entire body stiffened, but he didn't turn to face J.D.

"Put the pillow down and move away from her," J.D. told him.

"I can't do that. I have to finish it tonight. I have to keep my promise."

"I have a gun in my hand, and if you don't drop the pillow and move away from her, I'll be forced to shoot you." J.D. moved closer, one cautious step at a time. "Do it now."

Somer continued struggling, her hands clawing at the pillow.

"Damn it, Bryant, don't make me shoot you!"

But he paid no attention to J.D.

Should he just shoot Porter Bryant or should he tackle him?

J.D. wanted to shoot the son of a bitch, wanted him dead. But he holstered his weapon, rushed forward, and jumped the man who was engrossed in smothering the woman in the rocking chair. The moment J.D. grabbed Porter and jerked him backward, Somer Ellis gasped for breath.

Porter dropped the pillow as he scuffled with J.D., trying to free himself from J.D.'s powerful grip. As Porter struggled against being subdued, J.D. wrestled him to the floor. When Porter swung at him, J.D. grabbed both of his wrists and straddled him.

"Need some help?" Will Brannock asked as he entered the secret room.

"Help me get him cuffed," J.D. said, "before I beat the hell out of him."

Together Will and J.D. dragged Porter Bryant to his feet, shoved him face forward against the wall, and handcuffed him. "I've got him," J.D. said. "Go see about her." He inclined his head toward the woman now weeping hysterically.

"It's all right, Mommy, don't cry," Porter said. "Please, don't cry."

With all the fight gone out of him, a dazed look in his eyes and a peculiar softness to his expression, Porter resembled a pitiful child. A lost, lonely little boy crying out for his mother.

Will dropped to his haunches in front of Somer Ellis. "It's all right, Mrs. Ellis. You're safe now. I'm Special Agent Brannock with the Tennessee Bureau of Investigation."

She lifted the bundle in her arms. "Please, take it away. Please . . ."

Will took the blanket-wrapped skeleton, laid it carefully on the floor, and then reached out and untied Somer's bound ankles. He lifted her to her feet, and when he realized she could barely stand, he picked her up and carried her out of the dark, secret room inside the basement.

Chapter 35

Within an hour after Porter Bryant's arrest, the small, dilapidated church hidden in the woods five miles from the Chaney farm became the center of an in-depth investigation, the entire area swarming with law enforcement officers and crime scene personnel. Porter had been taken into custody and was on his way to jail. Somer Ellis had been whisked away and taken by ambulance to the hospital, where her husband was waiting for her.

In order to keep the secret room and its contents preserved so as not to compromise any evidence, the people allowed inside were kept to a minimum. And each person wore protective coveralls to avoid cross-contamination. J.D., Will, and Tam waited upstairs inside the church while the highly trained CSI crew went over the secret room with a fine-tooth comb. Garth had been pacing restlessly, going outside periodically and then returning to continue pacing.

When ME Pete Tipton arrived, he took possession of the shawl-wrapped toddler skeleton. After placing the child's remains in a body bag and turning it over to his assistant, Pete waited with the rest of them. Nobody said much, just an occasional comment about what a complete shock it had been to discover that Porter Bryant was the Rocking Chair Killer. They each knew Porter and all agreed that the man had appeared to be perfectly normal.

Garth said the least, mostly just nodding, adding an occasional yes or no to the limited conversation. He seemed distracted, as if his thoughts were on something else entirely. J.D. couldn't imagine how Garth felt knowing the little skeleton cocooned in the body bag belonged to his missing nephew, Blake Sherrod. When the child had been brought up from the basement, J.D. had expected Garth to at the very least look at the skeleton, but he hadn't. Maybe even the thought of it had been too painful.

An hour and a half later, Jada Irby, a member of the CSI team, came upstairs and walked straight to J.D. "I thought you'd want a preliminary report," she told him.

"Thanks. We appreciate that," J.D. said.

"We found five wooden boxes," Jada told him. "There are fragments of what appear to be blue cloth of some kind in each of the boxes."

"Baby blankets?" J.D. asked.

"Possibly the remnants of shawls or blankets."

"Are the boxes empty?" Tam asked.

"Yes." Jada looked at Tam. "We can't know for sure at this point, but we suspect that the boxes were used as coffins."

J.D. recounted in his head. Including Cody Bennett, there were six toddlers in all: Cody, Keith Lawson, Chase Wilcox, Devin Kelly, Blake Sherrod, and Shane Douglas. It was possible that Regina had not placed her son here in the church with the other toddlers and that was the reason there were only five boxes. "Did you say there were only five?"

"Yes, only five."

"And you didn't find any other skeletons? Just the one Somer Ellis had been holding?"

"Yes, just the one."

"Something doesn't add up," J.D. said. "If Regina Bennett killed her son and five of the six toddlers she kidnapped, there should be six boxes."

"Unless she buried Cody or hid his body somewhere else." Tam stared at J.D. "If that's the case, then there would be only five coffin-type boxes down there, which there are."

"Five boxes, but only four bodies," J.D. reminded her.

"Oh, that's right. So, where is the fifth toddler?" Tam asked.

"Excellent question."

"One that we'll be asking Porter Bryant."

"Do you think he'll tell us anything? He seemed really out of it when y'all brought him up from the basement," Tam said. "He looked at me as if he had no idea who I was. And he kept mumbling something about keeping a promise to his mother."

"Once he's been examined by a physician and a psychiatrist, we'll have a better idea if he'll be capable of cooperating with us." J.D. couldn't shake the feeling that the fact there was one less toddler skeleton than there should have been was somehow significant. How or why, he wasn't sure. But he had learned long ago never to ignore his gut instincts.

J.D. had been up all night. He not only looked like hell, but he felt like hell. Phil Hayes, accompanied by Chief Mullins, Commander Nicholson, and the county sheriff, would be holding a 6:00 A.M. news conference to announce the capture of the Rocking Chair Killer and the rescue of his fourth victim, Somer Ellis.

When J.D. had asked Tam to let him be the one to tell Audrey about Porter Bryant, she had given him a hard, scrutinizing glare. "I'm her best friend. I should tell her and be there with her when the announcement is made."

"Maybe that's the reason I should be the one to talk to her . . . because you're too close to—"

"Bull. Don't give me that crap. What's really going on with you? With you and Audrey?"

He had started to lie, to deny that anything was going on between him and Audrey. "I can't explain it. Let's just say that I know I should be the one there with her, that I should be the one to tell her that the killer was Porter Bryant."

Tam had studied his face for a full minute, and then said, "All right. You have until the press conference. I'll be on Audrey's doorstep at five minutes till six."

J.D. called Audrey when he was en route, apparently waking her. He told her only that he would be there shortly and that he had important information about the Rocking Chair Killer.

He arrived at her town house at ten till five, and just as he stepped onto her front porch, she opened the door.

"My God, you look awful," she said. "Have you been up all night?"

"Yeah, I have."

After moving aside to give him room to enter, she closed the door behind him and said, "Go on into the living room and sit down. I put on a pot of coffee right after you called."

"Let's just go straight to the kitchen. I could use that coffee as soon as possible."

He looked at her and saw the tension in her body and the uncertainty in her eyes. Then he scanned her quickly from head to toe. Her hair hung loosely about her shoulders, her delicate face was devoid of makeup, and the belt on her silk robe hadn't been tied, leaving it open to reveal the sheer silk pajamas beneath. He wanted to reach out and grab her, hold her close, and protect her. The last thing he wanted was to tell her that the man she had been dating for months was a mentally unbalanced serial killer.

He eased his open palm beneath her elbow and guided

her into the kitchen. Working together, they poured coffee into two mugs, and Audrey doctored hers while he took his black. They pulled out chairs and sat at the kitchen table. J.D. took a sip of the fresh, hot coffee, then set his mug on the table and scooted his chair until he was beside Audrey, close enough to touch her.

"Whatever it is, it's bad, isn't it?" She looked into his eyes.

He reached out and grasped her, his hands locking around her upper arms, his fingers tightening halfway between her shoulders and her elbows.

"Oh, God, J.D., you're scaring me."

"Don't be afraid, honey. You're safe with me." He hated knowing how much what he had to tell her would hurt her. "We caught the Rocking Chair Killer last night. We got there in time to save Somer Ellis."

"Oh, J.D., thank God . . . thank God."

"There's more, Audrey, other things you have to know."

A fine sheen of moisture glistened in her gold- and green-flecked brown eyes. "You found Blake's body . . . his skeleton, didn't you?"

"We found a toddler skeleton, yes. And DNA test results will prove his identity."

She pulled one arm free, lifted her hand, and caressed his cheek. "I'm so thankful that y'all were able to stop him before he killed another woman. How did it happen? How were you able to—?"

"It's a long, complicated story." He covered her hand with his, drew it away from his face, and then grasped both of her hands in his. "And later, when there's more time, I'll explain everything, tell you whatever you want to know, but for now, I'll give you the condensed version."

Her hands trembled. He squeezed them tenderly.

"You're scaring me again," she told him.

He lifted her hands to his mouth and rubbed each set of

knuckles slowly across his mouth, the gesture one of care and comfort.

"We've been working on a couple of leads, one concerning the car an eyewitness saw at the antique store where the last body was found," J.D. said. "And the other lead took us on a search for a boy named Corey Bennett, Regina Bennett's son and Cody Bennett's twin, who had been adopted twenty-three years ago." When Audrey's mouth fell open on a surprised gasp, he didn't pause, but kept talking, wanting to get it all out as quickly as possible. "Once we learned his identity, we put him under surveillance, and last night, he led us straight to where he was keeping Somer Ellis, where he had kept and killed three other women."

Audrey's eyes widened, her gaze fixed to his, her breath caught in her throat.

"Honey . . . Audrey . . . damn! Corey Bennett was adopted by Morris and Lynn Bryant when he was nine years old."

Audrey stared at him, her eyes expressing her thoughts. Puzzlement. Doubt. Disbelief. Reluctant acceptance. "Porter Bryant is the Rocking Chair Killer."

Chapter 36

A week later the test results came back from the DNA taken from the only toddler skeleton found in the church basement. At first, no one could believe that the toddler was Shane Douglas and not Blake Sherrod. No one except J.D. Wayne Sherrod had demanded that the test be run again, but had finally been convinced of the accuracy of the original findings. A dozen different theories popped up as to why the Rocking Chair Killer had skipped Blake, the fourth missing toddler, and had placed the fifth toddler in the fourth victim's arms. And equally as many scenarios were batted about as to why there had been only five coffin-type boxes found and why there had been no sign of another toddler skeleton. But these and other questions concerning the old Baby Blue cases were swept aside, at least temporarily, while everyone involved with Porter Bryant's capture celebrated the confinement of a serial killer.

With Porter tucked neatly away in jail, awaiting trial—if he wasn't declared legally insane before then and placed in a mental institution the way his biological mother had been—the CPD began tying up loose ends on the case. But for J.D., there were still too many loose ends on the Baby Blue cases for him to walk away without finding the answers.

When the DNA results identified the skeleton as Shane Douglas, he hadn't been quite as surprised as everyone else. His gut had warned him that something was off about the whole thing, that there had to be an explanation for why Porter had skipped Blake Sherrod and why there were only five coffin-type boxes in the church basement. The truth had been right there in front of him all the time, and on a subconscious level he had known what it was even before he finally accepted the most logical explanation. There were only five boxes because there had been only five toddlers, including Cody Bennett. And Porter hadn't skipped over the fourth toddler because Shane Douglas *was* the fourth toddler.

Regina Bennett had not kidnapped Blake Sherrod!

For the past few days since coming to terms with the obvious truth, J.D. had kept his opinion to himself. He needed time to dig deeper, to sift through the old files, to go over every scrap of information and evidence from the Blake Sherrod file.

But for today, nearly two weeks after Porter Bryant's arrest, J.D. had put his search into the past on hold so that he could attend Shane Douglas's funeral, which was being covered by local, state, and national press. He had told himself that the only reason he was going to the funeral was to represent the TBI. But if he was totally honest with himself, he had to admit that the main reason was Audrey. He needed to be there for her. The past ten days had been difficult for her, and although he had seen her only a few times when he had gone by to check on Zoe, they hadn't really talked again since he had told her Porter was the Rocking Chair Killer.

He would never forget her reaction. To say she'd been startled would be an understatement. She had looked as if someone had hit her between the eyes with a two-by-four.

And then, to his surprise, she had taken control of her emotions and quickly put up a cold, disciplined façade. No tears. No hysterics.

She should have fallen apart, should have ranted and raved and denied the possibility that a man she had dated for months could be a killer. In the past, he had occasionally seen the soft, emotional side of Audrey's personality and could only imagine the amount of strength it had taken for her not to fall to pieces.

Zoe had told him that she'd heard Audrey sobbing late at night, when she'd been alone in her bedroom. But J.D. suspected that those tears were not for Porter or even for herself. She'd been crying for her baby brother, still missing, his disappearance remaining an unsolved mystery.

Neither Hart Roberts nor Jeremy Arden had attended the church service for Shane Douglas, and neither came to the cemetery for the burial afterward. J.D. had halfway expected to see them both there. Tam had been there at Audrey's side during the funeral and even Garth showed up to pay his respects at the cemetery.

When J.D. walked up alongside Audrey at the gravesite, she didn't even glance at him, but she reached down between them and took his hand. Tam noticed; she shot a quick, hard glare his way. He understood Tam's concern and her silent warning. Audrey was her best friend and was extremely vulnerable right now.

Shane Douglas's mother, Grace, was flanked by Wayne Sherrod and her son, Lance. Weeping continuously and moving as if in a trance, Grace Douglas leaned heavily on Wayne, as she had done throughout the church service earlier.

The young minister spoke a few words at the cemetery, and when all was said and done, he issued an invitation to the small crowd of mourners.

"Grace would like for y'all to drop by her house this afternoon. Ladies from the church have prepared a meal for the family and friends."

As J.D. escorted Audrey and Tam to Tam's car, Audrey said, "I think I should go to Mrs. Douglas's home. Daddy will be there and—"

"I'm not sure that's such a good idea," Tam said. "Besides, I really need to get back to work and—"

"If you want to go, I'll take you," J.D. heard himself offer, the comment made from gut reaction and not through a logical thought process.

"Audrey, are you sure?" Tam asked, concern in her dark eyes.

"I'm sure." Audrey hugged Tam before turning to him and grasping his arm. "Thank you, J.D. I appreciate your offer."

During the drive from the cemetery to Grace Douglas's home, Audrey didn't say a word. Respecting her need for silence, J.D. remained quiet. A few cars and SUVs lined the side of the street in front of the Douglas house.

"Are you sure you want to do this?" J.D. asked her as he opened the passenger door and helped her from his Camaro. "Tam didn't think it was such a good idea."

"Daddy may need me," she said. "We thought we would be burying Blake, but instead . . ." She blew out a soft, sad breath. "Today has to be doubly difficult for my father."

An assortment of relatives and close friends who had come straight there from the church, skipping the burial, ate and talked and carried on various conversations. Audrey and J.D. introduced themselves to Grace's sister and brother-in-law as well as her son, Lance.

Someone had arranged a collection of photos depicting Shane Douglas from birth to thirty months old and displayed them on the dining room sideboard.

He had been a precious, rosy-cheeked blond cherub.

"He looks a little like Blake," Audrey whispered. "Only he was chubbier and his hair wasn't curly. Blake had curly hair."

J.D. draped his arm around her shoulders. "Let me take you home, honey. This isn't good for you."

"Soon," she told him. "I need to find Daddy first and make sure he's okay and see if he needs . . . anything."

J.D. knew she had been about to say "see if he needs me."

After declining an offer of food, Audrey and J.D. meandered through the crowd assembled inside Grace's home. When they reached the entrance to the hallway leading to the bedrooms, they saw Wayne Sherrod. He closed the door to the room at the end of the hall. A woman they had met earlier, Grace's cousin, came up to Wayne and said something to him.

"She's resting," Wayne told her. "She took more of the medication her doctor prescribed, so maybe she'll sleep for a while."

The woman nodded, patted Wayne's arm, and then returned to the living room.

When Wayne spotted Audrey, he stopped, the expression on his face devoid of emotion. Audrey pulled away from J.D. and approached her father.

"Daddy?" She gazed up at him with love and hope in her eyes, so obviously offering him comfort and sympathy.

"What are you doing here?" he asked, his voice cold and hard.

"I wanted to be here for you," she told him honestly. "I've been so worried about you. I've tried to call you several times. I thought maybe you'd stop by the house or at least call me." She reached out and placed her hand on his arm. "Is there anything I can do for you or for Mrs. Douglas?"

Wayne Sherrod withdrew from Audrey, detaching his

arm from her comforting touch. "There's not a damn thing you or anyone else can do." He walked past her and went into the kitchen without a backward glance.

Audrey looked as if her father had slapped her.

It took a great deal of self-control for J.D. not to follow Wayne Sherrod and knock the old fool on his ass. But that was the last thing Audrey needed. Instead, he slipped his arm around her waist and said, "Come on, honey. I'm taking you home."

For most of her life, Audrey had prided herself on not needing anyone. And yet in the deepest recesses of her heart, she had secretly longed for something always just beyond her reach, had experienced that inexplicable yearning to love and be loved . . . to need and be needed in return. She had learned at an early age, after her mother died, not to depend on anyone except herself. And as the years went by, she came to accept that her role in life was to be that of a caretaker, both professionally and personally.

As she sat in J.D.'s car on the drive from Grace Douglas's home to downtown Chattanooga, Audrey told herself that she could deal with the pain inside her. It wasn't as if today was the first time her father had rejected her, but oddly enough, his insensitive dismissal of her, his absolute refusal to accept her comfort, had hurt Audrey more than at any other time in her adult life. Yes, as a child, she had wept bitter tears over his emotional abandonment of her, but as the years passed and she matured, she had learned to accept what she couldn't change. But now as then, she had difficulty understanding why her own father didn't love her.

When J.D. pulled the Camaro to a stop in front of her town house, Audrey turned to him. "Thank you for bringing me home." She opened the door.

J.D. reached over and clutched her shoulder. "You shouldn't

be alone. Let me park the car and I'll come inside with you and stay for a while."

She glanced back at him. "You don't have to do that. I'll be all right."

"With Zoe off on that school field trip for the next couple of days, you won't have a perky, pesky teenager to take your mind off everything that's happened. So why not let her aggravating, argumentative dad take her place, at least for this afternoon?"

"Don't you need to go back to work?"

Why am I trying to send him away when I so desperately want him to stay?

"I need an afternoon off," he told her. "Besides, it's past four now, so most of the afternoon is shot."

Audrey offered him a hesitant smile. "If you're sure . . . ?"

"I'm sure. Invite me to stay for dinner, and I might be persuaded to prepare my specialty."

"Dare I ask what that is?"

"I make a superb BLT."

"In that case, please stay."

After J.D. parked the car, he escorted her up the steps and onto her porch. He took the keys from her unsteady hand and unlocked the front door. She removed her lightweight coat and hung it in the foyer closet. He followed her into the living room, took off his suit jacket, folded it, and laid it across the first chair he passed; then he loosened his tie and undid the collar button.

"Would you like something to drink?" she asked. "I have wine or—"

"Nothing right now," he said. "Let's save the wine to go with our sandwiches later."

"A glass of wine and a BLT. Hmm . . . interesting combination. I think I prefer a Coke with my sandwich and then maybe wine with dessert."

"Then I'll look forward to dessert."

J.D. grinned at her and the bottom dropped out of her stomach.

"Why don't we sit down and talk," J.D. said. "Or if you just want to sit quietly for a while, we can do that."

"Sitting quietly sounds good."

After she eased down on the sofa, she removed her heels, set them aside, burrowed into the cushions, and laid her head against the back of the sofa. J.D. sat beside her, removed his tie, folded it, and placed it on the coffee table. She felt a peculiar sense of comfort just having him there with her. Perhaps it was nothing more than being grateful not to be alone.

You don't really believe that, do you?

As they sat together in silence for several minutes, Audrey began to feel the tension in J.D.'s body, feel it as surely as if she was touching him. The relaxation she had envisioned them sharing had suddenly disappeared; instead the exact opposite was true. How could she possibly relax when some alien part of her longed for J.D. to hold her?

"I hope Zoe's having fun," Audrey said.

"Yeah, me, too."

"You two have come a long way in a short period of time."

"Mostly thanks to you."

Audrey smiled. "You've done your part, too."

"I've tried."

"That's a lot, you know. Trying."

"What happened?" When she looked at him as if she didn't comprehend his question, he added, "Between you and your father? The way he treated you today was unforgivable."

Audrey hugged her arms around her body and stared straight ahead, determined not to give in to her emotions as she so often did. "I'm not sure I know. He was never affectionate, not with me or with Hart, either. And even though he acted as if he thought the sun rose and set on Blake, I don't remember him hugging or kissing Blake, either."

"Some people just aren't able to express the way they feel, not in words, and not by being affectionate."

"I understand that now, even though it's difficult for a child to accept." Audrey closed her eyes. "I suppose he was a good father, in his own way. He never spanked me or Hart. He provided for us. He spent far more time at home with his family after Blake was born. And he was good to Enid, and I'm sure that wasn't always easy. Although her problems were never actually diagnosed, looking back, it's obvious that she had terrible emotional problems."

"It must have been rough for you and for Hart and your father when she killed herself."

"You have no idea." Audrey opened her eyes and looked at J.D. "It was as if our family was living inside a nightmare that just wouldn't end. First Blake disappeared and then Enid committed suicide and my father . . . I don't know what we would have done if Geraldine and Willie hadn't stepped in and looked after Hart and me. And Garth . . . Uncle Garth handled everything. There were weeks when we didn't see Daddy at all, and then when we did, he seemed like a stranger."

"You'd have thought that eventually he would have reached out to you. He might have lost his son, but he still had a daughter . . . a daughter who needed him."

Audrey clenched her teeth tightly. *I will not cry. I will not cry.*

Suddenly, while she was trying so hard to hold herself together, J.D. closed the distance between them, put his arms around her, and pulled her into a comforting embrace. As if responding to him was the most natural thing in the world, she wrapped her arms around his waist and laid her head against his shoulder. He leaned over just enough so that his chin brushed against her cheek.

She couldn't explain why she suddenly felt so safe, why it seemed that as long as J.D. held her, nothing and no one could ever hurt her again. Such a foolish thought, such an illogical feeling.

He splayed his hand across the center of her back and caressed her from neck to waist, his touch unbearably gentle. She relaxed against him, giving herself over completely to the pleasure of being in his arms. Warm, salty tears streaked her cheeks and spilled over her lips. The anger and pain and soul-deep hurt she had been holding inside for days on end poured out of her as she clung to J.D. Sobbing, moaning, holding nothing back, she allowed herself the much-needed emotional release she had been denying herself. And all the while, J.D. simply held her, stroked her, nuzzled her tenderly. How long he held her while she cried, she wasn't sure. All she knew was that when cleansing relief washed over her and she lifted her head to look into his eyes, she realized she wanted him.

"Audrey?" He whispered her name.

"Yes." Just one word, but that was all he needed in answer to his unspoken question.

He lowered his head until his mouth reached hers. She held her breath, anticipation spiraling through her. His lips brushed across hers, both eagerness and hesitation in the touch. She understood he was giving her one last chance to change her mind and that the next move was up to her. Overwhelmed by his restraint in allowing her the power to take what she wanted, what she needed, Audrey circled his lips with the tip of her tongue.

J.D. groaned, the sound coming from deep in his chest. "Be sure this is what you want." He grabbed her upper arms and pressed her down onto the sofa cushions. "If you don't stop me now, there won't be any turning back." He hovered over her, his hot gaze boring into her as he waited for her response.

She tried to speak, but couldn't force the words from her throat. Staring up at him, her mouth opening, her body trembling beneath him, she pulled one arm free of his tight grip and lifted her hand to his face. Her fingers traced the same path that her lips had made only moments before, pausing to dip one finger into the moist interior of his mouth.

J.D. sucked her finger in and Audrey panted as she eased her finger from his mouth. Visibly shaken, he drew in a deep breath and released it on a ragged groan before he kissed her. As his mouth covered hers, she felt him shift his weight and insert his knee between her thighs, effectively parting her legs. The kiss went on and on, robbing her of breath and all coherent thought. By the time he reached beneath her, unzipped her dress, and pulled it down to her waist, she had unbuttoned his shirt and yanked it loose from his pants. He kissed, licked, and nipped her throat and shoulder and blazed a trail down to the lace cups of her bra. While he effectively undid the back hook and deftly freed her breasts, she raked his back with her fingers, loving the feel of his hard muscles and masculine heat.

The moment his tongue flicked across one tight nipple, she whimpered and lifted her body up and into his erection.

They tore at each other's clothes, pushing up, shoving down, ripping apart until she felt the tip of his penis pressing against her mound.

"God, Audrey, I need to protect you." He growled the words against her ear.

"It's all right. I'm protected," she told him as she dug her nails into his firm buttocks. She was still on the pill even though she hadn't been involved in a sexual relationship for several years.

Her assurance snapped the final, tenuous threads of his control. He slid his hands beneath her hips, lifted her urgently, and thrust into her hard and deep.

Within minutes, she climaxed, the fury of her release shocking in its intensity. She had never reached an orgasm so quickly. His climax followed hers within seconds, his masculine roar of triumph sending aftershocks of pleasure through every nerve in her body.

Chapter 37

What could have been an awkward moment after they made love on the sofa, especially with both of them still partially dressed, became instead a romantic interlude. J.D. lifted himself up, shucked off his shirt, tossed it onto the floor, and then stood and dropped his pants and briefs. He kicked them aside and stood there in front of her completely naked. Without missing a beat, he reached down, hauled her to her feet, and dragged her wrinkled dress over her head and off. After going down on his knees in front of her, he kissed her belly. She shivered. He stuck his tongue into her navel. She moaned. He buried his face against her mound. She cried out. And then he kissed her hips, her thighs, her knees, and finally looked up at her and smiled.

"You're even more than I thought you were," he said.

"More what?" she asked as she reached down and urged him to stand.

He revisited the trail he had taken on his way down, only this time he took his time to maul her breasts on his ascent up to her mouth. With his lips almost touching hers, he told her, "You're more beautiful, more giving, more exciting, more woman in every way."

"Oh . . ." She was on the verge of telling him that he was responsible for her being all those "more" things when he unexpectedly swept her up into his arms. She gasped and then laughed as she draped her arm around his neck.

"I'm spending the night," he told her. "I just wanted you to know, in case there were any doubts in your mind."

No doubts, she told herself. *Not about being with him tonight.*

When he carried her into her bedroom and tossed her in the center of the bed, she looked up at him, and suddenly second thoughts did creep into her mind and she wondered if she was crazy for doing this. J.D. Cass was probably more man than she could handle. There was a primitive masculine streak in him a mile wide, and that frightened her. She would never be able to tame him or control him. But would she really want to do either? On some purely primeval level, wasn't that part of what attracted her to him?

"I'm glad you want to stay," she said, pushing aside all doubts.

He crawled into bed with her, inching his way slowly toward her like a large, powerful animal stalking his prey. When he covered her body with his, bracing himself over her with his hands on either side of her head, she reached for him, her fingers exploring his wide, muscular shoulders.

He gazed down at her, his eyes black with desire. The moment her lips parted, renewed hunger plain on her face, he swooped down and kissed her.

She returned the kiss and was amazed that she could be aroused again so quickly.

He lifted his head and smiled. "Don't plan on getting much sleep tonight, honey. I've had a few erotic fantasies about you and I'm planning on fulfilling every one of them."

"If we're playing true confessions, then I have to admit,

I've had more than a few fantasies about you, too, Special Agent Cass."

"Mmm . . . If we're going to fulfill all of your fantasies and mine, maybe we should get started right away." He circled her ear with the tip of his tongue. "The only thing we have to decide is who goes first."

"We can take turns," she told him. "Who knows, we may share some of the same fantasies."

"One way to find out." He rolled off her and onto his back. "Ladies first."

With a feeling of incredible feminine power surging through her, she tiptoed her fingers up and down his semi-erect penis and smiled when he moaned. Moving upward, she found his nipples and rubbed them with her index fingers.

He threaded his fingers through her hair and urged her head down to his chest. When she licked first one nipple and then the other, he moaned again, deeper and louder.

"Honey, I'll give you an hour or two to stop that."

"Oh, I don't think you'll last an hour," she told him, feeling quite sure of herself.

Hart sat alone in the dark room. He couldn't go on this way, knowing what he knew. Not now. It was only a matter of time before someone started asking questions, before someone stated flat out that Regina Bennett had not kidnapped Blake.

All these years, everyone had believed that Blake was one of the Baby Blue toddlers, abducted and probably killed by an insane woman who kept ending her terminally ill son's life again and again by murdering other little boys. If only it had been true. If only twenty-five years ago, Regina had sneaked into their house on a warm summer day and taken Blake from his bed.

If only . . .

He had tried to forget.

He had pretended it never happened. He had halfway convinced himself that Blake really had been kidnapped.

He had lied the day Blake disappeared. He had lied to his stepfather. And he had lied to Audrey.

He wondered if she had suspected the truth, at least back then, before the lies had replaced the reality, before everyone believed that Regina Bennett had taken Blake.

He shouldn't have lied. He should have told the truth.

Hart knew what had really happened to his baby brother.

Garth downed another hefty gulp of whiskey, coughed, wiped his mouth, and set the glass in front of him on the table. Peggy Ann came into the kitchen, her housecoat open all the way down the front, revealing her large, drooping breasts, her still-flat belly, and her dark furry pussy. He had left her in bed a few minutes ago, after he'd hammered into her until he came. He had no idea if she'd had an orgasm or not and he really didn't give a rat's ass. He had gotten what he needed and that's all that mattered tonight. But the short-lived oblivion had lasted only as long as his dick stayed hard. After that, all his troubles came rushing back, bearing down on him, crushing the life out of him.

Peggy Ann eyed the open bottle of Jack Daniel's on the table. "Save a little of that for me."

He reached out, ran his hand inside her housecoat, and squeezed her butt. "I'm going to get stinking drunk tonight, drunk enough to pass out," he told her.

"Go right ahead." She pulled her housecoat together and tied the belt, effectively concealing her naked body. "It won't be the first time you've slept one off in my bed."

"You're a good woman, Peggy Ann. A good friend."

She took a glass from the cupboard, sat down at the table

across from him, and picked up the whiskey bottle. "You're beating yourself up for no good reason."

"What do you know about it?" He glared at her as she filled her glass halfway with Jack Daniel's.

"I know you're carrying around a load of guilt and pain because of what happened to your little nephew. I know because you've cried in your beer and mumbled in your sleep a few times over the years. You think there's something you should have done or could have done to save Blake."

Garth stared at Peggy Ann, wondering if she actually knew the truth. Had he ever been stupid enough during one of his drunken blackouts to tell her what had happened that day, the day Blake disappeared? Surely to God, he hadn't.

"Blake wasn't one of Regina Bennett's victims," Garth said and waited for her response. "It's only a matter of time until everybody knows."

"Yeah, but you couldn't have known that before now. Nobody could have. It made perfect sense to assume that the Baby Blue Kidnapper had taken Blake the same way she'd taken those other little boys."

Garth breathed easier. Peggy Ann didn't know the truth.

No one else knew the truth. Only he and Hart.

Chapter 38

Hart had been awake all night. Thinking. Praying. He needed a drink, needed a fix, needed the courage to do what he should have done twenty-five years ago.

But you were just a kid. Only eight years old.

Kids do what grown-ups tell them to do, especially grown-ups they love and trust the way he had loved and trusted Uncle Garth.

He did what he thought was best for everyone, didn't he?

But lying had been wrong then and it was wrong now. If he had told the truth back then, would his life be any different now? He'd never know for sure. It was too late to change the past. But it wasn't too late to change the future.

I can't keep this secret any longer. If I do, I'll lose what little hold I have on my sanity.

He got up out of the chair where he had been sitting all night, walked to the windows facing east, and drew back the curtains. Dawn light spread across the horizon, where golden-tinged pink tentacles heralded a new day. A new beginning. A chance to right old wrongs.

Tears swelled up inside him, gathered in his eyes, and seeped steadily down his stubble-rough cheeks.

Before his courage evaporated like the morning dew, Hart picked up the phone and dialed his uncle's cell number. The phone rang and rang and rang. The call went to voice mail. Hart hesitated, then said, "We need to talk. I've made a decision that will affect us both. Call me as soon as possible."

Hart returned the phone to its base and then glanced at the wall clock in the dimly lit living room. He would give Uncle Garth until noon to return his call before he contacted Audrey. If he was going to do this—finally do the right thing—he would need to rely on his sister's strength to see him through the ordeal.

She had come into the house to get some Kool-Aid. She had mixed two packages of her favorites—lemon and orange—that morning before breakfast, so the gallon jug should be nice and cold by now. The back storm door shut behind her as she entered the kitchen. Immediately, she heard someone screaming and then someone else shouting. What was going on? Could Enid be having another one of her sick spells? No, probably not. Enid always cried. She never screamed. And the shouting voice belonged to a man. But not her father. Her daddy was at work.

Forgetting about how thirsty she was and how delicious the Kool-Aid would taste, Audrey left the kitchen and followed the sound of the voices. By the time she reached the foot of the stairs in the foyer, the screaming had stopped and had been replaced by hysterical sobs.

She took a hesitant step up the stairs and paused when she saw her stepbrother on the landing, his face pale, his eyes wide, his lips quivering. What was wrong with Hart? He looked funny. Odd funny. Not ha-ha funny.

Audrey raced up the stairs and when she came face-to-face with Hart, he stared right at her, but it was as if he didn't see her.

"What's wrong?" she asked.

He just kept staring at her.

And then behind them, the nursery door closed, but not before she saw Uncle Garth. Her gaze had connected with his for a split second.

Reaching out, she gave Hart a gentle tap in the center of his chest, thinking that would snap him out of whatever was making him act so odd. His only response was nonverbal. He began trembling as if he were very, very cold.

She grabbed him by the shoulders and shook him. "What's wrong with you?" She called out, "Uncle Garth? Help us. Something's wrong with Hart."

"It's my fault," Hart said. "It's all my fault."

"What's your fault?"

"Blake . . . my fault . . . all my fault."

"I don't know what you're talking about. What about Blake? What's your fault?"

Everything began to spin around and around. Audrey and Hart were swept up into a whirlwind, a dark tornado that twirled them around and around, deeper and deeper into its vortex. And inside that same tornado, the violent wind took Blake higher and higher until he finally disappeared.

Audrey's terrified cries woke J.D. instantly. He shot straight up. Then he turned and looked down at the woman beside him as she thrashed and moaned. Tears dampened her face.

She was having another nightmare.

J.D. caressed her cheek before cupping her chin with his hand. "Audrey, honey, wake up."

She struggled for breath. "No, please, no. Don't take him."

J.D. ran his hands down her throat, over her shoulders, and curved them around her upper arms. He gave her a gentle shake. "Audrey. Audrey, wake up. Whatever is frightening you isn't real. You're dreaming. You're having another nightmare."

Her eyes flew open. She stared up at him. "J.D.?"

"Yeah, honey, it's me."

"Oh God. It was awful."

He pulled her up and into his arms, holding her naked body against his, soothing his hand over her back, whispering comforting words to calm her. "It was just a dream. You're all right. You're safe. Nothing can hurt you." He placed a tender kiss on her shoulder.

She wrapped her arms around him and pressed her cheek to his. "Hold me, please, J.D. Hold me."

"I've got you."

And I'll never let you go.

Where the hell did that thought come from?

"Want to tell me about it?" he asked as he held her. "Is it the same dream you've been having for weeks now?"

She lifted her head and stared at him. "How did you . . . ? Oh, Zoe told you."

"She wasn't breaking a confidence. She told me because she was worried about you."

"Sometimes, the dreams make sense, as if I'm remembering what really happened that day, but sometimes they're all mixed up and crazy and don't make any sense at all."

"Dreams and nightmares are like that."

"I had thought that if we ever found Blake that maybe . . . maybe the dreams would stop." She pulled away from J.D.

"What a horrible mess . . . Everything is so . . . so . . ." She looked at J.D. "Porter Bryant, a man I thought I knew, a man I—"

"Cared about," J.D. said.

"Yes, I cared about him." As if only then realizing she was naked and her breasts were uncovered, she grasped the sheet and lifted it up to her neck. "Don't you want to know if I slept with him? You could have had sex last night—all night—with a woman who had been having an affair with a serial killer."

"You never slept with Bryant," J.D. said with absolute certainty.

She glared at him. "How did you know?"

"Because you said you cared about him, not that you loved him."

A pink stain colored Audrey's cheeks. "You're assuming a great deal."

"Am I?"

"Yes, you are, if you think I have to love a man in order to have sex with him."

"Don't you?"

"You think I love you?" She huffed loudly, her eyes bright with indignation.

"Yeah, I think you do."

"Why, you egotistical, conceited—"

He effectively ended her verbal tirade by kissing her as he toppled her onto her back. She struggled. He held her down and deepened the kiss. She writhed beneath him, halfway fighting him, halfway aroused.

He slid his mouth along her cheek and to her ear. "I think I love you, too."

The moment his words registered in her mind, he felt her immediate surrender and knew that she wanted him again, every bit as much as he wanted her.

* * *

Garth woke with the mother of all hangovers. He managed to get out of bed, stagger to the bathroom, and take a piss. He felt like holy hell.

He needed a shower and a shave. He needed a cup of coffee. He needed to come up with a plan. There had to be a way to convince everyone that although Regina Bennett had not kidnapped Blake, someone else had. He couldn't let the truth come out, not now, not after twenty-five years, not after everything he had been through with Hart.

He would figure out something and then talk to Hart. The boy would do whatever he told him to do. He always had.

But first things first. Shave, shower, and—

"Hair of the dog that bit you." Peggy Ann entered the bathroom and held out a large mug to him. "Irish coffee." She chuckled.

He took the mug, lifted it to his mouth, and took a few sips. "Thanks."

"Want some breakfast?" she asked.

"Maybe some toast and more coffee." He saluted her with the mug.

"Sure thing." She turned to go, then paused and said, "Oh, by the way, your cell phone's been ringing, but I didn't answer it."

"If it was anything important, they left a message."

"Yeah, that's what I figured."

Twenty minutes later, shaved and showered, Garth pulled on a clean pair of boxers—he kept a few things at Peggy Ann's for times like this—and removed the dry cleaner's bag from a pair of khaki slacks and a long-sleeved navy blue shirt. Dressed and his hair combed, he headed for the kitchen.

"I could use a couple of aspirin," he told Peggy Ann as he set down the empty mug he had brought from the bathroom. "And about a gallon of black coffee."

She opened a drawer beneath the kitchen counter, retrieved a bottle of aspirin, and threw it to him. He caught it in one hand, screwed off the cap, shook several tablets into his open palm, and tossed them into his mouth. Just as Peggy Ann put the refilled mug in front of him—only coffee this time—he noticed that she had laid his cell phone on the table.

After downing more coffee, he picked up the phone and checked for messages. When he heard Hart's voice, his stomach muscles knotted.

"We need to talk. I've made a decision that will affect us both. Call me as soon as possible."

God damn it! Didn't he have enough to worry about without Hart going nuts on him?

He listened to the second message. *"I'm going to tell Audrey the truth and ask her to go with me to tell Wayne. I want you to be with me when I tell them. It's what we should have done all those years ago."*

Garth clutched the phone with brute strength, his mind screaming, his body rigid with fear.

"What's the matter?" Peggy Ann asked as she set a plate of unbuttered toast in front of him.

Taking quick, deep breaths, Garth willed himself under control. He slid back his chair and stood. "I've got to go. I don't have time to eat anything."

"Duty calls, huh?"

"Yeah."

He took the time to kiss her before he left. "See you later."

"Sure thing."

Could he make it back to his place and stop Hart before he spilled his guts to Audrey? He had always been able to control Hart, but if he couldn't stop him before he spoke to his stepsister, then all hell would break loose. Whatever influence he'd had over Audrey when she'd been a child no longer existed. He had spent years worrying about those damn nightmares she'd had, afraid maybe she had seen more than he thought she had that day, that the truth might be locked in her subconscious. Eventually, he had stopped worrying about it; but if Hart told Audrey, Garth knew that there was nothing he could do to control her now.

Nothing short of killing her.

Fresh from her morning shower, dressed in aqua velour pants and matching scooped-neck top, Audrey hummed as she prepared cinnamon French toast for brunch. J.D. had suggested they shower together, but she had known where that would lead and told him they would shower separately. They had spent the entire morning in bed. Making love. Napping. Making love. Napping.

She needed some time alone, a breather from J.D., so that she could think straight. When he touched her, every rational thought went out of her head. Everything had happened so fast. Too fast? Probably. Did she regret what had happened? No, she didn't regret anything, not one single moment.

"I think I love you, too."

He had said it only once, but once had been enough. The question was, did he mean it? Or did he tell every woman he slept with that he thought he loved her? No, she didn't think he did.

But are you sure?

That was the problem. She wasn't sure. Not sure about J.D.'s sincerity. Not sure about her sanity. Not sure if they were beginning an affair or if she had been nothing more than a one-night stand. Make that one night and half a day.

Lost in thought, the ringing telephone startled her. She hurriedly flipped the slices of French toast browning in the square frying pan, wiped her hands on a dish towel, and lifted the portable phone off the base on the counter.

"Hello," Audrey said.

"Hi, sis. You busy?"

"I'm in the middle of fixing brunch."

"I . . . uh . . . need to talk to you."

"What's wrong?"

"Can you come over here?"

"Where's Uncle Garth?"

"I don't know. Out somewhere. I tried to call him earlier this morning to tell him . . . His phone kept going to voice mail. I told myself that if he hadn't called back by noon, then I wouldn't wait any longer, that I'd call you."

"Hart, what is it? Has something happened?"

"I can't tell you over the phone. Please, Audrey, please . . . I need to see you. I have to tell you . . ."

"Tell me what?"

"I need your help. I have to tell you the truth."

"The truth about what?"

"I know what happened to Blake."

"What did you say?"

"Uncle Garth made me promise not to tell anyone. He said if I told, they'd put her in jail or lock her up in the loony bin. I should have told the truth. Once everyone knows, it'll be better for all of us. It'll be better for me."

"Hart, what are you saying? Are you talking about Enid? Did your mother do something to Blake?"

The dial tone hummed in her ears.

"Hart! Damn it, why did you hang up?"

J.D. had no choice but to put his wrinkled pants and shirt back on, but he left off his underwear. Whistling as he came out of the bedroom, he thought about how he would like to spend the afternoon. A repeat of that morning. God help him, he couldn't get enough of Audrey Sherrod.

Something sure smelled good. Cinnamon.

Audrey was a fantastic cook, only one of her many talents.

He had known his share of women with phenomenal bedroom skills, but not one of them held a candle to Audrey. Not that she knew all the tricks, all the practiced moves that a woman such as Holly Johnston knew. There was a surprising innocence in the way Audrey touched him, explored him, tasted him, that had been far more arousing because he suspected that she had never experienced that type of wantonness with any other man.

"I'm hungry as a bear, woman," J.D. called to her as he entered the kitchen.

The empty kitchen.

Where was she?

A slip of paper beneath the salt shaker on the table caught his eye. He pulled the note from underneath the shaker, picked it up, and read it.

French toast in the oven. Coffee ready. Hart called. He's in trouble. I've gone to Uncle Garth's to see what I can do to help. Be back as soon as possible. She had written "love" and then crossed it out, then had written it again, signing the succinct note, *Love, Audrey.*

Hart Roberts was her stepbrother and she loved him, but he took advantage of Audrey's love, her tender heart, her compassion. It was time that Roberts and everyone else—other than her clients—stopped leaning on Audrey, stopped using her as a crutch. If Audrey couldn't bring herself to cut the ties, to end Roberts's blood-sucking dependency on her, then by God, he'd do it for her. He wasn't going to let anyone hurt her, not ever again. And that went for Wayne Sherrod, too.

J.D. left the delicious-smelling French toast in the oven

and the freshly brewed coffee in the pot. If Hart Roberts needed Audrey, that meant that Audrey needed J.D. Whatever trouble her stepbrother was in, they'd help him get out of it. But this would be the last time. After today, Roberts would have to get by without his sister being at his beck and call whenever he needed her.

Chapter 39

Garth unlocked the front door and walked into the living room. Hart stood by the windows, his back to him.

"Are you all right, boy?"

Hart didn't turn; he continued staring out the window. "You can't talk me out of it, so don't even try."

Garth pocketed his key. "If you're so goddamn worried about this, then we need to talk about it before you do something you'll regret. What good is it going to do anybody for you to tell the truth about what happened to Blake? It won't bring him back. It won't bring Enid back. All it'll do is destroy us, both of us, you and me, boy."

"Lying all these years has already destroyed me."

Garth moved quietly across the room and stood directly behind his nephew, only a few feet separating them. He couldn't let Hart tell Audrey and Wayne the truth. If he did . . . *He won't. You can talk him down, persuade him to do what you want him to do.*

"You don't want to hurt the people you love," Garth said. "Think what it will do to Wayne if he knows. And Audrey . . .

do you think she'll ever be able to forgive you? You don't want to lose her love, do you?"

"If Wayne knows the truth, maybe he'll stop blaming all the wrong people." Turning halfway around, he glared at Garth. "Audrey will understand. She'll forgive me. She remembers how things were. We were just a couple of little kids. We trusted you."

"You can still trust me. Haven't I always taken care of you? Didn't I take care of you and Audrey that day?" When Garth took a tentative step toward his nephew, Hart moved away from him, closer against the window.

"I called her," Hart said.

"Called who?"

"Audrey."

"What did you tell her?"

"I asked her to come here. She's on her way now."

"Damn it, boy, you can't do this. If you won't consider what will happen to you, at least think about me. This will ruin me. I've been a police officer all my life. I've done a lot of good for a lot of people. That has to count for something. If the truth comes out, I could go to prison for what I did. And you know what happens to cops when they're locked up with the guys they put away."

"You can't talk me out of this." Hart turned his back on Garth and faced the window. "I've made up my mind. I should be able to see Audrey from here when she drives up. She'll be here soon. She's never let me down."

"Neither have I," Garth told him.

"They won't send you to prison. You only did what you thought was best for all of us, especially for Mama. They'll understand."

"Yeah, maybe you're right. Maybe they will understand." Garth slipped his hand inside his jacket and carefully eased his Smith & Wesson from the shoulder holster.

He loved Hart, loved him as if he were his own son. He'd

spent the past twenty-five years taking care of his nephew, looking out for him, getting him out of trouble, helping him every way he knew how. And now the boy was going to betray him.

Hart wasn't leaving him with any choice. He couldn't allow him to tell anyone what had really happened to Blake.

Do what you have to do.

It would be easy enough to explain what happened. Hart was an alcoholic and a drug addict, a guy with severe emotional problems since childhood, a man tormented by his brother's disappearance and his mother's suicide. Finding out that Blake hadn't been one of the Baby Blue toddlers had sent him over the edge.

I can say that I wasn't surprised he took his own life, that I expected it for years, that I have lived in fear that it would happen eventually.

Garth crept up behind Hart and placed his left hand on Hart's shoulder in a comforting gesture. "We'll watch for Audrey together."

"And we'll tell her the truth together," Hart said.

"That's right. We'll tell her the truth." Garth brought the gun up slowly to Hart's temple. When he pressed the muzzle against his nephew's head, Hart lifted his hand and clutched Garth's hand that held the pistol.

Garth pulled the trigger.

Hart gasped and gurgled; and then as he slumped downward, Garth supported his weight for a moment before stepping back and letting his nephew's body fall to the floor. Not taking time to even look at Hart, he worked quickly. He had to make this look like a suicide, one that he had tried to prevent.

He had my gun. He pointed it at his head and said he couldn't go on living. He confessed that he had killed Blake accidentally and that Enid had done something with Blake's body in order to protect him. He said he thought she buried

Blake in the backyard somewhere, weeks afterward, maybe even the day she killed herself. Oh, God, I tried to stop him. I grabbed him from behind and had my hand on the gun when he pulled the trigger. See, his blood is still on me.

Yes, that's how he would explain Hart's death. A suicide.

He'd barely had time to set up the scene before he heard a car door slam. He glanced out the window. Audrey was there.

Garth reached for the telephone, dialed 911, and said, "Help me, please. Send an ambulance immediately. My nephew just shot himself."

The doorbell rang while Garth was making the call. He let it chime again and again. The door wasn't locked. She would let herself into the house.

"Oh, God . . ." Garth hurried over to Hart, dropped to his knees, and cradled his nephew in his arms.

The front door opened. He looked up, put a stricken expression on his face, and cried out, "Oh, God, Audrey, he's killed himself."

She rushed toward them and stopped suddenly as she looked down at Hart. "No, no . . ."

"I tried to stop him," Garth told her.

"We have to call for help," she said.

"I've already called nine-one-one, but it's too late. He's gone, Audrey. We've lost him."

"But why?" Audrey shook her head. "I don't understand why he would kill himself. It doesn't make any sense."

"He couldn't live with the lies," Garth said as he rose to his feet. "He confessed to me that he accidentally killed Blake and that Enid covered it up by pretending that Blake had disappeared. That's why she killed herself. Because she knew one of her sons had killed the other one."

Suddenly, Audrey's mind went back twenty-five years, to that fateful day.

She didn't understand why Hart was acting so weird.

"It's my fault," Hart said. "It's all my fault."

"What's your fault?"

"Blake . . . my fault . . . all my fault."

"I don't know what you're talking about. What about Blake? What's your fault?"

"I was supposed to take care of him. If I'd done what I was supposed to do, then it wouldn't have happened."

"What happened? Why was Enid screaming? Why is Uncle Garth here?"

"Blake's gone. . . .

"What do you mean he's gone?"

Ignoring her as if she weren't there, Hart ran toward the nursery, lifted his fists, and beat on the closed door. "Mama . . . Mama . . ."

Audrey hurried to him and when she laid her hand on his shoulder, he turned and stared at her, his eyes filled with tears.

"Where is Blake? What happened to him?" she asked.

"Mama . . . She didn't mean to. Uncle Garth said she didn't mean to. We can't tell anybody. . . ."

Audrey backed away from Garth. "You're lying."

"What did you say?"

"I said you're lying. Hart didn't kill Blake. You know he didn't. You were there that day. You know what really happened. If anyone killed Blake, it wasn't Hart."

"Are you remembering or just guessing?"

"A little of both."

"You're wrong, Audrey. I'm telling you that Hart killed himself because he'd been lying all these—"

"Stop saying that! Hart did not kill Blake. You know he didn't. If anyone killed Blake that day, it was Enid. Oh, God, it was Enid, wasn't it? And Hart knew the truth." With realization bright in her eyes, Audrey shivered.

"I'm not going to let anybody ask you and Hart a lot of questions that will upset y'all. I'll protect you, both of you. Just do what I tell you to do. Do you understand?"

She nodded. "Yes, Uncle Garth."

"And if you need to talk to somebody about what happened today, you talk to me, okay?" He searched her eyes as if trying to decide whether or not she understood. "If you don't do exactly what I tell you to do, I can't protect you and Hart. We don't want anybody thinking it was your fault, do we? If that were to happen, they would take you away, you and Hart, and there wouldn't be anything I could do to stop them."

Enid's anguished screams and mournful weeping replayed itself over and over again in Audrey's mind as she huddled near the fence in the back yard. Audrey squatted on her knees and curled up as small and tight as humanly possible, hoping no one could see her.

Blake was gone.

Uncle Garth said someone had stolen her baby brother.

But she knew that was a lie. No one had stolen Blake. He hadn't been kidnapped.

"You knew the truth, didn't you?" Audrey glared at Garth. "You've always known what really happened to Blake."

"Yes, I've always known," Garth admitted. "Enid didn't mean to kill Blake. He woke from his nap crying. He had an ear infection, if you remember. She told him to stop crying, to go outside and find you or Hart. And when he wouldn't leave her and clung to her, she shook him, and when he cried louder, she put her hands around his throat and strangled him."

"Oh, Blake . . . Blake . . ." She swallowed a mouthful of tears. "Did—did Hart see what happened?"

"No."

"Were you there when it happened?"

"I arrived afterward. I had stopped by to check on Enid. Wayne had asked me to run by on my lunch break because he was worried about her and he couldn't get away to go home. He said since Blake had been sick and fretful, she'd been more on edge than usual. When I arrived, I found Enid sitting at the top of the stairs. She was holding Blake in her arms. I couldn't help him. He was already dead. And before I could handle the situation, Hart came in the house to check on Blake."

"We have to do what Uncle Garth tells us," Hart said. "We have to!"

Audrey nodded. It was a sin to tell a lie. But if they just pretended they didn't know what happened to Blake, they wouldn't really be lying, would they?

"They'll take Mama away and do horrible things to her." Hart clutched Audrey's hand. "And Uncle Garth said he didn't know what they might do to you and me. We—we were supposed to be taking care of Blake. It's my fault . . . it's all my fault."

"No," Audrey told him. "It's our fault."

"We can never tell anybody. Promise me. Pinky swear."

Audrey lifted her hand, curled her pinky finger, and held it out to her stepbrother. Hart wound his pinky finger around Audrey's and they made a solemn oath to do what Uncle Garth had told them to do.

"Our baby brother Blake was kidnapped," Audrey said. "Somebody came into the house and stole him."

* * *

Oh, God, she remembered! All the nightmares had been real. Fear for herself and Hart had forced her to submerge the truth deep into her subconscious. As a child, she had been forced to lie and that lie had eventually become her reality.

"You remember, don't you?" Garth asked.

"Yes, I remember."

"Everything?"

"Yes, everything. How could you have done that to us, to Hart and me? You scared us to death. You made us believe that if we told the truth, we'd be taken away and punished."

"I did what I had to do to protect my sister," Garth said. "I told Hart why we could never tell anyone what really happened. When he agreed, I had him walk his mother back upstairs and stay with her while I carried Blake's body into the basement. I temporarily buried him at the bottom of the freezer. I managed to completely cover him with frozen food."

"How could you have—?"

"I didn't leave him there. A few weeks later, Enid and I took his body and buried him in the backyard and planted a rose bush on top of his grave."

"And all these years, Blake has been in the backyard, under the rose bush?"

"Yes."

"And you let Daddy believe, made us all believe that Blake had been kidnapped."

"It was best that way. Someone had already abducted three other toddlers, so I simply suggested to Wayne that the same thing had happened to Blake, that he was probably one of the Baby Blue toddlers."

"How could you have done that? To Daddy and Hart . . . and to me?"

"I'm sorry, Audrey. I'm really very sorry."

* * *

Garth might well have been sorry for what had happened, for what he'd done to protect Enid, but she realized that he was saying he was sorry because he knew that he couldn't allow her to live now that she knew the truth. Garth intended to kill her, just as he had killed Hart. With fake bravado, she stood up and faced the man she had called uncle for most of her life. A man she had trusted. A man her stepbrother had trusted.

"If you kill me, how will you explain it—two dead bodies? My father will—"

"Wayne is a fool. He'll believe whatever I tell him." Garth smirked, a wicked, frightening look in his eyes that told Audrey he had snapped. "You and I realized Hart intended to shoot himself. You got to him first and the two of you struggled. The gun went off. When he realized he had killed you, he shot himself in the head and I couldn't stop him, even though I tried."

"You think you have it all figured out, don't you?" Audrey knew that she couldn't expect help from anyone, that she was on her own, as she always had been. Only she could stop Garth from killing her.

As if sensing her intention to either flee or attack, Garth dropped down and reached for the gun lying beside Hart's body. Audrey dove forward, hit the floor with a painful thud, and while gasping for air, she grabbed Garth's hand as he clutched the 9mm.

Garth might be over fifty and not quite the man he had once been, but he was larger and stronger than she was. Unless she could find some advantage over his brute strength, there was no way she could take the gun away from him. Their struggle ended quickly, despite Audrey giving it everything she had. He wrestled the pistol away from her grasp, slammed the grip against her head, and jerked his hand back and into the air. Pain shot through the side of her head as blood seeped out of the burning gash and trickled down into her eye.

Suddenly she felt the muzzle against her belly. Acting purely on survival instinct, she head-butted Garth in the nose. When he yelped and jerked back, she reached down and grabbed his gun hand with both of her hands. Before he regained his equilibrium, Audrey found an unknown strength born of desperation and fear. She managed to turn the pistol away from her belly for only a second, but a second was all she needed. Garth pulled the trigger just as she gained momentary control. The weapon fired. The bullet went straight up and grazed Garth's shoulder and then sliced through his cheek. Moaning in pain, he shoved Audrey away from him as blood seeped through his shirt and jacket and dripped from the hole in his cheek.

Clearly disoriented, Garth stared at her as he rose to his feet and staggered backward. He aimed the gun at her where she lay on the floor.

By God, he might kill her, but she wasn't going to just lie there and do nothing. She struggled to stand and somehow managed to get up on her feet, fully intending to go down fighting.

Behind her the front door flew open. She kept her gaze on Garth's hand as she lunged toward him. Gunfire exploded in her ears as the bullets zipped past her. Garth grunted and clutched at thin air as bullet after bullet entered his body. Suddenly a big arm circled her waist and threw her face-down onto the floor before the man who covered her with his body aimed and fired one final time; but only after Garth had pulled the trigger of his own weapon one final time.

Audrey could barely breathe. The man lying on top of her was big and heavy, his own breathing ragged.

"Are you all right?" J.D. asked her in a hoarse, throaty voice.

"I—I think so."

He rose up and off her, grabbed her forearms, and dragged her to her feet. She swayed. Dizzy and slightly disoriented, she slumped against J.D. He slid one hand around her waist and used the other to holster his gun. And then he wrapped both arms around her and held her so tightly that she thought he was going to break her in two.

Holding on to J.D. for dear life, she turned her head and looked at Garth's bloody, bullet-riddled body lying on the floor, his 9mm still in his hand, held in a tight death grip. She jerked her head back around and buried her face against J.D.'s chest. As she shuddered uncontrollably, he kept her secure in his arms.

She lifted her head and looked up at J.D. "He killed Hart and he was going to kill me. If you hadn't shown up when you did . . ." The trembling began again.

He stroked her back, soothing her. "You're safe. He can't hurt you."

"I have to tell you . . . Garth . . . Garth killed Hart because . . . because . . ." She felt as if she couldn't breathe.

"You can tell me later. For now, don't talk, honey. Don't do anything except let me take care of you."

In the distance, Audrey heard the wail of sirens. The police would be there soon. And an ambulance. Garth had called 911 after he killed Hart.

"Oh God, oh God!" She clung to J.D. as the reality of what had happened replayed itself in her mind.

Hart was dead. Garth had killed him.

Garth was dead. J.D. had killed him to save her.

Chapter 40

Tam came and took Audrey home from the hospital that night. The doctor had wanted her to stay for observation, but she had wanted to go home. She had bruises and abrasions, a mild concussion, and three stitches in her temple where Garth had slugged her with the grip of his gun. And her clothes were stained with blood.

They had taken her to the hospital in the ambulance. She had gone alone. J.D. had told her not to worry, that he'd handle everything. He had stayed behind, of course, because he had to explain what had happened and why he had shot and killed Garth. Tam had arrived less than ten minutes after Audrey had been admitted to the ER, and Geraldine and Willie had come rushing in only a few minutes after their daughter. Audrey had answered their questions and Willie had told her she wouldn't have to make an official statement until tomorrow.

Nothing seemed real. She felt as if she were inside one of her worst nightmares and that eventually she would awaken. Hart wouldn't be dead. Garth would not have tried to kill her.

But it had not been a nightmare. It had happened. Garth had killed Hart and then J.D. had killed Garth.

Hours later, after her release from the hospital, Audrey and Tam sat side by side on the sofa in Audrey's living room. Tam had turned on only one lamp. They spoke in hushed tones, both of them in emotional pain and shock. Audrey kept reliving what had happened, trying to come to grips with the truth from the past and the horrors of the present. They talked and cried and sat silently. And sometime in the morning, they both fell asleep on the sofa.

Audrey woke to the sound of the doorbell ringing.

"Stay put," Tam told her as she went to the door.

Early morning sunlight peeped through the wooden blinds.

Audrey's head throbbed. Her eyes were swollen almost shut. Emotional pain radiated from her heart and transposed itself into a physical ache that spread through her entire body.

Before she could ask Tam who was at the door, J.D. walked into the living room. She tried to stand. J.D. grabbed her the moment she was on her feet, swept her into his arms, and sat down and held her on his lap. She curled her arm around his neck and laid her head on his shoulder.

When she heard the front door close, Audrey knew that Tam had let herself out, leaving her alone with J.D.

She lifted her head and looked at him. "Tam knows I'll take care of you," he said.

She sighed deeply, allowing J.D. to give her the tender, loving care that she so badly needed.

During the weeks since Hart's death, J.D. and Zoe had stayed with Audrey, one of them never far from her side. A man she had once disliked and thought a carbon copy of her father had shown her how very wrong she had been about him. He had held her when she woke from nightmares about Garth trying to kill her. He had kissed away her tears when she mourned her brother's death. And he had given her the comfort and pleasures of their slow, sweet lovemaking, each moment together a reaffirmation of life itself.

The police had found Blake's little body buried beneath the rosebush in the backyard where they had played as children, she and Hart and Blake. Her father and Grace planned a memorial service, and they reburied Blake in the cemetery beside his mother.

When she went to her father after the graveside service, longing to comfort him and afraid of his rejection, he had gripped her hand briefly. And with tears in his eyes, he had looked from her to J.D.

"Take good care of her," her father had told him before he'd turned and walked away.

It had been more than she had expected, less than she wanted. But J.D. had pointed out later that it was a start; and given time and patience, there was hope that one day she might have a better relationship with her father.

A week after they reburied Blake, they buried Hart near Blake and Enid. Her father and Grace had attended the funeral, as had Geraldine and Willie. And as difficult as it had been for Audrey to say good-bye to her stepbrother, it had been even harder for Tam. She had wept for her lost love, wept for Hart's child that she had aborted, and wept for foolish dreams that would never come true. Marcus hadn't come to the funeral with Tam, and Audrey hadn't asked her best friend why her husband wasn't there. But afterward, Tam had explained.

"We've separated. I've moved back home with Mom and Dad, at least for a while."

"Oh, Tam, why? You two love each other."

"I—I told him about Hart. And about the baby."

"I thought he would understand."

"He did. Marcus was wonderful."

"Then why—?"

"I left him. He didn't leave me. I have to work through some things on my own. I have to decide if I love Marcus enough to build a life with him, enough to have his children."

Audrey had arranged for Garth's burial and paid for everything. He was the third family member to be laid to rest in a month's time. And oddly enough, saying a final farewell to a man she had thought of as her uncle had been almost as difficult as saying good-bye to Hart. She had been consumed with a barrage of mixed emotions about so many things the past few weeks. Porter, who was now confined to Moccasin Bend for further evaluation. Her brother Hart, who would remain forever in her memory. And Garth, who had condemned them all to live a lie for twenty-five years.

J.D. told her she was a damn saint.

"Someone had to do it," she said.

"Yeah, but why does that someone always have to be you?"

"Because some of us are born to do these things, to take responsibility, to be the caretakers. You should know, my darling J.D., because whether you want to admit it or not, you're one of us."

"Why the hell would you say a thing like that?"

She stood on tiptoe and kissed him. "Because it's true. Just look at the way you accepted responsibility for Zoe."

"Of course I did. She's my daughter."

"Uh-huh, she is. And look at the way you've been taking care of me for weeks now, not to mention that you saved my life."

"Damn right I did." He pulled her into his arms. "You're my woman. I'd move heaven and earth to protect you."

She lifted her arms up and around his neck. "Do you still *think* you love me?"

He grinned. "Yeah, honey. I still *think* I love you." When she glared at him, he laughed. "And I *know* that I'm crazy about you, that I want you more than anything in this world. God, woman, don't you know I love you?"

"Yes," she told him. "I know. But I needed to hear you say it."

Right then and there, Audrey realized exactly what else she wanted from J.D. She wanted them to spend the rest of their lives together.

I'll give him six months to propose to me, and if he hasn't by then, I'll just have to propose to him.

Dear Reader,

When I originally plotted *Don't Cry,* I envisioned it as a single, stand-alone novel, a book to give my readers a break from the Powell Agency. While writing Audrey Sherrod and J.D. Cass's story, I became so fascinated with them and the people in their lives that I realized I wanted to tell my readers more about these interesting characters. I wanted to write a sequel. So, at this point a second book featuring Audrey and J.D. is tentatively planned and if my plans come to fruition, you can expect *Don't Say a Word* (working title) to be released in 2012.

At present, I've begun work on the next Powell Agency novel and the second in the Dead By trilogy. *Dead by Morning* (working title) is set for a May 2011 release and will feature Powell agent Maleah Perdue and former FBI profiler Derek Lawrence as the main protagonists. Those of you who have been following the Powell Agency novels are aware of the animosity between these two strong, stubborn characters. Forced to work together yet again to track down a killer who is murdering Powell agents and members of their families, Maleah and Derek must set aside their differences in order to unearth a deadly secret that threatens everyone associated with Griffin Powell and with Maleah's best friend, Griff's wife Nicole. The third and final Dead By novel, tentatively set for release in December 2011, will feature Nic and Griff and reveal all of the secrets from the mysterious past that Griff shared with Sanders and Yvette Meng.

I always love hearing from readers. You may contact me through my Web site at www.beverlybarton.com or by writing to me in care of Kensington Publishing. While visiting my Web site, you can enter contests, sign up for my e-mail newsletter, and check out a list of all my books and my upcoming appearances at book signings, speaking engagements, and conferences. Also, go online and take a look at my new Beverly Barton Official Fan Page on Facebook: www.facebook.com/beverlybartonfanpage.

Warmest regards,
Beverly Barton